Leigh stepped forward and took Aspen in her arms. "I don't know if you're going to hit me or run away, but right now I want to do this," she said as she tipped Aspen's chin up and kissed her. Her tongue teasing at Aspen's lips. Aspen could feel her lips open like the unfolding petals on a tulip. Her tongue reached out to taste Leigh. She tasted of passion and desire and Aspen pulled Leigh tightly against her. *To hell with the past,* she told her brain. *To hell with the past,* she told her conscience. Their tongues now investigating, probing and penetrating. Aspen couldn't get enough of Leigh's mouth. She wanted to taste all of her. She felt Leigh back her against a tree. "I want you, Aspen Brown and screw the consequences." She felt Leigh's lips as they kissed down under her ear and across her neck. Each kiss left a seared mark on her skin. She felt Leigh lift her shirt and she heard Leigh sigh as she took in Aspen's naked breasts.

As if her body was in control of her mind, Aspen felt herself push up on her toes. She wanted Leigh to take each breast into her mouth and she sensed Leigh absorbing her unstated desire. Leigh's lips were hot as she felt them wind around her swollen nipples. Then Leigh sucked each nipple into her mouth and the canopy of leaves that had offered her the protection from life's problems each time she ran to the woods burst in fireworks of yellow and red and green as her nipples silently screamed for more. Aspen rested her head against the hard bark that somehow felt like a pillow.

"I'm going to fall," she said through tight lips.

"I won't let you," Leigh said as she braced a knee between Aspen's legs. Aspen ground her hips on the knee. Her whole being seemed to be focused on that pressure that now demanded more.

Visit

Bella Books

at

BellaBooks.com

or call our toll-free number

1-800-729-4992

Aspen's
EMBERS

Diana Tremain Braund

Bella
BOOKS
2007

Bella Books, Inc.
P.O. Box 10543
Tallahassee, FL 32302

Printed in the United States of America on acid-free paper
First Edition

Editor: Cindy Cresap
Cover designer: LA Callaghan

ISBN-10: 1-59493-102-X
ISBN-13: 978-1-59493-102-4

This book is dedicated to Nan—the woman I've been looking for my whole life.

And to Miss Etta—who really lived the life described in the book.

And to Marjorie—the world's best psychologist and my friend who walked me through the steps of depression.

And to my editor—who pulled Aspen's Embers *out of the ashes.*

About the Author

Diana Tremain Braund continues to live on the coast of Maine in a house that overlooks the water. She and her dog, Bob, who is now six years old, take long walks on the beach. This is where she comes up with ideas for Bella Books.

You can e-mail the author at dtbtiger@yahoo.com.

CHAPTER ONE

Aspen Brown sat resolutely in the elbow of the red maple tree. Her back rested against the tree's scabrous coat. She scooted deeper into the camber. There was a scraping sound as her jeans dragged across the craggy surface and her jacket rubbed against the bark. The leaves served as a facial screen around her and rippled like the sails of a weathered ship. The nor'easter gained strength and the trunk wobbled like a sailor without sea legs.

Aspen pulled her jacket around her and buried her head deeper into her collar. The fabric's edges wiggled like butterflies around her face, slips of her black hair fluttered in the air like billowing flags under her hood. She shut her eyes. Her eyelids felt locked in place. She rested her chin against her hand. Aspen savored the humid air on her lips. The fingertips on her other hand, shaped like a tripod, rested against the limb, holding her in place. Aspen swayed with the rhythm of the tree as it rocked to and fro.

There was quietude to her being.

A quietude to her soul.

A quietude to her spirit.

A quietude.

She waited.

"Ya gotta come down."

Aspen didn't open her eyes. "Nope."

"Ya gonna be blown out of there. We'll be pickin' ya up in pieces tomorrow."

"I said nope!" She kept her eyes closed. No need to look. It was her friend Skeet Jones, who'd come to get her yet again.

"Storm comin'."

"I know. I can feel it."

"We all can feel it. Nothing special about that. Plus the weatherman said so."

"I didn't listen."

"So what's your point this time?"

"Just wanted to see how a tree feels when she's being thrashed about by a nor'easter."

"She feels fine, but you won't when you get tossed outta thar."

"I won't."

"Ya will."

"We'll see."

"Okay, then I'm comin' up."

Aspen opened her eyes. Skeet was seventy years old and lissome as a caterpillar. He was small for a man, but his shoulders looked like granite and his hands were knotted like tubers. His jeans were faded, from wear, not fashion. The collar on his blue jacket was pulled up around his chin. His baseball cap was pulled tight down on his head. His face was crinkles and pleats and was dark from age. She sighed, knowing that if he fell, Anne Jean—Skeet's wife and her friend—would kill her. "You serious?"

"I am."

Aspen inhaled deeply. "All right, but not because I want to."

"Tree'll be fine."

"Maybe." She pulled herself up and balanced her feet on the lower limb. "Maybe not." She turned toward the tree, resting her hands on either side of the trunk and stepped to the next branch. Aspen swung first one and then the other leg into the air, like a gymnast dismounting from a stationary horse.

They silently walked toward the path.

"Ya want to come for supper?" Skeet sent a stream of spit to the side of the path.

Aspen shuddered. She wondered why men spit. "I'll have to get Miss Etta Mae."

"I figured." The only sound was the scrape of their boots against the rocky path. "There's a new manager."

"I heard."

"Hear she's a woman."

Aspen shrugged. "Makes it worse. Supper the usual time?"

"Yup."

At the road, Aspen got on her bike. "See ya."

"Yup." Skeet climbed into his battered black Ford pickup truck. It looked as wintry and wrinkled as he did. She watched as it coughed its way down the road. He fished lobsters spring to fall and dragged for scallops in the winter. Skeet and Anne Jean had been the first people to welcome her family to Codyville Plantation. That was thirty years ago when she was two years old.

Aspen turned her bike toward home. She'd disliked every manager that the wood harvesting companies had hired over the years, but a woman was worse because she shouldn't be in the business of killing trees. She peddled past the driveway that said Burnt Brush Forestry Management Field Office, stopped and turned around. Face it, you're curious as all get out, she said to herself. The office was in the distance. Maybe if she stood in the shadow of the trees, she'd get a peek at the woman whom, she'd decided, either chewed tobacco and spit it out the corner of her mouth, or wore Armani business suits and black, low-heeled, Italian-made shoes and walked with her butt tucked tight as lips sucking on a lemon. Aspen skidded to a stop on the driveway, her tires spraying small pebbles into the air. *How childish is this? You're being a moron. Moron, maybe, but at least you'll get a measure of your enemy.* All wood harvesting managers had been her nemeses, and the sooner she got a look at this woman, the better she'd be at sizing her up. The September sun was fading quickly, and she had to get home, but not before she scouted out the enemy, she resolved as she peddled faster down the driveway.

The new company owned more than three-quarters of the woodlands in Codyville Plantation. They'd bought the land from the paper mill in Woodland a year earlier. The wood was harvested and shipped to the mill and turned into paper.

Soon after the management company bought the land, they'd held a town meeting and assured residents they would engage in sustainable forestry practices only, strategically cutting areas and planting more trees than they cut. In a year's time, they had kept their word. New seedlings quickly replaced the trees cut. They'd even agreed not to cut near a stand of mixed hard- and softwood trees where Aspen often found herself sitting. The trees escaped the ragged teeth of the saw over the years because they were home to a nesting pair of eagles.

For years, Aspen and others had tried to convince the former company to donate the eagle's nest and land to the town. They'd made the request of the new company, but the local manager rebuffed their efforts. Aspen had disliked the tall man with the scrunched up eyes the minute she'd met him. She'd heard plenty of complaints around town that he was aloof and unapproachable. Then one day he was gone and she hadn't heard the reason for his abrupt departure. Eventually the woman showed up.

Aspen could see a red Chevrolet pickup parked in front of the field office. The light was on inside. She skidded to a stop near a clump of trees.

"Evening."

Aspen jumped and turned toward the voice. "Evening." The woman was tall. Where Aspen was all elbows and legs, the woman was sharp edges and square. Her blond hair was feathered around her face, but it was her eyes that drew Aspen's gaze to her face. They were nut brown and colossal like almonds. They seemed to hold Aspen steady in her gaze. The woman's cheek wasn't puffed out from a wad of tobacco, and she had on tan cargo pants and a jacket, not an Armani suit.

"Can I help you?"

"You're the new manager?"

The woman's smile was gracious. "I am."

"Heard you were a woman. Not often town gossip is wrong."

The woman grinned. "I'm gossip already? I've only been here a short time."

" 'Fraid so."

The woman extended her hand. "I'm Leigh Wright."

"Aspen Brown." Her hand felt warm.

"Interesting name, but I bet you hear that all the time."

"I do." Aspen didn't feel inclined to say more.

"So what else they saying about me?"

"That's about it."

"You live around here?"

"About a mile up the road. My property adjoins the company's land. Mine and my neighbor Skeet Jones. He's on the other side of you. Other neighbors next to him."

"Not a lot though."

"No, most folks live on the other side of town, next to the ocean."

"But not you."

5

She narrowed her eyes. "When we moved here forest land was cheap, so my parents bought some."

"How long ago was that?"

"About thirty years."

"A good investment. Forest land is getting more and more valuable. Your parents still own the land?" Leigh leaned against her truck.

"No." Aspen changed the subject. She didn't like the direction the conversation was going. Plus she was talking way too much.

"You want to come in?" Leigh gestured toward the office. "Have a cup of coffee?"

"Nope. Gotta go." Aspen was surprised. She found that she liked Leigh's easy manner. She didn't seem in a rush to hurry their conversation. *Where did that come from? There was nothing to like about the woman.* She gripped the handlebars on her bike. Aspen stared at the woman. "So have you moved here yet?"

"I've been commuting from Presque Isle. That's where I was based. After the former guy moved out, the company had to do some things to the manager's house they own, so I didn't get moved in as quickly as I had expected."

"You plan on staying?"

"I do."

"The last manager was here less than a year. What's so different about you?"

"I've only been here a few weeks, but I like it around here," Leigh said resolutely.

Aspen nodded. Leigh's response did not demand an answer. Besides, the sun was gone and the twilight felt like a veil had surrounded them. "I gotta get going. I don't like riding my bike at night."

"Well, I'm heading back to my place. Would you like to toss your bike in the back of my truck and I'll give you a ride home?" Leigh looked at the sky. "A storm's coming up, and judging from those clouds, it's going to be a corker."

Aspen followed her gaze. She didn't like the fact that Leigh's face invited confidence. "I'll be home before it hits."

Leigh shrugged. "Well, any time." Leigh headed toward the office. "Stop by anytime," she called over her shoulder.

Aspen nodded. "Thanks." She put her foot on the pedal and pushed off toward the road. *I might not beat the storm,* she thought, *but damn I'm not about to ride in the same truck with her.* She looked again at the raging coal black clouds. Aspen eased to the side to let the truck behind her pass. Leigh tooted and waved. Aspen nodded. She had to tell Skeet and Anne Jean that she'd met the new manager. She looked up. A large bald eagle circled overhead. Aspen stopped her bike.

The eagle flying overhead was one of the nesting pair that lived in the old stand of trees she loved. She thought about how often she hiked the marsh after the hot days of summer had turned the earth into reddish-brown potter's clay, the soil dehydrated and bone-dry. Scant rain this summer had made the woods prickly and dry. She would cut to the side of the nest and climb a tree a distance away to watch the eagles feed their young in the nest they'd assembled at the top of a dead tree.

Aspen pushed off on her bike again and peddled hard, just reaching her driveway as the mist that had blanketed her turned to a soft rain. When she looked up, the clouds were churning around like the balls in a lottery draw. Once the storm took hold, she knew it would be breakneck and furious. Miss Etta Mae, who was in her run, leapt at the fence. Aspen opened the gate and let her out. A combination of long black hair and ballet grace, Miss Etta's long legs reached up into a slender and angular body like her owner's. Miss Etta happily barked. She was a combination Gordon setter and spaniel. Aspen had found her on the road two years earlier, saturated and starving, her one eye hanging from its socket. She had taken her to the vet and then posted notices around town, but no one claimed her. Miss Etta Mae moved in.

Aspen had named her after a favorite aunt who had died years before.

Aspen leaned her bike against the side of the house and went inside, Miss Etta on her heels. The last bit of light hung just slightly off to the west, then blinked before it nodded to sleep. The wind was already picking up. Nor'easters didn't reach the level of a hurricane when it came to wind velocity, but they came close. She needed to clean up.

"Come on, little girl. I'll feed you then you can ride over with me." She poured dry food into Miss Etta's bowl. Miss Etta daintily picked at each piece.

Miss Etta bounded into the front seat of the car and rested her chin on Aspen's thigh as Aspen turned on her windshield wipers. The rain was steady now. "You gotta be a good girl. No begging when you get there, okay?" Miss Etta seemed to huff in disagreement. Aspen retraced her steps. She drove past the driveway that led to the woodlot management headquarters and thought about the new manager. There was no question the manager was attractive, and there was a disarming friendliness about her. Aspen bit down on her bottom lip. *Stop that* she scolded herself. *The woman cuts trees and is your archenemy.*

She turned into Skeet's driveway. "Glad you're here," Anne Jean said from the screen door. Where Skeet was lank with flesh as tight as a leather glove, Anne Jean was hooplike and dense. Her brown hair was in ringlets, and the curls seemed to fly around her head. Her brown blouse clung to the rolls around her middle. She kept pulling it down over her green flowered skirt, which seemed to cascade wide around her legs. Aspen had never seen Anne Jean in anything other than a skirt. Inside, she squished Aspen against her in a firm hug. Anne Jean smelled of biscuits and yeast.

"Well, I'm glad to be here." Miss Etta danced around Anne

Jean's legs.

"She looks great." Anne Jean petted the dog.

"She's just fine."

"I'd say. She's the luckiest dog on the face of the planet. Besides, you living all alone in that big house without a dog or person didn't seem right."

"Well, I'd take a dog any day over a *person*," Aspen mimicked. Anne Jean playfully cuffed her on the shoulder. They'd had that discussion many times before.

"Come in. Supper's ready. Skeet's out back. Ornery cuss, I told him you'd be here any minute, but he had to go out there and fool with those damn traps." Aspen's mouth watered from all the smells in the kitchen.

"How long you been married?" Aspen knew the answer. She just liked to tease Anne Jean.

"Too long."

"Not too long." She loved the way Skeet and his wife picked at one another. Skeet was gentle surly to Anne Jean's effervescent exuberance.

"Probably not. Skeet said he found you up a tree."

"I met the new manager out at Burnt Brush." Aspen sat down. She didn't want to explain to Anne Jean why she'd been up a tree yet again. She'd tried over the years to explain to her friends that when her life seemed to spin erratically off its axle, sitting in a tree seemed to restore the harmony she needed to survive, except once when the trees offered her little comfort. Aspen had to will her mind not to think about that time.

"So?"

"I don't like her and I don't like what she does."

Anne Jean sighed, "Maybe she's different."

"Why? 'Cause she's a woman? She's no different than any male manager out there. Besides, it makes me nervous when they change managers because I get the feeling the company has plans for the land they aren't talking about."

"You're probably right, but this new company can't be worse than the original ones. When *they* started the mill over t' Woodland in the nineteen thirties, they bought up tons of woodland cheap. They'd cut those trees and truck them over to the mill and chew them up faster than a teenager munching on pizza." Anne Jean pulled buns out of the oven. The smell made Aspen's stomach do a dance. "That was one bad company. They just went through and clear-cut the land, leaving nothing but trails of dead stumps and young saplings and trees scattered on the ground. Looked most times like there'd been a major battle there. I was just a kid, but I remember. Then that fancy company from down south bought the mill and all of its land, and they managed it pretty darn good for a lot of years. At least they stopped polluting the river after the environmentalists like you got after them," she said as she turned back to the stove.

Aspen thought about the river that ran through the middle of Codyville Plantation. In the Seventies and Eighties, environmentalists had banded together to pressure the state into forcing the mills to install new equipment that would keep them from polluting the rivers and the air, but the rivers still carried the scars of the past. In the old days, logs were cut and tossed into the river. Some of the logs never made it because the weight of the run would force them down into the river's bed. In the late fall, when the river was at its lowest, the logs looked like underwater wooden bridges. As a kid, Aspen used to walk across that slippery bridge to see if she could reach the other side. Most of the time she tumbled into the river.

"Jobs were good, and it looked like we'd all settled in." Anne Jean busied herself with preparing supper. "Then that southern company up and sold their woodland to these guys. The way I figure it, these folks gotta do it right because they don't have a mill that produces paper." Anne Jean opened the oven door and took out a pot roast.

"Anything I can do?"

"Nope, just tell me about the new woman manager."

Aspen shrugged. "Not much to tell. I'd judge she's around forty." Miss Etta ran to greet Skeet. Her dog smile was wide.

"What're you two up to?" Skeet dropped an armload of wood next to the stove. He scratched Miss Etta behind the ear as she pranced around his feet.

"Just talking about the new manager." Aspen smiled.

"You met her?" Skeet turned to Aspen.

"I did." She stacked the wood next to the stove. "I can at least build up the fire." She opened the door and poked at the red embers with the shovel.

"Have at it, woman. Once the oven cools down, it's going to get chilly in here. This sure has been a cold August. Last year we hadn't even lit the stove by now. All summer we been starved for rain. Now here we got a nor'easter comin'." Skeet walked over to the sink and washed his hands.

Aspen rolled up newspaper and balanced kindling against it. She blew on the embers and soon the fire ignited.

"So what did you learn?" He dried his hands.

"Like I was telling Anne Jean, I'd say she's around forty, blond hair. She offered me a ride home." Aspen brushed off her hands and stood in front of the stove.

"You didn't take it?" Anne Jean held the potato masher up in the air like the baton of a music conductor who'd just finished directing a chamber music group. " 'Course you wouldn't."

"Nope, I told her I'd get home all right."

"You might'a learned something," Skeet said.

"Doubt it. That company has been closemouthed since they bought the land except for that one public meeting. Remember how we asked them if they had any other plans for the land? All they'd say was they were reviewing their options. I hate that expression. Seems to me if all they planned to do was cut wood, they'd say so."

"Like I said, why change?" Anne Jean asked. "Paper companies been making money off that land for years. So I expect this group's going to do the same." Anne Jean put the potatoes in a bowl and cut the meat. "Seems like they would just continue to do that."

"I'd felt more comfortable if they'd have said that's all they planned to do."

"It'll take me a second to make the gravy. Listen to it howl out there." The mist had turned into hard rain, and there was a rat-ta-tat-tat against the window.

"Going to be a good one," Skeet said.

Aspen signaled for Miss Etta. The dog plopped down next to Aspen's chair. "She's already eaten, so don't let that sorrowful look fool you."

Skeet tucked his napkin into the top of his shirt. "Seems to me if they were making plans to change stuff, they'd have said something from the beginning," Skeet said, returning to their previous topic. He spooned potatoes onto his plate and passed them to Aspen.

"It still makes me nervous every time there's a change in ownership," Aspen said. "Each time the new company pays more for the land. Some day the wood just isn't going to give them the profits they need to keep their stockholders happy."

"So what are they going to do?" Anne Jean asked.

"Don't know, but it seems to me they could do a lot of stuff with that land."

"I'm not worried," Skeet said around a mouthful of potatoes.

Codyville Plantation was a small isolated town in northern Maine. Its closest neighbor was thirty miles away. At its summer peak when the snowbirds returned, only a thousand people lived there. There was a small grocery store next to the pharmacy and a vacant lot where the clothing store had burned years before. The school where Aspen taught was nearby. There was a diner, a restaurant, a hardware store and a satellite bank with two tellers. Because the town was part of the county's unorganized territory, there was no town office, which was another way of saying that county officials were responsible for plowing the roads and providing fire and police protection. Other than that, county government, which was fifty miles away, pretty much left them alone. Most people either worked in the school, fished the ocean, worked in the woods or were retired folks from as far away as Boston and New York who had discovered the town years before with its ocean to the right and its woodlands to the left.

"So tell us more about the woman forester." Anne Jean was as curious as a mouse sniffing Limburger cheese.

"She say anything about the company?" Skeet asked.

"Not really. Mostly we talked about the fact that people knew she was here. She seemed amused by that, but not concerned."

"What she look like?" Anne Jean asked.

"I don't know. Tall for a woman. Kinda sturdy built."

"Don't matter what she looks like." Skeet stuffed a forkful of potatoes in his mouth.

"Well it does," Anne Jean shot back.

"And why is that?"

"Tells a lot about a person. You'd expect she'd be just the way Aspen described her. You wouldn't expect some woman in a frilly dress to be the manager of a woodlot."

Uh huh, Aspen thought to herself. *They're off again.*

"Might be refreshing to see a woman in a frilly dress out there," Skeet countered. "Why, it'd dress the place up." Skeet's eyes twinkled.

"You're just pulling my leg again," Anne Jean said affectionately. "I got plenty of blueberry cobbler."

Aspen groaned. "Wicked fine. You know I can't leave here without eating at least three pieces."

"Good." Anne Jean picked up her plate.

"Gotta go," Aspen looked at the clock. "I got classes tomorrow."

"Here." Anne Jean pushed a plate into her hand. "You won't

have time to cook for yourself, so I made up a plate for tomorrow night."

Aspen hugged her. "You're something else."

"I'll say." Skeet put his arm around his wife.

"Oh, go on, ya old fool." Anne Jean laughed.

"Who's an old fool?" Skeet was feigning hurt.

"Enough, you two." She hugged Skeet. "I want out of here before you two get going on each other again and before that storm gets raging."

"You want to spend the night?" Anne Jean was worried. Roads in Codyville were narrow and dangerous even when dry.

"Heavens no. Come on, Miss Etta." Aspen opened the kitchen door and felt the blow of wind against her face. "Wow, this one's going to be a real toad strangler."

"You be careful," Anne Jean called after her.

"I will," she yelled over the wind. She ran to her car, opening the door just as a gust of wind exploded, almost pushing the door into her. Rain pelted her face. Miss Etta jumped into the car as soon as Aspen opened the door. Aspen started the engine and put her windshield wipers on high as the car rocked back and forth. Miss Etta snuggled close to her leg. "We're going to be fine, girl. We'll take it real slow."

Aspen groaned when she saw the beat-up Honda Civic in her driveway and the flicker of candles in the kitchen windows. The wind was swirling hard around her, and rain was coming down in torrents as she held the door open with her leg. "Well, Miss Etta, we got company." She picked up the plate of food. "Come on, girl. Let's make a run for it."

Aspen wasn't surprised when she saw the battered car. It was storming, and that meant Cassie Jenkins was sitting in her kitchen. Storms were Cassie's enemy.

"I was thinking," Cassie said as soon as Aspen opened the

door.

"About?" There was never a need for introduction. She and Cassie had been friends since kindergarten. Cassie's mellow style blended well with Aspen's contemplative moods. On long summer days she and Cassie had sat in the trees in the woods or curled their bodies around the rocks that dotted the bay. They read books by Farley Mowatt and Rachel Carson about embracing the earth, while their contemporaries embraced beer, second-hand cars and making out at the pit.

After high school, Aspen went to college and Cassie stayed behind to marry Tommy Jenkins. He was a year older and was one of the ones who drank beer and raced second-hand cars up and down the road. Tommy fished lobsters. Their marriage ended when Cassie joined with Mary Tyler Moore to protest the treatment of lobsters. She even tried to get Tommy to quit working for his dad. After a while, the stresses of Cassie protesting on the streets of Codyville broke up her marriage.

Seated on her kitchen floor surrounded by candles, the light was flickering on Cassie's reddish-brown hair. Her nearly olive-colored eyes were closed. Cassie was petite and round, but not fat. She reminded Aspen of the gnomes people stuck in their backyards. The large red caftan Cassie was wearing hid her legs.

"Belly dancing."

Aspen put the plate of food on the table.

"Hungry?"

"I am. I forgot to eat."

"It's still warm."

"Who'd you have dinner with?" Cassie closed her eyes again.

"Anne Jean and Skeet."

"Then I won't even ask what's under the tinfoil. I know it's good. I'll have some."

"Do you want to explain belly dancing?"

"I do."

"Eat first, or explain belly dancing first."

"I can do both."

Aspen gave Cassie half the food Anne Jean had put on the plate. As usual Anne Jean had given her enough for two meals. She sat down outside the circle of candles. There was no rushing Cassie.

Cassie sighed. "I've decided that the women in town need belly dancing."

"Do they?"

"They do." Cassie balanced the plate on her knees and cut the beef into tiny pieces. Cassie had a theory that if you ate only tiny pieces, you fooled your stomach into believing it was full. "We're getting fat."

Aspen waited.

"What?" Cassie said between bites.

"You're not fat."

"Well, you don't see me as fat because I'm skinnier than most women around here, but to me, the bulge I see around my waist is . . ." Cassie paused dramatically. "Thirty years of growing fat."

"That's ridiculous. Besides, what do you know about belly dancing?"

"A lot." She picked up one of the books in front of her. "This one here not only talks about the history of belly dancing, but is a how-to book."

Aspen stared at the book. "I don't think a *how-to book* is going to get it."

"I'm not ready to show you now because I just got the books, but soon we'll be belly dancing."

"Not me."

"Why not?"

"Remember that time you decided we should take up tap dancing to lose weight? We tapped for days and months all over the kitchen, anyplace we could find a bare floor. Didn't lose a pound. Then the oil deliveryman saw us, and soon the whole town was laughing. About the only thing worse, you wanted to

16

free our spirits and tap dance in the nude, and like a fool I went along with it. My boobs were flying every which way. I was sore for days. Can you imagine what the town would have said if we'd been seen tap dancing naked?"

"Well, they didn't and so what? It didn't do any harm."

"Cassie, it did. For weeks, every time I walked into the classroom, the kids were doubled over in laughter. It took me quite a while to settle them down."

"Don't you think your kids know you're a wee bit strange? For God's sake, you sit in trees."

"That's different. Anyway, I met the new manager today," Aspen said to change the subject.

"So tell me about this *new woman*. What's she like?"

"I don't know, I just met her."

"Describe her."

"She looks like a woman." Cassie had a way of pricking her calm.

"Brown hair, black?"

"Blonde."

"Oh wow. Blonde would contrast nicely with your black hair."

"Now you're really being silly."

"Is she cute?"

"Nice looking. I wouldn't say cute."

"Is she—"

"Tall?" Aspen responded.

"No, silly. A lesbian?"

"How the hell do I know?"

"Well, you must have sensed something."

Exasperated, Aspen shifted on the floor. "I didn't sense a thing. All I want to know is if her being here means changes at the company."

"So is something changing?"

"I don't know." Aspen shrugged.

"So what did you think of her?"

17

"Same as her predecessor, I didn't like her."

"Maybe we should give her a chance."

"Why?"

"I don't know. Seemed like the right thing to say. Anyway, getting back to belly dancing . . ."

"Let's focus on getting you fed." Cassie furtively looked at the window. "Cass, I know you hate storms, but you're safe here."

"All right." She nibbled on a piece of meat. "This is really good. Cold, but good."

"Come on." Aspen turned on the kitchen lights. "I'll pop it in the microwave. You can eat. We'll talk about our day and then go to bed."

"Well, okay, but only if you promise me you'll try belly dancing once I learn."

"I promise." She had distracted her. That's all that mattered.

CHAPTER TWO

Leigh rolled over and pulled the covers higher on her neck and then peeked at the clock. Six a.m. She threw back the covers then swung her feet to the floor.

In the bathroom she studied the face in the unforgiving mirror. Those parts of her hair that she had slept on now stood at attention. When she was growing up, her sister Brittany had called it the *porcupine look*. She grabbed her toothbrush, but stopped when she heard the telephone.

"Yo," she said, the toothpaste dripping on the telephone. She wiped it off with her shirt.

"You've got toothpaste in your mouth. Go rinse and then I'll talk to you," Brittany demanded.

Leigh quickly finished brushing. "So why are you calling so early?"

She heard her sister snort. "I knew you were up. Do you still like your new place?"

Uh huh, she thought, Brittany never got to the point when she was unhappy about something. "The same as I told you last week. I've settled in. So what's not to like? It's a company house. It's furnished okay, and you know I don't care as long as I have a place to put my head."

"I don't agree. You don't have any ties to a place like that. It's not your home. There's nothing personal about it," her sister groused. Leigh groaned inwardly. "How do you expect to find someone?"

"Been there, done that, had this discussion. Now why did you call?"

"Don't be mean." Brittany, who was four years younger than she was, owned a dress shop in the Old Port district in Portland. She was silk and flowers to Leigh's denim and flannel. They hadn't been close until a few years earlier when their mother had gotten sick. After their mother died, they were like tandem sky-divers, dependent upon one another to survive. Their father abruptly left home when Leigh was eight. Growing up, Leigh resented her sister because she spent so many years parenting her while their mother worked two jobs. While her schoolmates were playing at the park and later driving around in their beat-up cars, Leigh was dragging Brittany to the playground or helping her do homework.

It was just after she had turned thirteen that she'd slipped out of the house to hang out with her friends after she thought her sister was asleep. When Leigh got home, the lights were on and her mother, who'd left work early, met her at the door. Brittany had awakened and called neighbors. Even now, Leigh still shivered when she remembered that night. Her mother didn't shout, but the look of defeat was so unmistakable on her face. That was the first time Leigh grasped how worn her mother really was. Leigh inhaled heavily. "So, you're calling why?"

"I'm leaving Harry."

"Does Harry know?"

"Well sort of, kinda. Oh hell, I don't know."

"Sorta, kinda?"

"He doesn't understand me."

"Well few of us do." Leigh tried to keep her manner easy.

"You're just being mean." Brittany pouted. "Harry loves me, but he isn't interested in me anymore."

"Have you tried to fix it? I think leaving is a bit excessive. Do you love him?"

"Of course I love him. It's just he's been preoccupied lately."

"How preoccupied can he be? He's superintendent of a wastewater treatment plant."

"He is not. He's a wastewater management engineer."

"He watches Portland's shit flow through the system."

"He does not. It's more than that. Besides, it's not his job that's distracted him."

"Another woman?"

"No, he has a new hobby."

"Harry?"

"Yes, Harry. Who do you think we're talking about? He's gotten into astrology."

"Harry?"

"Would you quit saying *Harry*?"

"Well, it sort of takes my breath away. I can't picture Harry concentrating on which moon is in the house of which planet or whatever that stuff is."

"Well he has and he does."

"When did this start?"

" A few months ago. He enrolled in this adult education class. When he first mentioned it, I thought it was great," Brittany huffed. "Not now! All he does is carry charts and stuff around."

"You're kidding."

"It gets worse."

"How much worse?"

"I can't get through the morning coffee and he's telling me what kind of day I'm going to have. And it's frightening, because lately when he says I'm going to have a bad day at the store—"

"You have one."

"You got it."

"Power of suggestion?"

"Hell, who knows? All I know is I go out of the house with pincers snapping at the air from rage." Brit was angry.

"Rage? Isn't that a little harsh?"

"I want to kill him." The words burst from Brittany's clamped jaws.

"Again, have you talked with him?"

"More times than you can imagine. So I'm leaving him."

"Forever?"

"Just for the weekend."

"And you're coming here." Leigh swallowed. She'd planned to camp in the woods over the weekend.

"Where else? I need my sister right now. I need to get away. Besides . . ."

"Besides?"

"Harry wants me to go to a conference in Boston."

"That sounds like a romantic getaway."

"Not this weekend."

"Is it for his job?"

"No, it's an astrology conference. He's all excited."

"Oh wow."

"Yeah, oh wow. We had it out. I told him I was not going to spend two days away from the store listening to a bunch of people talk about planets and whose star is falling."

"What did he say?"

"Kissed me on the cheek and told me to have a good weekend. So I'm leaving. When he gets home from work on Friday to pack for his trip, he will see my *I'm leaving* note and come looking for me."

"You're certain of that?"

"Well . . ." Brit was uncertain. "He'd better."

"I think that's a hell of a gamble. Talk to him until he hears you."

"I've tried. He won't listen. So I'll be there Friday. You doing anything?"

"Well . . ." Leigh stared out the window. "I had planned to spend the weekend backpacking the company land. There are some areas we want to cut and I need to check them out."

"So do it."

"You don't backpack."

"Not me, silly. I'll just hang around town, do some shopping."

"That'll take you five minutes."

"Leigh, I know you're trying to get out of this."

"Am not."

"I'll be fine. I don't need a babysitter. You've got to let go of that stuff. I'm not going to call the neighbors just because you're not home."

"Sorry." Leigh stared out the bedroom window. "Just, I always feel like I have to take care of you."

"Look, I need a place to light for a few days. I'm making a statement with Harry."

"Well, I just hope the statement doesn't end in divorce."

"Of course not. Harry needs me. He's just forgotten."

"Not to get your ire up, but there are worse hobbies. He could be fishing."

"At least he wouldn't always have me on edge about what the stars are saying about what kind of day I'm going to have. God!"

"Look, I'll be home around five. We can have dinner and then I'll head out in the morning, if you're sure you'll be all right."

"I'll be fine. Have you told them yet?"

"Not yet. The company plans to make the announcement on

Monday."

"How fitting. Tell a bunch of wood harvesters they're out of a job a few weeks before Labor Day. How weird is that?"

"Well, not the best timing, but the powers figure they'll start looking for work the next day. You lay people off on a Friday, they have two days to think about it, possibly get into mischief."

"Really?"

"It's happened with other companies. You can end up with a lot of vandalism."

"I didn't realize that. Do you have to tell them?"

"I'll be there, but my boss is coming down to say the words. The state plans to have its resource team there. They help displaced workers."

"Then what?"

"The local harvesting companies will hire them. They're the best trained."

"Then why all the gloom?"

"I've only been here a short time, but they're a great group, but I also understand where the company's coming from. You can't imagine what we pay in workman's comp. People really don't realize how dangerous the job is." She inhaled deeply. The layoff was bugging her. "The point is, my company did the numbers and realized that it's cheaper to hire private wood harvesting firms than to keep the employees."

"Why did the other company keep them on?"

"They didn't have the land debt we do. Besides, they got rid of the headaches by selling the land, but they still get to use the wood because they buy it from us."

"Sounds too complicated for me. I'm more interested in walking downtown Codyville and looking at the few stores and thinking about my life."

Leigh smiled to herself. "Sounds about right. You walk the downtown and look for bargains, and I'll walk the woods and think about my employees."

"We need to find you a woman."

"No, *we* don't." Leigh shuddered as she thought about the last time Brit had meddled in her life. Brittany had lured her to Portland promising her a quiet weekend, only to find she had planned a dinner party for Leigh and four single lesbians she'd met over the years. Leigh sucked in her breath.

"I know what you're thinking."

"Do not."

"Do too. You're thinking about the dinner party I held. Well, it wasn't so bad."

"Are you kidding? I felt like a pair of Italian leather shoes everyone wanted to try on. Why did you have to give them those cards with all my information on it?"

"It was just your telephone number and address."

"No, it wasn't. You had my birth date on there. The kinds of things I like. You even had a list of my dislikes . . ." The same frustrations she'd felt when her sister had subjected her to the party were still there.

"I put your birth date on there because it was coming up, and if they wanted to take you to dinner or something it would have been romantic."

"Romantic?" Leigh squeaked. "What's so romantic about your sister figuring you're so desperate she holds one of those Tupperware parties and you're the squeezable tupper? What's so romantic about women—"

"Enough, I was just trying to help." Leigh could hear the pout in her sister's voice. "After Kathy dumped you, you seemed so alone."

"First of all, Kathy didn't *dump* me. It was a mutual breakup, and frankly, dear sister, I've been quite content."

"Oh baloney. That's why you spend so much time in the woods?"

"I spend time in the woods because it's my job and because I like it." Leigh inhaled. "I go into the woods to relax. Something

I can't do around people."

"Well, seems silly to me. I relax best with people."

"You'd feel relaxed in the middle of Boston's Big Dig during rush hour."

"Now you're exaggerating. Besides, two of the women who were at the party got together. I get the cutest Christmas card from them thanking me."

"I think that's great, but just leave me out of any future matchmaking. I don't need a partner—"

"Of course you do."

"No! I don't!"

"You need to be in a relationship."

"I don't *need* a relationship. I don't *want* a relationship."

"You say that, but I know differently. You're lonely. You were made to be in a relationship. More than me actually."

"Leave it, Brittany." Leigh chewed on her upper lip, silent fury prowling inside of her.

"Anyway, getting back to Friday. I'll be there around three o'clock."

"I'll still be at work." Leigh smiled to herself. Brit had heard the resolve in Leigh's voice and knew better than to push. She returned to the reason she'd called.

"I want to get out of here before Harry gets home from work."

Leigh sighed. "Okay, the door will be unlocked."

"I hate that."

"Brittany, I live in the country. It's safe here, but more importantly—"

"I know, you've told me. Locks only keep honest people out." Brit's voice was singsong.

"Bingo."

"Do you want anything from here? Good wine? Bread?"

"Do not bring me lentils and wheat germ."

"I only did that once."

"And I had to throw them out when I moved. I still don't know what you do with them."

"I left you several recipes."

"Let's not go there." Leigh stared at the clock. "I have to get to work. I'll be home around five o'clock. Don't cook anything. I'll take you to dinner."

"Sounds good."

"So, it's agreed? We'll have dinner together Friday night, and then I'm gone for two days and you'll be all right?"

"It sounds like we're making a contract."

"No, just getting the terms of our agreement down. I don't want you to say that I dropped the ball or something."

"I'd never say that."

"You would."

"Forget it. I'll see you on Friday." Leigh heard the click.

CHAPTER THREE

Leigh turned her truck onto the highway, relieved that the week was over. She'd shut production down early on Friday and given them all a half day off. Leigh had worked for the company for more than ten years, and as their only woman forester, she wasn't worried about being fired. Besides, her boss, a gruff old woodsman in his seventies, liked her and she liked him. Jeff had started cutting trees as soon as he was big enough to hold a saw, working alongside his father in woodlots all over the state, including Codyville. Jeff often talked about the *good old days* when he spent his summers at the wood camps. Leigh knew it was tough work for a man, let alone a child, and she was surprised how Jeff recalled those days with such nostalgia.

Leigh thought about the boss she adored. Although he was surly and bristly, there was an endless glint of kindness in his teal-colored eyes. He was built like a moose through his arms and chest, with fingers as twisted as corkscrews.

Arthritis, that Jeff had nicknamed *Arthur I tis*, had seized his back and pushed his head forward like a turtle ready to snap at its quarry. He told people he wasn't a modern man like those movie actors in Hollywood who always talked about getting in touch with their feelings, but Leigh sensed Jeff was more in touch with his feelings than he realized. He just didn't know how to articulate them. The first time she'd tested her authority, Jeff had disagreed with her decision but had not overruled her in front of the employees. Years later they'd talked about that first time and he told her he took no issue with what she'd done even though he hadn't agreed.

Leigh groaned. Her sister's black BMW SUV was parked in front of her house. She'd hoped her sister and husband were wrapped romantically in each other's arms.

"I'm so glad you're here." Brittany pushed open the screen. "I have so much to tell you."

"Harry's coming."

"No, silly." Brittany wrapped her arm through Leigh's. "I can't wait to show you what I've done."

Leigh sighed. She hated those words. "What exactly have you done? Brittany Larkin, if there's a strange woman in my living room, you are dead meat. No, more than that, you're going to be tortured dead meat."

"You're so suspicious." Brittany pulled Leigh through the kitchen. "Ta da."

Leigh gasped as she stared at the flowery curtains that covered the windows in her living room. Her couch and chair had been moved to one side, and there was a large red wooden chair sitting where her favorite chair had once sat. Colorful cloth drapes covered every table, and a lamp that looked like someone had nailed together pieces of tin and then stuck a lampshade on top was perched on a table next to the red chair.

"I brought along a few things to cheer the room up." The room looked like it was a sunrise ready to burst out of the sky. "You're so monochromatic with tans and more tans, so I decided to bring along lots of color. Don't you just love it?" Brittany enthused as she squeezed Leigh's arm. "I didn't do much, although a lot is needed." Her sister pulled her into the bathroom. "Look what I've done in here."

Leigh blinked. Her white towels had been replaced with pink and orange ones. A wooden dog was sitting in the corner, an extra roll of toilet paper perched strategically on his head. *Was the dog smirking*? Leigh wondered.

"How long have you been here?"

"Since this morning." Brittany did a small dance around the room. "After we talked, I just had this wonderful desire to do something for you. All week I've been gathering stuff. 'Course, it's fantastic that my shop is next to this wonderful odds and ends store that has things like this great dog." She adjusted the roll of toilet paper on its head.

"What about Harry?"

"Who knows? He kissed me this morning and said he'd see me on Monday. I expect when he got home from work he read my note and is on his way here." Brit sounded confident. "Don't you just love it?"

"It's overwhelming." Leigh was able to get out.

"And beautiful. I just love this living room." She pulled Leigh back inside.

"Have you done anything else?"

"The next time I visit, your bedroom definitely needs work, and that spare room I'm sleeping in will undergo a complete makeover. So what do you think?"

"It's kind of overwhelming."

"You do like it?" Brittany frowned as she looked around the room.

"I . . ." The look of insecurity she'd seen so often etched on Brittany's face when they were growing up was there again like a perfectly etched lithograph. Their father drunk most of the time and then disappearing in the night. Their mother gone all day as a waitress and part of the night as a checker at a convenience store. Leigh had adopted a confidence borne of years of taking care of her sister. Brittany had developed insecurities borne of years of living with a sister who resented her role. "It's fine. I have only one request. I really like that chair over there." Leigh pointed to the chair that Brittany had buried in a corner. "Maybe we could move that more into the room? It's kind of where I sit every night."

Brittany sighed. "Well, if we must. It's so ugly. Hmm, wait just a second." She flew out of the room.

Leigh stood like a storm-weary survivor surveying the damage. *I hate it. I really, really hate it,* she said to herself.

"I threw this in at the last minute." Brittany held up a yellow and green throw. "Help me." She tugged the chair back into the middle of the room and put it next to the red one. She shook out the drape, and it floated to rest on top of the chair like a huge beach ball bouncing into place. "Wow! That does finish it off." She surveyed the room. "Come on. I'm starving."

"I need a shower."

"Of course, silly me. You shower and we'll go for dinner. I can't wait to get back here and just savor all these colors." Brit was happy. Leigh turned toward the stairs. Keep it inside, she told herself. Don't say what you think. Just shower and go to dinner. Leigh glanced back at the room one last time as she reached the top of the stairs. *Savor?* That's not the word she would have used.

"Wow, this place is nice. Linen tablecloths and napkins, candlelight. Who could ask for more? If the food is as good as you say, then this is one nice restaurant."

"Can I bring you drinks?" The waitress handed them menus.

Leigh looked at her nametag. "Melissa, I would love a glass of Beringer's white zinfandel." She looked expectantly at her sister.

"I'll have a piña colada with extra cherries and pineapple."

"I can add the extra cherries. Unfortunately, we're out of pineapple."

"Whatever," Brittany said dismissively. She waited until the waitress left. "No pineapple? I don't believe it."

"Brit, it's no big deal. I doubt there's much call for piña coladas here. I suspect most people drink either beer or wine." Leigh looked past Brittany. Aspen and another woman had entered the restaurant. She hadn't realized how attractive a woman Aspen was now that she wasn't buried under a jacket. Dressed in a lavender blouse and black slacks, Leigh marveled at how delicately beautiful she really was. The other woman was slightly heavier, but also attractive. She was wearing a bright pink caftan that was ostentatious to Aspen's conventional. The woman in the caftan marched into the room with the confidence of a woman who took charge of her life and the lives of others.

"You know that woman?" Brittany followed her gaze.

"The one in lavender. I briefly met her at the office earlier this week."

"She's beautiful. Who's that with her?"

"Couldn't say."

"She's looking at you." Brittany nodded toward Aspen.

Aspen said something to the other woman, who looked their way. The woman grabbed Aspen by the arm and propelled her toward their table.

"Good evening. Leigh, right?" Aspen said rigidly.

"Right and you're Aspen, a name one doesn't forget." Leigh was confused by Aspen's apparent reluctance. "This is my sister, Brittany Larkin."

Brittany stood up and shook hands. "Aspen, what a pretty

name."

"Thank you, this is my friend Cassie Jenkins."

"Join us," Brittany said.

"We don't want to interrupt. I'm sure you want to talk about family stuff." Aspen held back.

"Heck, we can do that any time." Brittany pulled out a chair. "Join us. Right, Leigh?"

"Of course." Leigh forced a smile.

"I think that'd be great." Cassie pulled out another chair. "I just love meeting new people. So, Brittany, right?" Aspen reluctantly sat down. "Do you live near here?"

"I live in Portland, well Yarmouth to be exact. I'm visiting my sister."

"I love your dress."

"Thank you. I own a woman's clothing shop in the Old Port District of Portland." Brittany glanced at Leigh. "Leigh hates when I talk about my store, but since you mentioned it, dresses are what I sell. I named it LeiBrit Boutique."

"Neat name."

"Lei is for my sister, and Brit, of course, is for Brittany. It sounded French, yet it combined our two names."

"I like it." Cassie beamed. Aspen looked like she had cramps. "Don't you, Aspen?"

"Yes, very nice."

"And I like your caftan. It's so sixty-ish," Brit said.

"I discovered them in high school and I've worn them ever since. They're not stylish like your dress, but it suits me."

"I say what works is great and hang what people think. Do you live here?"

"I do and have my whole life. I used to be married, but now I'm just looking." Cassie giggled.

"Well, I'm married," Brit replied curtly. "My husband is at a convention, so I decided to spend the weekend with my sister. I left him a *Dear Harry* note, and I expect he's on his way here right now."

"Oh . . ." Cassie looked away.

"It's a long story. I won't bore you with the details." Leigh was relieved. "What about you, Aspen? What do you do for a living?" Brit asked.

"I teach in the middle school."

"Aspen is one of our best teachers," Cassie enthused. "I job around. After Tommy the jerk—my husband, that is—and I divorced, I couldn't settle on any one thing, so I do all kinds of things. House-sit, dog-sit. You name it and I do it."

"Well, that's kind of fun and certainly not boring," Brittany said. "But you said you were *looking?*" Brittany mimicked. "Don't look too hard. Marriage isn't all that it's supposed to be."

"You aren't going to get an argument from me." Cassie waved to the waitress. "Melissa, how are you tonight?"

"Just great, Cassie. How are you, Ms. Brown?" the waitress asked more formally.

Aspen smiled warmly. "Fine, Melissa, and since it's been years since you've been in middle school, need I remind you that you can call me Aspen?"

The young woman blushed. "Sorry, it takes getting used to. Would you like something to drink?" She handed them menus.

"I'll have a cup of coffee," Aspen said.

"And I'll have one of those." Cassie pointed at Brittany's drink. "Why, this is just so great," Cassie said after Melissa had left. "Aspen mentioned that she had met you earlier this week. She didn't tell me how cute you were."

"She is kinda cute, isn't she?" Brittany said looking at her sister as if for the first time. "And she's single." Leigh glared at her sister. "Don't glare at me. My sister is a *lesbian*. I'm not supposed to out her, but this is different." Brittany looked around the room. "She was in a relationship with this awful woman. Five years later, they broke up. Thank God that one's over!" Leigh glared at her again. Why had Brit revealed that bit of news?

34

"Isn't that wonderful?" Cassie was obviously enjoying the information. "Not about the awful partner, but Aspen is a *lesbian* also," she said just as quietly. "This is so cosmic, the two of them lesbians." Aspen glanced at Cassie, her expression hardened. If thoughts could kill, Leigh decided, Cassie would be dead.

"Isn't this too much? I was telling my sister just the other day that she needed to find a partner." Leigh choked on her wine. There was a flicker of amusement on Aspen's otherwise motionless face.

"We're going to talk about something else," Leigh warned.

"Don't be silly," Brittany said. "We're just making conversation."

"I recommend we look at our menus." Leigh stared at her sister.

"Well, okay . . . so what do you recommend?" Brit asked.

"I've had several of the dishes. The haddock stuffed with scallops and shrimp is good. I personally love the prime rib," Leigh said, closing the menu.

"That haddock dish sounds wonderful," Brittany said. "What are you having, Cassie?"

"The haddock dish," Cassie said simply. "I've had it several times. The sauce is wonderful. What are you thinking of having?" she asked Leigh.

"Prime rib," Brittany answered first. "My sister is a carnivore. She would have been a wonder in the caves of old. She'd have gone out and killed the . . ." Brittany waved her hand in the air dismissively. "Whatever they killed in those days and would have dragged it home and fed the whole tribe."

"I eat other things." Leigh tried to suppress the frustration she was feeling with her sister. Already there had been way too much conversation about her. "I like meat," Leigh said reservedly. "Didn't I just recommend the haddock dish to you?"

"Oh, and she likes fish. Other than that, she is unwilling to really experiment with food. The last time she was in Portland . . ." Brittany turned away from Leigh's scowl. "I took her to this really wonderful French restaurant. Well, do you think there was a thing on the menu that she was crazy about? Finally, she settled for something with . . . I think it had veal in it. She hardly ate a bite."

"Do we have to talk about my eating habits?" Leigh glared at her sister yet again.

"I think eating habits are important." Cassie picked up on the theme. "I think they speak volumes about a person. Aspen here is an environmentalist. She sits in trees. She's protested. Sat down in front of bulldozer operators who were trying to mow down trees, but she eats meat. A real contradiction if you ask me."

"What does one have to do with the other?" Aspen demanded.

"Just that most environmentalists are vegetarians. They see eating meat as a contradiction to saving the earth and animals. You know all that stuff. Now, I, on the other hand, don't eat lobster, not because I'm opposed to eating meat, but because they are cooked alive." Cassied shuddered. "But that's another story."

"I think—" Aspen glowered at Cassie.

"Don't go getting your heater turned up," Cassie objected. "I don't mean *your not eating meat* as a criticism, but it gets to the heart of what I was saying."

"Which is?" Aspen asked.

"Just that you can't predict people."

"I agree," Brittany joined in.

Leigh now understood Aspen's stiffness. She was an honest-to-God, card-carrying tree hugger. *Well, the hell with her*, Leigh thought. She'd spent most of her professional life defending herself against the tree huggers and environmental morons, and she wasn't going to do it again.

"Ready to order?" Leigh was relieved at the interruption.

"I'll have the haddock," Brittany said. "And the salad with the house dressing."

"Me too," Cassie added.

"How about you . . . Aspen?" Melissa asked, her pen poised above her pad.

"I'll have the prime rib, the salad with the house dressing and the rice pilaf." She looked at Cassie, daring her to comment.

"How would you like that cooked?"

"Medium rare." Aspen continued to stare at Cassie.

"And you?" she asked Leigh.

"I'll have exactly the same thing." Leigh handed her menu to Melissa.

"Isn't that wonderful?" Brittany said after Melissa had left. "You both ordered the same thing. I just think that's too cool."

"Me, too." Cassie grinned, angling her head at Aspen, "Even though I know it was just to make a point with me. You know," she said, returning to their original conversation, "even though my marriage ended on a less-than-pleasant note, I really believe in relationships. It didn't sour me one minute. But Aspen—"

"Me?" Aspen squeaked out her interruption. "Just leave me out of this."

"Don't be ridiculous. There's nothing secret about it. Aspen was in this relationship a few years back which ended abruptly when Jackie announced she was moving to New York. She'd decided she was fed up with small-town living and left town. Didn't even ask Aspen to go along." Cassie turned to Aspen. "See? That little bit of information didn't hurt one bit, did it?"

"It will when I kill you later," Aspen said between clenched teeth.

"She's so silly."

"Leigh's the same way. After she and that other woman who shall remain nameless broke up, Leigh refused to even consider another relationship."

"Don't go any further," Leigh also warned.

"Leigh has this toenail theory."

Leigh blanched. "Don't you even go there," she admonished her sister.

Brittany threw her a look of disdain. "There's nothing wrong with it."

"I can't wait to hear," Cassie said.

"Well." Brittany looked at her sister. "Oh, quit giving me that look. I think this theory is great. Leigh believes you can judge how considerate your partner is by how she or *he* cuts their toenails." She glanced at Leigh. "People cut their toenails in the shower, in the bathtub, while sitting on the johnny. Most people just let them fall on the floor or in the bathtub. Not my sister. She cuts her toenails over a wastebasket."

"I cut mine in the bathtub," Cassie said.

"That's the problem, you leave them behind," Brittany said. "The little ones eventually go down the drain. The big ones poke your partner in the foot while showering."

"I usually ignore them, but you're right."

Leigh glanced at Aspen, who was trying to keep from laughing. Well at least the toenail story had loosened the woman up. "Brittany, you're going to pay for this."

"Don't mind her. Anyway, Leigh's theory is that a thoughtful partner would cut their toenails in a way that would leave no sharp points behind."

"I think that's wonderful." Cassie looked at Leigh. "Obviously, your former partner cut her toenails in a way that annoyed you."

"That and more," Brittany answered for her sister. "I won't go into all of that. Now my Harry . . ." Brittany took her elbows off the table as Melissa set salads in front of them.

"Could we talk about something other than toenails now that the food is here?" Leigh regretted the day she'd shared her theory with Brittany. It had come out of frustration after she and Kathy had had an argument.

"Sure." Brittany tasted the salad. "This house dressing is

wonderful. You can tell the quality of a restaurant by its house dressing."

"Really?" Cassie asked. Brit was in heaven. She had found a willing listener.

The rest of the evening, Brittany talked about her store, while Cassie talked about belly dancing. Aspen added little except to nod at the appropriate times or laugh when the story called for it.

"I'm sorry," Leigh said to Aspen as they waited outside the restaurant. Cassie had stopped to talk with some people and had drawn Brittany into the conversation. Leigh had stepped away from the two women and out the door. Aspen joined her.

"For what? It's obvious they're clones. I felt like I was at a tennis match. One would say something and the other would lob words back. They didn't miss a stroke."

"No, they didn't." Leigh was still fuming. "The conversation was pretty . . ."

"Strange?" Aspen finished the sentence. "Yes, but that's Cassie, and I suspect that's your sister." Aspen put her hand on Leigh's arm. "I didn't mean that unkindly about your sister."

Leigh laughed. "I didn't take it that way. My sister is *strange*."

"I guess in a way it's good they were together, because Cassie often goes off on avenues of bizarre, and your sister seemed to enjoy listening to her."

"My sister thrives on eccentric." Leigh stared at the stars. "And about that toenail thing . . ."

"Don't try to explain it." Aspen laughed. "I was watching you. The earth wasn't big enough to swallow you up, even though you wished it had."

"I wanted to throttle her."

"She loves you."

"Sometimes I think they mistakenly gave us the wrong baby

at the hospital."

"You're lucky. You have a sister." Leigh could hear the sadness in Aspen's voice.

"Most of the time, and by the way it was nice—"

"Now what are we going to do?" Brittany demanded. Cassie was behind her.

"Yeah, it's too early to go home," Cassie joined in.

"You guys do whatever," Leigh said, sorry for the interruption. "I have to be up extra early tomorrow."

"My sister's camping in the woods. Won't be back until Sunday."

"Really?" Aspen was clearly surprised.

"Yes, really." Leigh smiled.

"You're not going with her?" Cassie asked.

"Heavens no."

"Why don't we go shopping in Bangor tomorrow?"

"I'd love it," Brittany said eagerly. "Join us, Aspen?"

"Can't. Winter's coming on. I've got to get wood cut, split and stacked."

Leigh kept her face impassive. *A tree hugger who burns trees.*

"Aspen hates shopping. I know where Leigh lives, so I'll pick you up around ten."

"Fantastic."

"We'll see you tomorrow." Cassie linked her arm through Aspen's. "Sorry you can't join us, Leigh. Why don't you put your trip off until next weekend?"

"Not a chance," Brittany answered for her sister. "Leigh hates shopping just as much as Aspen. But I'm looking forward to tomorrow. 'Course if Harry is waiting at Leigh's house then I may have to adjust our plans." Brittany fluttered her hand disdainfully. "Oh, the heck with him. He can just hang around until we get back."

"Good woman. From what little you've said, sounds like he didn't care if he abandoned you for the weekend, so a few hours

40

of cooling his heels will make him more interested in you," Cassie said.

"Agreed," Brittany said excitedly. "I hadn't thought about it that way."

"Well," Leigh said quietly to Aspen as Brittany and Cassie finished talking about their plans. "It was nice having dinner."

"It was," Aspen said succinctly. "Have a good time backpacking. Most wood harvest managers only see trees for the dollars they represent, not their real value."

"Oh, my sister does," Brittany said. Leigh always marveled at how her sister could carry on a conversation with one person and eavesdrop on another. "She's very good at balancing what the stockholders want with her belief in the preservation of the forest. I've heard that lecture a thousand times."

"I bet you have." Aspen looked at Leigh. "It was a nice evening. Thank you."

"I enjoyed it. Thank you." An interesting evening, Leigh thought as she turned to her truck. Aspen was an enigma, lukewarm at times, cold and distant at others.

"Well, that was really a treat," Brit said. "I like her."

"Cassie?"

"Her too, but I liked Aspen."

"How could you tell? You and Cassie were so busy talking."

"I can tell. There's value in silence. I noticed she was attentive to the conversation and joined in where necessary. She kept looking at you. I think she kinda likes you."

"She was looking at me because she hates me."

"Don't be silly. Why would she hate you?"

"I cut trees. You heard Cassie. Aspen sees herself as the godmother of trees."

"So? What does that have to do with anything? That's what you do, not who you are. Aspen's smart enough to figure that out. Besides, we need both."

Leigh grunted. "About that toenail story, why did you bring

that up? We barely know those women."

"Simple, if you and Aspen fall in love, it's important she knows that up front."

"What?" Leigh nearly shouted the word.

"It could happen."

"And so could the earth falling off its axis."

"I saw how you were looking at her." Brit was smug.

"I was not."

"You were too."

Leigh yanked open her truck door so hard she almost lost her footing. She started the engine. "Could we just have silence, please?"

Brittany laughed. "You used to say that when we were young. I liked Aspen," Brit said after a moment. "She'd be just right for you."

"Leave it, Brit."

"I wonder where she got that name?"

"Who knows? She didn't have time to explain because you and Cassie were prattling, I thought you'd stop long enough to eat, but you didn't miss a beat."

"It's better than what you were doing, which was sitting there like a wart on a toad." Brit studied her. "She's a lesbian, you're a lesbian. I expect you two'll be going out soon."

Leigh groaned. "I'm going in the woods tomorrow and I'm going to forget this meal. Please, could we have just a few minutes of silence while we drive home?"

"Of course. I can do silence."

Leigh sighed. Her sister had a way of getting in the last word. *Poor Harry*, she thought. *No, lucky Harry.* He was off at a conference.

CHAPTER FOUR

Life was amazing and in perspective after a weekend in the woods. Leigh didn't feel any better about the layoff, but at least the foul mood she'd been in the day she'd left was gone. During her hours in the woods, she'd also thought about the woman with the ebony eyes, eyes that were dangerous yet bewitching. Leigh had dealt with the Aspen environmentalists of the world. Aspen was a card-carrying, going-to-jail environmentalist who couldn't see the forest for the trees.

Leigh tossed her backpack and tent in the back of her truck. She'd also thought about her sister. When they'd returned to Leigh's house, Harry wasn't there. For the first hour, Brittany ranted and raved about men, and when Leigh insisted Brittany call Harry, Brittany had a tantrum. When she suggested Brit go home, she tossed her a sour look. Saturday morning Brittany had gotten up, her hair all askew, and announced she was divorcing

Harry, selling her business in Portland and moving to Codyville to be a painter. That's when Leigh left for the woods. She didn't want to spend her weekend stuck in Brittany's emotional vortex, which seemed to range from mild irritation to black fury.

Leigh parked her car next to Brittany's.

"Welcome home!" Brit exclaimed.

"You okay?" Leigh studied her sister.

"Cassie and I spent every moment together. I just adore that woman. We've decided men suck. We've been shopping in Bangor and Ellsworth. She started to teach me belly dancing." Brittany's words were speeding faster than a NASCAR driver heading for the checkered flag. "I found out that Aspen's real name is Aspen. Her mother loved trees. Cass said that's where Aspen got her passion for the environment, and I guess it's a real passion because she's battled everybody from the paper companies to the state to save them. Her father abandoned her and her sister Willow when she was eleven and Willow was eight. Something like us, although we were younger. Her mother, like ours, had to scratch to get by, but Aspen and Willow both went to college. Anyway, Aspen went through some real pain after her mother died. I guess from what Cassie said, they were really close," Brittany linked her arm through Leigh's and started to pull her toward the house. "But the real tragedy occurred a short time after that when Willow died in an automobile accident. That was several years ago, and Cassie hinted at some stuff, but all I could figure out was that Aspen went through some really heavy pain in her life dealing with that loss. Cassie said she doesn't drink, so don't bother offering her a glass of wine. Maybe she's an alcoholic. Anyway, she's been in relationships, but not a lot. The longest one lasted, about four years. So . . ." Brittany stopped. "How was your weekend?"

"Not as exciting." Leigh laughed. "Hold on while I get my stuff."

"Of course." Brittany waited for her. "Don't ask about Harry. I haven't heard from the lug nut all weekend, and as far as I'm concerned, he's history. Cassie said not to think about him. Do you know that woman chose lobsters over her husband?"

"I beg your pardon?"

"I mean it. She got into that whole 'don't boil the lobster' thing that Mary Tyler Moore was involved with. I hadn't thought about it, but she's right. You throw live lobsters into boiling water, or chefs cut their backs down the middle—while they're alive I might add—and stuff them with that Newberg stuff. We don't do that with any other whatever you want to call them—living being, I guess. Anyway, I've decided to never eat another lobster and I'm going to insist that anyone around me also not eat any." She paused thoughtfully. "Anyway, she told her husband—"

"Let me guess, he was a lobsterman."

"You got it. She told him he had to choose between the lobsters and her."

"And he chose the lobsters."

"She was devastated at first, but now that she's into Zen and Buddhism, she said she'd never have grown if it hadn't been for lobsters."

"Frighteningly, somehow that makes sense."

"She volunteers at the library and spends all of her time reading."

Inside, Leigh saw the place settings and the decorated table in the dining room. "We're getting company?" Leigh counted six place settings.

"I wanted to have a welcome home meal for you."

Leigh sighed. All the way home all she thought about was a snack, a hot shower and bed. "And our guests are who?"

"I think it's *whom*, but never mind. Cassie and Aspen and a new couple I met, Skeet and his wife Anne Jean. You're going to love them. We had dinner there Saturday night and I wanted to reciprocate."

"Aspen's coming here?" Leigh allowed unhappily. "I had the feeling she didn't like me."

"You're an enigma, Cassie said. Aspen's curious."

Leigh shook her head. "What about Harry?"

Brittany's smile faded. "I told you I don't want to talk about him. When I get home, I'm filing for divorce."

"Is it possible he's gotten sick or hurt?"

"Not Harry." Brittany pulled rolls out of the oven. "He's somewhere in Massachusetts wrapped around some damn star or whatever it is that they do."

"Divorce?" Leigh asked. "Isn't that just a tad drastic?"

"Nope. I'm divorcing Harry. We're having broiled salmon and tomato, mozzarella and basil salad. I got everything in Bangor except for the greens and tomatoes, they're from Aspen's garden. We also are having wild rice pilaf with pecans and dried cranberries, and for dessert panna cotta with berry coulis."

Leigh's head was buzzing. Salmon? Panna cotta? "I want to talk about divorce."

"And I want to tell you about panna cotta." Brittany held up the recipe book.

"I'll pass." Leigh realized she was caught up in Brittany's whirlwind. "I'm going to grab a shower. I do have time for a shower, right?"

"Of course, but make it quick. They'll be here soon. Go, go." Brittany gently pushed her sister toward the stairs. "I can't wait for you to meet Skeet and Anne Jean."

Leigh picked up her backpack and carried it upstairs. She glanced furtively around her bedroom, fearful that some colorful scarf or other decorative touch had appeared, and was relieved to see there were no changes. She looked at her bed. It looked so inviting. Instead she stripped and showered.

"You look great," Brittany said as Leigh entered the room.

"Thank you." Leigh glanced down at her jeans and white shirt. Brittany was definitely in a good mood. She usually fussed

46

about what Leigh was wearing.

"Would you open the wine? I have everything ready. I can't wait." Brit was excited. "Skeet tells such wonderful stories, I couldn't stop listening."

"What kinds of stories?" Leigh uncorked the bottle.

"About when he was a young man. I don't know . . ." Brittany frowned. "Some people can turn a memory into a powerful story, while others make them sound like dull recitations of the past. He's just very colorful in how he describes things, and I adore his down east accent with the hard 'r's' and dropped 'h's'. And he's done everything from working in the woods to fishing. He even built the house he and Anne Jean live in. They have three children, all scattered. Not a single one stayed around here."

"Probably because there aren't any jobs."

"That's what he said. He said he didn't want his children to eke out a living like he had to. But for all his struggles, he wasn't complaining." Brittany took the salad out of the refrigerator.

"Probably because he's happy with what he has."

"You're right. Funny, I started out with a beat-up Plymouth Horizon. Now I drive a BMW. Harry and I started out in a tiny house. Now we have a huge house and I'm not happy."

"You're not happy right now." Leigh took wineglasses out of the cupboard. "Because you're mad at Harry."

"I couldn't care less about him."

"Maybe Harry's homesick. Maybe he fell down those carpeted stairs you have."

"He left for Boston."

"How do you know?"

"I know."

"Did he call?"

"Not exactly."

Leigh stopped pouring the wine and looked at her sister. "Not exactly?"

"I called my neighbor. She saw him put his overnight bag in

47

his car and leave."

"You had your neighbor spying on Harry?"

"Well, yeah." Brittany couldn't look her in the eyes.

"That's disgusting and sneaky."

"Of course it is, but what's a wife to do?"

"Talk to your husband!" Leigh almost shouted the words. "I'm sorry," she said more quietly. "It seems to me you're going through a lot and involving a lot of people just to see if your husband is going to do what you want."

"That's not fair, Leigh." Brittany smacked the salad bowl down on the dining room table. Lettuce bounced out onto the tablecloth.

"Then explain to me what's going on."

"I just asked my neighbor to check on when he got home and when he left." Brittany picked up the errant pieces of lettuce and tossed them back into the bowl.

"And?"

"He got home around three and left a half hour later."

"And?"

"I'm pissed. He reads my note and still leaves for Boston. Thank God for Cassie."

"And she did what?"

"I've been doing yoga and meditating."

"All in two days."

"We never stopped the whole weekend . . ." Brit declared. "I've enjoyed my time here, except for being mad at Harry. I can't believe he read my note and went to Boston."

"Have you considered the possibility that Harry didn't read your note? That he thought you might be at work? After all, you've worked late at the store before."

"How could he miss the note? I put it right on his dresser."

"You've said it before, a stink bomb could go off and not only would Harry not hear it, he wouldn't even smell it."

"I guess . . ."

48

"Why don't you call him? I'm sure he has his cell phone with him."

"I could." Brittany pondered the idea. "No, I can't. Cassie said it's like giving in."

"Cassie again. Cassie is divorced and maybe she doesn't do relationships well."

"One mistake doesn't mean she doesn't do relationships well. Besides—" Brittany opened the door "Our company is here."

Brittany greeted Aspen and Cassie. *Wow,* Leigh thought. Aspen was breathtaking in jeans and a white blouse. Aspen shyly smiled at her. Leigh felt warm inside. Embarrassed, she turned her attention to Cassie, who was dressed in a multi-colored caftan. *What the hell was that about?* she wondered as she again looked at Aspen.

"Skeet and Anne Jean are right behind us," Cassie said.

"Fantastic. Make yourself comfortable. We have wine, coffee, tea, whatever." Brittany opened the door again and greeted the couple.

"Leigh, this is Skeet and Anne Jean Jones, my sister Leigh."

"You're the woodlot manager," Skeet said, shaking hands.

"I am."

"Lots of rumors flying around about you."

"I expect," Leigh said with a laugh.

"You stop," Anne Jean chided him. "Leave the poor woman alone. He's just impossible." She looked tenderly at him. "He's just trying to get you all nerved up."

"I was just letting her know that people know she's in town and they're talking." Skeet feigned a hurt look.

"I'm not sure I want to know what they're saying." Leigh laughed as she picked up the bottle of wine. "How about a glass of wine? A bottle of beer?"

"Beer," Skeet said.

"Can I get you some coffee?" Leigh asked Aspen.

"Thanks."

"How about you, Anne Jean and Cassie?"

"Coffee, black please," they both said.

"Let's go into the living room," Brittany said. "We can visit in there."

"You guys go ahead," Leigh said. "I'll bring the drinks in."

"Can I help carry?" Aspen asked.

"That would be nice. Thank you."

"How was the camping trip?"

"Good. Beautiful out there."

"It is. I'd hate to see it change."

"What makes you think that it will?" Leigh asked as she opened the beers.

"Your investors paid lots of money for that land, and cutting wood and selling it isn't going to give them the return they demand," she said stiffly. Leigh sensed the steel door of coldness that had been so apparent when they'd met was back. She wondered why Aspen had come. Was this some kind of weird tree-hugger test?

"All I know is I'm responsible for cutting trees to feed the mills here and in other parts of the state. I've been told to plant as many trees as I cut. Which I'm doing."

"But that doesn't mean that something bigger isn't looming."

"As in?"

"I don't know. Some kind of development. It's happening elsewhere. Eventually the trees are gone, replaced with condos and expensive houses and silver hairs on golf carts. The trees slaughtered, the land wrecked."

"My company's into operating woodlots. That's what we do best," Leigh said just as stiffly. She wasn't in the mood to explain her company to a rabid environmentalist, no matter how charming her eyes were. "Would you mind carrying the cream and sugar?" For the first time since she'd met Aspen, she realized she didn't like her. "I have drinks," Leigh said. "I—"

50

She stopped. There were brightly colored paintings on two of the walls and some kind of round object that looked like a bent wheel rim on another.

"Surprise." Brittany's face was aglow.

"Wow." Leigh nearly dropped the tray.

"I knew you'd like it," Brittany said. "My sister just loves the touches I add to her life," she said to the others. "She's very into tans and variations of tan. You feel like you're dying in the desert when you're sitting in one of her rooms. So I added some color, a few scarves on tables and a new chair and now the new pictures, and voilà, we have perfection." Brittany swept her arms like a symphony conductor.

"I just love it." Cassie was excited. "She found the pictures in Ellsworth. The metal wall object in Bangor. Isn't this just the best, Aspen?"

"The best," Aspen said lukewarmly. Leigh detected a look of sympathy. *Well, she may be an inflexible tree hugger, but at least she has better taste than Cassie.*

"What do you think, Anne Jean?" Cassie asked.

"It's lovely. Lots of color, don't you think, Skeet?"

"I'd be wearin' sunglasses if I lived here."

"Hush," Anne Jean said quickly. "Judas Priest, he didn't mean that the way it came out. Besides, what do men know about decorating?"

"A lot." Skeet stood firmly planted in the middle of the room, his arms folded. "As a matter of fact, a lot of decorators are men. Kinda sissy men, but men anyway. Funny though, they seemed to be named Bruce for some reason. That one I don't understand." Skeet rubbed his knuckles against his prickly cheek.

"And how do you know that?" Anne Jean demanded.

"I read the magazines at the dentist's office. I ain't numb as a pounded thumb."

"Well." Anne Jean smiled affectionately at him. "You never cease to amaze me."

51

"Don't mean to be rude, Brittany, but I'd put you in a bait bag, stuff you into a lobster trap and dump you over the side if ya ever did this to my living room."

Brit was hurt. "Well." Brittany turned to Leigh. "If you don't like it, I can change it."

"It's fine. It just takes getting used to," Leigh said to cover the awkwardness.

"You apologize, ya old coot," Anne Jean said to Skeet. "You've hurt her feelings."

Skeet was embarrassed. "I'm sorry. I didn't mean anything by it. I was just sayin' if it was my house. Well . . ."

"It's okay." Brittany's smile was thin. "Frankly, I like the honesty. It hurt, but it's candid. My sister would grin and bear it, and my husband wouldn't notice."

"Well, if nothing else, you get honesty from this man," Anne Jean said. "One time we were in church, not that I get Skeet to church all that often. You remember Bertha May Miller?" She looked at Aspen and Cassie, who nodded. "She had on this hat she had made. It had all these lovely feathers and things stuck all over it. Anyway, Skeet leans over and tells her he'd wished he'd brought his gun so he could shoot it. Well, if you'd seen the look on Bertha May's face, she couldn't decide if she wanted to laugh or punch him. In the end she laughed, but everyone who overheard him say it just held their breath."

"It was the ugliest thing I ever saw." Skeet grinned.

"Skeet may be right," Brittany said thoughtfully. "We can undo all of this right now if you'd like." She started to pull a cloth off the table.

"Leave it," Leigh said gently. "It'll take getting used to, but it's fine. Why don't we relax and go into the dining room where we can talk until dinner's ready?"

"Sounds like a great idea to me," Aspen said.

❧

With dinner finished and their dessert in front of them, Leigh had run out of things to say to these strangers. Aspen had been silent, while Skeet told comical stories about life in the *olden* days, but now even he was running out of words. Anne Jean and Brit had shared recipes, and Cassie had talked about belly dancing. The rest of the meal they'd talked a lot about the weather, to a point that Leigh wanted to laugh at the tediousness of the conversation, but instead she felt self-conscious. Why had her sister subjected her to this punishment? She had nothing to say to these foreigners.

"May I be so bold as to ask exactly what your company's plans are for the future?" Anne Jean asked kindly.

Leigh looked straight at Aspen. "What we're doing now. Cutting trees, planting more trees."

"You plan on doing that for a while?" Skeet asked.

Leigh leaned forward. "That's what we do," she replied tightly. How could she explain to these environmentalists who she was, what she was? "I cut trees, but I respect them. Trees are elegant and majestic and it doesn't matter if it's an alder or an oak." She took a breath, warming to her subject. "They give us who they are to make our lives easier, but we give them life by planting thousands and thousands of them. I know we take, but we also give back, and that's why I can live with myself. When I touch a tree," Leigh's voice was soft, "it's not like touching someone you love, but it's just as mesmerizing. I know I'm a forester and I'm supposed to look at trees as if they are a commodity, but it's never been like that for me. Trees are the embodiment of everything that is right with the earth, and I value them. They give so we can live . . ." Her voice trailed off. Aspen was staring at her.

"Wow, that was so cool." Cassie broke the silence.

"I like that." Skeet nodded briskly.

"Me too." Anne Jean smiled knowingly. "How about you, Aspen?"

"Something to think about," Aspen conceded grudgingly.

"That's my sister!" Brit beamed. "But you know what?" She looked at the others. "My sister really believes what she says. I have heard her talk about this before, and each time my heart does a dance. I can feel her enthusiasm."

Leigh looked away, embarrassed. She hadn't planned to give them anything more than the company line of cutting and planting, but somehow she wanted Aspen to know her, to know who she was, how she felt. *How uncharacteristic of her was that?* An odd look had passed over Aspen's face.

"The evening went well," Leigh said as she stacked the dishes in the dishwasher.

"It was good, but . . ."

Leigh detected a taciturnity in her sister that she hadn't seen all evening. "You're not upset about what Skeet said about the living room?"

"Oh, I was at first. You know me, I just get all excited and I never think to take your feelings into account. I didn't even ask you if you wanted me to make changes to your house. I just did it."

"Brit, it's okay."

"You sure do put up with a lot just because Daddy left us and Mom was working all the time. I just bull my way through your life and you're okay with it."

"Most of the time, but on the important things I say no to you. This wasn't that important. Besides, I can always change it back when you leave."

Brit laughed. "You can and you will. You should take her out."

Leigh turned back to the dishwasher. "Who, Cassie?"

"No, not *Cassie*! You know who." Brittany handed Leigh more dishes. "She wants you to, you know. I can sense it."

"We're so different. I get the feeling she vacillates between sort of liking me and hating me."

"Are you afraid to get involved?"

"I don't know." Leigh leaned against the counter.

"I think you do know."

"Life's simple now. I have a job I like, a house that is . . ." Leigh smirked "Colorful. Why screw it up?"

"This weekend, when you were out there tramping in the woods, wouldn't it have been nice if someone like Aspen would have been with you?"

"Sure. Experiencing something new is a lot more fun when you can share it with someone. Especially someone you love," Leigh said wistfully.

"Are you attracted to her?"

"I just met her." Leigh looked at the floor. "Hell, I don't know."

"Then find out. I'm not asking you to marry her, just take her out for dinner. If you don't want to call it a date, go Dutch treat. That'll take the romance off the rose."

"That's silly."

"My thoughts exactly. That's why I suggested it. Just ask her out."

"What if she says no?"

Brittany laughed. "I don't think this is about partnership, or commitment or anything else. I think my big sister is a tad scared."

"About what?"

"About asking her out. Afraid she might say no."

"Well, maybe," Leigh said quietly.

"It's obvious she's curious about you and no doubt does consider you an enigma."

"Me? I'd say Aspen is the enigma, not me."

"Hear me out." Brittany shot a knowing look at her. "Just that you're an environmentalist and a forester. I'm not surprised she's curious."

Leigh laughed. "Curious? Curious about punching me in the nose to see if it'll bleed trees or corporate dollar bills."

"Why so sarcastic?"

"She's a card-carrying environmentalist. I cut trees. Is that so difficult to figure out? She probably thinks if we go out, she can convert me, take me over to the light."

Brit shrugged expressively. "I watched her tonight after Anne Jean asked you about what your company planned to do in the future. Aspen Brown's mind is percolating, and you did that. She now has to face the fact that you appreciate the same things she values. I suspect she doesn't quite know what to do with it, but she's curious. So, ask her out to dinner next Saturday night."

"I don't know." Leigh forced her hands into her pockets. "Naw, that won't work. Especially after she sees what the company does to some of her neighbors tomorrow. Hell, I'll be lucky to get served at the diner after that news hits the street."

"That's ridiculous! People will know it's not your fault. Put the blame on management. They're the ones doing this, not you. I think you're worrying about nothing."

"Just a bunch of men and women out of their jobs, that's all," Leigh said grimly. "I don't know, Brit. I don't think this is the time for me to get involved with anyone."

"Now who's being silly? Aspen is a bright, beautiful and, I might add, enchanting woman, and you owe it to yourself to get to know her. And if you don't, you're one big dumb lesbian."

Leigh laughed. "Well, when you put it that way, I guess I can't argue."

"So call her up and take her out. Besides, it'll give me something better to focus on other than Harry. And speaking of that damn fool, as Cassie calls him, I guess I have to face that issue tomorrow."

"What are you going to do?"

"Murder him, then throttle him and then yell at him."

"Sounds about right."

"Seriously, I don't know. At first I was angry with him. Then hurt that he hadn't called." Brittany took Leigh's hand out of her pocket and held it. "I'm just bewildered. I love him. I should be mad. I should be demanding a divorce. But I realized tonight when I saw Anne Jean and Skeet together, I really love the buffoon and I miss him."

"So what are you going to do?"

"Go home and find out what happened."

"Good," Leigh said quietly. "I vote for Harry. He's a kind man, and I think if he'd found the letter, he'd have called because he knows you'd come here. Go home, Brit. You love Harry. Fix it."

"I hear ya. Thanks, big sister. Now what about Aspen?"

"I'll call. I just don't think the timing is that great. What do I say? Hi, I just fired your neighbors. How about dinner and a roll in the hay? And by the way, I'm going to cut down a bunch of trees near your house."

"Well, you could, but I don't think that's going to go over well. Why don't you tell her the truth?"

"And the truth is?"

"You went for the overnight because you needed to meditate. It's something you've done your whole life because laying off those people is bugging you, more than you're willing to admit."

"You're right. I hate what the company is doing, and I hate the fact that I'm the one in the captain's seat as the plane is going down."

"The plane's not going down, it's just stalled. But I gotta tell you, I'm miffed at your company. Why didn't they do it when that other guy was here?"

"All I know is that the guy and the company didn't part well. Rumor has it he was fired because he was skimming logs. I don't even know how you do that, and I've not asked, because the company has made it clear it's not inclined to talk about it. But what irritates me is I wouldn't have left Presque Isle if I'd known this shit was coming down."

"I think it's lousy. The company should've left the position vacant until this mess was cleaned up."

"It's too late now. I get to be the villain."

"Don't be so hard on yourself. You're not doing it, your company is."

"Yeah, but the only thing those people are going to remember is that I'm the company. Tomorrow, after all the hotshots are gone, I'm the face they're going to see around here and . . ." Leigh held her thumb and finger an inch apart. "I'm this close to quitting."

"I suspected as much. I've seen the worry in your eyes. Are you going to quit?"

"I came out of the woods not knowing. On the one hand, I think I can make a difference here because I really like this place. The wood harvesting hasn't been managed well and I know I can do that."

"Let's make an agreement. I'll go home and fix my marriage and you stay here and turn a black Monday into a sunny Saturday." Brittany laughed. "And on Monday night or Tuesday, invite Aspen to dinner this weekend."

"I doubt that she'll accept after tomorrow."

"Well, you're not going to know unless you ask."

"Okay." Leigh smiled. "We are a pair, I'll tell ya."

"We are," Brittany said softly. "But the best part, we can do this together. I'm really glad you're my big sister."

"Me too, because I'd hate to think what your life would be like if I wasn't around to fix it." Leigh smiled. "I'm teasing. You'd probably be a hell of a lot better off."

"I doubt that. Right now the two Wright sisters, need to make *right* their lives."

"Oh, lousy pun, but you are so right."

CHAPTER FIVE

Monday morning Leigh gave her sister a hug and left her standing in the driveway. Brit was trying to decide if she was going to leave immediately or eat breakfast first. Driving to the office, there was a mass in Leigh's stomach the size of an oak tree and just as hard. Thirty workers out of a job on her watch. Only her secretary, Jane Savage, and two foresters would be left. She pulled into the driveway, Jeff's truck in her rearview mirror.

"Morning," Jeff said as he lifted a large briefcase off the front seat. "Can't say it's going to be a good morning."

"No."

"This is your first. It's never easy."

"I agree with that." Leigh unlocked the office door. "I understand the state folks will be here in a half hour. I can make coffee."

"Maybe later. I had several cups at the diner."

"Any gossip there?"

"Not that I heard. But then folks don't say much in front of strangers." Jeff pulled out an office chair and sat down. "Sit. You look as nervous as a cat in a dog pound."

"That's how I feel. You seem so calm."

"I'm not, but the job fell to me and I have to do it. Just as someday you're going to have to do it. It's not easy. I had a restless weekend thinking about it, but we've got stockholders to keep happy and, bottom line, cutting costs is one way of turning a negative into a positive. We paid a lot of money for this land because they've got plans for it."

Leigh studied him. "Plans? How so?"

"Don't know yet, but I've heard talk around the office. They paid top dollar for this panoramic view of the ocean, and I expect someday they want to develop it."

"You're the second person to say that to me in the past few days."

Jeff frowned. "Who?"

"A local woman I ran into at the restaurant on Friday. She basically said the same thing. I gave her the company line: *We manage woodlots*," Leigh said sotto voce.

"I'm speculating, but I think there's truth in that speculation."

"I wished I'd known this stuff before I transferred. I'm not certain I want to work for a company that's changing so fast, and I know I don't want to work for a company that isn't in the wood harvesting business."

"Hold your muffler. This is tough, but things will settle down and you'll be doing what you do best, getting trees out of the woods."

Leigh frowned. "We'll see." A car door slammed. "I expect that's the state people."

"Good. I spoke with them on Friday, but this will give me a chance to make sure we're all singing from the same hymnal." Jeff put more folders on the table as three people walked into the office.

Jeff straightened determinedly. "Jeff Grant," he said to the two women and man. "This is my colleague, Leigh Wright." Leigh listened to the introductions. "I've faxed you all summary sheets of what we're offering, so let's go over them." Jeff handed them each a black folder. Leigh wondered what it would be like to be handed a folder and told you're retired. Leigh shook off the image. She listened as Jeff went over the contents of each folder. This was going to be a long day.

"I hate to interrupt, but my secretary's just arrived and I want to talk to her. You folks stay here, and I'll talk to her in her office," Leigh said.

"Sounds good. Ask her not to call anyone," Jeff said without looking up.

"Jane's good. I've told her things and they haven't left this office."

"You didn't mention anything to her on Friday?" Jeff asked.

"I didn't, but she knew something was up. I let folks leave early on Friday."

Jeff grinned. "I heard. Had corporate talking."

"I expect, but they'd gotten the order done ahead of schedule and deserved the time off."

Leigh closed the door to her office. "Morning, Jane."

"Morning. I hope you had a good weekend with your sister."

"It was nice. How was your weekend?"

"Good, the family was home and we had a barbecue on Sunday. I see the company truck. I expect Jeff's here and there are two state cars parked next to his."

"State cars? How'd you know?"

"No mystery, the license plate."

Leigh shrugged, embarrassed. "Of course. I need to talk to you. Can we go into your office?"

"Do I have a choice?"

"Sure," Leigh said stupidly. Down east folks were direct, an idiosyncrasy she wasn't used to.

Jane glanced at the empty coffeepot. "I'm going to make a pot of strong coffee first, okay?"

Seated across from Jane, Leigh studied her secretary. She was in her late sixties. Her salt-and-pepper hair was cut short, her English face angular and pointed. She was as tall as Leigh was, and although she was past retirement age, Jane had made it clear when Leigh arrived that she had no plans to retire.

"How many?" Jane broke the silence.

Leigh wasn't surprised by the question. "All but you and the two foresters."

"That's more than I thought." Jane was upset. "Jeff going to do it?"

"He is."

"That's good. You don't need to be the one to say the words."

"Doesn't make it any easier."

"Did you know before you got here?"

"No, I didn't."

"Good. At least when they get mad, it won't be you who'll take the brunt of it."

"I guess. I've checked. Most are going to be hired locally. The Foleys over in Charlotte are looking for workers, so are the Hinckleys in Talmadge."

"What about the old-timers?"

"They're being offered a retirement package. I'm relieved about that."

"Me, too. Most of them are way too old to start over, but don't tell them that. Knowing them, they'll be in line applying for work in the morning."

"More power to them." Leigh stopped. There was chatter in the outer office as the men and women punched in. "Can we talk afterward?"

"We can. Look, I'm going to stay in my office until it's over. Any of them want to talk to me they can, but for right now, I don't want to be a part of that."

"Jane, I'm sorry. I really didn't know this was going to happen when I took the job." Leigh had to say it again.

"That's good because the guys like you. You're the first woman they've worked for, and it was tough for them not knowing how you'd handle yourself in the woods. You impressed them your first day on the job. In the end, most of them ended up liking you."

"Most?"

"Not all. A lot of them wouldn't have liked you even if you'd been a man."

Leigh smiled. "I'll talk to you later."

Leigh liked her driveway empty of cars. She opened the door to a quiet kitchen and poured herself a glass of wine. There was an envelope on the table. Leigh picked it up between two fingers, uncertain if she wanted to open it.

Dear Sis—I've been so preoccupied with my life that I didn't even think to wish you good luck this morning. I'm going back to Portland to try to fix my marriage. I went back and forth all weekend between hurt and anger and disappointment, but never once did I stop loving Harry. But more than Harry, I wanted to talk about us. Before Mama died, we were just sisters. Then all those nights we spent at the hospital and then at Mama's house sitting next to her bed waiting, I found my best friend. You are my touchstone, my mooring, Leigh. I know from you I get unrestricted love, and I cherish that, but more importantly, I cherish you. Thank you for being my sister—which you didn't have a choice with. Thank you for being my friend—which you choose to be every day. I love you.—Brit.

Leigh swallowed. A colossal nugget was stuck in her throat. "Glad you're there," she said as soon as her sister answered the telephone.

"I am."

"I liked the note." Leigh cleared her throat.

"I wanted you to know you're appreciated. We spend way too much time saying those words when someone's dead. Like with Mama, I never thanked her for working so hard for us, and I didn't want that to happen again."

"She knew."

"I hope. Anyway, I wanted you to know how much I appreciate you and you don't have to say a word, because I can hear it in your voice. So how was your day?"

"Not good, not awful."

"Did they try to tar and feather you?"

"Jeff did the hard part. I stood by and listened. Those who were ready to retire were grateful. The others . . . well the reaction was mixed. I guess that's to be expected."

"I guess."

"How are things back there?"

"You were right."

"About?"

"The note was where I'd left it, unopened." Leigh listened as Brittany talked about Harry's return and his suggestion that they see a marriage counselor. "I went out and bought steaks and other stuff. I decided to fix him his favorite meal. I turned off the telephone, took this very long and very hot bubble bath, then I did my nails . . ."

"Spare me the details." Leigh laughed.

"Anyway, things are fine, not perfect but fine. Have you called Aspen?"

"Not yet."

"Call her right now and then call me back."

"I will call her. I won't call you back."

"Why not?"

"Because you need to focus on Harry. I'll call you tomorrow."

"Grumble, grumble, but okay."

"Say good-bye, Leigh."

"Good-bye, Leigh, and call Aspen."

Leigh looked up Aspen's number and called. There was no answer. Disappointed, she hung up when Aspen's message clicked on. She opened her refrigerator and studied all the neatly marked blue-covered containers her sister had left behind. She shook her head. Her sister had even organized her refrigerator. Leigh saw the lights reflected on her kitchen window even before she heard the car. Aspen rolled down her window. "Are you afraid of dogs?"

"Only if they bite." Leigh laughed.

"Lick you to death, but not bite." She opened the car door. "This is Miss Etta Mae." A black dog bounced out of the front seat.

"Well, good evening, Miss Etta." Leigh scratched her ear as the dog sniffed first one and then the other boot. Her nose followed a line up Leigh's pants.

"Hi," Aspen said as she handed Leigh a bag.

"What's this?"

"Comfort food. I expect you haven't eaten."

"I haven't." Leigh saw several containers. "I'm sorry. Please come in."

"Okay if Miss Etta comes in, or would you rather she stay outside?"

"Please." Leigh held the door open. "The whole family is welcome."

"Good."

"I don't know what to say. You must not have heard about today."

"Oh, it's all over town." Aspen set containers on the kitchen table. "Can this be informal?"

"Of course." Leigh pulled out plates. "Will you join me?"

"Absolutely. I haven't had dinner either. Been mostly on the

65

telephone."

"I don't expect that I'm going to be elected mayor anytime soon."

"No, but then we don't have a mayor." Aspen laughed. "But they're not going to run you out of town either."

"That's a relief. But I don't understand this." Leigh pointed at the food.

"Anne Jean."

"I still don't understand."

"Anne Jean made this and ordered me to bring it over," Aspen said as she put more containers on the table. "Said you wouldn't stop in town to eat because you'd feel like Judas, so she *fixed you a plate*, as she says. Said you'd need a friend right now."

Leigh glanced at Aspen sideways. "You don't have to stay."

"I do, or Anne Jean'll never speak to me again." Aspen stopped opening containers. "Honestly, I didn't want to come, but she reminded me that you're here alone, without friends, your sister gone home." Aspen had a sheepish look on her face.

"It's okay. I won't tell her you dropped the food off and left." Leigh held her breath wanting Aspen to stay.

"I thought about that driving here, but now that I've seen you, you do need a friend."

"That bad?"

"You look a little gray around the edges."

"More than just the edges." Leigh turned away. After Jeff and the others left, she shook hands with each of the employees and thanked them. But it wasn't until she was driving home that she realized that when she went back to the office, the laughter and kidding from the men as they punched in would be gone, and she felt very sad.

"You okay?" Aspen touched her arm. Her hand was warm and comforting.

"Yes." Leigh cleared her throat. "Just tired."

"Come on. We'll eat and I'll leave. That way I keep my prom-

66

ise to Anne Jean, and you don't have to feel like you have to entertain me."

"No, really, I don't feel like that," Leigh said weakly. "This is nice."

"I'm going to get the candles your sister used the other night." Aspen went into the dining room. "A little shorter, but they'll do the job." She put them on the table. "Matches?"

"Over there." Leigh nodded toward the drawer.

Aspen lit the candles and opened a container. "Nothing special. Just Anne Jean's delicious fried chicken and . . ." Aspen opened another container, "potato salad. Anne Jean makes the best in America."

"And in there?"

"Dessert." Aspen lifted the aluminum foil. "Something called sticky pudding."

Leigh looked at the thick, dark chocolate. "Maybe we should start with that first?" she asked hopefully.

"Would that make you happy?" Aspen beamed.

"No, that's silly."

"Where is it written in American cuisine that you have to save dessert for last? It's a silly tradition that we're going to break." Aspen spooned pudding onto the plates.

"Oh wow!" Leigh said as she tasted the chocolate cake-pudding.

"It's good," Aspen said between bites. "Can we do one thing?"

"And that is?" Leigh sucked in some air, uncertain what Aspen would say.

"No talk about work."

"Sure, but I figured that's what you'd want to talk about."

"Folks have hammered it to death today. Teachers at school. Kids in the hall."

Leigh groaned. "I knew it'd be all over town. I didn't think it'd be the topic of discussion at school."

"What'd you expect? A lot of kids' fathers worked there. Within minutes of your telling the men, cell phones began to ring." Aspen scraped her plate. "I feel like licking the plate."

"So do it."

"If I were alone I probably would, but I feel silly." Aspen's smile was shy.

"Then I'll join you." Leigh picked up her plate and began to lick it. "Yummy."

Aspen laughed. "I haven't done this since I was a kid. This feels so good." Aspen touched Leigh's nose with the tip of her finger. "You have chocolate on your nose." Leigh swallowed to keep from making a noise. *What that hell was that?* The touch felt like electrical energy had zipped through her. Her insides were roiling. "And you're thinking about what?"

Leigh swallowed. "My sister." *Not true*, she amended mentally. "She'd go into cardiac arrest if she knew I just licked my plate clean. She says I'm uptight. Keeps lecturing me on being more *spontaneous*." Leigh shrugged. "Actually, I envy the Cassies and Brittanys of the world. They can do things like belly dance and—"

"Tap dance."

"Tap dance?"

Aspen told Leigh about her and Cassie's tap dancing experience.

"You really did it *naked*?" Leigh could hardly say the word.

"I did, once." Aspen blushed. "On my own, I never would have, but Cassie can talk me into some of the strangest things. I bellyache the whole time, but mostly I'm having fun. Maybe your sister's right. We both need to be less uptight."

"Just don't ask me to tap dance naked." Leigh grinned. "Aspen, thanks for coming over. It means a lot."

"It's okay."

"I don't know. I got the feeling when we first met that you didn't particularly like me."

"I didn't, but that's a topic for another day."

"I don't understand."

Aspen studied her. "Let's eat and talk about you."

"Really? You don't want to talk about the other?"

"I do, but not now. Tell me about you. Why'd you become a forester?"

"Only if you tell me about you and explain why you didn't or don't like me."

"I will," Aspen said. "But first you."

Leigh told Aspen about growing up in northern Maine and about the woman forester who'd come to talk to her seventh-grade class on career day. How after that, all she could think about was being a forester. She told her about college and graduation and about Brittany and her newfound interest in astrology and about their mother. She didn't talk about her father and the drunken fights she listened to as a child. "Wow, look at the time." It was eleven o'clock. "I don't ever remember talking so much about myself." Leigh smile shyly. "You're a good listener."

"You just needed to talk." Aspen smiled. The chicken container was almost empty and there was little left of the potato salad. "And eat."

"Did we eat all of that?" Leigh asked, surprised.

"Well, more thee than me." Aspen smiled.

Leigh stared at the mostly empty containers. "I was hungry. Now that I think about it, I didn't have lunch."

"Anne Jean said she didn't think you had."

"I really hope I get to know her and Skeet better. I like them."

"I'm lucky to have her and Skeet in my life. They're the best."

"Now it's your turn." Leigh looked at Aspen expectantly.

"You're going to have to wait. I have to get up for school tomorrow." Aspen put covers back on containers.

"I didn't realize I talked so long. That's not like me."

"You needed to talk." Aspen touched Leigh's shoulder. Leigh felt the charge again. Her shoulder tingled.

"How about dinner Saturday night?" The words seemed to rocket out of Leigh's mouth.

"I'd like that." Aspen put the containers in the bag.

"If you don't want to be seen in public with me, we could have dinner here. Or we could go to Ellsworth. There are some nice restaurants there."

Aspen put her hands on her hips. "I'm not afraid to be seen with you. Why would you say that?"

"Just that I . . ." Leigh scratched the back of her head. "I feel like I'm a carrier of the avian flu, and being with me means you're going to catch it and, well . . ."

"I must admit when Anne Jean suggested I come over here I wanted to tell her no, but she was right. I can't shoot the messenger just because I don't like the message."

"All I can say is thank you, Anne Jean," Leigh said quietly.

Aspen rested her hand on Leigh's arm again. "I'd be happy to have dinner with you at the restaurant."

"Okay." There was that damn heat again. She swallowed.

"Well." Aspen dropped her hand. "Come on, Miss Etta."

"Why the one eye?" Leigh nodded toward the dog.

"That's another story for Saturday night. Say six o'clock?"

"I'd like that. I'd like to pick you up."

Aspen smiled. "That would be nice." Aspen opened the kitchen door and Miss Etta ran outside. "Just think, tomorrow is a better day."

"Thank you." Leigh smiled.

"You have a kind smile."

She blushed. "Thank you." She looked away, confused.

"Well then, good night." Aspen closed the door behind her.

CHAPTER SIX

Leigh realized she'd spent hours thinking about what she was going to wear for her date with Aspen. Her uniform was either tan cargo pants or Levi's with a blouse and vest. *I wonder what Aspen will be wearing?* She reached for a pair of cargo pants. *What the hell are you thinking?* She admonished. *This isn't a date. Then what the hell is it?* She touched the spot on her arm where Aspen had touched her as she was leaving and remembered how hot her arm had felt. *That's not romance*, she chided herself. *You're just in need of some attention.*

Leigh picked out a white oxford blouse. Funny, she thought, after she and her ex had broken up, she'd refused to allow herself to think about touching another woman in that intimate way partners do. But the past week that was all she was thinking about, and the woman she wanted to touch was Aspen. The same Aspen who vacillated between furnace-blast hot and arctic cold when she was around her.

Leigh studied her image in the mirror. She needed color. She frowned. Her vests and jackets were black, brown and tan. She searched the overhead shelf and found the green vest her sister had given her for Christmas. Not bad, she decided as she studied herself in the mirror.

Leigh glanced at the clock. It was six. She was anxious to find out more about Aspen. *Anxious? Hell*, she thought. She was burning up. Tonight, she got to ask the questions.

Miss Etta rushed out the door and sniffed Leigh's shoes and pant legs.

"Wonder where I've been?" Leigh scratched Miss Etta's ear. Leigh looked up. Aspen was in the entryway. Her blue dress flowed down across her shoulders and over her breasts, making her body appear diminutive and fragile looking. It continued on down across her hips to her thighs and ended, just barely touching the floor. Aspen's feet were bare. Leigh found it hard to swallow.

Aspen smiled at her. "You look very nice."

Leigh glanced down at herself. "Hardly. You look terrific. That dress is . . ." Leigh searched for the right word, but all she could get out was, "Wow."

"Thank you." Aspen laughed. "I know it's *un-lesbian* to be dressed like this, but every now and then I like to wear a dress. No apologies." Aspen laughed, embarrassed by her disclosure. "I like the green vest."

Leigh sighed in relief. She'd almost gone back to the house to change. "My sister gave it to me for Christmas. This is the first time I've worn it."

"You wear that color well."

"Thank you." *What was that gulping sound?* "You ready for dinner?" She needed to change the subject.

Aspen picked up a shoe and slipped it on. Leigh resisted the urge to bend down and take Aspen's feet in her hands and caress them. Instead, she stuffed her hands in her pockets. *Where the hell was she going with all this desire?*

"Let me get my shawl and I'm ready. Miss Etta, you're going to stay here. You don't get to go to dinner."

"That disappointed look is just too beseeching. Okay if she comes with us?"

"You don't have to do that."

"I insist. She can't get into trouble, and besides, it'd be nice to have her along."

Aspen laughed. "If it's really okay, then come on, Miss Etta." The dog bounded out the door.

At the restaurant, the fiery dance her stomach had been doing earlier in anticipation of their date continued. Seated across from Aspen, Leigh was positively enraptured by the woman's liquid black eyes.

"What are you thinking about?" Aspen asked.

Leigh felt somewhat perplexed looking at Aspen. "My sister, she called this morning," she said finally. That wasn't exactly the truth, but how could she tell Aspen she was struggling to keep from dissolving into huge ebony eyes? "Insisted I call her immediately after I get home."

"Cassie did the same thing." Aspen frowned. "I suspect those two have been chatting it up on the phone since Brittany was here. Seems like way too much of a coincidence that we both get telephone calls just before we're ready to go out."

Leigh smiled. "Nothing's a coincidence with my sister."

"What was Brit like growing up?"

"Whoa, we're not talking about my sister tonight. We're talking about you."

"I thought you might have forgotten."

Leigh liked the way the candle made Aspen's eyes glisten. "I didn't."

"Well, where to begin?" Aspen leaned back in her chair. "Saved by the bell. Good evening, Melissa." Aspen smiled at the waitress who had approached their table.

"You look really awesome tonight . . . Aspen," Melissa stammered.

"Thank you, Melissa. I thought it might be nice to dress up."

"I'd like you to meet my Aunt . . . Linda sometime." Melissa seemed to have trouble getting her aunt's name out. "She's been hired as an instructor at the community college. She's an environmentalist like you, done some cool things down in Massachusetts. That's where she last taught. Anyway, I told her all about you and she'd like to meet you."

"Why, I'd love to meet her, Melissa. Feel free to bring her around any time."

"Any specials tonight?" Leigh asked. Melissa was staring at Aspen.

"Ah . . ." Melissa stuttered. "We have broiled veal chops with cheese, garlic and sage, and sautéed chicken breast with white wine and herbs. Tonight's special hors d'oeuvres are hot cheese, which is beaten into a very thick cream sauce and then placed into miniature pastry shells. It's delicious. I must say."

"I say let's start with the hors d'oeuvres you mentioned." Leigh looked at Aspen who nodded. "And two cups of coffee. We'll order dinner in a few minutes."

"Very nice."

Leigh placed her arms on the table and folded her hands together. "I think your former student"—Leigh nodded at Melissa's departing back—"is thunderstruck by you."

Aspen laughed. "Remember, she knew me when she was eleven or twelve and thought I was a boring *old* teacher. That's a very impressionable age."

"Hardly boring and hardly old. She sure was anxious for you

to meet her aunt."

"That she was, but you know, one environmentalist to another, I guess."

"Anyway. I'd like to start with you and me and why I got the feeling when we first met that you didn't like me. Did I read that wrong?"

"No, you didn't. Actually *didn't like* doesn't really describe it. I was prepared to hate you." Aspen looked ashamed.

"Hate? That's such a nasty word."

"It is."

"Why hate?"

"I've never liked any of the managers out there. The last guy was the worst. He was unapproachable, and when you did talk to him, he was so condescending. Then he left and I heard a woman was replacing him. I decided you had to be worse than the others. First, because you were a woman doing a job not even a man should be doing, and second, because as a woman, I felt you'd sold out."

"And now?"

"I was wrong. That night we had dinner at your house and you talked about your feelings for the environment, your passion came through. That was a difficult night for me."

"Difficult? Why?"

"I had to confront myself, and I didn't like me. It was easier to place you in a box, with all your male colleagues and assign labels to you—anti-environmentalist, murderer."

"Murderer?"

"Cutting trees."

"Ah."

Aspen was thoughtful. "I try to instill in my students that new ideas should be either embraced or rejected only after they're understood. I tell them it's part of their mental growth. I guess I need to practice what I teach."

"How do you feel now?"

"Confused. A lot of emotions twirling around inside me about you, your job, what it means to my town. It's hard to explain, but, Leigh"—Aspen leaned forward—"can we talk about something else? I'm quite embarrassed by all of this, and I really don't have an answer right now."

Leigh studied her. "Actually, I do understand," Leigh replied carefully. "So we agreed to talk about you. Let's start with your name. How did you come by Aspen?"

"My mother. She loved trees. She named me Aspen, my sister Willow."

"Your mother was a hippie?"

"Some people would say that, but mostly she loved trees. She grew up out west, and they were her favorite tree as a child. Aspens have leaves that flutter ever so gently in the wind. That's what she used to say." Aspen's smile was wistful.

"You don't seem like the fluttering type."

Aspen smiled. "I'm not. But it could have been worse. She could have named me Sun and my sister Moon. Two other things that she loved."

"Sun is nice. It shimmers, something like you." Leigh realized she was flirting. *Stop that*, she exhorted herself.

"Thank you." Aspen looked embarrassed again. "I'm glad she didn't because Sun wouldn't have gone well with Brown."

Leigh smiled. "I guess not. You were born here?"

"My parents moved here when I was two. My dad got a job on a lobster boat. He didn't stick around long after we moved here."

"Brittany told me you lost a sister." There was pain in Aspen's eyes. "I'm sorry. That was way too personal."

Aspen smiled. "It's distressing remembering. My sister died in an automobile accident shortly after my mom died. It wasn't a good year." Aspen studied her hands.

"Cheese in pastry cups," Melissa said. The interruption startled them both. Leigh realized she was leaning across the table absorbing every word Aspen was saying.

"These are wonderful," Leigh said taking a bite.

"Would you like to order?"

"I'll have the veal special." Aspen handed Melissa her menu.

"And I'll have the chicken dish."

"Very good."

"Now that we have the important things done, let's get back to *This is Your Life, Aspen Brown*," Leigh said.

Aspen smiled. "Not much to tell. I grew up here. Went to college in Maine, where I got my teaching certificate. Came back here to teach. People will tell you I'm an environmentalist, which is true. They'll also tell you I'm just a wee bit wacko, which is probably true. Mostly because I like trees better than people."

"Really?"

"Really." Aspen smiled.

"Why?"

"They don't talk back. After you've spent an entire day with middle school pupils, a tree looks mighty nice."

Leigh laughed. "I hadn't thought about that."

"I couldn't do your job," Aspen said quietly.

"Because we cut trees?"

"Yes."

Leigh shrugged. "I couldn't have done it way back when loggers used to cut and run. No appreciation for what the forest had to offer."

"I still couldn't do your job."

"If we didn't cut trees, where would our toilet paper and our paper towels come from? Where would the chair you're sitting on or the table come from?"

"I agree, and the alternatives aren't much better. I used to say plastic, but look what that's done to our landfills, our environment. Intellectually, I know how trees are a necessary part of our lives. If nothing else, the paper companies keep reminding us of that. I remember one year we'd picketed the mill in Woodland."

"About what?"

"They kept dumping their toxic liquid from the papermaking process into our river. It was the first company, not the southern company you bought the land from. I remember we were picketing, and this company flack comes out and hands us a piece of paper. Didn't say a word." Aspen laughed.

"What did it say?" Leigh was mystified.

"It was a list of all the products that are made either directly or indirectly from trees, and it concluded with one statement, *The next time you go to the bathroom, take along a roll of plastic.*" Aspen shook her head. "We kept on picketing. I don't know if the mill owner thought that would get us to quit or not. We didn't quit."

"I bet you've done your fair share of picketing over the years."

"I have." Aspen grinned. "I hope your company isn't next."

"Not unless you're going to picket us for cutting trees, 'cause that's what we do."

"I guess that depends. Who are the people behind your company, anyway?" Aspen asked darkly. "When your company announced it'd bought the land, I looked it up online. There was stuff about the staff, your president and about what you do, but nothing about your backers. You're a management company. That means someone had to put up the money to buy the land."

Leigh rested her chin against her hand and scrutinized Aspen. "It's a good company, otherwise I wouldn't be working for it," Leigh said. "But I really, really don't want to talk about Burnt Brush." Leigh's smile was gentle. "You agreed we'd talk about you."

"Not much more to tell," Aspen said after a moment.

"Well, there must be other stuff. Life, loves . . ."

Aspen studied her. "The first time I fell in love, it was a woman I'd met in college. I was a freshman. She was a senior. It was very romantic, or so it seemed at first. She was an engineering major. Soon our lifestyles diverged."

"Let me guess, you picketed the college and she didn't."

Aspen grinned. "Guilty as charged. It wasn't a Vietnam War protest. Those were important protests. Ours was kind of silly, but it felt right at the time. We wanted to make the dorms co-ed, so a bunch of us protested."

"And?"

"We lost, and the woman I'd been involved with went south like the protest."

"Sorry."

"Why? It wasn't meant to be. Anyway, there have been a few other women, but nothing that stuck. How about you?"

"My sister would say I have a closet full of romantic failures. My most recent break, a woman I'd met in Presque Isle. We lived together about five years."

"You still look a little bruised."

"Bruised, but not bitter. It wasn't meant to be," Leigh said thoughtfully.

"I think we ought to focus on more cheerful topics." Aspen grinned. "Let's talk about trees and the life they have inside them. Let's talk about little saplings that are trampled when a machine cuts across them."

"Are you serious?"

"Well, that seems like it *could* be a pretty innocuous topic."

Leigh cocked an eyebrow and chuckled. "It probably would be to most, but not to a forester and an environmentalist. Besides, we agreed to talk about you." Leigh took another pastry puff. "Maybe we don't talk about lost loves, but may we talk about likes and dislikes."

"That seems pretty safe. You first."

"I don't think so." Leigh feigned hurt.

"Okay, likes. I like you in green. It makes your eyes look absolutely enchanting."

Leigh wondered if Aspen could hear the gulp she'd just made. It sure sounded loud in her ears. "Thank you." She looked down, confused. Yikes, there was that heat again.

"I'm sorry," Aspen said softly. "I've embarrassed you. Sometimes my brain stops working and my mouth gets in gear. It's one of my least desirable traits."

"No, just . . ." Leigh said helplessly. "That dress you're wearing is *awesome.*"

"Now it's my turn to be embarrassed, but thank you." Aspen shyly looked away.

"Look—" they both said together. Aspen smiled and Leigh chuckled.

"We're flirting." Leigh responded evenly.

Aspen shifted uncomfortably in her seat. "I'm sorry. I started it." Leigh didn't say anything. "Umm, I'm not sure this is such a good idea."

"Why?" Leigh asked. "I know I'm attracted to you, and I wasn't sure how to say it. My sister knew it before I did. She's the one who suggested we go out."

Aspen shook her head. "Really? Cassie hammered me about the same thing, but I have to tell you what I told Cassie. I'm attracted to you, but I'm not at that place in my life right now. I decided a long time ago that I wasn't going to get involved with another woman. It's too complicated, and it definitely leads to a broken heart."

"It doesn't have to."

"No." Aspen's eyes held her. "But a forester and an environmentalist, that's more than a recipe for disaster. That's a God blessed entire meal of disaster."

"Are we that different? I agree, I cut down trees—" Leigh held up her hand to stop Aspen's response. "I don't physically cut them myself, but I'm responsible for their being cut. But that doesn't stop me from appreciating them. I would never be a forester for a company that cuts trees without thinking about the

80

future. The best part of my job is being part of a company where we raise saplings that eventually get planted. Yes, we cut, but we also replenish."

"But that's the point. You take in those huge machines that grab the trunk around the middle while a blade cuts through it. I know a tree doesn't feel it, but what if it does?"

"It doesn't," Leigh said matter-of-factly.

"But I feel for those trees. I've watched them being taken down. It's not like people around here who cut a few trees for firewood. You just raid and rip. I've sorry to be so dramatic, but I feel that's what's happening. I know a tree doesn't have feelings, but to me it's like pulling hair out by its roots. You see, to me, the pain is just as palpable." Aspen shivered.

"And the alternative? I don't want plastic to be the answer."

"I know, I know." Aspen groaned. "I hate the hypocrisy of it. I really do, but those trees have life."

"How did we get from flirting to the feelings of trees?"

"Because it's part of it. What I believe is me."

"I understand that, but—"

"How can there be a *but* in this one?"

"Flirting is not getting involved. It's just flirting," Leigh countered. She saw Melissa carrying the tray of food toward them and waited.

"Leigh," Aspen said after Melissa left. "You're a very attractive woman, and I've figured out I'm attracted to you." Aspen bit her lip apprehensively. "I almost cancelled tonight."

"Really?"

"Really." Aspen set her fork down. "Had I, we wouldn't be having this conversation."

"True, but we'd have been having it at some point, because buried in this brain of mine I knew that I was attracted to you. And do you know when I finally accepted that my sister was right?"

"When?"

"That same night when you put your hand on my arm as you were leaving. It should have been just a comforting touch, but Aspen, that touch singed me. I know that sounds dramatic, but that's what happened."

"I felt it." Aspen's voice was just above a whisper. "I didn't intend it that way. It was just a touch because you were feeling so sad."

"That's what made it so seductive. I haven't stopped thinking about you. I just didn't know what to do with it." Leigh stopped, disconcerted. "I mean I knew what to do with it, but I wasn't sure where you were coming from."

"My fingers tingled from the touch, but Leigh, I don't even want to go down that tortuous trail." Aspen took a shuddery breath.

"Why?"

"I can't."

"Can't or won't?"

Aspen stared at the fork in her hand. "Both."

"But why?"

"I just can't. It's complicated and . . ." Aspen put her fork down and looked at Leigh. "It's just complicated."

"Can't we just see where it leads us?" Leigh asked quietly.

"It's going to lead to disaster."

"Disaster is a broken heart. It heals."

"No, disaster is giving away a part of your soul. It never heals."

"Wow, someone really must have hurt you in the past."

Aspen didn't answer.

"Aspen," Leigh said gently. "Tonight, I stood in my closet trying to pick out something to wear, and I realized that my wardrobe is about as diverse as a ream of paper. Then I remembered this vest. My sister's right. I'm muted in everything that I do. But not now. You're a spark, and I want to see what it's going to ignite."

"This sounds like one of those bodice ripper books. It's not going to work."

"Why?"

"Because beautiful love stories happen only in books."

Leigh rubbed her hands on her knees. "I only ask this. Let's have dinner again. Let's go for a walk in the woods. Let's learn to trust who we are and trust being together. For the first time in a long time, I'm interested in a woman, and you've done that. Can we just have dinner again? No commitment, no expectation, no pressure."

"And even though we know it's going to lead to disaster because of your profession and my beliefs? Or life's past?"

"I don't know about life's past, but I want to gamble it's going to work."

"The idea of getting involved scares me," Aspen said.

"Me too."

"But you still want to go forward?"

"I have to."

"Have to?"

"Yeah, have to."

"So it's not just about touches that heat your arm?"

"It's more than that. I really looked forward to tonight. I must admit I didn't think we'd be talking about this, but maybe this is right for us. I find you intriguing and that's a good thing. *You did that.*"

"I too looked forward to tonight," Aspen said.

"I'd like to have dinner with you. Monday, Tuesday, every night. I'll cook."

"Wait, remember, I teach school every day to some feisty twelve-year-olds."

"I want to see the woods through your eyes, but I also hope you want to see them through my eyes."

Aspen studied her. "Well put, forest lady. Well put. But we also have to talk."

"Agreed."

"About what's going on."

"Agreed."

"About emotions and how we're feeling."

"Agreed. It's going to be difficult for me. You'll have to be patient. I don't do this well," Leigh said.

"I understand. We also have to talk about other things."

"Other things?"

"You need to know where I've been in my life." Aspen's eyes were reflective.

"The same here."

"I have a feeling your life was a lot less complicated."

"Not when you're living it."

"Agreed." Aspen smiled. "I guess it's always easier to think that your life's been more complicated than others. Easy to think, but not necessarily true."

"Aspen, the past doesn't matter to me. I really try to focus on the future."

"But the past shapes who we are, which also sounds like something out of a lousy novel, but it's true."

"It is."

"I'm willing to try, but you're going to tire of all that touchy-feely stuff, because I do talk about it."

"And you're going to tire of my reticence to talk about stuff like that, but I'm willing to try. I really want to try."

CHAPTER SEVEN

"I don't know what to think," Aspen told Anne Jean.

"To think or do?"

"What do you mean by *do*?"

"Do you like her?"

"Yes!"

"Are you attracted to her?"

"Yes. No. I don't know. Yes, I guess I am," Aspen said gloomily.

"Aspen, what's the problem?" Anne Jean put down her rolling pin. Aspen had stopped by Skeet and Anne Jean's after school. She was looking forward to her and Leigh's Saturday night together. They were seeing a lot of each other. At least two nights a week they spent at Aspen's house just talking, and when Leigh wasn't at Aspen's house, they were on the telephone. Her conversation with Leigh the night before still played like the cadence of a metronome in her mind. She knew she was attracted to the woman. *Hell, attracted?* She wanted to go to bed with her.

She'd shared few details with her friends other than she and Leigh had had dinner and coffee together a few times, but it didn't seem to matter, because they suspected. Cassie had called the night before and announced she was ready to become the wedding planner, and Anne Jean had called that morning demanding to see her. "I don't know," she said avoiding Anne Jean's gaze.

"I think you do."

"Really, and what's that?"

"You're scared."

"Scared. Of what?"

"Falling in love."

"Wait, haven't we taken a huge hop from attraction to love?"

"Not really."

"I'm sure you're going to tell me the difference."

Anne Jean gave her a dirty look. "Not with that attitude I'm not. You're the one who looks like the lobster that's been caught in the trap."

"All right, all right. I'm sorry." Aspen was contrite.

"Look, Aspen, I know you're scared. It's been a long time since you've been attracted to a woman."

Aspen stared at Anne Jean. "I *am* afraid."

"You're afraid she'll break your heart, and she might, but so what?" Anne Jean held up her rolling pin like a teacher with a pointer. "Then what do you do? Avoid what may happen? Keep from falling in love because you might get hurt?" Anne Jean patted the dough. "Are you afraid of the other?"

"Yes." Aspen's face crumpled. "I've been alone, but not lonely. I have all of you, my students. I have a very full life." Her voice trailed off. "Let's say," she said after a moment, "I allow Leigh into my heart, what happens if she breaks it? I'm worried, Anne

Jean! I'm terrified the depression will come back." Aspen pushed her chair back and rubbed her hands against her knees. *Stop! You're not going to have another anxiety attack.* She ordered her brain to take control, and then sat on her hands to keep them from twitching. "You know that I skirt that dark hole all of the time because I don't want to go there ever again," Aspen said grimly. "You'll be happy to know after I figured out I was attracted to Leigh, I talked with my therapist."

"Good! And what did she say?"

"Not what she said, but what she did. She made me walk through it, examine all aspects. She thinks I should do it."

"You should listen to her."

"I know, but it doesn't make me less scared."

"Nor should it, but, Aspen, for all your protestations about having your friends and your job, you don't have what's important," Anne Jean said patiently.

"I know what you're going to say, *I don't have love,*" Aspen affected a child-like cadence.

"No, Miss Smarty-Pants. You don't have passion."

"*Passion.*" A strangled noise emanated from Aspen's throat.

"That's right, passion."

"I didn't expect you to use that word."

"Why? Because I look like a ho-hum housewife?"

"God, no! Just that we've never talked about *passion.*"

"And maybe we should have. It's important in a woman's life."

"Passion."

"I'm not using any other word, and it's not something you get from your friends." Anne Jean's gaze spoke intensity.

"I don't know that I've really known passion. I've known lust. I've known the heat of the moment. I've known love," Aspen muttered.

"Passion isn't about doing the deed, although that's part of it. Passion is what you feel in here." Anne Jean pointed at her heart. "It's ardor and desire and longing and feeling safe and allowing yourself to be you, unafraid because that person who has passion for you loves you without reservation. You get to be who you are and they still want to be with you." Anne Jean wiped the flour off her hands and touched Aspen's shoulder "Women have loved you, but you won't let them in because you're afraid of who you are."

Aspen looked out the window. She didn't want Anne Jean to see the anguish in her eyes. "You're right."

"I know."

"How?"

"Ever since your sister died, you've been afraid."

"Can you blame me? You saw what that did to me. First Mama, then Willow. I almost didn't come back from that one. Anne Jean, I don't have to tell you about the hellhole I lived in. All I wanted to do was sleep, stay in my house, not see anyone."

"There was a lot of pain, but you did come back."

"Not before it almost destroyed me. If it hadn't been for you, Skeet, Cassie . . ." Aspen whispered as she took a breath.

"So you never love anyone again? Never feel passion?"

"It's worked for me."

"Until now."

"Until now," Aspen agreed reluctantly.

"Do you know for all his blustering and noise, I love Skeet more today than I did when we first kissed. And that was a pretty powerful kiss, I might add." Anne Jean picked up a star-shaped cookie cutter and cut patterns in the dough. "Aspen, the passion I feel for Skeet is the foundation of who I've become. I'm a better woman because of what lives inside of me for that man, and if I'd worried about if he died, or if he'd find someone else, or if he'd stopped loving me, I'd never have had this quality of life. My passion for him is what keeps my love alive, and for all his muted acknowledgement of emotions, I know he feels the same way."

"Anne Jean, I've settled into a life that's safe, predictable."

"You've settled into a life that's tiresome and predictable."

"That's not nice," Aspen said.

"But true. Look, I don't know if Leigh's the woman for you. And maybe with her, life could have a soft landing, maybe not. You'll never know if you keep throwing up all these barriers."

"She cuts down trees."

"So what! This woman has to have some good stuff in her. Otherwise you wouldn't be sitting here looking like a dog with porcupine quills in your muzzle. She has a job you don't like, but you've seen something else."

"I have," Aspen said. "When I'm around her I feel like my mind is on manual rather than idling on automatic. I have to shift gears to think. It's ridiculous."

"Not ridiculous."

"She doesn't know a thing about me. In fact, when we talk I always turn the conversation around to her and we end up talking about her."

"Why?"

"Because I want to know everything about her, but also because I'm afraid. I'm not ready to talk about all that's happened."

Anne Jean put the cookie cutter down and gently lifted each of the stars onto a cookie sheet. "You do have to tell her."

Aspen groaned. "I know."

"Why delay it?"

"Fear."

"That she'll run the other way?"

"That, yes, but there's something else."

"Aspen, your battle with depression isn't like you committed a crime."

"No," Aspen said flatly. "But it's a lifelong sentence. Maybe she won't understand and maybe once she finds out she won't—"

"What?" Anne Jean put the pan in the oven.

"That she won't like me," Aspen answered bleakly. "I'm afraid if she hears about my past, she *won't like me*, and that frightens me. What's strange, I usually don't care what most people think. I know she's a kind person. That layoff at the mill bothered her more than it would someone else who's into growing professionally in corporate America. I really care what she thinks."

"That's good, right?"

"Yes, good, but?"

"But?"

"Maybe she's too decent to accept what happened to me. Anne Jean, I almost imploded. The depression. That was such a sordid point in my life."

"Not sordid, Aspen. A low point, yes, but not sordid. You were suffering, real bad, but you got through it. You need to hold onto that, not the rest."

"I hope you're right." Aspen glanced at the clock. Miss Etta needed to be fed. "I love you, Anne Jean. I don't know what I'd do without you." She hugged her.

"Remember that Leigh is not your enemy. Give her a chance."

"I don't think I have a lot of choice. I say to myself that I'm going to stop seeing her before I get in deeper, then she calls and all I can think about is seeing her. This falling in love stuff is a real headache."

"True." Anne Jean walked her to the door. "But it's the best things we humans have going for us."

A tin of warm cookies sat on her front seat. Miss Etta's head rested on her lap. Aspen thought about her conversation with Anne Jean. She had to tell Leigh and she had to tell her Saturday night. Aspen turned onto her driveway and groaned when she saw the black pickup truck.

"I wonder who that is?" Miss Etta looked out the window.

"Aspen, this is my Aunt Linda," Melissa said getting out of the truck. The aunt had flaming red hair cropped close to her head. She was tall like Leigh, but where Leigh was angular and square, Linda was slim and sparse of meat. She was wearing a blue running suit with white lines and a white turtleneck. "Remember you said I could bring her over? She really wanted to meet you."

"Of course." Aspen shook Linda's hand. Melissa petted the dog.

"Nice to meet you," Linda said.

"Same here. Your niece has said some nice things about you."

"She'd better, or the family would disown her," Linda teased.

"And this must be Miss Etta. She's quite famous you know," Melissa said.

"Yes, that's Miss Etta and, no, I didn't know she was famous."

"Just all the kids know how you rescued her and all. It was a pretty neat story."

"Your dog is a celebrity." Linda's eyes were like sapphires, dark blue and sparkly.

"Come in," Aspen said. "Can I get you some coffee?"

"We're not going to stay," Melissa said once inside Aspen's kitchen.

"I'd love a cup." Linda pulled out a kitchen chair.

Melissa tilted her head, puzzled. Aspen suspected that Melissa thought they would only stay long enough for her aunt and former teacher to meet.

"Come on, sit," Aspen coaxed Melissa. "Do you drink coffee?"

"She does," her aunt answered for her. "Very, very white with milk." Melissa was embarrassed.

"I prefer milk with cookies. How about we both have a glass?" Aspen opened the tin of cookies. "A friend of mine made these."

"They look yummy." Melissa eyed the cookies.

"Why don't you start? I'll get our milk."

"Super." Melissa dug in. "This is a neat kitchen, it feels just

91

so—"

"Comfortable," Linda finished the statement.

"So, Melissa tells me you teach at the college," Aspen said, now seated, milk in front of her and Melissa, coffee in front of Linda.

"I was hired at the start of the semester. I teach computer science."

"A mystery field to me. I have a computer. I turn it on, write lesson plans and e-mails and the rest, as they say, belongs in cyberspace."

"It's a fun field." Linda became very animated as she talked about her job. She talked about computers and how they were the twentieth century's Guttenberg Bible. "It has had that much of an impact on the world, really. The Bible taught people to read. The computer has made the world a smaller place."

"Aunt Linda's really good," Melissa bragged. "She's won all kinds of awards in her field. She's even written papers on the subject."

"My niece has a bit of hero worship." Linda laughed. "In fact, I'm trying to get her into my computer science program. Being a waitress is a waste of her talents."

"I'm not always going to be a waitress," Melissa objected. Aspen sensed Melissa and her aunt had had this discussion before. "I'm saving my money so I can open a delicatessen in town. I think we're ready for it." Melissa looked shyly at Aspen.

"I think that's terrific, and you're right. The town is ready for a good deli."

"My college instructor helped me put together a business plan. I won't get rich, but I'll be doing what I like, and it'll be my own business."

"I still say that she should go into computer science. That way if the deli fails, she has something to fall back on," Linda insisted.

"Maybe at some point she'll be able to do both," Aspen said

gently. "I understand you're an environmentalist," Aspen said to change the subject. She wasn't about to get in the middle of a family dispute.

"I am. I did some stuff in Massachusetts that got some statewide media ink."

"That's why I wanted you to meet. Aunt Linda has done some really cool stuff, and I figured the two of you would have a lot in common." Melissa was more relaxed.

Linda talked about several of the projects the environmental groups she belonged to had worked on in Massachusetts. "So we had many successes, a few failures."

"I think that's great." Aspen reached for a cookie. The tin was almost empty. Melissa had been steadily eating.

"I find this purchase by Burnt Brush to be rather interesting," Linda said.

"Why?" Aspen was curious about what Linda had heard.

"From what I've heard around the college, they paid top dollar for the land, and a few weeks ago they got rid of all of their harvesters. I just think it's ripe for something to happen."

"As in?"

"They announce they're going to develop it. I don't know."

"Well, the manager assured me that that's not what they plan to do. Says they're into sustainable forestry."

"An oxymoron if I ever heard one," Linda scoffed. "Sustainable forestry practice, my butt. They figure if they tell the masses they're planting faster than they're cutting, we'll go away. It's crap. They're planting, but think how long it takes to grow a cedar or fir tree. Think how long it takes to replace the hardwoods they're destroying."

"Well, the company says that woodlots they've owned for years in the southern half of the state where they've planted seedlings are producing trees." Aspen frowned. She was defending Burnt Brush. How strange was that?

"I understand the manager is a woman."

"The first woman manager ever in Codyville. She's had her successes."

"And failures. The layoff for one."

"True." Aspen remembered the pain in Leigh's face the night of the layoff.

"Do you know her?"

"They've had dinner at the restaurant a few times," Melissa answered. "I know her because I saw her picture in the paper after she arrived."

Linda nodded. "Melissa tells me there are some pretty good hiking trails on the company's land."

"There are." Aspen smiled. Melissa had taken the last of the cookie pieces. "You have to hike in, but once there, you feel like you're the only person in the universe."

"I've been there with friends," Melissa said between bites. "We were just kinda hanging out. Not really thinking much about the environment, I guess."

Aspen smiled. "Some young people go out there. Not a lot though."

"Why not?" Linda asked.

"It's a long hike in. The kids would rather hang out at the local spots in town that're easier to get to." Melissa smiled at Aspen. "I'd love to go out there sometime with you and Aunt Linda." Aspen wondered how she had screwed up the courage to ask.

"I'd like that." Aspen smiled at her. Melissa relaxed.

"How about Friday?" Linda asked. "You have a workshop day, which means you've got the afternoon off."

"How did you know?"

"I have students working as ed techs in your school."

"Friday?" Aspen was surprised at how soon Linda wanted to go.

"How cool is that?" Melissa enthused.

"Pretty cool," Aspen said.

"Now that my niece has polished off your cookies." Melissa was embarrassed again. "It's time to go. How about we pick you up around noon? Melissa can pack a lunch."

"That'd be nice." Aspen shook Linda's hand. She smiled at Melissa. "I'm glad you ate the cookies. My friend Anne Jean made them and believes that food is best when it's shared," she whispered.

"Thank you," Melissa said.

"Well, little girl." Aspen eyed Miss Etta. "You're going to enjoy this probably more than me." Aspen picked up the telephone on the first ring. "Hey, Cassie, I'm great. I'm going for a hike with Melissa. You remember her from the restaurant? And her Aunt Linda?" She told Cassie about their impromptu visit earlier in the week and about Linda's environmental efforts in Massachusetts. "Anyway, they'll be here in a few minutes, although judging from those clouds we're going to have to hurry or we're going to be picnicking in the rain. Great, I'll see you Sunday."

Miss Etta barked and Aspen opened the door. "Linda, hi. Where's Melissa?"

"Something came up and she couldn't join us. She was really disappointed, but God love her, she packed a great lunch. It's in the truck. You ready?"

"I am. I hope you have rain gear." Aspen picked up her backpack.

"It doesn't dare rain on such an important day."

"Important?"

"Sure, I get to spend time with you and see one of your favorite places through your eyes. I'd say that's pretty important."

Aspen angled her head to look at Linda. Was the woman flirting with her? Impossible, she decided. They'd just met, but then she'd only known Leigh a few weeks, and they were definitely flirting. Aspen smiled to herself. Feast or famine. Years without an interesting woman in town and now there were two. "It's a beautiful spot as seen through anyone's eyes. I'm just disappointed Melissa couldn't come."

"As was she. I told her next time." Linda held the door open for her.

"Come on, Miss Etta."

"Is she joining us?" Aspen saw the surprised look on Linda's face.

Aspen frowned. "She doesn't have to."

"I love dogs, really. Just that I got a new truck and it has cloth seats. I'd hate to get dog hair on them."

"It's fine, really," Aspen said. "She's stayed home before." Miss Etta looked from her to Linda. Disappointed, Miss Etta walked to her bed and settled herself down with a firm plop.

"Well, then let's get going. I say we can do it all before one raindrop even hits us."

"I hope you're right," Aspen said studying the sky.

"Wow. Melissa was right. This place is spectacular." They were seated next to the river. "Hungry?"

"Not a lot. Would you like to hike first? We can come back here and have lunch, or . . . ." Aspen looked at the sky. "We could be having lunch in your truck." She wondered if they were allowed to eat in the truck. She thought about Miss Etta who looked miserable when she'd left.

"First, I have to show you what my niece prepared." Linda opened her backpack and put containers on the ground. "Melissa gave me a cheat sheet." She held up a piece paper. "This dish has autumn duck salad with green beans." Linda read off several more items. "And for dessert, chocolate peanut butter bites."

"I'm impressed. Your niece should open more than a deli. It

looks like she should have a full-scale restaurant." Aspen surveyed the food.

"How about that hike?" Linda asked.

They hiked to the narrowest part of the river and Aspen showed Linda where as a kid she used to walk across the river on the underwater log bridge. "I fell in a lot." She laughed.

Linda looked at the aging tree trunks. The ripple of the river made them look contoured and crooked. "You know we could force the paper company to clean this up. There's no reason for these abandoned logs to be here. Talk about polluting. This is polluting on a grand scale."

"I guess there's this expectation that after a time they'll just rot and disappear." Aspen realized she was seeing the logs through the eyes of someone who had not grown up in town. To the locals, the logs reminded them of a time when the river was the highway of the town, with boats and barges and river runs. Although the local environmentalists had fought the mill, demanding it clean up the river, no one had considered the logs. Somehow, they'd been burned into the memory of the town and were now part of its folklore.

"You said they've been here since the log driving days? When was the last river run?"

"I think the late forties, early fifties. I'd have to check at the library. They have several books there about the history of the logging business."

"I bet we could make a big deal of getting these removed. Probably even get statewide attention. Maybe national." Linda was studying the logs. "Are there more of these?"

"There are. Both upriver and down."

"This is an even bigger story than I thought," Linda said.

"Look, Linda, a word to the wise. Before you charge headlong into this, a lot of people like the logs, me for one."

"You? That surprises me. Clearly nature didn't put these here."

"True, but they've been here for my thirty years in this town, and for others a lot longer. I'm not sure you'll get support for any kind of forced clean up."

Linda scoffed. "We won't know until we try."

Aspen wiped the first few drops of rain off her face. "I think we have a more serious problem right now. We'd better head back to the campsite," Aspen said.

"This is just a shower. I don't expect it'll turn into much." Linda turned and followed Aspen.

They walked faster as the shower turned into a downpour. "I think we'd better pick up the food and head for your truck." Aspen pulled raingear from her backpack. "Sorry, I don't have any more in here."

"Wouldn't fit anyway and serves me right for being so cocky, but I'm with you, I think we'd better make a run for the truck." Linda grabbed containers and stuffed them in her backpack.

It didn't take them long to hike back to Linda's truck. Aspen stripped her rain jacket and hat off and tossed them on the floor in the back, mindful of Linda's concern about the new truck seats.

"How about we go over to your house and have that picnic?" Linda was shivering.

"I think that's a very good idea. You're going to catch pneumonia in those clothes. Do you want me to drive?" Aspen asked.

"I'm fine, really. Get the truck heater going and I'll dry off." Linda blew on her hands as she started the truck. "It's really cold out there."

"Strip down and I'll throw your clothes in the dryer." Aspen looked at Linda's size. "I doubt my robe will fit," she said as she directed Linda to the bathroom and handed her a blanket.

Seated in the kitchen, Linda looked very much like a naked woman under a blanket. "This feels wonderful," Linda said.

Aspen added wood to the stove. "You hungry?"

"I am."

"Good. I'll make a fresh pot of coffee."

They spent the afternoon eating and talking. Linda told her more about her environmental efforts in Massachusetts. "I even got arrested a couple of times," Linda said after she'd changed back into her clothes. Aspen decided she liked her better in clothes than in a blanket, because occasionally when Linda reached for some food, the corner of the blanket slid down, exposing a part of her breast.

"Really."

Linda sipped her coffee. "The last time was the most serious. The company we were protesting claimed some stuff." Linda shrugged dismissively. "You ever get arrested?"

"Nothing serious. Just civil disobedience stuff."

"You should try it, you might like it." Linda's lip twitched. "I'd love to be in jail with you."

There she goes again. This woman is flirting with me. Aspen mentally flinched, she had enough problems with a forester. "Well, let's hope it doesn't ever come to that."

Linda ignored Aspen's cautionary response. "Who knows? Maybe Burnt Brush will be the ones to test our environmental might. Now wouldn't that be fun?" Linda started to put covers on the food dishes. "I have to get going. I'm meeting my niece and some of her friends. Well, this has been fun."

"Except for the wet part, I agree." Aspen put the containers in Linda's damp backpack.

"It could have been worse. We could have drowned our lunch too," Linda joked. "I'm glad I put those tops back on the food."

"Me, too. Tell Melissa it was a terrific lunch and next time I hope she can share it with us."

"I'd like to do it again."

"Let's." Aspen smiled at her.

"I feel rather awkward here, but I'd really like to hug you,"

Linda said.

"That'd be nice." Aspen gave her a perfunctory hug, but Linda drew her into her arms. Her hand moved down Aspen's back and stopped just above the waist of her pants.

"Thank you for a great day," Linda said, her lips touching the top of Aspen's hair.

Aspen stepped back, uncomfortable with the intimacy of the hug. "It was fun."

"I'll call you." Linda ran to her truck. It was still pouring.

CHAPTER EIGHT

Aspen blew out the match and inspected her living room. Candles were flickering on almost every surface. When she and Willow were kids, her mother always had lit candles around the room in the evening, and she and Willow would lay on the floor to study the patterns the flickering light cast on the ceiling. She smiled as she remembered. Willow always saw lots and lots of chrysanthemums, while Aspen would point at the ceiling and draw an imaginary line with her finger of the leaves of a local oak or an exotic and foreign teak tree. Leaves she had seen in a book. She called it leaves from around the world. Most of the time the leaves from around the world emerged from her imagination.

One day her mother admonished her and told her that someday Willow would grow up and Aspen's imaginary leaves would be exposed. Years later she and Willow were home from college and her mother had lit candles in the living room. They were lying on the floor looking up at the ceiling, and Willow asked Aspen what leaves she saw. Aspen closed her eyes and drew the round and toothy edged leaf of the quaking aspen and the finger-long leaves of the shining willow tree. Aspen wiped away the tear that had rolled onto her cheek. She hated remembering those memories.

"Woof, woof," Miss Etta yipped.

"Am I too early?" Leigh handed her a bouquet of flowers.

"Not at all. I love flowers. Thank you. Let me put these in water."

"Good and here's something for you, little lady." Leigh held up a beef-basted rawhide bone. "Okay if I give it to her?"

"I think she'd take your arm off if you didn't." Miss Etta hopped on her hind legs. Leigh handed her the bone, and she crawled under the kitchen table.

Leigh hung her jacket on the hook next to the door. "I'm glad you suggested having dinner here. I enjoy eating out, but this is nice."

"Well, I thought so too." Aspen handed Leigh coffee. "Let's sit in here. How was your week?" Aspen asked, seated on the couch.

"Good. I love the candles. This is nice." Leigh settled herself on the couch. "As to my week, it's getting better. The crews actually are working out well. How about you?"

"I met a really neat woman. Remember when we were at the restaurant and Melissa said she wanted me to meet her Aunt Linda? Well, they stopped by earlier in the week. Linda and I went for a hike in the woods yesterday."

"Yesterday? It poured yesterday."

Aspen laughed. "That it did. I wore my rain gear, but she didn't and got soaked. We ended up finishing the picnic here. Anyway, fascinating woman. An environmentalist. She's done a lot of stuff in Massachusetts. I think you two would like each other. She mentioned you as a matter of fact. Said she'd like to meet you."

"Great." Leigh sipped her coffee. "Is she a lesbian?"

Aspen smiled. "Why? Are all environmentalists lesbians or are all lesbians environmentalists? Actually, we didn't talk about it, but yes, I expect she is." Aspen remembered the lingering hug when Linda was leaving.

"Sorry." Leigh exhaled noisily. "So did you have a good time?"

"Well, yes, in a bizarre sort of way. As I said, she was soaked to the skin and I made her strip down so I could throw her clothes in the dryer."

"That must have been fun."

Aspen laughed. "I guess that does sound rather funny. She's a lot bigger than I am, so I gave her a blanket to wrap up in and we finished the picnic. Really a fascinating woman."

"You said that," Leigh said curtly.

"Are you all right?"

"Sure," Leigh said, looking at her. "My week was less interesting. I did get a call from my sister."

"Me too. I guess she and Cassie have cooked up some kind of get together in a few weeks. Your sister said something about coming up here and the four of us having dinner."

"I tried to dissuade her, but Brittany's a freight train when she gets going. Said Cassie just *loved the idea*. She's insists on coming up on the sixteenth. Then she and Cassie plan to spend Sunday together. Something about a belly dance lesson."

"Cassie's still doing it, I guess. How are things between Brit and Harry?"

"Good. At least she says things are fine. They're still going to counseling and she's getting gung ho about astrology. I think part of the reason for the visit is she's done charts on all of us. I can't wait," Leigh added grudgingly.

Aspen laughed. "Charts? I've never had a chart done on me. It should be fun."

"I think it's weird, but that's Brit. But this dinner makes me a wee bit nervous."

"Why?"

"Like my sister told you at the restaurant, after Kathy and I broke up, Brit took it upon herself to plan a lot of dinners."

"That sounds nice."

"Actually, they weren't. They were sort of like *check out the valuable heifer at an auction.* I was the heifer."

"Oh."

"Yeah, oh."

"I take it all these women were single and lesbian?"

"Yes, to both."

"Nothing took?"

"Just a lot of fancy footwork on my part to elude them. She even had the audacity to hand out business cards with all my vital statistics on it."

Aspen put her hand over her mouth to try to hold back the laughter.

"Go ahead and laugh. I can now, but I was fuming at the time."

"Vital statistics, as in . . . ?"

"What I liked and didn't like. She even put on there that I hated mushrooms and broccoli."

Aspen couldn't hold back the laughter. "You're kidding."

"I wanted to hang her on a hook. She said she did it in case they invited me for dinner, then they'd know what not to cook. She had my clothing sizes on there. In case they wanted to give me a gift. One woman gave me underwear for Valentine's Day."

"What did you say?"

"Thank you, I think. I don't remember. I was so embarrassed by the whole thing. My sister thought it was sweet."

"So did they have little hearts on them?"

"You're toying with me, aren't you? Having a little fun at my expense." Leigh's grin was wide.

"Just a little. More coffee?" Aspen asked picking up the pot.

"Thanks."

"So did they have hearts on them?"

"Yes, and, no, I didn't wear them." Leigh looked away self-consciously.

"I'm sorry. I *am* having some fun at your expense."

"It's funny now. Then I was just mortified. I really did want to throttle my little sister."

"I can imagine. She and Cassie are so much alike. Cassie's had her moments of meddling in my life."

"I bet. Can you match my Valentine undies story?"

"No, that one's pretty unique, I have to say. You mentioned Kathy. You've never said why you two broke up."

"Over my job, actually." Leigh laughed.

"Your job?"

"It was more complicated than that, but, yes, my job was involved. Kathy was . . . I didn't dress, eat or think right. I loved hiking in the woods. She loved hiking around the mall. She didn't like Brittany, and she hated what I did. Anyway, this vice president's job came up at my company and I was up for it. Kathy wanted me to take it. It meant a desk rather than fieldwork What can I say? I'm a forester and I like what I do. Anyway, it came down to crunch time and I had to make a decision. I took off for three days and went for a hike in the woods. When I came out, I told corporate no. Kathy sort of exploded. She left faster than a hurricane hitting the Gulf Coast."

"How'd you feel?"

"Relieved. Things weren't going well before she left. What she wanted and what I wanted just never seemed to mesh. She was an advertising account executive for a television station in Presque Isle, I was a forester. She wanted more, I wanted less."

"Not less, just what made you happy."

"Probably. Anyway, she moved out. Three weeks later she wanted to move back, but I'd already decided to transfer here. I just needed to get out of Presque Isle."

"Well," Aspen said getting up. "Presque Isle's loss is Codyville's gain. Come on, dinner is ready." She picked up the coffeepot. "I have to tell you though, I wish I'd had that business card your sister handed out."

"Why?"

"We're having broccoli for our vegetable tonight."

Leigh groaned. "You really are going to have fun with this at my expense."

"I am. I really am."

"Anyway, getting back to Linda, I was thinking the three of us should have dinner some night," Aspen said.

"Sounds fine."

"You don't sound very enthusiastic."

"It's fine, really." Leigh straightened determinedly. "I guess I'm just jealous because you took that walk in the woods with her. It's something I'd like us to do. It's silly, really," Leigh said, clearly self-conscious.

"I'm sorry," Aspen said simply. "We're going to take that walk in the woods. It's important, but I really want you to meet her. I know you two will like each other."

"And my job doesn't bother her?"

"Doesn't seem to."

"Really?"

"I think she just wants to get to know you, Leigh. We've had forest managers around here for years, but you're the first one I've taken the time to get to know, and it's made a difference. I'm not as rabid anti-company as I was prior to meeting you."

"Really?"

"*Really!*" Aspen said with a smile. "Well, not totally *anti*. I'm willing to listen is probably how I should put it, and I think Linda is too. She's done some outstanding things in Massachusetts." Aspen then related some of the battles that Linda had been involved with.

106

"Sounds fascinating."

"I get the feeling you're prepared not to like her."

"I don't know her," Leigh said evenly.

"She is who I am, only she did it in Massachusetts." She was surprised at Leigh's reaction. She was also surprised that she found herself now defending Linda to Leigh.

"She sounds like one of those radical environmentalists you see on television."

"I hate that word."

"What, television?"

"You're being cute." Aspen's sarcasm hung in the air. "Just because we disagree with people who pollute the air or kill our earth, why are we labeled radical?" Aspen realized her tone was more biting than she intended.

"I'm not labeling you a radical."

"Really?"

"There's a difference. From what you've described, Linda laying down in front of a bulldozer and being part of a human chain to stop something is radical. You don't do that. I think environmentalists can accomplish just as much without all the posturing."

"I've lain down in front of bulldozers. I've never been part of a human chain to stop something, but if I believed strongly enough, I'd do it. What makes her different?"

"Sounds to me like she'd carry it to the extreme. She'd be the one who'd pound spikes into trees, like they did out west, so that when a chainsaw cut through it would break the chain and hurt the operator, possibly killing him. Look, Aspen, I respect you as an environmentalist. I just have a real problem with fanatics."

"And just because Linda has taken some aggressive steps to stop the destruction of the earth, she's a fanatic? I think you're busy attaching labels, rather than looking at what business is doing to our country." Aspen glowered at her.

"And I think that it's fanatics like Linda who give people like

107

you a bad name. Look, Aspen, I agree that if it hadn't been for people like you, this country would be in a whole lot worse shape. But I think the real change happened because of people who pushed the boundaries, but didn't cross over. I applaud what the environmentalists have done, but I think the fanatics have done more to hurt your cause than help." Leigh's face was red.

"And I think, to coin a cliché, the end justifies the means. I think what Linda has done is brave and downright admirable."

"You're kidding! She admitted she broke the law. She's proud she broke the law!"

"So! I broke the law and corporate America breaks the law every day and we call it doing business. I think she did what she had to do to stop some really terrible things from happening to the environment, and I think she deserves a medal."

"I think she deserves a good thrashing."

"What? You thrash people who don't agree with you?"

"No! But I think—"

"And I think you need to leave because it's clear that you and I live in two different worlds. You're not an environmentalist, you're a—"

"A what, Aspen? Can't say it? Well, I agree I need to leave, and frankly I'm not interested in having dinner with Linda now or in the future."

"Fine, I'm sorry I brought it up." Miss Etta was leaning against Aspen's leg, she was trembling.

"Thanks for dinner," Leigh said as she grabbed her jacket and stormed out.

"I think that went extremely well," Aspen said as she blew the candles out in the living room. She was still replaying the conversation in her head. How did they get from Valentine undies to radicals? She stared at the picture of her sister on the sideboard. Aspen inhaled deeply. "Ah, Willow, I wish you were still here.

You always seemed to keep me going in the right direction. I miss our talks." Aspen closed her eyes, feeling depression settling on her shoulders. The same depression she'd felt after her sister died. She closed her hands and tightened her fists. "Come on, Miss Etta. We'll do dishes in the morning," she said to push back against the loneliness. Miss Etta barked. Aspen saw the headlights in her driveway and waited at the door. Miss Etta ran out to greet Leigh, Aspen frowned, how different it was for a dog, Miss Etta had already forgiven.

"I'm sorry. I don't know what happened." Leigh stayed next to her truck. Afraid Aspen would order her to leave.

"Come in. I really don't want to end this like that." When Leigh had stormed out, Aspen had felt scared for the first time in a long time. Scared that she'd never see Leigh again.

"Aspen, I'm sorry," Leigh said. "Can I give you an apology hug?" Aspen stepped into her arms. "I stormed out like a child. I don't do that, and I foolishly got angry at a woman I don't even know. I really feel like a jerk."

"Well, I didn't help matters any." Aspen swallowed. The hug was what she had so missed by not having a woman in her life. She wanted more. *Stop it*, she said to herself. *Stop it! Leigh doesn't have a clue as to who you are.* She stepped back and felt Leigh's arms reluctantly drop from around her.

"Truce?"

"Double truce. Coffee? Tea?"

Leigh pulled out a kitchen chair and sat down. "Nothing, thank you. I think . . ." Leigh chose her words. "I'd like to go for that walk in the woods. Now, rather than later. I think we need to resolve a lot of stuff between us. Philosophical stuff, practical stuff. Can we do that?"

"I'd like that."

"Good, as in the next couple of days?"

Leigh was studying her. "I can't tomorrow. I promised Cassie that we'd do some stuff together. How about Saturday?"

"Good, that's what I was hoping you'd say, but I didn't know if maybe you and Linda might have planned a hike or something," Leigh added, afraid to say more.

"No, not at all. I'll pack lunch, nothing fancy."

"I'd like that."

"Me too." Aspen's hands were clasped in front of her. She spread her fingers apart and rested them on the tablecloth. There was silence.

"Well, I'd better get going." Leigh stuck her hands in her pockets. "Aspen, I'd like to get back to where we were. I feel awkward now and I don't like that. How about dinner on Friday night?"

"I'd like that."

"Good, I like what was happening before. I don't want to lose that. Well . . ." Leigh said finally. "I should go."

"Can I have a good-bye hug?"

"Of course." Leigh sighed. The woman smelled so good. "I should go," Leigh said again. She reluctantly dropped her arms.

"I guess . . ."

After Leigh left, Aspen stared at the closed door. The hug, she realized, was unsettling and she wanted more. *No!* She sharply told herself as she turned off the kitchen light. *You can't have more until you tell Leigh where you've been, who you've been. You have to tell her on Saturday.* "Come on, Miss Etta. It's time for bed."

"Linda, hi." Aspen was surprised to find Linda's truck parked in her driveway.

"I took a chance you might be here."

Aspen frowned. She and Cassie had spent the day cleaning junk out of Cassie's garage. She turned down supper with Cassie because she wanted to grade papers. Linda pulled bags out of the truck. Miss Etta was also curious. "Come in." She was irritated.

110

The woman kept dropping in.

"Doggie, go with your mama," Linda said pushing Miss Etta off her pant leg.

"Miss Etta, come. What's in the bags?"

"A surprise." Linda's face glowed. "I have Greek olives and French bread and wonderful Italian salami. All the fixings for one of the best Italian sandwiches you've ever eaten. I'm not a gourmet cook, but I can sure fix one mean sandwich. And," she said, holding up a bottle, "one of the finest Chilean wines you've ever tasted. You do whatever you have to do, and I'll fix our sandwiches."

Aspen groaned inwardly. She'd have to be up at five to get her paperwork done for school. "This is nice, but first I have to fix Miss Etta's supper."

"Well, I had to do something to make up for that aborted walk in the woods. By the way, I was wondering if you were doing anything Saturday. The long-range weather said it's going to be a beautiful day. How about another hike?"

"Sorry, I've made plans, but I'd love to another time. By the way, I mentioned to Leigh that you'd like the three of us to get together and do something. She thought that'd be fun." Aspen bit down on her lower lip. She thought about the night before.

"Great," Linda said. "Here." She handed Aspen a glass of wine.

"Sorry, I don't drink."

"Really, you don't drink because you don't like the stuff or . . ."

"I don't like the stuff." Funny, she realized she didn't want to tell Linda about that side of her life.

"That's fine. It means more for me." She put both wineglasses in front of her.

"I'll make myself a cup of tea." Aspen put water on to boil.

"This is so nice," Linda said. They were seated at the kitchen table. "I've got to tell you, Aspen, I have an ulterior motive for being here."

"Really?"

"Really." Linda smiled. "I'd like to get to know you better. My niece said you were a nice-looking woman. She didn't tell me how beautiful you are." Aspen looked down. "Sorry, I've embarrassed you," Linda said intently. "Melissa adores you and she still recalls some of the stories you had them read on the environment. It really impressed her."

Aspen was relieved Linda had changed the subject. She smiled. "They don't remember why I made them read it, but if they walked away with an appreciation of the environment, that's good."

"I can't remember a teacher that I had in school who had such a profound influence on my life. I got into this whole environment thing after I got into college."

"I did early on. My friend Cassie, you haven't met her yet, and I used to read Rachel Carson, among others. Now Cassie is just as passionate about saving the environment." Aspen then told her about Cassie joining Mary Tyler Moore's fight to save the lobster.

"I like that. I believe in whatever it takes to save the environment."

"Do you really?"

"I do. Your friend putting her marriage on the line is worthy of a medal. You must also believe that."

"I do, but I also know she has regrets." Aspen shrugged.

"I have one philosophy. I never look back and I refuse to regret."

"Wow, you're a better woman than I am."

"Try it. It does work. Anyway, how about dinner Friday night?"

"I've got a commitment that night also. I'm free Thursday night if you want to do something early since I have classes Friday morning."

"Well, I'm disappointed, but Thursday it is. I see that I'm

going to have to get on your dance calendar weeks ahead of time."

"Usually, it's pretty easy. This just turned out to be a busier than usual week. I'd like to have dinner. Maybe Melissa could join us?"

"Dinner it is, at my house, and if she's not working I'll invite her. I did bring dessert," Linda said opening another bag.

"Flan?" Aspen exclaimed. "Where did you get flan?"

"In Harrington. There's this really cool Mexican restaurant. It just opened. I had dinner there with some faculty members and we had flan."

"I adore flan," Aspen said eyeing the containers.

Linda handed her a spoon. "Nothing formal, flan out of the carton. Anyway, bon appetite."

"Oh, yeah!" Aspen said digging into the creamy custard.

"This was nice." Aspen tried to hold back a yawn. "I have to get up early."

"You're just so easy to talk to." Linda reluctantly got up. "Keep all of this stuff." She gestured at the remaining Greek olives and Italian salami.

"Take some with you. There's enough here for another three meals."

"Good. Every time you eat a Greek olive, you can think of me."

Aspen laughed, uncomfortable with the too serious tone Linda again had taken. She liked the conversation before when Linda had talked about herself. "Anyway, thanks for the food, the visit. It was nice."

"I liked it too. Well . . ." Linda said taking Aspen in her arms. "One of my favorite moments in the day. You smell so good." Linda held her tight.

Aspen pulled away.

"I'm sorry. I didn't mean to come on so strongly. But, Aspen, you have to know I'm attracted to you. It's so nice to find a woman who speaks my language. I don't have to explain to you who I am or why I do what I do. I really like that."

"Linda, I . . ."

"Don't say anything," Linda said taking Aspen's hand and kissing the top of it. "Just be aware that I like you a lot. But I'm also willing to take this slowly. Give you a chance to like me, *a lot*. Your dog seems to like my pant leg *a lot*," Linda said pushing her down.

"Sorry, Miss Etta likes everyone's pant leg. Miss Etta, stop," Aspen ordered.

"I'm just not used to it. One of my exes had a dog that also had some undesirable traits. I spent a few weeks training her. She's a great dog now. That was one of the better things to come out of that relationship." Linda grinned. "Anyway, see you on Thursday."

Aspen stared at the closed door. *Oh, dear,* she thought. She had tried to tell Linda that she liked her, but not in any way that would lead to a kiss on the hand. "Well, Miss Etta, it looks like that's something Ms. Linda and I are going to have to talk about on Thursday night." Linda was fun and funny, but a forester named Leigh Wright, whose easy manner had an unsettling effect on her had already complicated Aspen's life. "Come on, squirt. Time to go to bed."

CHAPTER NINE

Aspen was dumbfounded at how keyed up she was. They were just going for a walk in the woods. Nothing different than the dinners and other walks they'd taken, she kept telling herself. But then she'd think about the night before and the candlelight on Leigh's face. It was so sexy that Aspen wanted to reach over and stroke Leigh's cheek. All she could think about after she'd gone home was kissing her all over. And as much as Aspen had wanted to—was burning to—she couldn't do it because she was terrified. She knew she was the one that kept holding back, holding them both back. Each time they were together, she wanted to tell Leigh about that corner of her life that was as black as ink. "I'm not a whole person," she whispered to the kitchen. *I want to tell her*, she repeated like a chant. *She needs to know who I am. But what if telling her drives her away?* She'd come close several times, then the evil ghost of dread would seize her and she would remain silent. *Why are you so scared?* Hadn't Anne Jean told her to trust Leigh, to tell her? Somehow Leigh had crept up on her and now she wanted her more than any woman she'd ever wanted. How odd, she thought. She thought about her dinner with Linda Thursday night. Melissa had to work, and so it was just two of them. She'd tried to tell Linda that she wasn't at the same emotional level, but Linda kept telling her to wait. She was confident about where they were going. When she'd left she'd kissed Aspen ever so lightly on the mouth. Thinking about that kiss, Aspen realized it hadn't moved mountains, not even an ant hill.

Funny, the one she wanted to kiss was Leigh, but other than lingering hugs, it hadn't happened. She knew she was holding back until they resolved their differences. She was relieved she and Leigh were finally going for a hike. Trees were a piece of her and how Leigh fit into that life's scheme troubled her deeply. Aspen sighed. All week she had wavered between thrilled and anxious. She had tried to analyze each level of emotion. Leigh was a forester, someone who made her living off the very life forms she stood ready to protect. And thrown into Aspen's maze of emotions was this: What if Leigh failed the test? Test? When had it become a test? Aspen wondered. It was just a walk, but what if . . .

Miss Etta heard the car engine and growled. Aspen glanced at the clock. Leigh wasn't due for another hour. She shook her head when she saw Cassie's car.

"Hush," Aspen said to Miss Etta, who was jumping at the door.

"Are you surprised to see me?" Cassie rushed in.

"Should I be? Miss Etta, go lie down," Aspen said. The dog walked over to her bed and, with a groan, dropped onto her stomach.

"Well, I know you told me to butt out of your life, but I just had to bring this over. It's for good luck." Cassie held out her hand.

Aspen eyed the braided hair with red ribbons on either end. "What's that?"

"A horsehair braid. It's an ancient good luck charm. I read about it in a new book I just got from the library," Cassie said, admiring the braid like it was a caftan she'd just bought. "I had to go over to Vanceboro to get it. Do you know there aren't any horses around here? The farmer was really nice and let me cut a swatch out of the horse's tail. I took just a little bit. I could tell he thought I was a bit ditzy, but I gave him ten dollars, and ditzy or not, he took the money. I've braided it and everything. I just put the red ribbons on because I thought it added a certain amount of panache."

"What am I supposed to do with that?"

"I don't know." Cassie turned the braid over in her hand as if examining it for the first time. "It didn't say anything like putting it under your pillow or wearing it around your neck. There were tons of other good luck charms that the ancients used, but this was the only one I could get a hold of quickly. Some are really quite difficult to come by, like the tooth of a bat or a swallow's heart. Some would have meant I would have had to kill an animal." Cassie shuddered. "I couldn't bring myself to do that. But I thought, what harm is there? It just might bring you good luck." Cassie dropped the tail into Aspen's reluctant hand.

Aspen glanced at the braid. She wasn't quite sure if she should laugh or yell at Cassie for being goofy. "Thank you." She put the braid on the table.

"I'm relieved. I thought you'd think it was just another one of my silly things, but, Aspen, it can't hurt. You like this woman. More than that, I know you're attracted to her. I'm not going to explain it. I just know."

"You want coffee?" Aspen wasn't prepared to talk about her feelings.

"Love it. I can gulp down a cup in a few minutes."

"What are your plans for today?" She handed Cassie her cup.

She didn't want to think about the horsehair braid.

"I'm going over to the grange hall to sign a contract. I'm going to rent it." Cassie was clearly excited. "It's been vacant forever."

"Why are you renting the building?"

"To teach belly dancing. Three women already have signed up."

Aspen groaned inwardly. "Cassie, is it a good idea? I mean the expense and all?"

"Oh, it's a gamble, but what isn't? I've also talked to some other women who said they'd come if I started the course. I wanted to use the gymnasium at the school, but I couldn't afford it. Someone suggested the grange hall. I only have to pay for the electricity and the heat. I figured that was a good deal."

"Cassie, I know you're trying it, but teach a class?"

"I've gotten a bunch of videos and I've been practicing. You've been with Leigh so much lately, *and don't think I don't know that*, I haven't been able to show you."

"Are you sure you want to do this?"

"I play the videotapes and we all learn together. The only reason I'm charging ten dollars is to pay for the utilities. What's the harm of women wanting to exercise in a fun kind of way?"

Aspen was surprised at the tenacity in her friend's eyes. "Nothing." Aspen turned away. This wasn't the first time that her practical side had collided with Cassie's dream world. In the past Cassie had stumbled, but most of the time her ideas and schemes seemed to bring a lot of fun to a lot of people. "Nothing at all. I think it's great."

"You do?" Cassie enthused. "Great, because I told a couple of the women you might join. They were just thrilled! A lot of them are mothers of your students."

Aspen held her breath and counted to ten. She did that a lot with Cassie. "I'm not going to dance around in my underwear with mothers of some of my students."

"We don't dance in our underwear. We'll be wearing skirts." Cassie finished her coffee. "Gotta run. Leigh's going to be here in a few minutes."

"You're right." Aspen followed her to the door. "I guess we're all having dinner together in a few weeks. I've talked with Brit a few times. She's planning quite a meal."

"I guess."

Aspen studied her face. "Is something wrong?"

"Gosh, no, Aspen. I just gotta go." Cassie picked up the horsehair braid. "I did wash it before I braided it. I know how finicky you are." She put the braid in Aspen's hand. "I want you to find happiness, and we do whatever we need to to make it happen. And maybe, my friend, it will hold back those sad demons." Cassie's voice was soft.

Aspen sighed inwardly. How could she be upset with her? "Cassie, I love you." She held her friend close. After her sister had died, she'd battled depression, and for a time she was unsure if she'd ever win. Afterward, she'd realized that it had also been a difficult time for Cassie and Anne Jean. Throughout the ordeal and for years after, Cassie had refused to use the word *depression* and had called that time Aspen's *sad demons*.

"I know." Cassie hugged her. "I also know people think I'm foolish, but they just see that side of me. You see the whole of me." She held Aspen away from her. "All I want is for you to be happy. What's the harm in getting some ancient luck in on this?"

"None." Aspen laughed. "But I'm not going to put it under my pillow tonight," she said staring at the braid that was again lying in her hand.

"That's okay. Just call me tonight. I'm anxious to hear. I know Brittany's also been bugging Leigh for a telephone call tonight. We want to hear about the walk."

"Would you two stop and leave us alone?"

"No, we won't. I love you and Brittany loves her sister, and we think you two were just meant for each other. And we're

119

really excited because if you two get together, we'll almost be in-laws. I know I'm not your physical family, but I'm your spiritual family, so that counts."

Aspen groaned. "You keep this up and the two of you are going to jinx any chance Leigh and I might have."

"So there is a chance?"

"No." Aspen inhaled deeply. "I don't know. Oh hell."

Cassie squeezed the hand Aspen was holding the horsehair braid in. "For luck," she said quietly. "Give me a call tonight." She closed the door.

"I'm not going to call you!" Aspen yelled at the closed door. She looked at the amulet and then at Miss Etta. No, she decided, it couldn't be a Miss Etta toy. She dropped it in a bowl in the living room. Out of sight, out of mind, she decided.

Miss Etta barked. Leigh got out of her truck and pulled her jacket down over her jeans. She truly is a handsome woman, Aspen decided. She frowned, there was that stirring she'd felt of late. Stop it, she ordered the passionate side of her brain. Miss Etta ran to greet Leigh.

"Good morning. It's going to be a great day in the woods." Leigh scratched Miss Etta under her chin.

"Come in. I've got everything ready." Leigh handed her a bag as she stepped through the door. "What's this?"

"Éclairs. I got them at the bakery in Machias. I go when I'm desperate for sugar."

Aspen laughed. "I stay away from there. Her bakery is my downfall." Aspen looked in the bag. "Oh wow. They're huge!"

"I know."

"I'm not going to put these in the backpack. It'll squish the chocolate. So you, Ms. Leigh, will just have to carry them."

"I can. Are we ready?" Leigh picked up the backpack.

"I am and so is Miss Etta. She's known all day we're going for a walk."

"How so?" Leigh put the backpack on the backseat. Miss Etta

jumped on top of it.

"The backpack," Aspen said, seated in the truck. "She knows that when it comes out, we're headed for a walk."

"Very smart dog." Leigh grinned.

Funny, she thought as Leigh started the truck. All morning she'd felt spleeny as she anticipated their walk in the woods, but now that she was with Leigh she had mellowed out. They chatted about their day as they drove to the trail parking lot.

Leigh picked up the bag and the backpack and slung it over her shoulder.

"I can carry that," Aspen said.

"As well as I, so how about I carry it in and you carry it out?"

"A lot lighter coming out?" Aspen smiled.

"Who's to say? You might find all kinds of rocks, and the backpack could weigh twice as much on the way out. I'm not dumb, ya know," Leigh teased.

"I never doubted that for a moment. At least let me carry the éclairs. That way if we get separated Miss Etta and I will have something to munch on."

"Smart lady." Leigh handed her the bag.

The walk through the woods did not require any talk and Aspen was relieved. She liked that Leigh seemed comfortable with silence. Miss Etta ranged left and then right as she sucked in the fall smells. Today was a study in contrasts, her love of the woods and Leigh's job. And that was what she had ordered her mind to concentrate on. The forest had a heart and Aspen heard its beat, and unless Leigh heard that beat, well, she wasn't going to predict what *unless* meant.

Aspen looked up at the sky. She loved the way the sunlight sliced through the forest's canopy. The ground looked like spotlights on a theater stage as they stepped from one circular light to the next. There was the alternating crunching sound as they stepped from broken twigs and dried leaves to dried grass that rustled as they walked.

"As you know, there is a great picnic area at the end of this path," Leigh said over her shoulder. "I expect you've known it your whole life."

"I have." Aspen followed Leigh. She smiled to herself. Wasn't that where Linda had abandoned her dignity to race back to the warmth of her truck during the downpour? She decided not to mention it to Leigh.

"The first time I saw it, it took my breath away," Leigh's voice brought her back to the present. "I get the feeling most folks don't come out here."

"They go to the ocean. It's easier to get to."

"Point well taken," Leigh said as she followed the path. "The first time I came here, I sat and listened to the river. Rapids have their own rhythm and, wondrously, their own cadence. Almost like listening to the constant beat of a drum. Next spring I want to bring my canoe and run the river."

"That's fun."

"You've done it?"

"Many times, although not lately."

"Well, maybe we can do it together. You can be my teacher." Leigh turned to see her reaction and Aspen, who had been looking at a finch in the tree, bumped into her.

"Sorry, I was looking at something else." Aspen swallowed. *How could a bump feel so good?* she wondered. "I'd be happy to run the river with you in the spring," she said as they resumed their walk, but not before she saw the surprised look on Leigh's face also. *What's going on?* she asked herself. *A bump should not feel so sexual.* She heard the whooshing sound and was relieved the river was just ahead.

"Good. Come on. I want to show you my favorite place to sit." Leigh was still muddled by their body contact. "I had a picnic here by myself earlier this year," Leigh said shyly. "Seems silly to picnic by yourself." Leigh set the backpack down.

"Why?" Aspen sat on the grass cross-legged. She put the éclairs between them. "I do it all the time."

"When I was growing up, a picnic was a social event. It wasn't something you did alone. My mom was usually working, so the neighbors would load all the kids in this old Volkswagen bus and we'd meet other neighbors at a lake. They'd talk and the kids would swim. Good memories . . ." Leigh stared at the river. "There I go again talking about myself."

Aspen laughed. "I think it's okay to picnic alone. Miss Etta and I do it all the time." She pulled sandwiches out of the backpack. They needed distraction. "Hungry?"

"I am." Leigh sat next to Aspen.

"Well, I'd love to tell you I'm a gourmet cook, but that's your sister, not me. So we have messy tuna salad sandwiches that need to be eaten right now. We have pickles." She handed another package to Leigh. "There's also potato chips and store-bought cookies." Aspen frowned. "I hope you're not disappointed."

"I adore tuna. I never quite know what to do at a nine-course meal. It makes me nervous when I sit down at a table and it has more silverware on it than I have in my whole drawer."

Aspen smiled. "Agreed." She bit into the sandwich. "Today we talk about you the forester and me the environmentalist."

"Well, no holding back, Ms. Brown." Leigh took a bite of her sandwich. "This is great, not gourmet, but better. It's good."

"Don't change the subject," Aspen teased.

"I notice you like to change the subject a lot." Leigh smiled warmly.

"I do and that's different."

"Okay, you're on . . . I'm a forester, I don't see that as a contradiction to you the environmentalist." Leigh's voice was persuasive.

"How can you say that?" Aspen cocked an eyebrow. "You cut trees, environmentalists want to save trees. I'd say the contrast was deep and wide."

"Not really. Throughout history and long before man did his number on the earth, the woods would burn, usually from a lightning strike. It was nature's way of fertilizing itself. Sure it looked horrific—fires do—but the rebirth of the woods fed a whole bunch of ground animals and other little critters. In a way, we do the same thing."

"That's a stretch," Aspen bit into her pickle. *Stop talking and let her explain*, she scolded herself. She'd promised herself she wasn't going to argue.

"Not really a stretch. I think woodlot owners have gotten a bum rap. Oh, I know at one time there were owners who were lousy at what they did. They'd cut and run and then grab up more woodland and cut and run again. But any company that wants to stay in business can't do that. They cut in a controlled fashion so that the forest is continuously fertilizing and renewing itself. Aspen, we have to or the mills would swallow up the wood and eventually, like oil, it would disappear. After we finish here I'll take you to one of our sites. Then I'll take you to another site where schoolkids spent an entire day planting seedlings. Death, yes, but rebirth also."

"The part I can't agree to is death."

"But all trees die eventually. We just hasten the time line."

"That's the point, hastening the time line. I think that's wrong." Aspen tried to keep the frustration out of her voice.

"I don't think there's a wrong. I think there's just an *is*. If we could live without what trees produce, then I would buy your argument. I really believe there's a common ground between a sustainable yet productive forest and preservation. I think we can do both."

"And I don't. I have wood furniture in my house because plastic is worse, so that's a compromise or a hypocrisy, whatever. Leigh, I grew up here. I saw what the mill owners did. It's only recently that foresters have been hired and things have been done differently. In the meantime, our forests were raped and murdered." *Don't take your anger out on her,* she amended hastily. "I'm sorry. That was harsh."

"No, it was honest." Leigh looked at her intently. "That's not happening now. I wouldn't want to be a part of something like that. I think we can enjoy it all." Her arms swept open as if encompassing the whole forest. "I think we can keep this beauty, yet provide product we can live with. I love everything about where we are. This was given to us to delight in, but also to use. Aspen, I cherish all of this. Every twig, every pine needle, every tree, I honor it all. I take, yes, but I also give back, with respect."

Aspen stared at Leigh. Her passion for the forest was real, and understanding that was like a finale of fireworks going off in Aspen's brain. But she couldn't give in. Giving in meant accepting cutting a tree to build coffee tables. "I doubt we'll ever agree."

"Agree? I don't expect that," Leigh said gently. "Just be on a level playing field. I would hate to think what I do and what you believe means that we can't see each other. I wanted this walk to set those differences aside," Leigh said expectantly.

Aspen smiled. "Me, too." Aspen liked the way Leigh looked at her. There was a rush in the area below her stomach. *Whoa, no rushes,* she thought to herself. God, she wanted her. *But not now,* she thought as she ordered her desire spot to cease and desist. Miss Etta lay quietly at her side, her one good eye staring at the rest of Aspen's sandwich. Aspen broke off a piece and gave it to her. Miss Etta swallowed without chewing.

"Tell ya what. When we finish here we'll go right to the area where we're cutting," Leigh said to fill in the silence. "I'll show you what we're doing. Then we'll go to another area where the kids planted some trees. Now . . ." Leigh held up her hand to stop Aspen's response. "There're more there than what the kids planted. My company's been planting seedlings ever since we bought the land. I like to involve the elementary school kids because it teaches them several things—that we cut wood, but we also plant in anticipation of preserving the forest." The tension between them was there, ready to be stroked. "You're beautiful," Leigh said quietly. "I've never seen you in your element before. You're radiant."

"Leigh." Aspen swallowed, embarrassed. "I don't want to go there."

"Why not?"

"There's just so much—"

"There's nothing."

"I can't talk about it right now," she whispered.

Leigh sat back. "I'm sorry." Leigh was clearly embarrassed. "I shouldn't have . . . I'm sorry. It's just that this place is so you."

"I'm not ready to deal with anything other than the flirting we've been doing. I'm just not ready, please—"

"Be patient," Leigh finished the sentence. "I can if I have a sense that you're in the same place. I can't have read these past few weeks wrong, could I?"

Aspen swallowed and looked down at Etta who was watching her. "You didn't."

"Good." Leigh's eyes were a bonfire of passion. Aspen looked away. She was afraid that those eyes would singe her soul and scorch her heart. "Well . . ." Leigh cleared her throat. "How do we get back to before I made a regal mess out of this? I know. How about those éclairs? We're going to need sustenance for the hike." Leigh's voice trailed off.

"You're on." She handed the bag to Leigh. *They had to talk about the past*, she said to herself as she put wrappers and bottles in her backpack and closed it. She took an éclair. "This is wonderful and messy," she said licking the chocolate from her lips. "I told you I could eat these every day, but I'd weigh three hundred pounds if I did." She tried to match Leigh's light tone even though the éclair felt like it was sticking to the back of her throat.

They finished the éclairs in silence and silence followed them as they hiked through the woods. Aspen occasionally glanced down at Miss Etta, who was again zigzagging across the path, but mostly she couldn't take her eyes off Leigh's back. Leigh's body oozed energy and intensity as she moved along the path. Aspen sensed Leigh's symbiotic connection to the woods, a relationship that confused her. This woman cut trees and it was wrong. Aspen stopped walking. *How hypocritical was that? Didn't she buy wood to feed her stove? But that's different,* she argued. *Her taking was for sustenance.* All her life she'd hated the woodlot owners. Now here was a woman who said she could do both—take and preserve—and her body seemed to scream: *This is where I belong!*

"You okay?" Leigh's words startled her.

"I'm just having an argument with myself."

"About?"

"Hypocrisy."

"Me?" Leigh was puzzled.

"No, me, and I need to think about that." Aspen stepped past Leigh on the trail.

"Oh." Leigh had questions that Aspen wasn't prepared to confront. She had to sort through the emotions raging inside her. She was definitely attracted to this woman. *Attracted? Hell, she was burning up inside.* And now that same woman had made her confront her own pretense of virtue. In the past, she'd refused to think about the twelve cords of wood delivered to her door each fall that would be eaten alive by the fire in her stove. It was a necessity to survive, and didn't she afterward go out and thank the trees? But that was the rub, because she had ordered her mind not to think about the life of those trees. *You're a hypocrite, Aspen Brown, a huge, elephant-size liar and hypocrite.* Aspen's internal anger ignited. She needed to think.

"We're here."

Aspen looked around as if awakening from a trance. "This isn't where you cut wood. This is where you've planted."

"I thought it best we start with what's being renewed before we tackle what's being removed." Leigh's voice was diffident.

Aspen looked across at the acres and acres of seedlings. Columns and columns of tiny trees. "I . . ."

Leigh stepped forward and took Aspen in her arms. "I don't know if you're going to hit me or run away, but right now I want to do this," she said as she tipped Aspen's chin up and kissed her, her tongue teasing at Aspen's lips. Aspen's lips opened like the unfolding petals on a tulip. Her tongue reached out to taste Leigh. She tasted of passion and desire, and Aspen pulled Leigh tightly against her. *To hell with the past*, she told her brain. *To hell with the past*, she told her conscience. Their tongues investigating, probing and penetrating. Aspen couldn't get enough of Leigh's mouth. She wanted to taste all of her. Leigh backed her against a tree. "I want you, Aspen Brown, and screw the consequences." Leigh's lips kissed down under her ear and across her neck. Each kiss left a seared mark on her skin. Leigh lifted her shirt and sighed as she took in Aspen's naked breasts.

As if her body was in control of her mind, Aspen pushed up on her toes. She wanted Leigh to take each breast in her mouth, and she sensed Leigh absorbing her unstated desire. Leigh's lips were hot as they wound around her swollen nipples. Then Leigh sucked each nipple into her mouth, and the canopy of leaves that had offered her the protection from life's problems each time she ran to the woods burst in fireworks of yellow and red and green as her nipples silently screamed for more. Aspen rested her head against the hard bark that somehow felt like a pillow.

"I'm going to fall," she said through tight lips.

"I won't let you," Leigh said as she braced a knee between Aspen's legs. Aspen ground her hips on the knee. Her whole being seemed to be focused on that pressure that demanded more.

"Please make love to me," Aspen said as Leigh's lips kissed a trail down her stomach. One hand held Aspen against the tree, while the fingers on her other caressed Aspen's nipples. Aspen inhaled deeply. Leigh backed her even tighter against the tree, the bark inflexible against her spine. Leigh's hands moved away from her nipples and tugged at the elastic of her pants, the cool fall air lingering first on Aspen's hips and then her thighs as Leigh pulled her pants down to her feet. Leigh's lips continued to follow until they came to rest at the core of Aspen's passion. First there was Leigh's hot breath and then her tongue as it first stroked and then encircled her. Aspen lurched forward, and Leigh's strong arms caught her and held her tightly upright. She pushed down against Leigh's tongue silently exacting, seeking and ordering her not to stop. Leigh read her desires, and her lips and mouth encircled every part of her, sucking and pulling until Aspen shouted to the trees, her body thrashing and vibrating. "Oh, my God!" she screamed to the blue jays and the chickadees. "Oh, my God," she screeched to the Goddess of all trees. Her knees gave way, and her body slowly slumped to the ground. "Please don't stop."

"I'm not going to." Leigh's body followed her to the ground.

Leigh's fingers entered her just at the edge of her passion. Then as if her body was totally disconnected from her mind, Aspen pushed down, demanding more, and again Leigh read her body as if it were a cherished familiar book. Leigh's fingers slid fully inside of her. *How long has it been?* The words roared through her mind. She seemed to fill up as Leigh found her G-spot and began to at first caress, and then with an urgency that began to throb through her whole body, Leigh's fingers moved with a rhythm that matched Aspen's racing heartbeat. She inhaled and held her breath as the rhythmic beat of Leigh's fingers pushed her higher and higher. There was an explosion inside of her that seemed to blow all of her cells apart. "Oh, my God," she heard herself scream again. Her body thrashed against the dried leaves, against the hard earth that had been days without water, against the dead grass that alternately cushioned and caressed her beating hips. Then there was a firestorm of blasts as she hit the pinnacle of her climax and then started to fall downward. She rested her head against Leigh's shoulder. Leigh's chest moved in rhythm with her own breathlessness and the pant of Leigh's exertion and passion blew gently against her ear.

"Are you all right?" Leigh asked.

"More than all right." Aspen couldn't believe that was her voice. It belonged to someone else. Leigh moved and straightened onto her back.

"Come here." Aspen turned on her side and rested her head against Leigh's shoulder. She curled into her body.

"No one's ever made love to me like that," she said after a while.

"Good." Leigh kissed the top of her head.

"I want to make love to you."

"Yes, but not now. Right now I just want you to savor the passion. There's no scorecard is there?"

"I guess not. Just that before it was sort of expected."

"Probably. But I don't think it has to be."

"Honest?"

"Honest."

"I could fall asleep right here."

"Good, then do it." Leigh moved, searching for something. She closed her eyes and then opened them ever so slightly as her jacket was put over her arms.

"That feels good."

"Take a nap," Leigh whispered. "I'll be right here."

Aspen raised her head. Even with Leigh's body and her jacket, there was a chill as the day moved toward night. There was a soft glow of orange just to the west. She looked at Leigh, asleep next to her. Aspen liked the way her long blond eyelashes rested against her skin. Her mouth slightly open, she was snoring ever so quietly. Miss Etta was curled up in her other arm. Aspen moved and Leigh opened her eyes.

"Good morning."

Aspen smiled. "More like good evening, and we'd better get going or we're going to be here all night."

"Would that be so bad?"

No, just that we don't have any blankets, and it's going to be cold tonight."

"I could build a fire."

Aspen pondered that. "Do you want to stay here?"

"Only if you do."

"It'd be nice, but I can't do that to Miss Etta. I can go without dinner, but I know she wouldn't be happy."

"Ah, life is calling us back."

"Is that so bad?" Aspen said as she sat up, suddenly shy in her nakedness. She reached for her shirt and slipped it over her head.

"Yeah." Leigh pushed herself up on her elbows. "It is."

"Why?"

"Because now we have to start thinking about life. An hour ago all we thought about was making love. Now you're going to think about what I do for a living and how that fits with your life. You're going to fret about whether I fit into the scheme of that life."

Aspen frowned. "I am. It's already started. Leigh, I don't know what happened, but right now I need to know what it means."

"Whatever you want it to mean."

"I can't use the 'L' word."

"Nor should you."

"What do you want?"

"Just what we have. Two women who are bursting with the hots for each other making love. I'll settle for that right now."

"And later?"

"Later always has a way of taking care of itself."

"I wish I could feel that confident," Aspen said as put on her pants. She stuffed her underpants in her pocket.

"You don't believe that."

"No." Aspen smiled down at her. "And I don't believe that you do."

"Well, what do you want right now?"

"This minute. I don't know."

"No, in the next week. The next month."

Aspen looked at her shyly. "To make love to you with the same passion you shared with me."

"Then that's what we'll do, tonight, tomorrow, next week. We'll make love to each other, but we won't talk about love."

"You can do that?" Aspen stood up. Leigh pulled herself upright and straightened her jacket.

"I can if I have to. What got me into trouble before was this." She gently kissed Aspen's lips. "And I suspect it will get me in trouble again."

"Oh, it will." Aspen was more confident now that the pressure of talking about future commitments had been lifted from her. "Spend the night with me."

"I will and we won't think about anything else. I want to make love again and again and then on Monday you'll go to school and I'll go to work. We'll take it one day at a time. Agreed?"

"Agreed," Aspen said, disoriented. Leigh wasn't asking anything of her. There were no demands that she had to give anything more of herself. Or were there? She looked quizzically at Leigh. Was she falling in love with this woman?

"What are you thinking?"

"That I'm hungry and so is Miss Etta."

Leigh smiled. "Good. So am I. Come on," she said as she held out her hand.

CHAPTER TEN

Monday morning, Leigh had reluctantly pulled herself away from Aspen with the promise they'd spend the night together. After their time in the woods, they'd gone back to Aspen's house where they'd showered together and then spent hours exploring each other's bodies. Aspen, for all of her quiet demeanor, was an ardent lover and, Leigh smiled to herself as she remembered, a noisy lover. Leigh thought about how many times while making love Aspen kept yelling *Oh my God!* Leigh wondered how often God's name was spoken in the heat of passion.

She'd sensed a shift in Aspen's mood as sunlight began to spill through the bedroom windows and the reality of the day settled upon them. Aspen had to go be a teacher, Leigh the manager of a woodlot. She had gone back to her house to change clothes and made the mistake of answering her telephone.

"Dinner's all firmed up." Some day her sister would start with hi, she decided.

"That's fine." Leigh moved the phone to her other hand.

"Cassie and I've been talking."

"That doesn't surprise me. I get the feeling you two talk a lot."

"Don't be sarcastic," Brittany said. "We want to help you with Aspen."

"Help me?" Leigh was flustered. Did Brittany and Cassie know about the weekend? Would Aspen talk about something so intimate?

"This thing with Aspen."

"What are you talking about?" Leigh demanded.

"I love you to pieces, but you're not always sensitive to a woman's needs."

Leigh smiled. That's not what Aspen had said. "I beg your pardon." Leigh's worry turned to irritation. "I think I'm very sensitive."

"You know what I mean."

"No, I don't know what you mean."

"Just that Aspen has had a lot of things happen to her. Cassie told me all about it. Her mother died. Her sister dying right after that."

"I'm aware of that."

"Did she tell you?"

"Tell me what?"

"Cassie didn't go into details, but I got the feeling that Aspen went over the edge. Maybe a nervous breakdown or something."

"I don't think people have nervous breakdowns anymore."

"You know what I mean. She lost it."

"Lost it how?"

"Cassie wouldn't say."

"Brit, don't mess with this thing between Aspen and me."

"So there is a *thing* going on."

"No." She was frustrated her sister had called and interrupted her thoughts of Aspen. *Keep control*, she said to herself, *keep control*.

"You were supposed to call me after the hike. So what happened?"

"We talked. I like her and I don't need you meddling."

"I'm not meddling," Brittany rushed on. "Cassie and I are on the offensive. We want to head off any problems so something can go on."

"Let's focus on you and Harry."

"Things are wonderful," Brit enthused.

"I think that's great."

"I've finished your horoscope, more directly your birth chart."

Leigh groaned.

"Don't groan," her sister said. "I hate it when you groan. I thought you wanted to support me. I thought you wanted Harry and me to get back together." Brit was in her shotgun mode. "A horoscope is a good thing. It's when you go overboard, like daily reads, that's when it goes wrong. Plus we're into honesty."

"You have to be honest in astrology?"

"Well, yes, but I'm not talking about astrology now, you silly goose, I'm talking about counseling. The psychologist said we have to tell each other the truth, so I told him I didn't like the daily read because I felt it jinxed my day, and he's been good about it. Anyway, I'm almost finished with Aspen's chart. I think you and Aspen are compatible." Leigh looked at the clock. She was going to be late for work.

"I gotta go."

"You've got another five minutes. Besides, you're the boss. You can be late for work, so don't rush me. Anyway, I just love this whole horoscope thing. It's made me much more sensitive to people."

Leigh bit back a response. "Look, Brit, I have to get to work," she repeated firmly.

"How are things there?"

"Good. The foresters are working with the logging companies. Things have transitioned well."

"Well that's good. Anyway, everything is planned for a week from Saturday."

Leigh ran her hand through her hair. Now that she and Aspen had spent the night together, she wanted more time alone with her, and her sister was going to complicate her life. Honesty? Didn't her sister just say the counselor had instructed that she and Harry be honest with each other? Well then, honesty it is. "Brit, how about let's put this off until next month? I've got things to do at work." Well, she thought, it wasn't entirely honest.

"Can't. It's all planned."

"This is not like some kind of state dinner. You can change the date."

"Can't."

"Would you stop that. Of course you can."

"Nope," Brittany insisted.

"Why?"

"It's a surprise."

"I hate surprises."

"Not for you, silly. Well, I guess somewhat for you, but not entirely."

"What the hell are you talking about?"

"I can't say anymore. I promised Cassie, and quit swearing. It's going to be a fun evening. Then on Sunday morning Cassie and I are going to practice belly dancing.

Well, so much for almost honesty. "Brit, you're like a runaway dog sled."

"I am and I think it's great." Brit sounded happy. "Someone

has to take charge of your life."

"Brit, I love you," Leigh said. "Come for a visit. But I don't need someone to take charge of my life. I'm doing just fine."

"I'll see you in two weeks and don't worry—"

"Look," Leigh said speaking over her. "I've got to go. I really am late for work."

CHAPTER ELEVEN

"We have to talk." Aspen was seated at her kitchen table.

"Okay." Leigh set her backpack on the floor. The flap fell open and some socks rolled out. Leigh hastily pushed them inside. Aspen's face was a roadmap of stress. "How was your day?" Leigh asked uncertainly.

"Wasted." Aspen eyed the backpack. "I left school at noon. My principal thought I had the flu. I didn't. And your day?"

"Just as wasted. I was supposed to start a new cut site, but I just sat in my office. Jane finally got my head out of my ass and told me to get out there to make certain the crew was cutting in the right area. After a few hours, Jane decided I was sick and ordered me home. I went to my house, put a few things in my backpack and came here."

"We need to talk."

"You said that. Can I have a cup of coffee first?"

"Of course. Let me get it for you," Aspen said getting up.

"I'll get it. So what would you like to talk about?"

"You, me, us."

"Okay."

"So say something," Aspen groused.

Leigh held her hands up in surrender. "What would you like me to say?"

"That you've gotten cold feet and decided that this isn't what you want. I don't expect that backpack over there is filled with tomatoes from your garden."

Leigh laughed. Aspen couldn't resist her own joke and laughed too.

"No, it's full of clothes. I thought because you'd invited me to stay here tonight, it would save me having to go back to my house in the morning. Did I read that wrong?"

"You read it right when we said it this morning. I'm not certain it's right now."

"Ah."

"Yes, ah."

"Have you gotten cold feet?"

"I don't know."

"Aspen, I'll do whatever you want. If you want me to leave, I will. If you want us to slow this down, I will. Just say what you want."

"If I knew that—" Aspen looked at the ringing telephone. "Damn."

"Don't answer it."

"I hate ringing telephones." Aspen snatched it up. "Linda, hi, tonight? No, I can't. I've got a major school project due by tomorrow. Friday? That would be fine. Listen, why don't I call you later about the time? Good, I'll do that." She hung up the phone. "That was Linda."

Leigh nodded.

"She'd like to have dinner."

Leigh nodded again.

"Is that all you're going to do is nod?"

"I don't know. What do you want me to do? Are you concerned about telling Cassie and Brittany about us?"

"Well, that too." Aspen pondered the question. "Do we tell them?"

"I would rather not, but I expect we'll have to. Probably on the sixteenth, when we all have dinner together. They're going to meddle, you know."

"I know." Aspen rubbed her eyes with the palms of her hands. "This weekend wasn't how I expected things would develop between us. I know there isn't any kind of script for this, but I really didn't expect we'd make love this soon. We sort of jumped to the end, without really exploring the middle."

"We've been flirting for weeks."

"I know and I'm just as guilty. The whole thing has been so romantic, and I realized I really missed that in my life. That intimacy of getting to know someone. The hours we've spent on the telephone, the times we've been together. I didn't realize how much I'd craved that attention. I just didn't think it would go to the next step this fast."

"Where did you expect it would go?"

"I don't know. I know it's been getting more intense, but I thought we'd have this talk first. Making love has complicated things."

"I take responsibility for that. It was just that I looked at you out there in the woods, and I don't know. It just happened."

"I could have stopped it, but I didn't want to."

"I thought the whole day was pretty spectacular."

"It was, but it was wrong."

"Wrong, why?"

"Leigh, tell me what you want."

"You," Leigh said quietly. "I want to be with you."

"Why?"

"I think," Leigh began readily. "I think you're the woman I've been looking for my whole life."

"Oh, God, we need to talk." Aspen again ran both hands through her hair. "About something that happened to me before. I want you to listen, and if you find you can't deal with it, then I want you to pick up your backpack and leave. Will you do that?"

"What can be so bad that I would choose to leave?"

"You haven't heard it yet."

"Aspen, what's wrong?"

"I need to tell you something because you need to hear it from me rather than from someone in town. I know Cassie won't tell Brittany directly, but God love her, in her need to safeguard me she sometimes says more than she should."

Leigh studied Aspen's appearance. Her hair looked like it had been finger combed. Her lips were clamped tight. Leigh thought about the night before and how those delicate lips had felt on her body, on the center of her passion. Leigh mentally shook her head. She had to stay focused.

"I told you about my mother dying and then my sister dying shortly after that."

"Aspen, you don't have to talk about his."

"*I do!*" Aspen nearly shouted the words. "It's something that's going to come out eventually," she said more quietly, "and you have to hear it from me first."

"It's not going to matter. Everybody has secrets."

"Yes, but some secrets are worse than others," Aspen added quickly. "You have a right to know my secret, so please let me finish." Aspen's voice was hushed. "I lost first my mother and then I lost Willow." Aspen closed her eyes. "In just a few short months my entire family was gone. My mother's death was difficult. My sister's death paralyzed me. Willow was killed in an automobile accident. It was like she was there and then she wasn't. Everyone else was there for me—Cassie, Skeet, Anne Jean. But I just kept tumbling deeper and deeper into this hellhole of depression. I developed anxieties. I couldn't drive my car. I had paralyzing dreams at night, and days were different kinds of sinister dreams. I returned to teaching, but I couldn't focus. It was like an out-of-body experience. My principal insisted I take a leave of absence, which I did.

"When I started to stay home, a major depression seized hold of my brain and started to squeeze it. I had these feelings of hopelessness and guilt. Guilt that I was alive and my sister was dead. But the hardest part was the fatigue, I'd end up for hours sitting in a chair and I could never remember what I was thinking about. That's when I decided to just stay in bed, and although the insomnia was unnerving, it was followed by stupefying exhaustion. I would sleep, but I was always tired. I was determined to handle it myself." Aspen laughed bitterly. "I didn't want people to think I was weirder than I am. But then the vicious circle of memories would start again. I was having flashbacks. I pulled away from people. I loved feeling the mental pain of anguish, and I embraced that as ardently as I embrace my trees. Afterward, I learned that I unconsciously wanted this to be my penitence for being alive." Aspen's fingers were clasped, her knuckles white, her breathing was raspy. Aspen put her head in her hands. Her words were muffled. "It was a quagmire. Anyway, Anne Jean started asking questions. I lied to her as easy I'm sitting here telling you what happened. Told her I was fine, told her I had a cold, I had a migraine. You name it, I had everything but what I had, which was depression."

"What happened?" Leigh asked anxiously.

Aspen's eyes were like a veil of memories had been pulled over them. "I refused to answer the telephone, wouldn't open the door. Anne Jean came, Cassie came, I pretended I wasn't home, which was stupid because my car was here. Miss Etta"— Aspen looked affectionately at the dog—"came into my life afterward." Aspen petted Miss Etta who had not left her side as she told her story. "Funny, my scream for help came in the strangest way, I started to cry and I couldn't stop. I called Anne Jean, hysterical. I begged her to take away the mental pain. Instead she took me to the doctor. I was put on antidepressants, which helped, but mostly talking it over with my therapist helped more." Aspen rubbed her eyes. "It took months and months of counseling, but I finally got it back together."

Leigh felt shaky. When Aspen said she had a secret, she hadn't realized the depth of it. Depression? "How long ago was this?"

"A couple of years now," Aspen said softly. "You notice, I don't drink, not that I was addicted to alcohol, I just figure one weird mental thing could lead to another. I see my counselor. That's where you can find me on Wednesday afternoons. I go to the medical center in Princeton. People around here are used to my being there and I don't really think about it, because it's part of what I do every couple of weeks. It took me a long time to accept that I'll never be cured and I have moments even today when I get that feeling inside my head, but I know the signs and I'm never ever going to allow myself to go . . . Leigh are you all right?"

Leigh's insides were churning. She needed to get out of there. Was she going to have to live that nightmare again? "I need time to think about this."

"You don't have to stay," Aspen whispered.

"I know." Miss Etta nudged Leigh's hand. She pulled away. "I need time to think about this."

"I understand." Aspen picked up the backpack and handed it to Leigh. "It's okay."

"Honest, I just hadn't thought about this."

"I know, really. It's okay."

CHAPTER TWELVE

Leigh wanted to run. While Aspen was telling her about her depression, Leigh felt like she was watching the skin of an onion being peeled back, and with each peel a tiny membrane was exposed until Aspen got to the final membrane which was thinner and more tenuous than the rest. Aspen had shown her that thin sheath and told her the promises she'd made to herself, but Leigh was afraid. She'd seen that thin membrane before with her father. *I just need time to think about this*, she kept telling herself as she drove away. The past was rumbling down on her. The whole time Aspen was telling her, Leigh couldn't stop the flashbacks of her father shutting himself inside her parents' bedroom for days, refusing to go to work, refusing help. And then the fights as her father buried his mental pain in bottle after bottle of booze.

Leigh rubbed her hands through her hair. Drunken days and nights were followed by hours of sobbing and the promises that he would get better. Leigh could never let loose the memory of the pain on her mother's face, as she summoned the energy to keep the family together. Her parents didn't know to seek help, because in rural Maine families dealt with *those problems* behind securely closed doors. And neighbors only spoke of the problem in whispers, never out loud. Leigh had hated her father. She hated the stink of sour booze that coursed out of his pores for days afterward and she despised his bleary-eyed indifference to her and Brittany. That was when she started to pray to God that he would die. Leigh scoffed as she thought back to that childlike innocence.

She also thought about the night God answered. Her father never came home. She'd felt a child's guilt that she'd killed her father, but growing up, she never had the desire to find out if he had died, or if he'd permanently fallen into a bottle. Later, she'd figured out that her father suffered from depression, but it didn't ease the pain of those childhood memories. Listening to Aspen, it reminded her of the promises she'd made to herself to never go through that malicious cycle again of depression and alcohol and a father who was never there. *But this is different*, she told herself as she turned into the driveway of her office. *Aspen is willing to deal with it, not turn to alcohol. Aspen is honest about who she is, what this almost did to her.* Then she would think of her father and she would stop. *I just need time to think about this*, she kept repeating.

She rested her head against the steering wheel. Her eyes felt heavy. When Aspen had insisted on telling her the secret, Leigh had told her the past didn't matter, but it did, because she was sitting here instead of holding Aspen in her arms. She stared at her office, too tired to work. She put her head back against the seat and closed her eyes.

Leigh awakened with a start. She was cold and tired and had to go home. She pulled to the end of the driveway. Right was Aspen's house, left was home. Aspen's driveway was just ahead.

She didn't remember turning. She drove past it. *Go home*, she willed herself. Go home and go to bed. *Aspen warned you that she'd faced a litany of problems that almost unraveled her life and she's given you a way out.* "Damn." Leigh slammed her hand on the steering wheel, the smack sending uncomfortable tingles up her shoulder. She stopped and stared at the driveway in her rearview mirror. *Where the hell was she going?* She pulled to the side of the road and turned her truck around. *Don't go in there*, she cried. *Go home, think this through, wait until tomorrow and then call her. Don't act on impulse*, she ordered herself. "The hell with it," she said as she turned into Aspen's driveway. Aspen, she realized, had triggered a desire in her that no other woman had, not even Kathy, and damn it, she was not going to run from it now.

Miss Etta was at her truck within seconds jumping at the door. Aspen was standing in the doorway, neither moving toward her nor retreating. She stared at Aspen as she got out of the truck. If there were to be regrets, she decided, then let those regrets be later, not now. "I don't know where this is going to go," she said as she walked toward her. "But I know one thing. I want more than just a weekend. I want tonight and tomorrow night and all the nights afterward, and if it gets complicated then we'll deal with it. Is that what you want?"

"Yes," Aspen said as she folded herself into Leigh's body. Leigh could smell shampoo and desire and passion. She crushed Aspen to her body and kissed her.

"Tell me again, why are we going to dinner with this woman?" Leigh was lying on the bed watching Aspen dress.

"She wants to meet you."

"Goody."

"I hear sarcasm."

"She wants to size up the competition."

"That's silly." She would have to tell Linda that she and Leigh

146

were now in a serious relationship.

"If you recall, Linda called that night—" Leigh knew Aspen was still struggling with that night. Leigh got off the bed and took her in her arms and kissed her. Aspen smiled. "Anyway, she wanted to go out to dinner tonight, and I mindlessly said yes. I called her on Thursday and told her that you and Cassie would be joining us."

"And she was ecstatic, right?"

"She was fine with it. Said she's looking forward to meeting you."

"I bet."

"Are you going to get dressed?"

"I am." Leigh grabbed pants and a shirt off a hanger. "Is Cassie coming here?"

"Not exactly."

"When are we going to tell them?" Leigh was thinking of her sister. All week, she'd called her from work so Brittany wouldn't call her house and wonder where she was every night.

"Soon." Aspen turned and looked at her. "This is so new. I'm just not prepared to deal with those two right now. All the questions, the knowing looks."

"You've said it yourself. This is a small town. I'm surprised Cassie hasn't heard."

"If she has, I'd have heard from her." Aspen pondered telling Cassie. "We'll tell them next weekend. Your sister will be here. That way we can face the grand inquisitors together."

"It's fine with me," Leigh said buttoning her blouse. "So I take it she's meeting us at the restaurant?"

"She is. I told her I was picking you up, and she was fine with it. Besides, she had some kind of meeting to go to with her belly dancing group, so it worked better for her."

"How's that going?"

"Fine, I guess. She seems excited. That's all she talked about."

"I'll be done in a minute." Leigh slipped on her shoes.

Seated at the restaurant, they were waiting for Linda. "This is so nice," Cassie enthused. She was dressed in a bright red caftan with her hair streaked pink. She looked like a candy cane. "How do you like my new look?" She looked at them expectantly.

"Why the pink streaks?" Aspen asked.

"I decided I want my hair to complement my wardrobe. It's not permanent or anything. I can wash it out. I can change the color with my clothes or my mood."

"What do you think, Leigh?" Aspen's eyes were playful.

"I like it, although I think the red and pink would be better at Christmas."

"I hadn't thought about that." Cassie ran her fingers through her hair. "I'm so looking forward to meeting this woman."

"There she is." Aspen waved.

Leigh looked at the woman. She was wearing black slacks and a crisp white blouse under a black leather jacket and carrying a small bouquet of flowers.

"Aspen, hi," Linda said, touching her shoulder. "I brought these for you."

"Ah. How nice." Aspen glanced at Leigh, uncomfortable. "This is my friend, Cassie Jenkins and Leigh Wright."

"Nice to meet you." Linda sat down and tried not to stare at Cassie's hair. "Excuse me," Linda said to a passing waiter. "Could you put these in water and bring them back?"

"Of course."

"Your niece isn't working tonight," Aspen observed.

"Not tonight. She's at a party with friends." The waiter put the flowers on the table.

"Would you care to order drinks?" the young man asked.

"I'd like to order a bottle of wine for all of us, Steven," Linda said, glancing at the man's nametag. "Do you ladies have a preference, or may I order?"

"I'll just have coffee," Aspen said quietly.

"You sure you don't want to try just a glass? They have some great wines listed here." Linda read the names of a few.

"Just coffee, thank you."

"Coffee for the lady and this Shiraz for the rest of us," Linda said, pointing at the wine list. It was the most expensive bottle on the list. "I'm really thrilled to meet you, Leigh, you too, Cassie. You're a bit of a celebrity here," she said to Leigh.

"Celebrity?"

"Our college president is talking about starting a forum for young women and your name's been mentioned. He wants to take you and other women who are in nontraditional-type jobs into the high schools to talk with the female students. Show them there are men's high-paying jobs that women can do."

"I think it's a great idea," Cassie said. "Don't you, Aspen?"

"I do."

"It's not a new concept." Linda smiled at Leigh. "Other schools have done it. It's just new here. Anyway, your name was mentioned as one of the speakers."

"I'd be happy to help out. We did something like that in Aroostook County . . ." Leigh waited as the waiter put the bottle of wine and glasses on the table. Linda smiled benignly as he poured wine in the glass in front of her and waited until she tasted it. This woman is all about appearances, Leigh decided.

"Very nice," Linda said to the waiter. "I'm sure you're all going to enjoy it. The waiter filled their glasses. "Give us a minute. We haven't even looked at the menu."

"I'll be back with your coffee," he said to Aspen.

Leigh studied her menu, relieved at the silence. Rarely did she have an immediate dislike of someone, but that was what she was feeling with Linda.

"I'm going to have the shrimp scampi. How about you, Aspen?" Linda asked.

"I've had that here. I think I'm going with the—"

"Well, I'm having my usual, vegetarian lasagna. It's my favorite," Cassie said over her. "So, Linda, do you like teaching here?"

"I do. I like the area a lot, but the students are so-so."

"How do you mean?" Aspen asked.

"They're mostly nontraditional students, so they have different issues to deal with. In Massachusetts, the students were mostly high school graduates. Here, they're older and come with a lot of baggage—daycare needs, transportation needs. They need more time off from school, and we spend more time counseling them. It's just different."

"It's tough here," Cassie said. "A lot of kids can't afford to go on to college, not even the community college. They have to work first, save their money. A lot of the young women are single parents. Thank goodness there are programs to help them get back into school." Leigh was surprised at how passionately Cassie defended the students.

"There are. Anyway, let's order," Linda said distracted by the waiter who waited pen in hand.

"What are you having, Leigh?" Aspen asked.

"The rib eye steak, medium rare, baked potato with butter and sour cream and blue cheese dressing on my salad."

"I'll have the same." Aspen smiled and closed the menu.

"So, Leigh, how did you get into the game you're in?" Linda asked after she and Cassie had ordered.

Leigh told her about wanting to be a forester and her career. "I've been with this company for ten years and they're a good company to work for."

"I understand your company is into sustainable forestry practices. What does that mean to your company?"

Leigh patiently explained the company's philosophy. *Was Linda really interested? Or was this leading up to some harangue?*

"And how does that jive with you, Aspen? You, too, are a bit of a celebrity."

"She is," Cassie enthused. "Do you know how many times she's taken on the corporate polluters? Tons of times, and each time she's backed them down."

"First off," Aspen said quietly, "I'm not a celebrity, and second, I did not back anyone down. We did it as a group."

"But you're our ringleader. If it hadn't been for Aspen," Cassie said to Linda, "it'd never have gotten done. She's the one who organized the protests, got people off their butts."

"That's what I heard. Sounds impressive."

"But what about you?" Aspen asked, embarrassed by the attention. "You told me about some of the things you've accomplished in Massachusetts, but I know Cassie and Leigh are interested. Tell them about the time you did the human chain at that construction site."

Linda laughed. "It was a group effort also. This developer wanted to put fill in a marsh that was in the middle of a Canada goose flyway zone. This was some time ago, and I was a lot younger. Anyway, a bunch of us linked arms in front of this bucket loader and refused to move. It stopped construction. That was the first time I got my picture in the paper for getting arrested. I'd like to take credit for coming up with the idea of the human chain, but I followed the lead of those who had organized the protest. Anyway—"

"Shrimp scampi for you. Vegetarian lasagna for you," the waiter said, putting the dishes in front of them. "And two rib eye steaks, medium rare. Anything else I can get you?"

"So," Linda said to Leigh after he had left. "Aspen tells me that you're an environmentalist yourself."

"If environmentalist means I care about planet earth, then, yes, I am."

"But you cut trees."

"I do."

"And you, Aspen, have a reputation for being a fierce fighter when it comes to protecting the trees, yet you two are friends."

Leigh suppressed a smile. She suspected Linda was trolling. She wanted to know if they were more than just friends. "I'm curious. How does that work?"

"We—" Aspen said.

Linda's statement was pointed. "You two must have some ferocious discussions."

"Not really," Leigh said. "In fact . . ." Leigh thought about their lovemaking.

"Actually," Aspen blurted. "It does lead to some interesting discussions, but not insurmountable and certainly not *ferocious*."

"How so? It's clear you're split on this issue. You, Leigh, kill trees. You, Aspen, save trees. How can that work?"

"We've agreed to disagree." Leigh looked at Aspen, who smiled.

"And we've agreed," Aspen said looking at Leigh, "that even though there are differences, we each come to this friendship carrying our pasts—our burden of truth so to speak—and our present, and we just have to work through those." Leigh knew Aspen was thinking about the depression.

"I think it's great," Cassie said. "And there's a bonus. Leigh has this really cool sister by the name of Brittany. Anyway, she and I have become friends. I just love her to death." Cassie talked about Brit's interest in astrology. She also talked about her belly dancing classes and invited Linda to join. Leigh was relieved. Cassie decided the conversation belonged to her for the night. A couple of times Linda tried to turn it back to the two of them, but Cassie would answer and be off on another subject.

"Dessert?" Steven asked.

"Not for me," Leigh said.

"Me, neither," Aspen added.

"I'll have the pecan pie with whipped cream," Cassie said.

Leigh did a mental grimace. Dessert meant more minutes with this super-ego dyke. *There, she said it.* And saying it in her brain made her feel better. It was clear that Linda was trying to impress Aspen. When Cassie wasn't dominating the conversation, Linda talked about the protests she'd been a part of. Leigh suppressed an urge to belch, sort of like a public statement about what she thought of Linda and her protests. Instead she covered her mouth and burped, just a little bit.

"This is my treat." Linda grabbed the check.

"We can't let you do that!" Aspen said.

"I insist. This has been a really nice evening. Please, it's something I want to do."

Aspen glanced at Leigh looking for help. *If the ninny wants to pay for it, let her,* Leigh mused. She wasn't going to arm wrestle her for it. In fact, she decided, she wished she'd ordered more bottles of wine. She smiled to herself. *You're just being childish. Good, I should have been more childish.*

CHAPTER THIRTEEN

"I've been here for more than an hour cooking," Brittany said as Leigh walked through the door. "Cassie called and she's going to be a little late. How was your week?"

"Fine." Leigh turned away from her sister. For all of her insensitivity to life, Brittany could read her like a manuscript, and she wasn't prepared to talk about all the hours she and Aspen had spent together.

"You're going to love the menu. Some I did at home. Look at this wonderful French bread I brought. And we're going to have grilled pork tenderloin with black bean and mango salsa and braised cauliflower with garlic and tomatoes." Brittany turned back to the stove. "And I'm not going to talk about dessert, because it's really special."

"That's great, Brittany." Leigh looked at the mail she had picked up. There were bills to be paid.

"I had just the most wonderful day. Harry was supportive of my coming up here."

"Uh huh."

"There's an astrology conference at the end of the month in Baltimore. We're going."

"That's good."

"Is something wrong?"

Leigh looked up, confused by her sister's question. "Wrong?"

"Yes, wrong. You act like you don't want me here."

"Don't be silly." Leigh tossed her mail on the counter. "Of course I want you here. I'm just a little preoccupied, that's all."

"A problem at work?"

"I had a message from my boss, Jeff, just before I left the office. There's going to be a company-wide meeting Friday at our corporate office in Farmington. I have to go."

"What's the meeting about?"

"Don't know. He said the company's working on a new project."

"You're not going to be transferred?" Brit exclaimed.

"Would that be so bad?"

"Well, yes. What about Aspen?"

"What about Aspen?"

"Leigh Wright, you're being an ass. You know Cassie and I would love for you and Aspen to get together."

"Is that what this dinner is about?"

"Pour us a glass of wine. We need it." Brittany stirred the vegetables. "You really are—" They both heard the car. "Good, Cassie's here." Brittany wiped her hands on the dishtowel. "You're obviously in some kind of foul mood."

"I'm not," Leigh said, exasperated.

"When you come home and study your bills like you're preparing for a final exam, then there's something going on in your head that you don't want to talk about."

"Am I that transparent?"

"Aren't we all with the people we love? I'll greet Cassie." Brittany opened the door and Miss Etta strutted in. "Aspen, hi." Brit was surprised. "I thought you were Cassie."

"Should I wait outside since I'm not Cassie?" Aspen was teasing.

"Of course not." Brittany took her jacket. "I'll just hang this in the closet."

Leigh stared at Aspen. "You're so beautiful," she whispered.

"So are you," Aspen answered just as quietly.

"Let's ditch this party and go to your house." Leigh was leaning toward Aspen. She willed herself not to grab her and kiss her.

"We can't do that."

"What are you two talking about?" Brittany said from the kitchen.

"Ditching this party and going to Aspen's. That way you and Cassie could have a wonderful visit and we wouldn't bug you."

"Don't be silly. This party is for all of us. I just wish Cassie would get here." Brittany looked out the window. "She's bringing some of the stuff," she added hastily.

"Brit, is there a problem?" Leigh asked.

"Problem?"

"Yeah, you brag about how you can read me, I sense something's going on."

"There's nothing going on. I'm just disappointed Cassie's not here. It would have been fun cooking with her." Leigh frowned at her sister.

"Is there something I can do?" Aspen asked.

"Nope, just relax." Brit waved her toward a chair.

"Coffee?"

"Please."

"So how was your week?" Leigh asked.

"Good."

"School going well?" Leigh handed her the coffee and smiled.

"Absolutely." Aspen sipped it and looked at Leigh.

She was melting under Aspen's raven-black eyes. How often in the past week had she looked into those eyes and felt herself dissolving into Elysian fields of passion? *Not now*, she said to herself. Not while her sister was stirring a pot just a few feet away. She looked away, but not before she caught the slightest of smiles on Aspen's lips. She's teasing me, Leigh thought affectionately. She knows my sister is making me feel uncomfortable and she's playing with me. Leigh stared at her, her eyebrow cocked. Aspen took another sip of her coffee and stared back.

"I would hate to be a school teacher." Brittany's words seemed to jar them both.

"I beg your pardon?" Aspen looked at her.

"I'd make a terrible teacher. Hell, that's one of the reasons Harry and I haven't had any children. I'd make a terrible mother. I just don't like those foul-smelling little rug rats running around, disturbing my life, disturbing my marriage."

Aspen laughed. "They don't smell."

"They have a body odor not quite as bad as a dog's, but similar," Brittany insisted.

"Brittany, what are you talking about?" Leigh asked.

"If you don't believe me you can read about it online."

"I think Harry should ban you from the Internet."

"Ban, shman. He'd never do that. I've been reading a lot of stuff on the Internet."

"Like what?" Leigh asked suspiciously.

"We'll talk about it later."

"I think we should talk about it now," Leigh persisted.

"We'll talk about it later," Brittany said through tight lips.

"Should I leave? Go into the other room so you two can talk?" Aspen asked.

"Absolutely not. Brit, whatever you have to say, just say it."

"I will when the time's right." They all heard the car. Miss Etta barked. "Get the door, would you, Leigh? I can't leave this dish right now."

Leigh threw a questioning look at Aspen, who shrugged.

Cassie breezed into the room wearing a mint green caftan, her hair streaked dark green. She looked like a giant green bean. "Sorry I'm late." She put a tray on the counter. "Leigh, Aspen, glad to see you and I'm so glad you're here." She hugged Brittany.

"Your hair is green," Brittany said, surprised.

"It's my new look." Cassie turned from side to side like a high paid model. "I decided that my hair should match my caftan. It's just a rinse."

"I like it. It's not something I could do, but with you it works."

"Do you still like it?" she asked Aspen.

"It's nice," Aspen said indifferently.

"How about you, Leigh?" Cassie asked.

"It's . . . nice. Like Brit said, you can get away with it."

"Anyway." Cassie took the cover off the tray. "I couldn't get Greek olives, but I got these wonderful black ones. Should I put this on the table or in the refrigerator?"

"On the table. We're just a few minutes away from dinner."

"It smells wonderful in here." Cassie sniffed the air. "Aspen, I've called you several times. I thought you'd dropped off the face of the earth. In fact, I stopped by your house after school last week, but you were gone." Cassie's eyes shouted worry.

"I'm sorry, I should have called you. I'm okay, really." Aspen felt contrite. She stupidly had not thought about how her absence—not even a telephone call—would trigger that kind of worry in her friend. "I'm fine, really," she said gently.

"Something going on at school?"

"No, just . . . preoccupied, I promise to do a better job of staying in touch," Aspen replied.

"How was your week?" Leigh asked to distract Cassie. Aspen smiled gratefully.

"Wonderful, several women and I painted the inside of the

grange. I've considered starting classes on the weekend. The response has been that good. Anyway, Brit, are you sure there's nothing I can do to help?"

"Go sit. I'll be in in a minute."

Leigh saw the dining room chairs. "Ah, Brit?"

"Do you like them?"

"What have you done to my chairs?"

"I recovered them." She set the meat on the table.

"But you've only been here an hour."

"A little white lie. I found the fabric and knew it would go in here."

"They're flowers." Giant red flowers flowed over the sides of the chairs. "This dining room set belongs to the company."

"Well, if your meeting in Farmington means you're moving again, then the next manager can take them off. I just tacked them over the fabric that was there."

"Brit, I . . . ."

"Meeting in Farmington? Moving?" Aspen asked.

Leigh looked at Aspen. "There's a meeting next week at company headquarters. My boss called late today, but I'm not moving. That's something my sister's decided."

"Are they talking about changes?" Aspen asked apprehensively.

"No." Leigh looked fiercely at her sister. "Jeff left a message saying there's a managers' meeting. It's no big deal. My sister's the one making it a big deal."

"Stop glaring at me. Sit, sit," Brittany said to everyone. "Leigh glares when she's upset. But she's right. They don't usually move managers around on a whim. More than likely they're talking about another acquisition. That company buys up land faster than I buy dresses for my store. Here," she said, handing the pork tenderloin to Cassie. "I want you all to try this new dish and let's talk about something less stressful. I want to hear more about belly dancing," Brittany said to Cassie.

159

Dinner over, Cassie and Brittany carried dishes into the kitchen. "Are you all right?" Aspen had been unusually quiet during dinner.

"Just worried."

"About?"

"Your meeting. When your sister first said that you might be moving, I got this sinking feeling. It was almost claustrophobic. I was just surprised by my reaction."

"Surprised?"

"I don't want you to move." Aspen rested her fingertips next to Leigh's. "I really don't want that to happen."

"It's not going to," Leigh said carefully. "But I like the fact that it mattered."

"It did." There was a noise in the kitchen.

"Happy birthday to you," Cassie and Brittany sang. Aspen was shocked. "Happy birthday to you," they continued to sing.

"Don't blame Cassie," Brittany said as she set the cake in front of Aspen. "I take full responsibility. This was my idea alone. That's why I insisted we have dinner tonight."

"As in killing her for revealing my birthday?" Aspen glared at Cassie.

"She tried to persuade me not to do this, said you hated parties," Brit interjected.

"She's right." Aspen frowned. "Did you know about this?" she asked Leigh.

"Nope. But Brit loves parties, and it's something she does regardless of the event. She means only good things for people, really. She even threw a birthday party one time for someone who didn't show up. Anyway, please forgive her."

Aspen frowned. "I just hate celebrating my birthday."

"I wanted to do something nice for you, and even though Cassie warned me that you hated birthday parties, I feel like you two are family." Brittany looked at Cassie and Aspen. "I didn't mean anything bad by it," Brit said uncertainly.

Aspen sighed and then smiled at Brittany.

"I . . . we . . . have gifts for you." Brit picked up a package, still unsure of herself. "But they require an explanation. I . . . we . . . came up with this gift more for Leigh than you, but it seemed appropriate because I thought you'd like to read it together." Brittany looked down at the tissue-wrapped package in front of her. "Cassie and I've been talking and we think you're just right for my sister. So that's why I'm here, that and to celebrate your birthday," Brittany added quickly. "I think my sister needs to be more sensitive to your needs. More aware of your . . ." Brittany turned away, embarrassed. "Well, some of that stuff."

"Really, you and Cassie are matchmaking?" Aspen was smug.

"Well, matchmaking sounds so pedestrian. More like we're going to nudge this big baby in the right direction." Brittany leaned over as if talking to Aspen confidentially. "Sometimes she needs a little help. I don't know how many times I've had a dinner party to introduce her to interesting women." Brittany glanced at her sister. "Of course that was all in the past. Long before she ever came up here."

"I didn't realize you were so shy." Aspen suppressed a laugh.

"I didn't either."

"Well, she is." Brittany ran her fingers over the package. "Anyway, I was listening to one of those talk shows and they were talking about being sensitive to each other's needs. They were talking mostly about men and women, but it got me to thinking. I expect women have problems in that area, too." Brittany looked directly at her sister.

"Brit, what are you talking about?" Leigh demanded.

"Just that some men . . ." Brittany glanced at Cassie as if seeking her support. Cassie was staring at the tablecloth. "Aren't great lovers. Then I went online and did some reading and discovered that although you'd expect that a woman would be just the most sensitive person in the world, not all lesbians are great lovers."

Leigh had just taken a mouthful of coffee. She coughed and coffee dribbled down her chin. She wiped it with her napkin. "Brit, shut up."

"Are you okay?" Aspen was clearly amused.

"I won't shut up," Brit said to her sister. "We want you to have this." Brittany handed the gift to Aspen.

Aspen looked quizzically at Leigh. "Dare I open this?"

"I don't know," Leigh grunted. "Knowing my sister it's a copy of—"

"The Joy of Lesbian Sex." Aspen pulled the paper off.

Leigh's cheeks were on fire. For a moment she thought she'd stopped breathing. "Brittany, I'm going to kill you." Her voice sounded strangled even to her. Leigh looked at Aspen who had her hand over her mouth. "Aspen, I'm sorry, I—"

"Don't. It's all right," Aspen said between peals of laughter. "I've always hated birthdays," she said between gasps. "But not this time." She held her sides as she laughed. "This is the most . . . I don't know how to describe it, the most . . . no, the weirdest birthday gift I've ever gotten." Tears were rolling down Aspen's cheeks. Cassie looked frightened. "It's okay, Cassie, you can laugh."

Cassie put her head back and laughed.

Relieved, Leigh also laughed. "Are you really okay with it, Aspen?"

"I am. This is *the* birthday present. I'll remember it for a lifetime. It's okay, Brittany, I think this is wonderful."

"Well, I'm relieved." Brittany hadn't quite grasped the humor. "Now for the really neat treat." She handed wrapped packages to Aspen and Leigh.

"What's this?" Aspen said still wiping her eyes with her napkin.

Leigh groaned. "I know." She opened hers. Inside was a blue

folder with her name embossed in gold. "Nice presentation." She held up the folder.

"I did astrological charts on you and Leigh, and this is my gift to you. Look at the detail in this," Brit said reading over Aspen's shoulder. "Your ascendant is Taurus." Brit pointed triumphantly at her sister. "Let me introduce you to a Taurus," Brit added. "Note your shyness is a screen to keep others from discovering your intense needs to be perfect in all details of your work, and to enjoy sex to the fullest." Brit nodded at her sister in triumph. "Another reason why you needed that book." Brit pointed to another line on the page. "You're a nonconformist seeking new and exciting lifestyles. You are easily depressed and need several ongoing interests to keep you happy, and on and on."

"Wow." Aspen paged through the document. "Can I read this later?"

"Oh, yes." Brittany was pleased. "I knew you'd enjoy it. You two are going to learn stuff about yourselves and each other. Harry and I read each other's and it was the most uplifting experience I've ever had."

"Uplifting," Leigh grumbled.

"And I have one for Cassie." Brit presented her with a similar folder.

"I can't wait. I'll share mine with you, Aspen," Cassie said looking through it.

"I'd love to read it." Aspen smiled at Cassie. "Thank you, Brit. You took me by surprise with the whole birthday thing, but I do appreciate it."

"See? I told you she wouldn't be mad at me," Brittany said to Cassie.

"You were right." Cassie looked to Aspen for approval.

"But, I might add, if you do this next year, I'll have your head." Aspen grinned.

"Don't worry about next year. It's all there in your horoscope," Brittany rattled on.

163

"Well, that sure cuts down on the mystery of life," Aspen teased.

"Oh, it doesn't tell you specific things like what you'll be doing next year on October sixteenth, but it has what I call windows of opportunities."

"Well put," Aspen mused. "Windows of opportunities."

Leigh was relieved when the rest of the evening turned to discussions about school, education and politics. Somehow even a discussion about the Iraq war seemed less threatening, she decided.

"Well, I've got to go." Aspen picked up her gifts. It was almost midnight.

"Me, too," Cassie said. "Brit, this has been wonderful." She squeezed Brit's hand. "I was worried about the party, but you pulled it off with aplomb."

"I told you to trust me. Come on, I'll get your coats," Brittany said to Cassie.

"Well, it's been quite a night." Aspen smiled at Leigh. They were alone.

"I'll say."

"That book should come in handy." Aspen was amused.

"I thought we'd done pretty good without it. I'm going to miss you tonight."

"Me too," Aspen whispered. "When do we tell them?"

"I don't want to tonight, not with that book staring at me. Actually, as far as I'm concerned, never would be too soon."

"I can't do that to Cassie. She's going to hear—"

"Well, here we are," Brittany said. "Miss Etta wanted out, so I let her, okay?"

"It's fine."

Brit handed Aspen and Cassie their jackets. "Leigh and I will walk you to your cars." Brit opened the kitchen door and Miss

Etta danced in.

"I'm going to the grange tomorrow with Cassie. Why don't you join us?" Brit said to Aspen.

"I'd love to, but I have things to do for my class tomorrow. But thanks."

"I wish you'd come, Aspen. I'd love to show you what I've learned," Cassie said.

"Another time, I promise." Aspen touched her friend's face. "Cassie. Thank you. This really was a nice birthday."

"I'm glad, Aspen. But really it was Brit's doing."

"And I thank you." Aspen hugged Brit.

"I gotta get in. It's chilly out here." Brit returned the hug. "I'll see you tomorrow, Cassie."

Cassie waved as she drove away.

"Do you really have class work tomorrow?" Leigh asked.

"Not really. I hope you can come over."

"I'll make sure Brit gets off to the grange and I'll be over. Do I get a hug? Everyone else seemed to get their share."

"You do," Aspen said then stepped into her arms.

"God, I want to kiss you." Leigh glanced at the house. "She's probably cleaning up," she whispered in Aspen's ear.

"You don't really believe that," Aspen said against Leigh's neck.

"No." Leigh stepped back and smiled. "Knowing my sister, she's watching us."

"No question in my mind." Aspen laughed. She touched her fingers to her lips and touched them to Leigh's cheek. "See you tomorrow."

CHAPTER FOURTEEN

"Is it true?" Cassie demanded. She was sitting in Aspen's driveway when Aspen got home from school. "Are you and Leigh sleeping together? Why didn't you tell me?" Cassie was irritated.

"Wait. Miss Etta is driving me crazy with all of her barking." Aspen opened the door to the run. Miss Etta hopped on her back feet, exhorting Aspen to pet her.

"Why didn't you tell me?" Cassie insisted.

"Because it was just too new," Aspen said.

"Too new? You two are sleeping together . . . Least that's what I heard in town."

Aspen had wondered how long it would take now that Leigh's car was parked in her driveway nearly every night. "I don't have an excuse."

"Well, that's at least something. I called Anne Jean. She

hadn't heard a thing, and I was surprised because she usually hears stuff before me."

"Who'd you hear it from?"

"Some of the mothers in my belly dancing class, which by the way, I now understand why you haven't been attending." She knew it wasn't so much that Cassie cared whether they were sleeping together, but that she didn't know about it.

"I'm sorry. We just weren't ready to talk about it."

"Brit was beside herself when I told her. She thought the reason she hadn't heard from Leigh was because she was tied up with that meeting tomorrow in Farmington."

"Well, she has been."

"But she's also not been home."

"That's true too."

"Are you in love with her?"

"I'm going to make a pot of coffee. Would you like some?"

"Yes, and stop avoiding the question."

"I'm not really." Aspen put beans in the coffee grinder. "I don't know."

"You don't know?" Cassie said. "How can you not know?"

"I don't want to think about love. Love complicates life, and right now I don't have either the desire or the will to do that." Aspen got up as Anne Jean's ancient truck sputtered to a stop and then discharged a loud bang.

"I brought cinnamon rolls. I just knew you'd have a pot of coffee on. Cassie, I'm glad you're here."

"Sit, everyone." Aspen surveyed her friends. They were looking at her with expectant eyes.

"What?"

"Aspen said she doesn't know if she's in love with her," Cassie said to Anne Jean.

Anne Jean just nodded.

"It's too early," Aspen said.

"So is there some kind of time line for falling in love?" Cassie

167

asked.

"No." Aspen sat down. "Oh, wow, these are still warm. Perfect comfort food." Aspen folded her hands on the table and waited. "Questions?"

"When did it happen?" Cassie leaned forward, the sleeves of her burgundy caftan draped over the table. At least her hair wasn't dyed burgundy, Aspen thought.

"We knew when we went for the walk in the woods."

"Wow, what a birthday present." Cassie looked away in embarrassment. Aspen knew she was thinking about the book she and Brittany had given them. "Wait. You knew the night of your birthday and didn't tell us?"

"I'm sorry. We just . . . oh, hell, there's no excuse, really." Cassie snorted.

"Are you happy?" Anne Jean asked.

"I am. She's remarkable."

"And the other?" Cassie was still irritated. "Did you tell her?"

"I did, and she said it doesn't matter."

"And the forester and the environmentalist thing you fretted about?" Cassie asked.

"If she can accept the other, what right do I have to question her job?"

"That's a good one." Anne Jean was pleased.

"Thank you." Aspen smiled at her friend. "It's—" Miss Etta barked. It was Skeet. "Ah, more company."

"Well, looks like a convention," Skeet said as he walked in.

"Got coffee and cinnamon buns."

"That's why I'm here. She's been cooking them all morning. Dropped most off to the library bake sale and brought the rest over here. Man's got to travel mighty far today to get some good cinnamon buns."

"Oh, you poor soul." Anne Jean was amused.

"Sit. Coffee is done."

"So," Aspen said after everyone had cinnamon buns and

coffee in front of them.

"I hope you're not carping on her about that forest lady," Skeet said between bites.

"We're not *carping*," Cassie said. "We're asking her questions."

"Ya happy?"

"I am, Skeet," Aspen said without missing a beat.

"That's all we have to know. The rest is nosiness." He licked the frosting off his fingers.

"Details are not nosiness," Cassie insisted. "It's friends wanting to make certain friends aren't making a mistake."

"It's nosiness."

"It's not."

"Pure and simple."

"All right, you two," Aspen said with a laugh. "She's all those things a person is supposed to be and more, and right now we're just enjoying getting to know each other."

"See, it's just that simple." Skeet reached for another bun.

"That's your second. You're not going to want supper tonight," Anne Jean admonished.

"I smelled that chicken soup cooking. Of course, I'm going to want supper. I'm just not going to want dessert."

Aspen smiled to herself remembering the dinner she and Leigh had shared the night of the layoff. They'd licked their dessert plates clean. "Sounds right to me."

"Well, how about some details?" Cassie's looked furtively at Skeet.

"Not much to tell. I like her and she likes me. It's been a whirlwind, really."

"Well, that was quite evident," Cassie said.

"And I'm sorry." Aspen looked at her three friends. "It's been a long time since anyone has interested me, and I admit that I've been a bit distracted of late."

"Distracted?" Cassie protested. "Try a damn hermit. We

haven't seen you once."

"Possibly, but not out of meanness. It was like there was no time between when we got together and today. It happened so fast."

"Your face looks relaxed for the first time in a long time, and your eyes are dancing again. You look happy, Aspen," Anne Jean mused.

"I am, Anne Jean, I truly am," Aspen said serenely.

"So that's all that matters." Skeet glared at Cassie.

"I agree," Cassie said. "I just want Aspen to be happy, and if talking about it helps her, then what's so wrong with that?" she asked the other two.

"Nothing," Aspen answered for them. "It's just that sometimes things are so new that you're just not prepared to talk about them. I guess that's where I'm at right now."

"When Brit heard, she wanted to come up immediately. She wants to celebrate."

"Celebrate what?" Skeet asked.

"She called it a *demoiselle* engagement party. Don't ask." Cassie held up her hands.

"I don't think that's such a good idea." Aspen frowned.

"Have you ever tried to stop Brit when she's on a mission?"

"Actually, I've not," Aspen said.

"Well, I haven't either, but I get the impression that she's an earthmoving machine stuck in high gear that's about to flatten everything in her path, although Leigh did persuade her to put off her visit for a while," Cassie said. "Anyway . . ."

"What?" Aspen was annoyed at all the questions.

"Tell me just this one thing and I'll shut up." Cassie glared at Skeet, daring him to say something. "Have you used the 'L' word yet?" Cassie asked.

"No, and I don't think we're going to for a while. She's had her relationships that've been bad and so have I. We're older, and I hope, a little wiser. So, no, we haven't."

"But what are you feeling emotionally?" Cassie persisted.

"See, that's what I mean." Skeet threw Cassie a dirty look. "She tells you she's happy, and the next thing you want to know if she used the 'L' word. First of all, why can't people say what they mean? I don't get the 'L' word," he said.

"It's how people refer to the word *love*, without coming right out and saying it," Annie Jean said.

"Why don't people come right out and say it?" Skeet asked.

"Fear," Cassie said succinctly.

"Fear of what?"

"Getting hurt," Cassie said. "Saying it too soon and the other person not saying it is the dilemma."

"Well, I like words that say what they mean, not a single letter."

"I can't argue with that," Aspen said.

"All right, have you and Leigh talked about love?" Cassie asked.

"We haven't."

"And I think that's fine." Anne Jean's eyes were on her. "You'll know when it's right. No one has to rush to say the word, or any other word for that matter."

"You're right, Anne Jean," Aspen said soberly. "It'll get said if it's right—" Aspen's phone rang.

"Aren't you going to answer it?" Cassie asked.

"My answering machine will pick up." Aspen's fingers were itching to pick up the phone.

"What if it's Leigh?"

"You go ahead and answer," Anne Jean said getting up. "You two come with me. We're *all* going home." She looked at Cassie, who shrugged but got up.

"Just a second, Anne Jean, Skeet and Cassie are leaving." Aspen waited.

"Is it her?" Cassie stared at the telephone.

Aspen nodded.

171

"Good, let me talk to her." She held out her hand.

"Not now." Anne Jean gently pushed Cassie toward the door.

"Our being together is all over town," Aspen told Leigh. Her friends were gone. "Did you learn anything more about the meeting tomorrow? Well, you'll know more tomorrow." Aspen listened. "I have an idea. Since it's all over town, how about dinner out? Good. I can't wait for you to get home."

CHAPTER FIFTEEN

Driving was her time for meditation. Leigh thought about the past week and the reaction now that the town knew they were together. It was evident the night before at the restaurant. Their waitress, Melissa, had been polite but nervous. Afterward, Aspen said she suspected her former student had wanted to say something about the rumors, but was too shy to do so. Leigh didn't believe it. She suspected Melissa was chock full of questions from her Aunt Linda, who had also heard about the relationship. Leigh inhaled deeply. She really didn't like Linda and suspected if she weren't around, Linda would be camped on Aspen's door. "Well, that ain't going to happen," Leigh said to the windshield.

She thought about Aspen and quivered inside as she thought about what happened after they'd returned to Aspen's house. Their night was a whirligig of orgasms. Aspen, for all of her quietude, was the Jolly Green Giant of lovemaking. Her passions reached to the clouds and beyond, and she knew no bounds. Leigh shivered as she remembered.

Leigh rolled her head around trying to relax the tension in her neck. She didn't need to think about passion, she needed to think about the meeting she was headed to. All week, she had sensed that Jeff was holding back, not wanting to even hint at what the announcement might be. She turned into the parking lot, snapped on her identification badge and walked to the side door where she was let in by a security guard.

In the conference room, Leigh greeted several of the other managers and shook hands with Jeff and another man he introduced her to. She poured herself a cup of coffee and picked up a croissant. "Leigh, nice to see you," Bill McKinley, the company's Houlton woodlot manager said as he poured himself coffee. "Love what they're talking about doing up in our neck of the woods. Means more money for all of us," he said as he walked past her to greet another manager. *My neck of the woods? More money for all of us?*

"Can I have your attention, please?" It was the company's president, Jay Hollingdale. Jay was in his early sixties with silvery white hair and matching mustache. He was Ivy League polish in L.L. Bean clothes. "If you could all find a seat, we'll begin." Jay waited. "Good morning and welcome. Today is a great day in our history." Jay turned on the PowerPoint. "As you know, there is little land remaining in southern Maine for any kind of large-scale development, but north of Bangor is different. There's some pretty decent acreage, and we own a lot of it. In the past, our mission has been to cut and plant trees. I've called it reinvesting in ourselves, and that's what our stockholders wanted to hear. However, a term that has become a mantra for business is *bottom line*, and that's what our investors want to know. In the end, what is the *bottom line*? Well, we've looked at that question very seriously and the result . . ." Jay clicked to map. "Is development."

Leigh stared at the map. There was a circle over the area she managed stamped *Development*. A similar circle covered the company's lands in Aroostook County. No wonder Bill was so happy. She set down the croissant. *God, Aspen was right.*

"We own more than a million acres in the state, with most of it in northern and eastern Maine. Some of the land is only good for cutting trees. Other parcels, like those in Leigh and Bill's district, have been marked for development because they have more to offer. The people who've bankrolled Burnt Brush want to make more money, and we're not going to do it cutting trees. Over the past three years, we've studied each of our holdings and decided that though good, they could be better. That's why we bought the land in Leigh's area with its picturesque views of the ocean. Bill's area was chosen because of the potential for hunting and fishing," the president said pointing at the map again. "Our goal is to continue to harvest wood. That's our backbone. Our bread and butter, if you will. But the plan in Codyville and Houlton is to build a country club with beautifully designed golf courses and campgrounds. We also want to build lots of houses. We hope to have the permits in place almost immediately and then proceed with construction in Leigh's district beginning in the spring. Bill's project comes later. We want to have a portion of the house lots in Codyville carved out by the summer of next year and begin construction on the country club around the same time. The campground will go quickly. We plan to open it in the spring. This is an ambitious time line, but we've been working with the governor's office. It's an election year, and he'll be there tomorrow when we make the announcement in Codyville. The governor has put the full resources of his agencies at our disposal. Any questions?"

"Won't we have to get the locals to buy into this? I hear you about the governor, but the locals are the ones who will make this easy or hard," Bill said.

"That's true. We've hired personnel who will shepherd this through not only the permitting process, but the public relations stages, and they will be working on parallel tracks, hopefully making things happen at about the same time. As you can see"—Jay pointed at the circle over Codyville—"about five thousand acres that're in Leigh's area"—Jay smiled at her—"are slated for rezoning and development, while the remainder of the wooded area will remain zoned as is, for the time being. The same with Bill's area." Leigh continued to stare at the map. "And we have similar projects planned in the future for land we own in Hancock and Piscataquis counties."

"Anything for Somerset County?" the manager there asked.

"Not really. Our holdings are smaller and much of the wood harvesting there is to supply our customers in southern Maine. Right now we're focusing on Leigh's chunk and Bill's chunk. We expect opposition from the environmentalists, but we've also hired one of the best public relations guys in the state, Tom Webster." Jay pointed at the same chubby man Jeff had introduced her to earlier. He was Portland haute cuisine, not woods crew brown bags, Leigh decided. "We're prepared to come out swinging, but what we have to our advantage is time. The final development, meaning all of the house lots, won't be completed for another ten years. As you can see from this map, the house lot part has been divided into increments of one hundred. We build one hundred, and as soon as we sell a portion of those, we start on a second development segment, so local folks shouldn't get their knickers in a twist. About our announcement tomorrow, we're not going to put it all out there for public consumption. We're going to announce Leigh's development first and talk only about the country club and about one hundred house lots, not all the houses we eventually plan to build there. If the project goes as well as we think it will, we'll announce our development plans in Bill's area next year. Any more questions?"

"I think we're going to have folks with their *knickers in a twist* just from our local environmentalists," Leigh said.

"No doubt, but we have a strategy to neutralize them almost immediately. Most of them don't have money behind them, so they can't afford to fight us in the courts. Oh, they'll carry placards and protest, but that's it, really." Jay was confident. "Jefferson and Aroostook counties are the poorest counties in the state, and what we have to offer are jobs. There's nothing else happening for those folks, so I think a lot of the locals are going to sign onto our project. It's environmentally clean and it's going to pour much needed capital into two counties that are desperate for development."

"That seems like an awful long time line," Jeff said.

Jay nodded briskly. "That's the time line we plan to announce tomorrow, but if things go well with the permits, we hope to expedite it. Anyway, we're sending you home armed with press packages. All information is embargoed until after the governor's announcement tomorrow. In a minute, I'm going to turn this over to Tom who is going to talk about public relations. Even you managers where development isn't happening need to toe the company line. We're selling this not just locally, but to everyone in the state. We want support for it, and I think we can get it," Jay said.

"How much wood harvesting area are we going to lose?" Bill asked.

"Good question. Once the development gets into the final stages, you and Leigh won't be harvesting as much. You can't have a multi-million dollar country club or three hundred thousand dollar houses and woodcutting machines driving through the neighborhood. So wood harvesting operations will be scaled back. Leigh's county is going to be the pilot project." Jay clicked on a map of a subdivision. "This portion here," he pointed, "is where the country club will be built, along with an eighteen-hole golf course. From this vantage point, you have nearly a one hundred and eighty degree view of the ocean. It is spectacular up there, folks. It's what sold us on the property."

Leigh rubbed her hands together and wondered what the hell she would be doing as the manager of a golf course. Is that what Jeff meant by *new and varied responsibilities?* She stole a look at him, but he was watching Jay.

"Around this country club will be upscale houses," Jay continued. "Several of the environmentalists have asked that this old stand of trees with the eagle's nest tucked in the middle of it be donated to the town." Jay pointed at it. "We're not in the business of giving land away, but it'll never be developed. It's a concession on paper, but realistically, we can't do anything with it anyway," Jay said placatingly. "This idea has been in the works for a while. As you know, we did away with our harvesters in Leigh's area and we're running the numbers on each of your areas, and if we can save money then we'll be shifting to outside labor there also." Jay's eyes were on her. "I expect Leigh feels like a sacked quarterback, but she's standing at the entryway to one of the biggest developments in the state, and I can tell you we're excited about this. Any more questions?"

Yeah, she thought, *how the hell do I get out of this?* "You might be underestimating the local environmentalists, Jay," Leigh said tentatively. "They've been pretty aggressive." She was thinking of Aspen. "There have been instances where the environmental groups have banded together across the state, sometimes even nationwide, to stop something from happening here."

"We're not underestimating them," Jay said confidently. "We expect opposition, no question. But we also think we can get people on our side, and certainly our having the governor there tomorrow is a plus. Anyway, I'm going to turn the meeting over to Tom who is going to talk about our media strategy."

Tom picked up his briefcase and set it on the boardroom table. He handed out folders. "Good morning." He smiled. "I can see in the future that I need to leave my gray suit behind and dig out my flannel shirt and jeans. I feel like a vegetarian at a meat packer's convention." A few of the managers chuckled. "This is the media kit we'll be handing out tomorrow." Leigh opened the folder he handed her. There was a press release and an architectural rendering of the country club. Leigh glanced at the drawing. The country club included an outdoor swimming pool and tennis courts. The golf course was to the right of the building. "As you read down the press release, we have quotes from Jay and the governor, and we're focusing on the important things like jobs and future development. The next sheet"—Tom held it up—"deals with the numbers. During the construction phase for both the country club and the houses, we plan to hire more than two hundred people locally. Also, you will note once construction is complete, we will hire around seventy-five full- and part-time people, everything from the manager for the country club to a greenskeeper. We even plan to have a golf pro. This is one of the largest projects this little county has ever seen. As you can see from this third sheet." Tom held it up. "This is a six hundred million dollar project. When it's all done, seventy-five million for the first phase. We're planning on targeting markets in Boston and New York. This project is a plus not only because it's environmentally safe, but it's an economic tool for future development. We expect that downtown Codyville will move from the one or two stores that are there now to high-end, upscale shops that will cater to the discriminating buyer. Everything from clothing to comfort stores that sell things like candles and home accessories. We've been told that once the houses have been built, a big-box store like Wal-Mart or Target would consider building something on the outskirts of town. Of course that then leads to more shops and eventually a mall. It's all there in the numbers we've crunched," Tom said enthusiastically.

Leigh stared at the papers in front of her. Brittany was going to love it. Aspen was going to hate it.

"And what about Codyville?" Leigh asked.

"What about it?" Tom asked.

"Right now it's an unorganized territory. There is no formal government. It seems to me that with what you're proposing, Codyville is going to have to petition the state to become a formal town with local government and all the things that go along with that, including paid police and fire departments. More people mean more problems."

"That's true, but it's not our job to make those decisions for the community."

"I don't know," Leigh persisted. "It's going to cost more to live there. How is that going to play with the locals? You add police and fire coverage, you have more expense. You add trash pick up, and there's more expense. You add—"

"I get the picture," Tom said amicably. "But we're also talking jobs, and that means money to pay for those kinds of services."

"That's true," Leigh said. "But—"

"I can see where you're going with this, Leigh," Jay said. "But right now we're focused on what's going to happen tomorrow. If Codyville residents decide they need a local government, we'll be there to help them, but right now we're confident the majority are going to be focused on the jobs the project has to offer."

"But I think it does, Jay," Leigh countered. "It has to do with a way of life. You're talking about adding hundreds more people, judging from this drawing. You may be talking about building a couple hundred houses over the next few years, but the plan you've shown us clearly is marked for future expansion beyond that." Leigh pointed at the map. "If I understand what I'm looking at, you're talking about house lots there, there and there. How many exactly?"

"About five thousand."

Leigh swallowed. "Five thousand houses? Jay, I think you need to be prepared for some large-scale opposition. You're not talking about adding a few structures. You're talking about adding two towns."

"As I said before." Jay was no longer smiling. "It's an ambitious plan, but not an impossible plan. Right now, we're dealing with a country club and some houses. That's what we're unveiling tomorrow. There is nothing else on the table."

"I think—" Leigh insisted.

"I think—" Jeff stared at her. His eyes warning her not to ask any more questions. "That we need to stay focused on what is in front of us. I know where you're coming from, Leigh. I worked in Codyville Plantation when it had one hundred people and the only wood that was cut was to keep houses warm. Each change was marked with pain from growth, but it happened, Leigh, and in the end, Codyville Plantation adapted and changed with it." Leigh nodded and looked at the papers in front of her.

"As I was saying . . ." Tom then talked about the press conference and the meeting afterward with the governor's staff.

"How many other managers will be there?" John Stevers, the company's woodlot manager in Hancock County, asked.

"You'll be there along with Greg from our Penobscot office." Jay nodded at the man sitting next to Leigh. "The rest of you I know are disappointed you're not going to have to work on Saturday," the president joked. "Any more questions for Tom? Good. Remember, Tom is our go-to man for all questions about this project. You two"—Jay nodded at Leigh and Bill—"are going to be bombarded with questions from the media. I expect more to you, Leigh, at least right now. Bill, you need to be prepared because your media will be asking if we have similar plans there. I want all of you to refer all calls to Tom." Jay glanced at the clock. "Our lunch should be here in about fifteen minutes. Why don't we take a break now? But let's be back in our seats promptly at noon."

"What the hell are you trying to do, get yourself fired?" Jeff guided Leigh toward a corner of the room.

"Right now," Leigh whispered, "I don't think losing my job is such a bad idea. Once that project is done, they're not going to need managers. They'll be able to manage what little cutting

181

they do right from here. So I'm out of a job no matter what."

"No, you're not," Jeff growled. "Just keep a lid on it until we can talk privately."

Leigh studied Jeff's face. "All right, but just until we've talked."

"I'll be up tomorrow. We'll talk after the press conference."

"Hey, Jeff, what do you think?" Bill said as he approached them. Leigh excused herself.

This isn't fair, she fumed as she drove home. For the first time since she'd been hired by Burnt Brush, she hated her job. If Jay thought that Codyville would welcome him with a parade, he was deluding himself. She'd been in town long enough to know that Codyville folks had no desire to become the recreation mecca for the rest of the state.

And what about Aspen? Leigh wondered. She'd never go along with the project. Leigh turned onto the Hardscrabble Road that led into town. Aspen would be a formidable opponent. Aspen Brown would be *her opponent*.

Leigh dialed Aspen's number. "Hi."

"Where are you?" Aspen was worried.

"On my way back." Leigh shifted in her seat. "Look, something has come up and I can't stay there tonight. Is that all right?"

"Sure, I'm disappointed, but okay . . . Is everything all right?" Aspen asked suddenly.

"Just all right."

"Things are bad?"

"Look, I can't say anything right now."

"Are you going to the office?"

"I am. I have a ton of paperwork. Aspen, I'm sorry."

"Somehow . . ." Aspen started. "Somehow I get the feeling that we're both going to be sorry," she said as she hung up.

It was midnight. Leigh had been at the office since her return from Farmington, and although she was able to clear some paperwork off her desk, most of the time she'd sat looking out the window at the sooty black night and thinking about Aspen. She was tired and she had to go home and get some sleep. Tomorrow, or rather today, she thought was going to be a long one. Staring out at the night, she knew she had to tell Aspen before the press conference. But what about the embargo? She asked herself, again. The hell with the embargo! She mentally yelled at the night. Hang the job and hang Jeff, she decided as she turned toward Aspen's house.

Aspen opened the backdoor and Miss Etta bounded out, barking as she ran toward the truck. Leigh could not move even as the dog jumped at the truck's door.

"Leigh?" Aspen said staring at her through the truck's window. "Are you all right?"

It took every ounce of her energy to open the door. "No."

Aspen put her arms around her and held her. "Is it that bad?"

"Yes," Leigh said against her shoulder. "It's worse than bad."

"Come in. Miss Etta, hush." Aspen's hand was on her arm. It exuded strength and urgency. "You're cold. Come on. I'll heat up some coffee." Aspen pulled Leigh's jacket off her and threw it on the floor. She pushed Leigh toward the woodstove, bent down and stirred the embers and then added wood. "How bad is it?"

"Everything you dreaded and worse."

"When are they making the announcement?"

"Tomorrow, rather today," Leigh said warily. "The governor's coming up."

"Of course he is. It's an election year. They certainly didn't give much time for anyone to organize any opposition." Aspen set the cup of coffee in front of her. "Drink," she said.

Leigh sipped the coffee. The heat filled her mouth and rolled down her throat. "I'm sorry."

"For what? Working for a company that's ambitious and wants to make money? It was bound to happen sooner rather than later. When I heard how much your company had paid for that land, I just knew there'd be changes and the changes would not make some people happy around here. So how bad is bad?"

"I'm not supposed to talk about it until after the announcement." Leigh put the cup down.

"I'm not going to pretend that I don't want to hear tonight, because I do." Leigh could hear the frustration in Aspen's voice.

"I'm sorry," Leigh said miserably.

"Stop saying that."

"What else am I going to say?" Leigh looked Aspen in the eyes. "What am I supposed to do? Pretend that nothing happened? I can't do that, Aspen. The wheels are turning, and after tomorrow's announcement, Codyville is going to embrace a whole new life."

"Tell me," Aspen said quietly. "There's nothing that I can do about it tonight."

Leigh studied Aspen's eyes. How different they were from the night before when they'd made love. Then her eyes were delicate and tender. Tonight they were anxious and afraid. "They are planning a full-scale development that will include a country club and golf course and row after row of very high-priced houses. The plan is to start next year and build in stages. They have a ten-year project in the works."

"And the wood harvesting?"

"It eventually will be phased out because there won't be enough trees to harvest."

Aspen sat down in the chair opposite Leigh. "That bad."

"That bad."

"Do they really think they can do this?"

"They do. They have the governor on their side."

"And a Democrat at that," Aspen said faintly.

184

Leigh just nodded. "I'd better go."

"No," Aspen said quietly. "Come to bed."

"Are you sure?"

"Yes."

The sadness that had been circling her all evening began to close around her. "Aspen." Leigh's expression hardened. "We have to think about beyond tomorrow."

"Yes, we do, but not tonight."

CHAPTER SIXTEEN

Leigh opened the office. The morning air had a nip to it. The severe wind the past few days had stripped dry leaves from the trees, and now instead of the rich colors of fall, the trees stood naked, their brown, red, orange and yellow leaves a thick mat on the ground. She thought about Aspen and the night before. Soon after Leigh had arrived at Aspen's house, they'd gone to bed, but Leigh's sleep was punctuated by nightmares of trees falling on her. When the alarm rang, Aspen's voice was calling her, but it sounded far away. Leigh tried to rub the gloom from her eyes. She didn't want to get out of bed. Was this what her father had felt? She pushed herself out of bed. She didn't want to think about that. They said little as they dressed. The connection she and Aspen had shared waking next to each other each morning was gone. In its place was absolute fear of the future. Standing alone in her office, the world a colorless gray, Leigh wondered about her future with a company she no longer liked.

"I figured you'd be first," Leigh said to Jeff as he got out of his truck.

"You figured right."

"Coffee?"

"Had gallons on the way up, but thanks. Jay and the rest will be here in a few minutes. He wants a final meeting with us before the governor arrives."

"Any more surprises?"

Jeff eyed her. "You're angry."

"That pretty well sums it up."

"I promised myself I would stand for the next hour because of the way my back feels, but somehow we both need to sit and talk. So sit," Jeff said gruffly. "I know you're angry, but you've got to get past that."

"Why?" Leigh said still leaning against the counter.

"Because you have a future with this company, and I don't want you to blow it because you're burning with anger right now. When you reach my age you learn to tamp those emotions down and sit on them." Jeff was studying her. "Look, I don't want you to accuse me of some of that *politically incorrect* stuff because I don't want to have to measure my words. I just want to say what's on my mind." He paused. "Leigh, you're a woman in a man's job, and that's a rarity here in Maine. When Jay offered you that promotion a year ago and you turned it down, he wasn't happy. He wants to move you up. I told him it'd be okay because you'd get there soon enough." Jeff rubbed his brow with his arthritic hand. "I know you were disappointed when we did away with the crews, but I knew you'd adapt. Let's face it, it's the future no matter if we like it or not. Leigh, I'm not good with words, but you're damn good at what you do, and you're better than most men. You have a real instinct for this job."

Leigh sat with her arms folded over her chest. "What do you want me to say?"

"Nothing. I know this announcement has you steamed, but you can make it work."

"How? As a manager of a golf course?"

"No, not *as manager of a golf course*," Jeff threw back at her. "As a manager then as a vice president of a hell of a good company, and maybe someday president. Right now this company makes millions. After today's announcement it'll be making more millions."

"Somehow if that's supposed to make me feel better, it doesn't, Jeff. I don't care about millions or the millions more on top of that, and I don't want to be a vice president, and I sure as heck don't want to be the president."

"Even if it means you can keep Maine pretty much like it is?"

Leigh scowled. "I don't understand."

"Look around you. More and more of these companies are looking at development. Look at that company down south. They announced last year they planned to build a resort bigger than anything we've got in this state. Looked for a time like it wouldn't get developed because so many people were lobbying against it. I read in the newspaper last week they reached a compromise with the state and the environmental groups. They get to develop a portion of their land, but in return they agreed to put non-development covenants on the rest and from what I read, that's a huge chunk. So if they had plans to make that resort even bigger, they can't. The local folks got some concessions, but a lot of them still are grumbling because they feel like everyone sold them out, and who knows? Maybe they did. This is Christmas future for Maine, and if people like you and me don't stick around, the Ivy League types like Jay will be our ruination."

"So I sign on and become part of that? I don't think I can do that."

"You like it here. I know you do. I got the feeling you've settled in and plan to stay. You walk, and Jay and the state get to decide what's best for this town. You stay, you get to lobby Jay and the bean counters. At some point Jay's going to have to compromise with the environmentalists, and it's going to be a lot more than those old trees with the eagle's nest in the middle of it. You can help make those compromises, or you can run away and leave the town to a few outsiders."

"I don't know," Leigh said thinking about Aspen. "I suspect the environmentalists right in this town are going to put up a hell of a fight."

"They are and so is Jay. Look, the company owns the land and they can pretty much do what they want, but you get to be inside and help guide the future. Development is coming. It's just a matter of how we control it."

"How about I quit and you whisper in his ear and guide the future?" Leigh said sarcastically.

"Suit yourself." Leigh could see the disappointment in Jeff's eyes. "But you walk, this little town may have some good fighters, but it ain't got someone inside who already is sympathetic to their cause. And as to my part, this ain't my town, Leigh. Besides, I don't have any fight left in me. You decide," Jeff said, getting up.

"I'm sorry. I'm taking my frustrations out on you."

"I understand." Jeff stood over her. "Look, Jay's a good man, but he's no forester. He comes to the job through the back door with his degrees in business. He's been good and managed the company well, and he's got ambitions, but he's also got age working against him just like me. So he needs people like you. Jay doesn't have a clue how people here are going to react. He's Massachusetts, not Maine. There's going to be development, Leigh, but you can either make it work or you can quit and watch it eat up the state."

"Why doesn't that make me feel better?"

"It's not supposed to. You stay, there'll be development but not on the grand scale they talked about yesterday. Right now the opponents are going to demand that nothing gets built, but the company can pretty much do what it wants to. Jay's no dummy. He's read about what's been happening in other states, and he knows this can be either his greatest achievement or his worst nightmare. So in the end, he and the environmentalists are going to have to compromise. They all say no now, but it's going to happen."

"So I keep my mouth shut and make this work, even though I don't feel good about it?"

"There's no other choice. We don't need more Jays and more bean counters, we need folks like you and me who love what we're doing. I've seen changes that I hated, changes that I thought would destroy this state, but she just kept rolling, and I'd say she's a better state for it. But we're getting to a point that some of these new changes ain't going to be good for the state. And I think this is one of them if it's allowed to grow the way Jay says it will."

"I—" She heard the vehicles outside.

"Let's leave it at that. We'll talk more after they leave, agreed?"

"Agreed." Leigh wasn't sure if she'd agreed to her future or her past, but right now she had to face Jay, and she needed to think about what Jeff had said.

Leigh stood in the background behind the crowd of L.L. Bean shirts and khaki pants, Jeff at her side. Jay and the governor were at the front next to the radio and television microphones. The speeches were short and full of great predictions about the future.

"How much is this going to cost?" a woman reporter asked.

"Seventy-five million dollars." Jay failed to mention that that amount only covered the first phase. Neither he nor the governor talked about the future.

"Is this good for Maine and for this area?" the same reporter asked.

Leigh inched forward. She wanted to hear the answer. "It is," Jay said. "Not just for Maine, but for Codyville Plantation and the people who live here."

"We're talking jobs," the governor added. "By the time this is completed, there'll be something like seventy-five jobs for people who have watched the economy here shrivel up. And there'll be collateral jobs as other businesses are built to complement this development."

"Jobs that don't pay any money," the same woman said.

"That's where you're wrong." Jay looked directly at her. "The jobs pay good money, and they offer something folks haven't had around here in a long time, benefits."

"Any other questions?" Tom stood next to Jay.

"How do we know those jobs won't go to outsiders? You just laid off a whole bunch of people," the woman reporter persisted.

"We did phase out the wood harvesting part of our business here," Jay said smoothly. "But ninety percent of the people who worked for us have found jobs."

"Was that layoff preparatory to your making this announcement?" she asked.

Tom started to say something, but Jay put a hand on his sleeve. "Actually it wasn't," Jay said calmly. "That had more to do with the economics of workman's comp and escalating insurance costs. No one wants to lay people off, but from a business point of view, it had to be done, but I might add"—Jay held up his hand to stop the reporter's next question—"we were confident the employees would find jobs, and that happened."

"Governor, we're seeing more and more of these announcements. What does that mean for the future of the state?" one of the male television reporters asked.

"A future," the governor said. "We have to grow and change, and the one thing we have to offer is some of the prettiest views in America. Just look around you," the governor said as he, too surveyed the view. "This is what people want to see, and this is where they want to be. That's going to help Maine's economy."

"Anyway," Jay said to the reporters. "The governor has to get back to Augusta, so we'll take just one more question."

"Do you expect opposition to this proposal?" the same woman reporter asked.

The woman's questions were starting to rankle Jay. "We expect opposition, but we feel that once people get a sense of how this will make Codyville Plantation a better community, a lot of that will go away. As a matter of fact, we'll be holding several meetings over the next few weeks, and we're looking for local input. This project won't be a success without the help of the people of Codyville, and once they see what's happening, they're going to want to be a part of this."

"One more question, Governor." The woman reporter wasn't finished. "There's talk that Maine's trying to do away with the mills and the wood harvesting. Is this part of your economic strategy for the future?"

"Not at all," the governor said unwaveringly. Leigh marveled at the governor's patience. "This is going to complement what we already have. Maine needs to grow, and to grow we have to have a diverse economy. Industry is a part of that, as is tourism. Developments like these add to that healthy economy that the state needs to survive. This is not a negative. This is a positive, and we are seeing entrepreneurs like Jay and others asking what they can do to make Maine an even better place to live. I think we have to thank Burnt Brush, and I think the folks around here, once they've had a chance to study the plans, will do just that. This project means jobs, and right now Jefferson County is running ahead of the nation in unemployment. That's why I've put the resources of my office behind this. Look, folks, what makes this plan great is Jay's willingness to work with everyone."

"I promised the governor that we'd take a mini walking tour of the site, and, of course, everyone is invited to join us." Jay guided the governor around the press and toward another section on the hill.

"Jay looks happy," Leigh said to Jeff. He was next to his truck.

"That's why they spend so much time planning. Although I don't think he was prepared for some of those questions that woman reporter was asking. She was starting to get under Jay's skin."

"I know she's local, but I don't know her."

"Almost seemed like she'd been prepped."

"I haven't been to enough of these dog and pony shows to know." Leigh shrugged, but she too had gotten the feeling that the woman knew more than the others.

"How you doing?"

"Just all right."

"Look, they're going to send the governor back to Augusta, and then we're going to have a strategy meeting with his staff. You going to be around afterward?"

"I can be, but really, Jeff, I'd like to think about what we talked about."

"Makes sense. You gonna quit or chew on it awhile?"

"Chew."

Jeff smiled. "Good."

"Anyway, looks like they're breaking up up there." Leigh nodded toward the governor. The entourage walked toward them and the governor shook hands with each of the reporters.

"It was Leigh," the governor said as he approached her.

"Leigh Wright."

"Well, Leigh, you've got a good company here."

She nodded.

"Well," Jay said after the governor was gone. "I want to thank you for coming," he said to the reporters.

"I understand there's a meeting with the state folks. Can we join you?" the female reporter asked. The woman wasn't ready to leave.

"Actually, this meeting is just for the state folks to get acquainted with the project. In your packet is a list of the meetings we'll be holding, and, of course, you're all welcome to attend." Tom then guided the reporters to their cars like the Pied Piper he was. The rest of the staff and state people went inside the office.

"Hi, I'm Sandy Baskins," the woman reporter who'd asked the tough questions said. They were standing in the parking lot.

"Leigh Wright."

"I know. I expect I'll be seeing a lot of you."

"I don't wish to be impolite, but I have to defer all questions about the project to our public relations spokesman."

"Oh, I don't mean that." The woman smiled at Leigh. "I've been on a two-week vacation, so I haven't been around much. I'm a friend of Aspen's." The reporter laughed. "You should see your face. Don't worry, Aspen called me this morning and gave me a heads-up. I also know you two are *an item*. I'm glad."

"We're not exactly *an item*," Leigh protested. Why was she explaining herself and her arrangement with Aspen to this stranger? "It's not like—" She bit back angry words. *Why would Aspen talk to a reporter?*

"Don't worry. Your secret's safe with me. Like I said, Aspen's a friend of mine."

"So that's why you knew what questions to ask." Leigh was irritated.

"It helped, but I would've asked the same questions anyway."

Leigh glanced at the closed office door. "I've got to go."

"If they ask you what we were talking about, and they will, just say I was trying to pump you, but you told me to call the PR guy. They'll love you for that."

"I will."

Sandy got in her car and waved. Leigh sighed. Aspen, a reporter and Jeff. How much more complicated could her life get?

CHAPTER SEVENTEEN

Aspen spooned blueberry muffin batter into paper cups. Cooked muffins sat nearby. Miss Etta barked. Sandy had called after the press conference and said she'd be over. She owned the Jefferson County Weekly. Aspen had called Sandy after Leigh had left for the office. Although Leigh had said the information was embargoed until after the press conference, Aspen didn't think that company mandate applied to her.

"Glad you called." Sandy hung up her coat.

"I didn't know if you'd heard or not."

"I had, but never assume. I take it from the number of muffins you're making, it's not going to be just you and me."

"I invited a few people. I figured they'd want to hear what the governor had to say firsthand. It's the usual cast of characters, Cassie, Anne Jean and Skeet. You might not know Linda Sappier. She teaches at the college. Her niece is Melissa. She works at the restaurant."

"I do know Melissa."

"Linda's been involved in several environmental battles in Massachusetts. I think she's going to be a great addition to the team."

"You're going to need her. This one's big, Aspen."

"I figured that."

"I spoke with Leigh."

"Was she okay?"

"She looked stressed and I don't even know the woman. I thought she was going to hide behind a tree when I told her I knew the two of you were seeing each other. I never even thought that she didn't know we were friends." Sandy chuckled.

"I never thought to tell her. Everything has happened so fast between us."

"Once she'd realized I wasn't going to chew her up, she seemed nice."

"She's better than nice. She's downright remarkable."

"I like that," Sandy said.

"We got here as fast as we could," Anne Jean said. Skeet was behind her. "It smells good in here. Sandy, hi. I'm glad you're here."

"I'm making blueberry muffins." Aspen put a pan in the oven. "Not like yours, Anne Jean. Mine come compliments of Mr. Pillsbury."

"There's nothing wrong with that."

"They're just not as good as yours."

"I'll make coffee," Anne Jean said.

"So what you got for us?" Skeet asked Sandy.

"I'll tell you this much, Skeet. This gets built, you'll be golfing."

"Shhh, I will not. Golfing?" Skeet was clearly disgusted.

"They're planning on building a country club and eighteen-hole golf course right between yours and Aspen's property.

Pretty soon the word you'll be hearing is *fore,*" Sandy said, playfully cupping her hands around her lips and pretending to yell.

"Wow," Anne Jean said.

"It's a double wow. They also plan to build what they called *upscale* houses for the *discriminating* buyer. In other words, houses we couldn't afford. And they carry a hefty price ticket. Three hundred to four hundred thousand."

Skeet whistled.

"They're talking about building a campground down near the river."

"As in tents?" Anne Jean asked.

"As in motor homes and those monster trailers people can't seem to leave home without."

"The road that goes in front of our houses can't support that kind of traffic," Anne Jean said.

"Sounds like someone else is here." Aspen looked out the window. "Good, it's Cassie."

"What have I missed?" Cassie hurried in. "Oh no, muffins. The last protest we had I gained ten pounds eating your muffins," Cassie teased. "Who else is coming?"

"Linda and Melissa."

"What about Leigh?" Cassie asked.

"She's at the office with the governor's staff."

"Not that. How's she taking it?"

"She's upset. These still are hot." Aspen didn't want to talk about Leigh.

"I hear another car." Skeet opened the door. "It's Melissa and must be that aunt of hers."

Aspen greeted Melissa and introduced Linda to everyone. "Okay, everyone," Aspen said after they were seated. Linda was at the counter pouring coffee for herself and Melissa. "I'm going to turn the meeting over to Sandy."

"Thanks, Aspen." Sandy handed out papers. "I made a copy of the information they included in their press kit. Aspen listened as Sandy talked about the development. "Questions?" Sandy asked.

"Their time line?" Skeet asked.

"They plan to break ground next year."

"That's pretty ambitious. I know we're an unorganized territory, but seems to me they're going to need an awful lot of permits," Anne Jean said.

"They are, but the governor's on board. They even had what they called a strategy meeting with state officials after the grin and grip part this morning. They wouldn't let us in. Top secret stuff, I guess. We're the company's first development project."

"Why does that worry me?" Cassie asked.

And me, Aspen studied her hands. Leigh was at that meeting. *Was she going to walk out? Tell her boss she couldn't, no, wouldn't, be a part of a massacre of the land?*

"It should," Linda said. "They work the glitches out on us and then go do it better somewhere else. I've seen it happen in Massachusetts. In fact, I've been a part of stopping development down there," Linda bragged.

"Good. We're going to need all the help we can get," Sandy said. "This is what I've learned so far about the company. They've been in the wood harvesting business since nineteen-seventy. A guy named Jay Hollingdale is the president. Harvard graduate with a degree in business." She talked about the structure of the company and more about the development. "I can't find out who their backers are, the people with the money, but I'll keep digging. But what we have to remember right now is there's going to be people around here who are going to buy into this project."

"Why would anyone do that?" Melissa asked.

"Jobs and money," Linda answered.

"Of course, the governor was all smiles," Sandy said. "I did make note of the staffers he had with him. It included folks from every department that pertains to either development or construction in the state."

"Which suggests?" Cassie asked.

"That this project is big," Sandy said.

"Wow," Cassie said.

"Yeah, wow," Sandy said. "The governor said if this goes through, we're going to get a new road, not the two-laned black-top job we now have. I can tell you they didn't even come close to sharing all they plan to do. Right now, I expect we're just seeing the icing, the cake part comes later."

"As in?" Skeet asked.

"A hell of a lot more houses. I don't think there's going to be much land left after they're done."

"What do we do now, Aspen?" Cassie asked.

Aspen jerked. "I'm sorry, what did you say?" She had been thinking about Leigh again.

"I asked, what do we do now?" Cassie made a rude noise.

"That's what you guys have to decide."

"Well, it's obvious we have to stop this," Cassie said to the others. She glanced at Aspen.

"Agreed," Skeet said.

"So we do what?" Aspen smiled. Melissa was itching for a fight.

"I'd suggest," Linda said, looking at the others. "We wait."

"Wait?" Cassie and Melissa said together.

"The company is planning on holding meetings. I think we need to hear what they have to say." Sandy nodded. "Then we need to hear what the local folks have to say. That way we'll know how many are with us."

"I think we need to start now," Cassie said.

"I think we need to organize," Linda said glancing at Aspen. "But I don't think we should show them how much opposition there might be. I know I'm the new kid on the block, and I expect all of you could rally folks and we could walk around with placards outside the company's office on Monday morning, but why? The first meeting is in a week. I say let's wait until after that then let's pull in all the folks who listened to what the company had to say and didn't like it. That's what we did in Massachusetts."

"What do ya think, Aspen?" Skeet asked.

"I think Linda's right."

"Sounds right to me," Anne Jean added.

"Right now we need to answer Sandy's question, give our reaction and say no more," Linda said looking around the group. "Aspen, you've been the spokesman for these types of things. I think it wouldn't be a bad idea if Sandy quoted you in her article."

Aspen sat at the now empty table. Sandy had peppered her with questions, and Linda and others had helped with the answers. After they'd left, Linda had remained behind. She'd suggested the two of them have dinner before the company's public meeting. She liked Linda and what she had brought to the group. It felt good to have someone else take charge. Linda was right. Had they been left to their own past practices, they would have been in front of Burnt Brush on Monday marching around, placards in hand. Linda's suggestion they delay until they took stock of their support made sense. Plus she liked Linda's certitude. She was the outsider, but she was fast becoming an integral part of their group.

Aspen sighed and picked up plates and stacked them in the sink. Funny, she thought as she put the muffins away, right now she didn't feel like being alone. How strange. Most of her life, she preferred trees to people, but not now, now she wanted Leigh. Together they would make it all go away. But what if they couldn't? What if it consumed them? She felt another wave of gloom, like a long-lost family member embracing her. *It's okay*, she told herself. *It's okay to be depressed.* Years of counseling had taught her to accept her depression and deal with it. But was it okay? How could she protect Codyville Plantation from a developer more interested in making money and not protecting the beauty that had been so a part of her town's landscape. A landscape made up mostly of trees. Fight them they would, but would they win? The company owned the land and the governor was already in their pocket. Who would help them? And if they lost? Could she live with that loss? Could she watch the machines grab trees that stood in the way of house lots and brutally pull them from their roots? Or would she try to stop the machines? Aspen rubbed her forehead. And what about Leigh? Leigh would have to quit now. She couldn't work for a company that violated everything she said she believed in. There would be no more cutting and planting. There would be only taking and more taking. Leigh could not live with that, and Aspen could not love a woman who agreed to that. Love?

Miss Etta barked. "Hush, there's no one out there. How about I take you outside?" she said as she opened the door.

"Hi." Cassie's voice startled her.

"Cassie?"

"Who else?"

"I didn't hear you drive up. Is anything wrong?"

"Not with me." Cassie stared at Aspen.

"Why are you here?"

"Because of you."

"Me?"

"Yes, *you,*" Cassie mimicked.

"Want something to drink?"

"No. Had too much coffee earlier."

"Do you want to sit down?"

"Yes." Cassie pulled out a kitchen chair. "How long have you known?"

"Known what?" Aspen didn't look at her friend.

"That you're in love with her?"

"I'm not in love with her, Cassie. We agreed that love was not something we'd talk about right now."

"Oh yeah, you're in love."

Impatient with her friend, Aspen asked, "And you came to that conclusion, why?"

"First, you let a stranger take over the meeting, and the whole time we were talking strategy you weren't here. I could see it in your eyes. You didn't think the rest of us were watching, but you might as well have painted it in big red letters on a billboard. *You love her.*"

"I do."

"But you're not happy."

"No."

"Because of this project."

"Yes."

"Do you have the ability to answer in more than one-word syllables?"

Her friend was definitely irritating her. "Yes, I do. Cassie, there were problems before, there are insurmountable problems now."

"I admit this project complicates things, but I don't think it's impossible."

"Cassie, I adore you, but sometimes . . ."

"I know, sometimes I'm just too cheerful. It's my histrionic personality."

"Where'd you come up with that one?" Aspen chuckled tiredly.

"Histrionic personality? I read it in a book some time ago. I like the way it describes me. Anyway, this isn't about me. You love her then it's okay, right?"

"I don't know. This one's a deal breaker, especially if she keeps her job."

"Why can't you be like that Washington, D.C., couple? I can't remember their names. He's a Democrat and she's a Republican or vice versa. They've been married for years. He liked Clinton, she liked Bush. I bet they had some really interesting dinnertime conversations. Or like that Republican governor and actor in California. He's married to a Democrat, a Kennedy Democrat at that."

"This is different. This problem between us isn't some Republican and Democrat having interesting dinner conversation. This goes deeper."

"It doesn't have to."

"Unfortunately, it does. This project is big and I know it's going to turn into a lousy battle."

"Aspen, I'm not doing my turtle trick, pulling my head into my shell. I know we're going to have a battle, but I don't want to see you lose what you have with Leigh." Cassie's voice was sad. "And I don't have to remind you that this project is like something I've encountered and the price I paid. I made the man I loved choose, and I wasn't prepared when he didn't choose me. And there's no going back."

"I'm sorry." Cassie's pain was palpable. Tommy had remarried two years after he and Cassie had divorced.

"Me too, but there's no fixing Humpty Dumpty." Cassie shrugged. "I don't want you to make the same mistake."

"But you drew attention to an important cause and you were right."

"A lot of good it did me."

Aspen sighed. She could see clearly the emotional bruises in her friend's eyes. "I really *am* sorry, Cassie."

"Funny, I won on principle, but I can't cuddle a principle. In the end, I'm not so sure what I would do today if someone I loved was on the other side of the battle line, but if I took up that fight, I would think more in terms of compromise."

"Whoa. Compromise? It's a little early for that." Aspen was surprised how fast the words came out of her mouth.

"Don't be so sure. You've never risked this much before. Ask yourself what price are you willing to pay?"

"I have no choice, Cassie. This development is the saw in hand getting ready to cut down all those trees that I've spent years protecting. Somebody has to say no."

"But maybe there's a compromise where you and Leigh can both win. You admitted you love her. Protect that and protect the land."

"I don't know if I can."

"You can, Aspen. Fight for the trees, but keep that woman."

"What happens if I have to choose between Leigh and what I believe in? Somehow compromise feels too much like selling my soul to the devil, and the devil's name is Burnt Brush."

"Talk to her. Tell her how you feel. Aspen, don't make the same mistake I did. I don't want you to have to live with similar regrets," Cassie said. "I believe if you're forced to make a choice between winning it all and Leigh, you'll make the right choice. I believe in you, Aspen."

"Well, let's just hope I believe in myself," Aspen muttered. She had to shrug off the gloom. "You're something else, Cassie Jenkins." Aspen smiled.

"I am and I'm a damn good friend too." Cassie gathered her cape around her shoulders and patted Miss Etta on the head.

CHAPTER EIGHTEEN

Driving toward Aspen's, the press conference behind her, Leigh remembered that first night they'd all had dinner at the restaurant and how Aspen had worried about how much money the company had paid for the land. She had assured Aspen that her company cut wood. *Get your head out of the trees*, she groused as she turned onto Aspen's road. Aspen's fears were fact, and now Leigh was faced with a choice: sign on or quit. She thought about Jeff. He had been so confident that if she stayed she could make a difference. But why would the company listen to her? They had a game plan and it would take an incoming missile to blow it off course. Jeff seemed to think she was that incoming missile. She pulled into Aspen's driveway and Miss Etta greeted her.

"Hi there, little girl." The dog hopped around. "I see your mama." Leigh resisted the urge to rush to Aspen as she had done on previous nights. Instead she walked slowly toward her, Miss

Etta running just ahead. "Hi," she said shyly.

"Hi."

"I'm not sure what to do."

"How about we start with a hug?" Aspen did not move.

"I'd like that." Leigh slowly took her hands out of her pockets.

"We start with you putting your arms around my waist." There was a tease of a smile on Aspen's lips.

Comfort washed over Leigh. "I can manage that." She put her arms around Aspen and pulled her close. "I was so scared," she whispered against Aspen's hair.

"Me too."

"You? Why? You didn't do anything."

"I was scared about how I might react. Funny, I'm not really angry at the company, but I am in the mood for a good fight." Aspen stepped back. "A group of us got together today. We're organizing a protest."

"The protest is expected. Jay talked about that on Friday."

"They don't think we're going to be able to do much, do they?"

"They expect opposition. I don't think they think it's going to be that big a deal. They really believe the majority of folks are going to buy into this," Leigh added reluctantly.

"Really?"

"Yeah, really. Anyway . . ." She shrugged expressively.

"What's wrong?"

"I shouldn't be telling you this stuff. Your reporter friend told me you'd called her."

"I did."

"Even though I said we weren't supposed to talk about the project," she replied tightly.

"I didn't feel that applied to me."

Leigh just nodded. "Well, then what do we talk about, Aspen?"

"Cassie said I should think about compromising," Aspen said

the words quietly.

"Oh?"

"If push comes to shove and the company gets its way, to find areas of *compromise*." The word was as bitter as alum.

"That's a thorny word for you." Leigh considered her.

"It is," Aspen said after a minute. "I'm not sure I can do that."

Leigh leaned against the door jamb. "So what does that mean?" She sensed a shade had dropped between them.

"I'm hoping you're going to tell me you quit."

"I haven't."

"And are you?"

"I've thought about it. Jeff said that I could do more inside the company than on the outside."

"I don't understand."

"Like Cassie, he thinks there's plenty of room for compromise and the company is going to have to give a lot to get what it wants. He thinks I can help define what some of those give ups might be."

"And if he's wrong?"

"I don't know. I haven't thought that far ahead," she said helplessly. "This feels so awkward."

"I know."

"Funny, I came here to talk about something else."

"What?"

In the past, Leigh had bathed in Aspen's unwavering gaze. Tonight she wanted to run from those eyes. "It's not important now. Look, I think I should go." Leigh hesitated, she wanted Aspen to tell her to stay. To tell her it was going to be okay.

Aspen just nodded.

Leigh heard the knocking. She'd fallen asleep with a book on her chest, the light next to her bed still on. She put on her sweats and ran down the stairs.

Miss Etta was through the door first. "Aspen, I—"

"Don't talk. Just hold me." Aspen seemed to fold into her arms.

Leigh closed her eyes and pulled Aspen tightly against her, her coat cold against her arms. "Are you all right?" Leigh searched her face.

"I don't know." Aspen leaned her head against Leigh's shoulder. "I have to tell you something." Leigh's muscles tensed. She was prepared for the bad news. "I've fallen in love with you. Cassie, Anne Jean, Skeet, everyone seems to have figured it out."

"I think those people are fantastic!" Leigh exclaimed. "I've fallen in love with you, but I was afraid. You'd set those conditions about being together but not talking about love. I thought it was just me."

"You're going to find that I'm great at setting all kinds of rules, but I'm hell on wheels when it comes to breaking them."

"And the project?"

"We'll make it work together," Aspen said hopefully.

"I want to live together here or at your house. I want to tell the world that we are a couple. I'm just bursting." Leigh embraced her. "I feel so good, I want to climb a mountain and as they say shout it from the treetops."

Aspen laughed. "But, we have to talk," Aspen said. "About the future and Codyville and your company."

"We will, we have too, but right now I want to kiss you."

Aspen sighed. "What's stopping you, lady forester?"

"Not a thing, lady environmentalist."

Leigh's passion erupted. There was no interlude and no moment of exploration. She pulled Aspen to her and kissed her again, her lips demanding more. A low growl formed in Leigh's throat as Aspen responded. Aspen pulled back, gasping.

Then Aspen's mouth was on her with an energy that amazed Leigh. Aspen's hands slipped up to Leigh's cheeks and she pulled her mouth even closer. An unquenchable thirst spilled over in

Leigh and her desire roared like the ocean. They had made love before, but each time seemed so new. Aspen was fierce as she kissed Leigh's eyes, her cheeks, her neck. She slid her hands under Leigh's sweatshirt. "We're not going to make it to the bedroom," she growled. Leigh savored the raw heat of Aspen's hands as they massaged first one and then the other breast.

They kissed again, their tongues seeking each other's sweetness, exploring, pushing the boundaries of boldness. Breathless, Aspen pulled her down onto the floor. Leigh shivered.

Numb with desire, she pushed her breasts against Aspen's fingers and cried out when Aspen took her fingers away to pull Leigh's sweatshirt off. There was desire in Aspen's eyes just before she leaned down to kiss Leigh's breasts, her tongue caressing first one and then the other nipple.

Leigh gasped as Aspen pulled her to her. The cloth on Aspen's coat rubbed against her breasts. Leigh gulped. Never had cloth felt so sensuous. "I want to feel you all over," she murmured in Leigh's ear. Aspen fumbled with the string on Leigh's sweatpants. Burning with desire and impatience, Leigh reached down and ripped the string apart, lifted her hips and pushed her pants down. Aspen's eyes smoldering with passion, she pulled the sweatpants from Leigh's legs.

Aspen tore her jacket off and pulled her shirt over her head. Leigh could not stop looking at her breasts. They were small, the nipples brown and puckered. Aspen lay across her, their hips together, their lips on a search-and-rescue mission of pleasure, the fabric on Aspen's pants felt sensuous. Aspen pulled her even tighter against her as she traced her tongue down Leigh's neck, down her arms, to her shoulders, where she took tiny little nips. Her tongue continued to slither down to Leigh's wrists and then to her fingers. Aspen took one and then another into her mouth and sucked. Leigh's excitement quickened as Aspen's mouth bathed her in ecstasy.

Aspen placed gentle kisses on Leigh's chest and then on each nipple. Leigh's nipples puckered again like spring buds on a young sapling as Aspen's tongue explored, pulling even more sweetness from her body.

Leigh's breathing was ragged. Her chest heaved. Desire exploded between her thighs. "Aspen, please, don't linger, please, don't linger. I need you," Leigh whispered between kisses. Aspen's groan was almost a sob as she moved down Leigh's belly drawing a trail with her tongue around her belly-button. Her mouth moved lower and licked at the curls of hair below. Aspen's tongue trailed farther, finally sinking deep inside Leigh's folds, bathing in her wetness. Aspen had found the center of her being, a hot fountain ready to erupt in huge splashes of desire, and Leigh wanted more, needed more. She shivered and pushed her hips against Aspen's mouth. Groaning, Leigh dug her fingers deep into Aspen's wrists.

Then as if she was no longer in control of her body, Leigh's muscles clenched as an orgasm shook her.

"I'll never get enough of you," Aspen whispered against her lips.

Leigh lay back panting. Aspen's tongue again found her and she was again racing higher and higher, another orgasm within inches of her fingertips. "And I you," Leigh screamed as her body thrashed and as Aspen's tongue dug deeper into her.

Then, as if sensing a subliminal plea in Leigh, Aspen's fingers slid in and pushed deep. Leigh gasped. She wanted to take all of Aspen inside of her as she climbed the mountain of ecstasy. Again and again, Aspen pushed her to the summit and then over the top. Leigh was burning inside, burning from Aspen's touch. Burning from Aspen's embers.

"That was incredible." Leigh gasped as Aspen's fingers slid out of her. "I haven't had an orgasm like that . . . that was incredible." Leigh looked at Aspen's red face and the mouth that had just feasted on her. "I want to make love to you," Leigh said pushing Aspen onto the floor. "I want you to feel the incredible pleasure you just gave me. Aspen, I'm so in love with you it scares the hell out of me."

"And I love you." Aspen's eyes were inviting.

"Wow, what a great way to wake up." Leigh smelled the coffee. She was stretched out on her bed. Miss Etta's head curled on the pillow next to her.

"You were sound asleep." Aspen cuddled next to her.

Leigh groaned as she shifted on the bed. "We're going to have to stop making love on the kitchen floor, or I'm going to need a new back."

"Was it that unpleasant?" Aspen smirked.

"Heaven's no. I think my back doth protest too much," Leigh teased then sat up. "How about I make breakfast?" Leigh frowned. "Although, I'm not sure what I have here. I've been spending so much time at your house."

"That is a problem. I took a quick inventory when I went downstairs." Aspen raised an eyebrow. "Spoiled milk, so it's a good thing we drink black coffee. I'm not certain how long the eggs have been in your refrigerator, so I pitched them. The bread looked like it could serve as a penicillin culture and the juice had an unusual hairy mold growing in it. There was a can of tuna, but Miss Etta ate that."

"Let's go out for breakfast."

"You know what I'd like to do?"

"What?"

"Let's get something from the diner and take it out to our favorite spot by the river. Leigh, we need to talk," Aspen said soberly.

"You're on." Leigh grabbed Aspen's hand and pulled her up. "You shower first. I'll get coffee."

∼∽

211

Aspen rested her back against a tree and balanced the Styrofoam container on her knees. "This feels so right."

"It does." Leigh bit into her bacon and gave half to Miss Etta.

"You're going to spoil her." Aspen petted Miss Etta's head.

Leigh nodded agreeably. "Is it okay?"

"It is. Miss Etta deserves to be spoiled, given how hard life was when she started."

"Good, then I plan to spoil her and you."

"Not me, but it's a nice thought." Aspen smiled wistfully.

"You're sad."

"Not so much sad as pensive, I guess. Leigh, you'll have to get used to that. My battle with depression didn't just start after my sister died. I discovered through counseling that it's always been a part of my life, but people just thought I was moody or standoffish. And I ignored the moods. I thought I was just deviated from the norm when it came to social things."

"I'll learn." Leigh straightened. "Aspen, I can deal with the pensive, the sad. We can deal with it all."

"And what do you get out of all of that?"

Leigh pondered the question. "You and love."

"Is that enough?"

"Yes. Is it for you? My love, that is?"

"Very much. I was thinking how much easier life would be if we'd met ten years ago, maybe even five years ago."

"I don't know," Leigh said thoughtfully. "Ten years ago, I might not have understood how important this really is." She waved her hand expressively. "I might not have tried so hard to make this happen."

"Really?"

"I don't know, Aspen. Speculating about the past and the *what ifs*, is just as hard as speculating about the future. I'd like to think it would have worked, I just don't know."

"I'm scared about the future."

"I know." Leigh looked straight at her. "We have to try

harder than most couples to make this work. I know my company has added a huge hurdle, but not a barrier. I want to gamble we can make this work."

"And if your job clashes with everything I believe in? Then what, Leigh?"

"We find a way around it."

"I wish I was as certain. It seems like forever that I've fought for what I believed in. Clean air and water, protecting the environment. I know this has become a cliché, but it's true, we've only been given one home and we have to take care of it. I can't stop now because of your company. I have to fight your company and you. Codyville isn't Bar Harbor. We don't want a country club and golf course. We don't want all of those homes built."

"Is there room for compromise?"

"Oh, God. Is that the only word people seem to say these days?" Aspen shifted uncomfortably.

"I don't understand?"

"Cassie talked about compromise yesterday in the context of losing her husband and over her battle about boiling lobsters. I knew she regretted losing him, I just never understood how much. She does have regrets."

"Regrets?"

"Yeah, and lots of them. I don't want that to happen to us. I'm scared, Leigh. I'm scared that because you're in my life, I might not fight your company as hard as I would if you weren't. I'm scared that you'll see a side of me you won't like and leave. I'm just scared. Yet last night I showed up on your doorstep. You'll also have to get used to my being impulsive. I tend to sprint into something and worry about the consequences later."

"I'm so glad you did."

"What would have happened to us if I hadn't?"

"I don't know." Leigh was honest. "I thought we'd talk after a few days, try to figure this out. I tend to sit and examine things until they're almost mummified."

Aspen's eyes softened. "Not me. That was pure impulse last night."

Leigh laughed. "I vote for impulse. That's something else I need to get in my life. So what do we do now?"

"Cassie said when it comes to this project, I need to think about compromise." Aspen was thoughtful.

"How do you feel about that?" Leigh set her breakfast aside. She rested her chin on her hand. Aspen had more to say.

"Compromise sounds so final. What if I compromise and things get built? Years from now, do I look at you and wonder if the compromise was worth it? Or what if I compromise and you and I later break up. How angry will I be that I compromised? I would always wonder if I had fought just a little bit harder, stayed a little bit stronger and not compromised, would it have happened?"

"And what if you fight hard and it's still built and you've sacrificed our relationship? There's a middle ground somewhere. Let's not use the word compromise. Let's call it something else."

"Selling out?"

"I wasn't exactly thinking of those two words." Leigh's brow puckered.

"I'm sorry. That was harsh. So what do we call it?"

"I don't know. Maybe we could call it broccoli," Leigh teased.

Aspen giggled. "But wait, broccoli is only distasteful to you, not me."

"Then let's call it liver or mushrooms, or—"

"Liver, I do find that distasteful."

"See? We already agree."

Aspen broke off a blade of brown grass and rubbed it between her fingers. "And what if you quit and we fought this battle together?" she asked tentatively.

Leigh rubbed her finger against her lip. She too had been thinking about that. "And if we still lose?"

"We'd have been in the fight together."

"Aspen, what if Jeff is right?" She held up her hand to block the blitz of protestations from Aspen. "Hear me out. He feels I can and will be more effective inside the company than out."

"God, I don't know." Aspen signaled Miss Etta to eat. The dog was buried up to her ears in eggs. "What if he's wrong? What if Jay, or whatever his name is, decides it's his way and hang Jeff's theory? Then what, Leigh? We face each other across a picket line? Is that what you want?"

"No! That's not what I want. You know that, Aspen. I love you. I don't want that."

"Then quit your job." The words hung in the air like dust particles. "Is this project that important to you?"

"No, Codyville is important to me." Leigh cocked her head. "That's what's been bugging me. Codyville is the first town I've ever lived in that I care about, and I don't want to see anything happen to it."

"Then quit and join our group!" Aspen said again.

"And lose?"

"Lose? How can we lose?"

"Aspen, the company owns the land." Leigh cupped her hands as if holding the concept inside. "It can do whatever it wants with it, because the governor has put the resources of his agencies at Jay's disposal. Somewhere, your group is going to have to talk about compromise."

"I won't compromise!" Aspen's tone was bitter.

"And I will, because I don't want Codyville to become Bar Harbor North. When Jeff first talked to me about staying on the job, I didn't understand it, but I do now. Jay will have his way unless your group and Jeff and I all stay on point. Jay is going to get some things, but not all."

"You really believe that?"

"Not because I want to, but because it's reality."

"And what about us?" Aspen's eyes were sad.

"We win."

215

"How, Leigh? Last night seemed so right."

"It was. It really was, and so is today and tomorrow." Leigh leaned toward her. "Aspen, I ask only this. Give us a chance."

"I want to." She stopped, her words stuck in her throat. She swallowed. "I don't feel good about this. What happens if your company does something that puts us at odds with each other What happens if it leads to a huge fight? Then what?"

Leigh studied her. God, she loved her. "I don't know. Aspen, we are not going to be able to figure out all of the *what ifs*. We just have to trust in each other."

"Wow, our life's balance is hanging on one word. Trust." Aspen rolled the word around in her mouth. "And if you're forced to make a choice, or I am?"

"If I have to choose between you and the company, never doubt for a minute, Aspen, I would choose you. I love you that much. Can we just live with that for right now?"

"And if I have to choose between you and the trees?" Aspen's words hung out there like a funnel cloud in the distance.

"Let's not try to figure out the *what ifs* of that one." Leigh's voice was subdued. "I think we have to trust each other, trust that we can make this work, regardless of who's making the rules right now."

Aspen stared at the river. "Leigh, I love you so much, but I don't know if I can live with . . . what's the other word you came up with for compromise?"

Leigh chuckled. "Liver."

Aspen smiled. "Liver. I can't wait to share that one with Cassie." Aspen sobered. "Leigh, I can live with this for right now, but know that I can't . . . no, that I *won't* sell my soul to Burnt Brush."

"Nor will I," Leigh said quietly.

Aspen rubbed her hands against her knees. "I think . . . we should . . . live . . . together."

"Wow, no prequel, no introduction. You *are* full of surprises."

"I've been thinking about it. You've been practically living at my house anyway, and this is unlike any other relationship I've ever been in. The pressures are there for it to fail." Aspen rushed on. "I think with the stresses of the development and everything else, we need to be together, under the same roof." Aspen's voice was low.

"I don't want to think about failure." Leigh stared at Aspen's hands. They were compulsively rubbing against her knees. She took Aspen's hands in hers to calm them. "I want to live together, but for the right reasons, not because of the *stresses of development*. I want to do it because we love each other and living together will make that love even better."

"For that reason too, but I think we look at it as . . . insurance. I think . . . I think we need to live through this together." Aspen nodded slowly. "Not me living in my house, you in yours, and then we talk about what's happening in our lives. We need to live through each other's moods and hope that in the end, we . . . our love, survives."

"You feel that intensely about it?"

"I do."

"Then we do it." Leigh stroked the back of Aspen's hands with her thumbs. "I don't want to attach a reason to it. I say let's do it and define our reasons as we go along."

Aspen's face was tense. Leigh studied her. "Come on. Miss Etta can have a ball with all the food." Leigh pulled Aspen to her feet. "I want to climb a tree with you."

"Really?"

"Very really." Leigh kissed Aspen on the lips. "Let's finish talking about this in a tree. It's where we belong and, Aspen, I'm willing to take one day at a time."

CHAPTER NINETEEN

Aspen put on a skirt and blouse. She was having dinner with Linda before the company's first meeting with the public. Miss Etta was lying on the bed, watching her. It had been more than a week since the announcement.

"I can't take you to dinner." Miss Etta dropped her head onto her paws. "Don't pout." Aspen ran a brush through her hair and studied her face in the mirror. Love was definitely the right prescription for her, she decided, and so was living with Leigh. She put the brush down. She was looking forward to dinner with Linda and discussing strategy with someone who'd been in the trenches, something she couldn't do with Leigh. When she'd told Leigh she was having dinner with Linda, she'd grunted.

❧

"Your niece isn't working tonight," Aspen said, seated at the restaurant.

"No, but she's going to the meeting," Linda said. "She's all excited, this being her first *protest*." Linda was obviously thrilled at her niece's interest. "In fact, I've been meeting with her and several of her friends after class. They are a wild bunch of kids. It's been a blast talking strategy with them. I love their enthusiasm. In fact, some of them will be there tonight."

"I think it's great you're involving young people in this. We need them. You should have asked your niece to join us. Her friends too," Aspen said.

"I was more in the mood for dinner alone with you." Linda ordered coffee for Aspen and a glass of wine for herself and waited until the waitress was gone. "I think we have a lot to talk about," she added.

"Me too. I can't tell you how excited I am working with someone with your experience. I feel good about that. So, where should we start? Tonight's meeting? Future strategy?"

"Let's start with disappointment."

"I don't understand?" Aspen's mind was percolating. *What did disappointment have to do with strategy?*

"By my calculations, I was about two months too late."

"I—"

Linda waved off her objection. "No need to explain, in fact, I'd prefer you'd not. That's just way too much pain to endure."

"Linda, I never—"

"You know what? You didn't even give us a chance." Linda was impatient.

"Us? I don't remember an us." Aspen was surprised.

"Not in so many words, but you knew how I felt."

"Linda, I've never given you the impression that I wanted anything more than friendship. I've been very clear about that." Aspen sucked in her breath. She didn't want to fight.

"Oh, I don't know. The kiss on the lips, you didn't exactly run from the room. Look!" Linda stopped Aspen's response again with a look. "There's no point in talking about it. Obviously I'm disappointed. I think you made a lousy choice, and when our group opens with both barrels blazing, your friend, Leigh, is going to be in the middle of the crossfire, and she's not going to survive. She calls herself an environmentalist, but stays with a company that is anything but." Linda threw her head back angrily. "Ya know, her kind makes me angrier than the corporate polluters because she's smart enough to figure out a way around the environment. So it looked like she's giving in, when all she is doing is taking."

Aspen was shocked at Linda's acrimony. "First, that kiss was a peck that, well, never mind, but second, there's not going to be any crossfire. That's not what our group is about. Protest, yes, Disagreement, absolutely. But not crossfire." People were staring. "Linda," Aspen said, lowering her voice, "I think this was a bad idea." She gathered her cape.

"Wine for you, coffee for you," the waitress said tentatively, looking from Aspen to Linda.

"I'm sorry," Linda said after the waitress had left. "Don't leave, please."

Aspen sat rigidly in the chair.

"I'm sorry," Linda said again. "My disappointment got the better of me."

Aspen still didn't move. "Linda, I don't know what to say."

"How about"—she held up her glass—"to you and Leigh, and to my being a good sport about it?"

Aspen cautiously picked up her cup and drank. "Thank you."

"I'm sorry," Linda said again. "Sometimes my temper gets ahead of my brain. I shouldn't have said any of that. But Aspen, I am disappointed. I thought with a little more time you'd feel the same way. Besides, I figured you couldn't resist my charms."

Aspen blanched. "I—"

"The last part was a joke. Please take off your cape. I promise, no more drama queen stuff tonight. Let's talk about the meeting," Linda said distractedly. "And let's order." She waved to the waitress. "So what is our game plan?" Linda asked after a moment. "Do we pepper them with questions? Do we call them liars to their face? What's protocol?"

"Honestly, I don't know." Aspen still felt unnerved. "This is the first time we've had a company come hat in hand asking us permission to destroy our land. I'd say it's more wait and see. See what they have to say. Take your cues from that."

"How's Leigh taking it? I expect this is sort of getting in the way of her *you can cut trees and be an environmentalist*. I'm not being sarcastic," Linda protested. "Just curious how she's handling it."

"It's been difficult, but she's handling it okay." Aspen clearly didn't feel comfortable talking about Leigh with Linda. "Anyway, I'm glad you're on board, Linda. I think your background and experience is going to help." The words lacked feeling.

"I hope so. I hate these kinds of developments. They start small and then take on a life of their own. I don't buy their, *we're only going to develop a small portion of our land* crap. They see dollar signs. Why else are they doing it? Anyway, I'm glad we finally can have dinner together. Let's eat," she said as the waitress put their dinners in front of them. "Then let's go to war."

Aspen greeted several of her neighbors as she walked into the hall. There was a buzz in the air as people looked at the maps on the wall.

She spotted Cassie, Anne Jean and Skeet in the front row. Aspen smiled at parents of her students and stopped to talk with Linda and Melissa, who were seated farther back. There were several young faces around them. No doubt the kids Linda mentioned. Aspen thought again about the meal and shivered. Linda had an angry side she didn't like.

"I saved you a seat," Cassie said when Aspen finally sat down. "How was dinner?"

"Good." She didn't want to talk about what had happened.

"If I hadn't had my belly dance class, I'd have joined you," Cassie said looking around.

"Is Leigh here?"

"I haven't seen her. Only the chunky guy in the gray suit and tie. He's been fiddling with a PowerPoint presentation."

Aspen nodded.

"May I have your attention?" the man asked. "My name's Tom Webster and I'm here to talk about some pretty exciting stuff that means economic development for this town. I'm going to talk for about fifteen minutes outlining the scope of the project and then answer questions."

Leigh and two men came in the side door. One was older and, from the way his body hunched forward, arthritic. That must be Jeff, she decided. He looked just like Leigh had described him. The other man looked Ivy League in a blue flannel shirt, chinos and Birkenstocks. Aspen smiled at Leigh and caught an imperceptible wink as Leigh turned her attention to Tom.

"As you know," Tom said, "Burnt Brush announced last week that it's prepared to undertake one of the largest development projects ever for this area. A project that will provide hundreds of jobs during construction and seventy-plus jobs once completed. Although a lot has been speculated about since we announced our plans, tonight you get the facts." Tom smiled at the group. "Rumors abound, and I've heard everything from ten acres to all of our land." Tom held up his hand to emphasize. "All we are developing is about ten percent of the timber land we own. So harvesting will continue to be a prime mover for this company." Aspen scoffed at his numbers. *Ten percent now*, she thought, *eventually one hundred percent*. Tom went through screen after screen of diagrams, artist's drawings and propaganda.

222

"Any questions?" Tom asked as he finished up. "I just ask that you state your name. We're the new guys on the block, so knowing your name will help. By the way, Burnt Brush plans to set up an office downtown, so if we don't get your questions answered tonight, feel free to stop by the office once it's open. We also have flyers we will be handing out at the end of the meeting with the telephone numbers of key personnel, so if you don't get a chance to ask a question tonight, you can ask it later. Any questions?"

"My name's Linda Sappier and I'm an instructor at the community college here in town. You say ten percent now. Is that all you plan to develop, or are there plans that you're keeping secret from us?"

"That's what we plan to build. This is a new venture for us, and to say that we're going to develop more isn't something we know right now. We want the character and identity of the wooded area we're talking about to remain the same. There will always be trails and wonderful places for people to hike. It would not be in the interest of the company or the community to build so many houses that people who come here complain about city living. That's not what this is about. This is about small-town living and small-town values. That's what we plan to market. Folks who sell their homes in Boston do not want to move to a mini version of Boston."

"You didn't answer my question," Linda said. "If this is as successful as you believe it's going to be, do you have plans to build more houses in the future?"

"What you see is what you get." His smile was forced. "Any other questions?"

Aspen listened as her neighbors asked about the impact on the river and the surrounding areas. She also listened as people talked about the pressure on the town's tiny infrastructure and the burden on the schools. Tom had regained his composure after Linda's question and moved through the rest of the questions with ease.

"Any more questions?" he asked.

"Aspen Brown. There's a very old stand of trees and an eagle's nest that the town has been asking for. What happens to it?" Aspen asked.

"It will remain under resource protection. We won't develop that land."

"I expected you'd say that," Aspen shot back. "I'm not talking about the pressure on it from development, but from the hundreds of people who will be moving here who don't have a clue that the eagles are on the Federal Endangered Species List and therefore protected by the government."

"First off, under resource protection, the status quo will be maintained, so the eagles are off the radar screen as far as people bothering them. We plan to put up signs during the nesting season notifying folks that there's a hefty federal fine if they harass the eagles. As to more people using that area, yes, that's going to happen. I walked that stretch of land myself the other day and it's beautiful, and people who move here I expect will be doing the same." Tom held up a hand to stop Aspen's next question. "But I might add, most of the people who will be moving here will be retirees, and I suspect will be ecologically and environmentally savvy people, so I'd be surprised if they'd harass the eagles."

"But what about the children and grandchildren who follow? How do we know they won't *harass* the eagles?" Linda's question was biting. "You may be marketing this to one segment of the population, but that doesn't mean you're going to stop other people from moving here and building. I think those are the stresses that Aspen's talking about."

"And stresses we are very aware of." Aspen's head turned to the voice that was coming from the side of the room. It was the Birkenstock man. "My name's Jay Hollingdale, and this is Leigh Wright, as most of you know, and Jeff Grant. Jeff, some of you may remember, was here when the first company owned the land, only a lot younger and with a lot more hair," Jay joked. There was polite laughter. "He was a harvester along with his father." He stood next to Tom. "To answer your question." Jay turned to Linda. "We are just as concerned about that kind of development, and that's one of the things we've been talking about with the governor's office. We can't stop people from building here, but we can certainly make it more difficult. If you look closely at the first map . . . Tom, would you bring that back up, please? If you look at that," he said pulling a laser pointer from his pocket, "we own most of this area, and like Tom said, we plan to continue harvesting it. So, although we're proposing a development with more people, we don't see that it will stretch the ecological and environmental resources. Will it stress the infrastructure? You bet, but in a good way. Right now we're talking with the state about a new and wider two-lane highway into town. We also plan to have good roads into and out of the development area. All pluses for the town."

"Good, by your definition," someone yelled from the back of the room.

"And good by the town's definition," Jay said smoothly. "And as to that stand of trees you're concerned about, Ms. Brown, that's one of the things we can negotiate. We want to keep it resource protected so that peoples' activities will be restricted, but we're open to other suggestions."

"How about giving that land to the town?" Anne Jean asked.

"As I said, we're open to any and all suggestions." Jay smiled.

"I like the idea. Let's talk about jobs," a voice yelled from the back of the room.

"There'll be plenty of them," Jay said looking toward the man who had made the statement. "And, of course, spin-off opportunities for folks right here in this room in the form of stores and other support businesses. Right now your downtown is mostly empty storefronts. Think about the day when there'll be a drugstore or a clothing store. How about a medical clinic? All possibilities."

"Skeet Jones," Skeet said, standing. "You're goin' to build a golf course and club house. What's to keep someone from building a resort with that? That would change the character and identity of our area even more."

"We're not interested," Jay said evenly.

"But what's to keep someone else from doin' it?" Skeet said.

"Nothing." Jay smiled. Aspen was getting tired of Jay's smile. "Admittedly anything is possible, but again, land is the issue. Codyville Plantation is a good-sized town, but we own most of the land."

"And you wouldn't think about selling that to a developer for big bucks?" Linda asked. "You just said *anything's possible.*"

"I did—" Jay's exterior calm had been penetrated.

"If I could jump in here," Jeff said from the side of the room. Heads turned to him and away from Jay. "As Jay said, some of you old-timers know me because my dad and I worked crew here for many years. I used to be the earnest kid in the oversized green shirt." Jeff took his place next to Jay. "There ain't nothing going to stop development, whether it's this company or the next. I don't like the way Maine's going. I hate all these flat-landers coming in with their fancy cars and fancy wines and eating all that funny food." There were chuckles of agreement. "So change has happened already, and change is going to happen again. What you folks have to decide is, do you want to do change with this company that's been here a year and that's come to you and said this is what they plan to do, or do you change with some unknown company that's not interested in preserving this area? Burnt Brush has a manager living right here, and she plans to stay here." Leigh's face remained impassive. "And a company, I might add, that said it's going to do only a fraction of development on its land. Or do you want a company that'll come in here and develop and run?"

"You saying Burnt Brush's going to sell if we don't go along with this?" Cassie asked. "Why, that's blackmail."

"No, I didn't say that at all." Jeff smiled at her. "What I'm saying is that everything has a price. So if Burnt Brush isn't going to develop this land, then someone else might come along someday and offer the company a hefty price and do it themselves. That ain't blackmail, that's reality."

"Sounds like blackmail to me," Cassie said petulantly.

"You can call it what you like, but it's reality," Jeff answered her kindly. "So it's really up to you folks. Look around you. It's happening. It's happening down south and it's going to happen here. The rest of the world has discovered Maine, and they want to live here. Will it change the character of the neighborhood and state? You betcha. Can you be a part of it and make it work to your town's advantage? You betcha again."

"Are you planning on selling?" Linda asked.

"No, we're not," Jay said. "But Jeff's got a good point. Everything is for sale in this world, and I guess we all have to decide what we want. Do you want to make the town a part of this development project? We're not going to do this in secret or behind closed doors. We plan to appoint a citizen's advisory committee to work right along with us, and it's going to be made up of people from right here in this room."

"I betcha Aspen won't be on that advisory committee," Melissa said quickly.

Jay smiled at Aspen. "We would love to have her join us." A flush crept up Aspen's neck. She hated the attention.

"But what about that resort?" Anne Jean persisted.

"We have no intention of building one," Jay said. "Put the development diagram up, would you, Tom?" Jay waited as Tom flicked through the pages on his computer. "As you can see," he said pointing at the diagram with his laser. "There'll be a country club and golf course, but the way we've designed it, it'll be surrounded by the houses we plan to build."

"That's all very nice, but you still haven't told us what you plan to do with the rest of your land," a woman said from the side of the room.

"Cut wood," Jay said succinctly.

"Forever?" Linda asked.

"For as long as it's lucrative." There was a low grumbling across the room.

"That's not an answer," Linda insisted.

"But it's what we know now," Jay countered. "Do we have more development plans on the drawing board? Not as we speak."

"What about after ya speak?" Skeet asked.

"Not now and not in the future," Jay answered. "I'd like to introduce you to our manager, Leigh Wright, who is available to answer questions, day or night." Jay smiled at her. "Leigh, why don't you come up here?" Leigh woodenly took her place next to Jeff. Jeff touched her arm and Leigh smiled gratefully at him. "For those of you who don't know her, this is our woodlot manager, Leigh Wright," Jay said. "And at our company meeting last week, Leigh asked many of the same questions you folks have asked."

Jay looked around the room. "We know this is going to make a difference to your town, and we want to be sensitive to that, but Jeff's right, if we don't do it, someone else will. Only that next person may be a developer who couldn't give a hoot about the woods. We give a hoot about the woods because that's our bread and butter."

"Then why change?" Leigh's secretary Jane asked the question. "Mr. Hollingdale, I've never met you, but I work for you. Well actually, I work for Leigh. Why change?"

"Well, Jane," Jay said smoothly, "to survive. We need this development to survive as a company. This development is taking place by a company that appreciates the character and quality of this town. Yes, the town will change, and yes, more people will live here, but the people who want to live here are making a life-change decision. They're moving here because they want what Codyville Plantation has to offer, and that's what we want to preserve." Jay glanced at his watch. "Look, folks, it's nine o'clock. We promised you that this would last only two hours, and I intend to keep that promise. Tom, Jeff, Leigh and I will remain right here, and those who want to stay and ask questions can do so. Leigh's going to put a sign-up sheet on the table for those who want to join our advisory committee. Next to the sign-up sheet is a fact sheet, which we invite you to take home with you. If there are no more questions, I want to thank you for coming. Those who want to ask questions, come right up here. We will stay as long as it takes."

There was a low rumble as people started toward the exit.

"What do you think, Aspen?" It was Linda. Somehow she had gotten through the crowd that was heading for the exit.

"Not good," Aspen whispered.

"I think it's all bullshit, frankly. That line, *join with us or the next guy's going to be worse*, is just a little too much to stomach."

"I agree."

"I've got to go because I have an early class. When's our organizational meeting?" Linda asked.

"How about tomorrow night?"

"Good, I know folks at the college who will join us, and Melissa and a bunch of her friends want to sign on."

"I expect we'll hold it right here then," Aspen said. "I'll talk to Cassie. She's already using the hall, so I expect she can get it for the meeting."

"I'll see you then," Linda said as she touched Aspen's arm. "By the way, dinner was a delight and, Aspen, if it doesn't work out with . . . well, I'm here," she whispered.

Aspen stared at Linda's retreating back. Unnerved, she

looked for Leigh who had people three deep around her, as did Jay and Tom. Jeff was by himself taking in the crowd. Aspen suspected he didn't miss much. Jeff's eyes settled on her. He did not smile.

"What do you think?" Cassie asked excitedly. "I can't wait until we blow these guys out of the water!"

"I suggested to Linda we have our organizational meeting tomorrow night. She said she could get people from the college." Aspen was still reeling over Linda's parting remark. "She said Melissa plans on bringing some of her friends. Let's announce it on the radio and see how many folks show up. Can you get this place for us for say around six o'clock?"

"No problem," Cassie said. "I'll do it right now."

"This ain't good," Skeet said looking at the front of the room. "No."

"You say jobs and that gets people's attention, and there's nothing wrong with that, but I think this group don't understand the opposition to this. I think they think they can just wave the old stand of trees under our nose and throw out the threat of some outsider comin' in and developing this, and we're all goin' to roll over and kiss them on the mouth. But we ain't about to do that," Skeet said.

Aspen smiled at Skeet's imagery. "No, we ain't."

"Leigh looked so miserable," Anne Jean whispered. "And what was that stare about from Jeff? It looked like he was trying to communicate with you telepathically."

"Don't know." Aspen frowned. Jeff had made her feel uncomfortable.

"Look at that poor woman." Skeet nodded at Leigh. "Looks like she's the squirrel backed into a corner by three mean coyotes." She had three women all talking at once to her. Leigh was smiling and nodding and even getting a chance to answer.

"You know what she needs?" Anne Jean said looking at Leigh.

"I expect you have some idea."

"Some homemade chocolate chip cookies. Follow us home and I'll give you some."

"I'm sure she'll appreciate it. I'll be just a minute. I want to make sure that Cassie's lined up the hall for us for tomorrow night."

"The way she's talking over there, I'd be surprised that she hadn't. Cassie can part rivers and move mountains when she's a mind to," Anne Jean said.

"No question about it. Look, I think we need to split up the call list. Make sure we get as many people as possible at tomorrow night's meeting. Agreed?"

"Agreed," Anne Jean and Skeet said together.

"See you at the house," Anne Jean whispered as she squeezed Aspen's hand.

CHAPTER TWENTY

"I'll be over in the morning," Jeff said quietly to Leigh. The few stragglers that had stayed after the meeting to ask questions were gone. Jay was talking to Tom.

"Okay," was all Leigh could get out before Jay joined them.

"I want to thank you two," Jay said shaking hands with them. "I think this was a good meeting. What'd you think, Jeff?"

"Seemed good."

"How about you, Leigh?" Jay asked.

"I think it went well, but there were some pretty passionate questions tonight."

"Passionate, but not unexpected," Tom joined in.

Leigh shook her head. "I think we need to be prepared."

"Prepared, yes," Tom threw out. "But not paranoid. Yes, there was concern, but I didn't see any out and out, *no, you can't do that in my town*, speeches. In fact, I thought folks were fairly accepting. Even those with questions."

Leigh shrugged.

"You don't agree?" Tom asked.

"I don't."

"Then I have my work cut out for me." Tom was confident. "I'm hired to sell this, and that's what I've got to do over the next few weeks and months. Any help you can give me, Leigh, will be greatly appreciated."

"Leigh's on board with this." Jay patted her on the arm. "She's here as our point person for any local issues that may arise. Jeff's also available. We have two very good resources here and I want you to use them," he said to Tom. "Well, I have a long drive back to Farmington. Tom's staying over, and I guess you are too, right, Jeff?"

"I am. Leigh and I are having breakfast in the morning."

"Good idea," Jay said looking at the lone man standing at the back of the room. "Looks like this gentleman wants to lock up."

"I've got to be going too," Tom said. "You guys like to grab a cup of coffee or something?"

Jeff smiled. "First, there's nothing open at this hour, and second . . ." Jeff looked at Leigh. "I'm tuckered. I just need to talk to Leigh a minute about our meeting tomorrow, and then I'm going over to the motel."

"One thing for sure," Tom said putting on his coat. "We're going to change that."

"Me having breakfast with Leigh?" Jeff frowned.

"There not being a place open after nine o'clock. Once this development happens, there's going to be plenty of fast food restaurants. I'd expect even a bar or two. I'd say Codyville is ready to wake up to the twenty-first century," Tom said smugly.

"I don't cotton much to that man," Jeff said. Tom was gone.

"Nor I." Leigh was subdued.

"Never trusted a man in a gray suit. I always expect he's trying to sell me a long-term annuity."

Leigh laughed. "So we're having breakfast tomorrow?"

"I was watching your face during the questions, and a few times I thought you were going into cardiac arrest with the answers. I want to finish that conversation we started. I don't expect eating at the diner is such a good idea. How about breakfast at your place? I plan to head back to Farmington early, so I'll be over about seven. Is that all right?"

"That's fine." Leigh kept her face impassive. She hadn't yet told the company she had moved in with Aspen. It had happened so fast. A quick stop at a convenience store was in order. She didn't have any food at the house.

Driving to Aspen's, Leigh thought about the meeting. Jay and Tom hadn't just hedged some of the answers. They'd out and out lied. Leigh rubbed her eyes as she parked her truck. Of late, life was an interminable case of acid reflux.

"Glad you're here. I thought Jay would keep you forever." Aspen kissed her.

"Me too."

"You have chocolate chip cookies waiting for you." Aspen held up a plate.

"Anne Jean."

"Bingo."

"Comfort food."

"Bingo again."

"Does she have a sixth sense?"

Aspen smirked. "What do you mean?"

"She seems to sense when cookies or sticky pudding are needed. Or does she just have an arsenal of stuff?"

"Probably both. For Anne Jean, eating is a comfort. It's been like that for as long as I've known her. They have some great kids, but growing up they caused Skeet and Anne Jean the same amount of anxiety that kids cause most parents, so when things

234

got tough, Anne Jean got cooking. I think it was a damn good way to relieve stress, a hell of a lot better than depression," Aspen said quietly.

Leigh took her in her arms. "There's no right or wrong path."

"No," Aspen said against Leigh's shoulder. "But sometimes we can choose to take an easier one than we do."

"Probably, but that's true of all of us."

"Anyway, you up for some cookies?" Aspen said changing the subject.

"I am."

"Right answer, Wright, because I sure as heck am. I even waited until you got home before I ate one. How virtuous is that?" Aspen joked.

"Extremely virtuous." Leigh loved Aspen's playfulness.

Aspen poured two glasses of milk. "So let's see, the most important thing that happened tonight is Jay dodged the future development issue. Hell, he lied!"

"He did, and thank you for not bringing it up." Leigh bit into one of the cookies. "Oh, this is good."

"I promised you I wouldn't, but Linda tried to hold his feet to the fire."

"I noticed. How was dinner?" Leigh was too tired to talk about the project.

"Good." Aspen picked up another cookie.

"Is there something you want to tell me?"

"No." Aspen stopped, unwilling to say more.

"Aspen, did she make a pass at you?" Leigh's expression was tight.

"No, we mostly talked about the project." *Well, that wasn't completely true. They did talk about the project.* "She's pretty passionate. She may be what the group needs."

"How so?"

"Just that, I don't know. I think the group needs new leadership and I think Linda is probably the one to take that role."

"I would imagine the group would want you. They've known you, been through a lot with you."

Aspen shrugged. "Maybe it's time for a change. Anyway, she's gotten a lot of young folks from the college interested and I think that's great. She's already meeting with them. She has a lot of energy. Some of them were there tonight."

"I saw some young faces in the audience, for that she's to be applauded."

"You like that?"

"Of course. They're our future protesters, and frankly, I think this is a good one for them to get a hold of. Plus, they're going to learn from a couple of pros. I still think Linda's a little too militant for this area, but I trust you if you say she's okay."

Aspen picked up their milk glasses and rinsed them out. "Jay's nuts if he doesn't realize people will figure they got some future plans." Aspen was done talking about Linda. "If this goes the way the company hopes, the pressure will be on to develop the rest of the land."

"You're right." Leigh yawned.

"You look exhausted. Let's go to bed."

"No argument from me. It was amusing watching Linda weave her way through the crowd to get to you after the meeting. Reminded me of a salmon swimming upstream."

"She wanted to confirm our meeting tomorrow night."

"And there's nothing more?" Leigh kept her voice light.

"No." Aspen looked at her intently.

"Nice looking woman, if you're into redheads."

Aspen chuckled. "I'm not into redheads. I'm into blond-headed foresters who cause me to have heart palpitations."

"Good, because I'm really into a woman with black hair and long, sensuous eyelashes that makes me hot just thinking about her."

"Hot?"

"Ablaze," Leigh said taking her in her arms.

"Good. Are you planning on doing anything to stoke up that heat?"

"In a big way," Leigh said. "Funny, I'm not as tired as I was."

Leigh picked up the groceries she needed and headed to her house. She was late. Jeff had said seven, and it was already six forty-five. Leigh turned into her driveway and was relieved Jeff wasn't there. She turned up the thermostat, then started the bacon and scrunched up the plastic bags and tossed them under the sink. She heard Jeff's truck.

"Hungry?" She took his coat.

"I am.

"Coffee's almost ready."

"You've not been sleeping here."

"How'd you know?"

"I was by earlier and your truck wasn't here."

"I could've just run to the store for something."

"Could've, but you didn't."

Leigh smiled. "You're good."

"It's the woman who was asking all the questions. The one down front."

"It is." Jeff was uncomfortable. "Do you have a problem with that?"

"Nope, just that it's a woman who's one of those environmentalists."

"She is. How'd you know about us?"

"I've heard things around town, and I also saw the way she looked at you during the meeting. When the questions seemed to be going against the company, she turned to see how you were doing. I don't know." Jeff shrugged. "I just saw more in her eyes than concern."

The coffeepot beeped. "I can have my resignation in by this afternoon."

"Why would you do that?"

"I thought that's what you'd want. Aspen Brown is very much a part of my life, and she's an environmentalist. I just figured that combination would definitely demand a resignation."

"Not with me. I think it's why you shouldn't quit."

"I don't understand." Leigh poured the coffee.

"You've finally found someone you care about and I'm glad. I've been worried about you."

"Worried?"

"Yup, worried. You're too good a woman to go through life alone. I was worried that you'd be alone after you and that woman up north broke up."

"You knew about that?"

"It's a small town. We're a small company. It's none of our business who you live with."

"Jay know?"

"I expect."

"You're pretty incredible."

"Not really." Jeff cleared his throat. "The question is, how do we handle this, aside from your quitting?"

"That one I want to hear." Leigh turned the bacon and put the eggs on.

"Right now, Jay wants to make Codyville a model for future development. I noticed, like you, he sidestepped questions about future development and even shaded the truth somewhat."

"Shaded? He was lying to those folks, Jeff."

"He was, but people do. The question is, can Jay do what he says he's going to do? I think not."

"Really?"

"Yup. Right now he's got this plan and he's been listening to all those paid yes men telling him how brilliant he is. He's never faced organized opposition. But we have. I've seen what the environmentalists can do when they set their minds against something, and in most cases the stuff they've done has been good for the state."

"Can't argue that one."

"I know I go robin round the barn a lot, but what I'm saying, Leigh, is Jay's going to get some of what he wants, but not all. There will be development, but better you and I have a say in it, and that's what your environmentalist friend needs to understand."

"Even when that development is wrong?"

"Is it so wrong? I'd say what he's planning long-term, yes, but short-term, no."

"I don't understand." Leigh put eggs and bacon in front of Jeff.

"Looks good," he said. "Look around you, Leigh. We got people here can't find work. There's nothing wrong in offering a man or a woman a job."

"No, but what if they don't want that job?"

"They do. Just no one's asked them. Jay's asking. When we had that layoff, you were relieved because the employees were going to other jobs. How'd you have felt if Jay had announced that layoff and there'd been no place for those people to go?"

"Lousier than I felt."

"That's right. People here want jobs, but there's not a lot around. Some of the jobs the company's offering ain't bad. Some will be just above minimum wage, but he's promised that all full-time people will have company benefits, and I believe him."

"But I feel like we're giving the town away to the company and to really bad development."

"Jay's not the devil. The poverty around here is."

"So we sign on to jobs and sell off what? Pristine beauty? A way of life?"

"No, we don't have to do that either. Leigh, look at the basic proposal. Jay's not lying. They're only talking about using ten percent of all the property we own. That leaves the rest to be harvested."

"But you saw the drawings he showed us in Farmington. It's not going to stop at just that initial project."

"That's what they believe, but they're wrong."

"Why don't I feel confident about that?"

"Because you ain't lived as long as I have. People around here will glom onto some of it, but in the end, the company is going to have to compromise big time. That plan they threw up on the screen in Farmington is just that, a plan. By the time this project gets off the drawing board, it's going to be a lot different. You saw that last night. We never discussed an advisory committee in Farmington. That was Jay's first compromise, and it ain't going to be his last. He jumped on that like a ladybug on an aphid because the questions were running against the project."

"That did surprise me. Heck, I didn't even have paper to sign people up." Leigh sipped her coffee. "Funny, I hadn't thought about it that way, I mean about the rest of the project," she added quickly.

"Well, you should because it's all there. Sure, he sidestepped questions about future development because he's less confident about that. Sure, he's got that Tom fella to do his sugarcoating to make that bitter pill go down easier, but it's not going to happen."

"I don't know, Jeff." Leigh still was not convinced.

"Do you like living here?"

"I do. It's unlike any other place I've been. There's something about this town that seems to just fit me. I felt it the day I arrived."

"So you quit. What are you going to do for work?"

"Find another job."

"You will, but not around here. The companies that harvest the wood are just too small. They couldn't afford to hire someone with your talent and experience. You'd be a forester again, not a forest manager."

"Is that so bad?"

240

"No, but it's where you started. You could move somewhere else, but that would complicate your life."

His statement didn't demand an answer. Leigh pushed her finished plate away.

"You could stay," Jeff ventured. "Don't be out there pushing it, and don't be bad-mouthing it. Let the experts stop it, and in the end you're going to be the manager of a woodlot. Maybe one not quite as big as what you started with, but one for sure."

"The experts?"

"That friend of yours for one."

Leigh nodded. "That's part of the problem," Leigh said quietly.

"You two talk about this?"

"A lot. That's why I know that for her, compromise isn't on the table."

"It will be."

"Really?"

"She ain't stupid, is she?"

"No, Aspen's not stupid."

"Then she's going to figure out that to stop the bigger project, she's going to have to compromise. We own the land. We can pretty much do what we want as long as we follow state law. She's going to figure that out mighty quick. We get some and she and her group gets some. It's just that simple."

"You're amazing."

Jeff grunted his disapproval.

CHAPTER TWENTY-ONE

Leigh sat with her feet on the stool. Miss Etta curled in her lap. The book she was reading was propped against Miss Etta's back. When she'd gotten home from her meeting with Tom and a group of business leaders, she'd found Aspen's note saying that something had come up and the meeting would run longer. She'd been attending a lot of meetings lately and so had Aspen. "Well, Miss Etta Betta, it seems like you and I are spending a lot of time alone together," Leigh scratched the dog's ear. Miss Etta wiggled on her lap and rolled onto her back, her black furry feet waving in the air, her dark pink tongue hanging out the side of her mouth. She stared at Leigh with her one good eye. Leigh smiled as she thought about Aspen telling her how she'd found the waif on the road, injured, alone and starved. Leigh scratched her chest. Miss Etta inhaled. "So, little Miss Scamp, if you could talk, would we talk about development or would we talk about other things?" Miss Etta licked her hand and then scrambled off her lap and onto the floor. She'd heard Aspen's car first. Leigh opened the door and was disappointed when she saw someone with Aspen.

"Gosh, it's cold out there," Aspen said. "I have this book I need to give Linda." Aspen went into the living room.

"Nice to see you again," Linda said offering her hand.

"Same here," Leigh said.

"Well, we had a good meeting. Sorry you can't join us."

"I'm sure Aspen will tell me all about it." Leigh looked like a bum in her torn running pants and old sweatshirt. Linda's jeans were crisp and newly ironed. The woman was studying her.

"Here it is," Aspen said handing the book to Linda. "Anyway, I loved it and I think you'll enjoy it also."

"Thanks, I'll see you tomorrow." Linda hung onto Aspen's hand just a beat too long. "Nice seeing you again, Leigh."

"Same here," Leigh said. "Tomorrow?" Leigh said to Aspen after the door was closed.

"A bunch of us are meeting with a staffer from the state. He's responsible for helping your company move through the maze of paperwork. He won't make the final decision, he's like the coordinator. He makes sure all of the paperwork is done from the various agencies."

"I expect Jay and the others are in touch with this person, but we sure as heck know nothing about him at my level." Leigh shook her head.

"In the end it'll be up to the state to rezone the acres Burnt Brush needs for the development. If you can't rezone it, you can't develop it. We formed the Codyville Non-Development Council. That's the group that's going to meet with him."

"Non-development council. I expect that's a first in the state." Leigh smiled.

"Probably." Aspen laughed. "By the way, I'm sorry for the last-minute meeting."

Leigh shrugged. "That's okay. Who's on the committee?"

"Me, Linda, Anne Jean, Skeet, Cassie, two wood harvesting guys, some others," Aspen said hanging up her coat. "We didn't want to overwhelm him with everyone in our group."

"Do we ever get to hug?"

"Of course. It's been a while." She put her arms around Leigh's neck.

"It seems like forever." Leigh kissed her. "I've missed you."

"Me, you. I was hoping for some quiet time alone. I'm beginning to doubt that." Leigh frowned. "Either you're at a meeting or I'm at a meeting. I feel like . . ."

"You're living alone?"

"Well, somewhat." Leigh smiled sheepishly.

"There's nothing I can do right now," Aspen said helplessly. "We're getting organized, and once that's done, maybe there won't be a need for so many meetings."

"I'm not complaining. I just feel we never see each other."

"I worry about that too." Aspen touched her finger to Leigh's lip. "But this is important."

"I know." Leigh sighed. "I promised myself I wouldn't do this."

"Do what?"

"Whine." Leigh held Aspen's hands in hers. "I think we're doing pretty good. We've done a great job of coordinating schedules, and I know I look forward to weekends when we're together. I'm just not prepared for the unexpected, like emergency meetings. That's when I look like Orphan Annie. Plus . . ."

"Plus?"

Leigh looked shamefaced. "Just that Linda gets to see more of you lately than I do."

"But I appreciate you more." Aspen stood on her tiptoes and kissed her. "I'm not happy with the unexpected, but I love you, Leigh Wright, and if we can make this work under the worst of situations, then think about the possibilities for the future. Just trust in that."

"I'll try. Can we go to bed?"

"I need a shower," Aspen said kissing Leigh again.

"I've had mine. I'll warm the bed."

"That's the best offer I've had all night."

CHAPTER TWENTY-TWO

"We've been thinking," Cassie said. They were seated around Anne Jean's table waiting for the others to join them, including the state official. Skeet was outside working on his truck. He'd held up some part when Aspen arrived, called it cussed and stuck his head back under the hood.

"Do I have to brace myself for this one?" Aspen grabbed the edge of the table and grinned.

Anne Jean laughed. "No, just that lately our meetings don't feel like they're going anywhere. Sometimes I feel like we're singing to the choir. We know how our group feels, but do we really know if we have the town's support?" Anne Jean asked. "I was getting my truck fixed last week down to the garage and I overheard several men talking. They were excited about the project. Said it's what we need. They're tired of the hard economic times this town keeps going through."

"Well, we're still getting organized." Aspen rested her chin on her hand. "I just figured most folks in town were on our side, but I guess we don't really know."

"Anne Jean and I have been talking about it, and I don't think we really do know how the majority of townspeople feel, so I suggested we do something dramatic," Cassie said.

"Dramatic how?" Aspen asked.

"I don't know." Cassie ran her hand through her hair. It had yellow streaks in it to match her yellow caftan. Aspen found she was getting used to the rainbow of colors.

"How about a Save the Trees rally? It would generate media interest." Aspen pondered the idea.

"I like it," Cassie said. "We've talked about doing that once we got our ducks in a row, but maybe now is better."

"Maybe," Aspen said. "I wonder if we shouldn't plan something for as early as next week to counter their PR guy's golden promises."

"I'm for it," Anne Jean said getting up. "Sounds like more folks are here."

"Aspen, share your idea with them," Cassie said. Jeremiah Wilkins, a wood cutter, Paul Compton, owner of the convenience store, and Kathy Bangs, a local artist, were there, along with Linda.

"We've been chatting." Aspen looked to Cassie and Anne Jean for support. "And came up with the idea that we need to do something dramatic to get folks' attention. I suggested we hold a rally next week."

"I think that's great. How about a rally right on company land?" Linda joined in.

"Not a bad idea." Aspen grinned.

"We'll get arrested. That's private property," Paul said.

"So, we get arrested." Linda shrugged.

"I've never been arrested," he persisted.

"It's great fun. They march you off to jail and you're bailed within minutes." Kathy smiled. "I was arrested a lot during the Vietnam War protests." She patted Paul's hand. "Don't worry. Just consider it an experience."

"Kathy's right," Linda added. "I've been arrested dozens of times. The trick is to get off, regardless of the charge."

"Regardless of the charge?" Paul squealed.

"Sure. Hey, this is about winning. Winning, I might add, at any cost. The environment deserves that kind of commitment." Linda waved her hand dismissively. "What I can't figure out is why you joined?" Linda said. "Seems to me that you're going to lose customers once it's known you're part of this group."

"I moved here from Boston ten years ago because I wanted to get away from urban life. I really like it here. I just hadn't thought about getting arrested." Paul ignored Linda's tone.

"You don't have to." Aspen gave him a reassuring smile. "You'll be our behind-the-scenes guy, stuff envelopes, that kind of stuff." Paul's face showed relief.

"Well, I don't think they're going to have us arrested," Linda said matter-of-factly. "They'll probably send us a message through the cops that they won't tolerate us doing it again on their land, but they aren't going to do anything. I say we go for it. I love rallies. It stirs people's blood and garners a lot of media attention."

"When should we do this?" Jeremiah asked.

"I was thinking Tuesday or Wednesday night," Aspen said.

"Can we do that?" Kathy asked. "I mean are we prepared to do that?"

"It's a gamble, but I think if we lobby the newspapers and other media hard for stories about the rally, people will turn out," Aspen said.

"Won't we look bad if no one shows up?" Paul asked.

"I can do my part," Linda said. "I can assemble faculty members and students from the college. My niece Melissa called. She wanted to be here tonight but had to work. I've met with her and a bunch of her friends. They're ready to help. I'm sure we can get at least fifty people out there, so the cameras will be happy."

"I think Linda's right," Cassie said enthusiastically. "I've been talking to my belly dance group and they want to help, without the costumes, of course." She chuckled. "I think we need to do something splashy to get the company's attention."

"We agree, it's a good idea," Anne Jean said going to the door. "But now we need to meet this state guy."

"I don't have any classes Tuesday night. Let's hold it then," Linda whispered. "How does that fit with your schedules?" They all nodded in agreement. "Good, how about we meet Sunday? That way we can have a full day to discuss strategy."

"That's fine with me. So let's talk after he leaves," Aspen said. Anne Jean and the state guy stepped into the kitchen. *Ho boy*, she thought, she was going to have to tell Leigh she had yet another meeting.

CHAPTER TWENTY-THREE

Aspen was uncomfortable at the podium. She'd never gotten used to speaking in front of large groups and most often stayed away from them. She pulled her cape tighter around her shoulders. October was coming to an end and the night air felt cold. On Sunday, they'd called several state environmental groups and a couple of their officers had agreed to attend and even speak. They'd also notified the company they planned to hold the rally on their land and had not received a response. The group had argued back and forth hours before the meeting about holding it there without company permission. In the end, the majority agreed they would.

"You look great," Linda said smiling at her.

"Thanks."

"How about coffee at my house after this?"

"Good. Let's invite the others." Aspen looked across at the

crowd that had gathered. She hated speaking in public, but after her crash, her therapist had urged her to do it. Now she was facing all those faces, and she couldn't control the grasshoppers that were bouncing around in her stomach.

"I'll take care of it." Linda smiled.

Aspen checked the microphone on the sound system and looked at the agenda. She would speak first, followed by the executive director of the Sierra Club and the president of the Nature Conservancy.

"Looks like we've got company," Linda whispered. Aspen saw the sheriff's deputy. "I'll go talk to him." A second deputy was on the other side of the crowd and moving toward Linda. *Oh wow*, she thought. Paul was right. The company was going to throw them off their land. Linda talked to the deputies and then shook hands with them. Linda greeted several people as she made her way back to the podium.

"So?" Aspen asked Linda.

"They're here at the company's request to maintain order and nothing else. They have no intention of stopping the rally, nor did the company ask them to."

"Good."

"There's one proviso." Linda scowled. "The company is requesting that their spokesman be allowed to say a few words when we're done."

"Really?"

"I told the cop he'd probably be booed because there's a pretty partisan crowd here, but the company said it was willing to take that chance."

"Stupid," Aspen whispered.

"Anyway, I told them to have at it. I don't expect there's anything they can say that will change peoples' minds. So why don't we get started?"

Aspen fumbled as she clicked on the microphone. Funny, she thought, Linda hadn't asked her if she agreed to the company speaking. "Good evening. I'd like to start by saying thank you for coming tonight. For those who don't know me, I'm Aspen Brown, and I'm opposed to this project. First, I'm going to talk a little bit about the scope of the project for those of you who haven't heard or read about it. Then we're going to hear from two environmental groups who are going to talk about how this type of development has ruined the other half of Maine. I learned a few minutes ago that the company has asked that one of its spokesmen have an opportunity to speak and we've agreed." Aspen stopped as a collective groan flowed through the crowd. "It's okay. We can stay a few extra minutes to hear what they have to say." Aspen talked about the plan and then introduced the people from the Sierra Club and the Nature Conservancy, who talked about other development projects in the state and their impact on the environment.

"As we promised, a company spokesman wishes to address us. I'm not sure . . ." Aspen said, searching the crowd.

"I'm, here," Tom said coming from the side of the audience, Leigh by his side.

"Good evening," Tom said to the group. "I want to thank you for allowing us to speak tonight." Tom nodded to Aspen. "My name's Tom Webster and I'm the hired mouthpiece for the company. I've also been given other names since this project started, but we're not going to use those tonight with all the kids in the audience." There was polite laugher. "This is my colleague, Leigh Wright. A lot of you know her. She's the manager of our Burnt Brush field office. I'm not here to defend the plan. The plan doesn't need defending, but I am going to read a letter from the president of the company."

Tom pulled a piece of paper out of his jacket. "Our president apologizes for not being here tonight and asked me to read this letter. "Good evening," Tom read, "Thank you for letting us speak with you tonight. As you know, we're excited about this project and we're looking forward to the future. We want to share some positive news with you. Right now we are in negotiations with the governor's office to hand over to the town and the state that stand of old trees and the eagle's nest that so many of you have been asking for. The cost will be one dollar." The crowd gasped. "In addition, we are prepared to put fifty thousand dollars into an annuity, and the payment from that will help maintain the parcel once the rezoning has been approved by the state and construction begins." Tom read. "So in closing, I would like to say that we see Codyville Plantation as our partner in this development opportunity, and we look forward to working with all of you in the future. Respectfully, Jay Hollingdale." The press was scrambling to get to the podium, but not to talk to Aspen.

"The bastards are good," Linda hissed in Aspen's ear.

"That they are." The press seemed to engulf Tom and Leigh. Leigh looked like she was going to be ill.

"What happened?" Cassie asked.

"They stole our thunder." Aspen was taken aback.

"Why did you let him speak?"

"I didn't. Linda did, but it doesn't matter. They had a right to. This is their land!" Aspen fumed. "We played right into their hands."

"Can we fix it?" Anne Jean said stepping up next to them.

"We can." Linda glanced at Aspen. "They've won the first skirmish, but not the battle." Linda was angry. "Look, Aspen and I are going to my house. We need to talk. We'll catch up with you guys at our meeting tomorrow night." Cassie and Anne Jean were surprised as Linda pushed Aspen toward her truck. "Hop in. I'll bring you back to your car later," Linda said.

"Sorry I whisked you away like that, but we really do need to talk," Linda said as she drove away from the company's parking lot.

"I forgot, I said I'd talk with some of the reporters after the rally." Aspen was numb. First from the announcement and then their abrupt departure.

"The reporters asked me for a reaction, and I told them that the company's announcement was not unexpected and that we were fine with it, but it didn't change the underlying message, which was we don't want Burnt Brush turning Codyville into downtown Portland."

"When did you say all of that?"

"While they were rushing to talk to the company flack. You were talking with your friends. I just figured that we needed some immediate damage control."

"You're good."

"Not good, just practiced. These companies like to one up you all the time. Eventually they run out of offers. I just didn't expect it from these guys, but I should have guessed. Public relations is public relations whether here or in Boston. The name of the game is who gets the last word, and this time the company bested us, but not next time."

They parked in front of a small bungalow near the edge of town. "Do you own this?"

"I do. I bought it shortly after I moved here."

"It's a nice house. I knew the folks who used to live here."

"Did you? Well, it's just the right size," Linda said holding the kitchen door open. "How about coffee?" she said turning on the pot. There were two cups sitting next to the coffeepot. Linda opened the refrigerator and put a plate of grapes, apples and sliced cheese on the table.

"You were expecting company," Aspen said eyeing the plate.

"Not expecting, hoping," Linda said with a smile. "Please sit down."

"The others could have joined us."

"They could have, but I really wanted time alone so we could talk. Then after what happened tonight, I figured we really needed to talk. Come up with a counter strategy. Get attention back on us. Anyway, let's take this time to brainstorm some countermeasures before we drop them on the group. Is that okay?"

"Sure."

"I know you take your coffee black."

"I do." Aspen laughed. "So are you enjoying being here?" Aspen said while Linda was getting their coffee.

"I am." Linda put a cup in front of Aspen and sat down. "I didn't expect this kind of involvement with the community quite this quickly, but I'm glad that I'm a part of it."

"Your niece seems as committed. I was sorry she couldn't be there tonight."

"She wanted to, even threatened to call in sick, but I told her it wouldn't be a good idea if the news cameras panned the audience and there she stood. I convinced her that there would be lots more rallies."

"Melissa is a good kid. I noticed the young faces in the audience. I was glad to see them there."

"All Melissa's doing. I can't take credit for that. Well, this is nice," Linda said taking a piece of cheese. "We never seem to have time to talk. It always seems like someone is around."

"I'm sorry about that, Linda." Aspen was embarrassed. "I should have invited you for dinner. It would've given you and Leigh a chance to get to know one another."

Linda shrugged. "Anyway, I figured this was as good a time as any to talk." Aspen listened as Linda talked about her ideas for countering the company's offer including media coverage as well as other rallies, only without the company input. All of the things she suggested, Aspen decided, could have been discussed in front of the group.

"I also think we need a contingency plan."

"Contingency plan?"

"In case we don't stop them."

"I don't understand."

"Just that." Linda rested her arms on the table and made a

teepee of her fingers. "Aspen, in the real world, environmentalists sometimes have to be more proactive. Out west, environmentalists pounded spikes in the redwood trees to stop them from being cut. Things like that." Linda's words dangled in the air.

"Violence?"

"No, not violence, *action*."

"Linda you mentioned something about Massachusetts." Aspen contemplated her. "About something happening there. Are you talking about vandalism?"

"I am." Linda sat up straight. "And I'm quite proud of it."

"What happened?"

"It was a project like this. The developers had the backing of the state. We did everything right, went through the hoops, filed things in court to try to stop it. You name it, we did it. They had a lot of money. Anyway, it got down to the wire, public hearings, the whole thing. And then their headquarters mysteriously burned."

Aspen's eyes were wide. "Burned?"

"To the ground."

"I read about that. It was about five years ago."

"Made national news," Linda boasted.

"Did you burn it down?" Aspen could barely say the words.

Linda's face hardened. "Aspen, we won. The developer compromised. Said he didn't want anyone to get hurt."

"Did you burn it down?"

"The police said yes. In the end I was never charged."

"I remember now. Several people were arrested, but I think only one guy went to jail."

"Yeah, he was a good guy. He's out now, still gets involved with causes, God love him."

"Linda, that's not what we're about."

"Maybe not now, but we could be in the future. Aspen, this isn't a classroom exercise. This is the real world. And in the real

256

world, people do whatever to win."

"Linda, I don't know."

"You're shocked. That surprises me."

"Really?"

"Yeah, actually. I've read about your activities."

"You have?"

"Sure. In our library at school. There's a file there on the environment. Your name is throughout it. Newspaper clippings, press releases. I know you've usually used mostly passive protest, but you've had your moments of civil disobedience—sitting down in front of the bulldozer. That kind of stuff."

"True, but not destruction of property. You believe in that?"

"I do, and a lot of people across this country feel the same way."

"I don't know, Linda." Aspen wanted to go home. She glanced at the clock. "I have to get up early for school." Aspen was agitated. "I need a ride back."

"You're upset." Linda put a hand on her arm. Aspen pulled away.

"I am." Aspen had to get out of there.

"Hey, it's okay, but once you get over the shock, Aspen, you're going to agree with me, especially if it looks like we're going to lose this battle." Linda was confident.

"I need to go." Aspen was insistent.

"Aspen, think about what I said. We're in this to win, and winning means at any cost."

"What was that all about?" Leigh demanded as soon as Aspen opened the door.

"That's what I'd like to know. How in the hell did we get from my rally to your company's rally?"

"That's not what I'm talking about. I'm talking about that Linda person. First you were there and then you were gone. For more than an hour I might add."

"We went to her place for coffee."

"Well, even Cassie and Anne Jean were surprised. Anne Jean didn't say much, but Cassie said Linda told her they weren't invited. You've got a few people upset tonight."

"I didn't do anything wrong."

"Who's accusing you?"

"Well, it sure sounds like you are."

"I would just like to know what the hell happened."

"And I'd like to know why your company one-upped us. I really didn't like that. The least you could have done was given me a hint it was coming." Aspen seethed.

Leigh held her hands up. "I didn't know it until late today. If you'd check your damn cell phone you'd find I called you several times. I even called here at the house." Leigh pushed the button on the answering machine. "*Hey, babe, it's important you give me a call before you head for the rally.*" They both listened to Leigh's message.

"I'm sorry," Aspen said. "I was late at school and I just rushed home, fed Miss Etta and then rushed to the restaurant."

"And your cell phone?"

Aspen dug into her pocket. "The battery's dead."

"Give it to me." Aspen dropped the phone in Leigh's hand. She plugged it into the charger.

"Thanks," Aspen said.

"You're welcome. Now can we talk about Linda?"

"There's really nothing to say. I think she's lonely. All she has is her cousin Melissa and family. She mostly talked about herself." Aspen couldn't look Leigh in the eyes.

"No questions about us?"

"Not really." Aspen held her breath. She didn't want Leigh to ask her about Linda's reaction to the company's announcement. She had to think about what Linda had said. The words kept ping ponging off the walls in her mind. Vandalism. Fire. Was

Linda really about that?

"Why doesn't that make me feel better?"

"Well, it should. Look, I'm sorry, but it happened so fast. She suggested coffee, and I said sure not realizing that it would be just the two of us. The next thing I know we're telling Cassie and Anne Jean good-bye. It was a very awkward situation all around."

"Cassie says she's got the hots for you and I should be careful. I've suspected it, but Cassie saying it makes me more uncomfortable."

"Cassie, as you know, has a very overactive imagination. If a man spends more than two minutes talking with her, she figures he has the *hots* for her. It's just Cassie."

"Does she have the *hots* for you?"

"No, and outside of our meetings, I don't plan to see her again." Aspen bit down on her lower lip. She thought about Linda's declaration and she was scared. Linda hadn't said that she'd actually burned the building, but she wasn't condemning the arsonist either. Was Linda a mirror of their future? Would Aspen burn something down just to win? She was petrified by the emotions whirling around inside of her. Should she tell Leigh? She looked at her. No, she couldn't tell Leigh. She couldn't tell anyone.

"I'm sorry." Leigh dropped her head "I honestly had a rush of jealousy when I saw you ride off with that woman. I feel so insecure about this relationship because of my job and everything, I just boiled over. It's not something I do."

"It's okay. I'd have felt the same way," Aspen said taking Leigh into her arms. "Can we just go to bed? I'm really exhausted."

Leigh kissed her on the top of her head. "We can."

Aspen smiled at her. "I love you, problems and all. Trust that, would you, please?"

Leigh kissed her. "And I love you."

CHAPTER TWENTY-FOUR

"I think we should do something for Halloween," Cassie said.
Aspen was still at school when Cassie called. "Like?"

"A small party. You hear from Anne Jean?"

"I did." Anne Jean had called that morning just as Aspen was
getting ready to leave for school, clearly upset by the company's
intrusion into their rally the night before. Anne Jean suggested
they meet Sunday morning for a debriefing. Aspen agreed. She
stopped short of telling Anne Jean about Linda's revelation. She
just didn't know what to do with it. Anne Jean said she'd call the
others and tell them about the meeting.

"She tell you about the meeting?" Cassie asked.

"She did and I'll be there. Anyway, I hope just a small party.
You know how I avoid big social events."

"I know. You feeling all right?"

"Yes, Cassie, I'm fine. I love you, but you worry more about that than a nervous young fella asking a girl out on their first date. I'm fine and things are fine between Leigh and me. So stop worrying." Cassie fretted often about Aspen's depression. "Anyway, how small a party?"

"Just a few of us, here at my house."

Aspen glanced at the calendar. "Halloween is three days away. Can you plan a party in such a short time?"

"I can and I will as long as you and Leigh promise to be there."

"I can't speak for Leigh, but, sure, I'll be there. I expect it'll be just the regular crowd."

"And some folks from our group. You'll know everyone."

"I'll ask Leigh when she gets home."

"Aspen?"

"Yes."

"What was that thing with you and Linda?" Aspen smiled. Unlike Anne Jean, she knew Cassie would ask.

"I don't know. She suggested we have coffee. I thought she meant all of us. Anyway, the next thing I know, that company guy's schmoozing our audience, and after that, I'm in a car headed to Linda's for coffee. It just happened."

"I think she has the hots for you," Cassie said matter-of-factly.

"I understand you told Leigh that." Aspen was annoyed.

"I might have mentioned it. Truth be told, I'm not real crazy about Linda. She has just too much of a take-charge attitude to suit me. We've gotten along pretty good over the years doing our protests without her. She comes in here with all of her big city ways and makes me feel uncomfortable."

If you only knew, Aspen thought glumly. "She's part of the group." Aspen said without enthusiasm. When Linda told her about the vandalism and the fire, she couldn't get past the shock. The next day during a break between classes, she had gone online and reread the news accounts of the incident. She was more determined than ever after reading them that she needed to talk to Linda. Aspen needed her to really understand that *winning at all cost* did not include burning down buildings.

"For now, I just don't trust her," Cassie went on. "What do we really know about her other than she's Melissa's aunt? Anyway, we can deal with her later." Cassie was through with that topic. "So you're on for the party?"

"I am. It'll be a nice diversion." Aspen sighed. "God knows we need one, but nothing big and fancy, Cassie. I don't want to hear you put a notice in the newspaper saying there's a party at your house."

"It's too late. Deadline for putting a notice in has come and gone."

Aspen groaned. "Don't tell me you'd thought about doing that."

"No, but I wanted you to think that I did." Cassie laughed.

Aspen was relieved that Friday had finally arrived. She still had not talked with Linda. She had called and left messages, but Linda had not responded. Cassie had called that morning saying she'd moved the party to the grange. She said she wouldn't have to clean her house and move furniture. Aspen frowned. Cassie had a way of inviting one person and telling them to invite their friends, and soon the numbers grew like black flies at a barbecue.

"Hey, darlin'," Leigh called from downstairs.

"I'm in the bathroom."

Leigh kissed her on the back of the neck. Aspen smiled.

"I'm glad you're home early."

"I told everyone to go home at four o'clock," Leigh said kissing her again on the neck.

"Glad this week's over." Aspen turned and kissed Leigh on the mouth.

"Me too. How about we skip the party and just stay here and

find out what kind of trouble we can get into?"

"I know what kind of trouble we can get into. But I promised Cassie."

"Call her and tell her I fell and broke my leg. No, that won't work because I won't have a broken leg the next time I see her. Tell her vandals broke into the office and wrote Happy Halloween on the wall." Leigh scratched her ear. "No, that won't work. Any break-in would be major town news."

"Welcome to Codyville," Aspen said with a chuckle. "Anyway, Cassie left a message and said she moved the party to the grange." Aspen studied Leigh's reflection in the mirror. She liked the lines of her mouth.

"How big is this party?" Leigh asked.

"I hate to think. She said she didn't have time to clean her house."

"I've been to Cassie's house." Leigh stripped her shirt off. "It doesn't need cleaning."

"I know. So I don't know what to expect. I almost called and cancelled. I hate big parties."

"Why?"

"I don't feel comfortable around a lot of people, never have." Aspen was restless. "Just another one of my funny little quirks."

Leigh put her arms around her. "If you don't want to go, that's fine, but if you do then I'll be right there with you. We do this together."

Aspen sighed. "That's why I didn't cancel. That and the fact that Cassie has her heart set on our being there."

"Oh, my God, look at the cars!" Aspen said as they pulled into the driveway. "I may still change my mind about this." Aspen was quivering inside. She felt anxious.

"We're fine," Leigh said confidently. "Does she know this many people?" She squeezed Aspen's hand reassuringly.

"Cassie knows everybody."

"How'd she get so many people here at such late notice?"

"Who knows?" Aspen said halfheartedly. She pulled next to a green pickup. There was music coming from inside the hall. She groaned when she opened the grange door. The place was packed. There were black and orange crepe paper stringers hanging from the ceiling. A song was playing in the background, something about a creepy purple people eater. Aspen recognized several people from their protest group and waved. Another group dressed as belly dancers were there. Obviously they were part of Cassie's group. Aspen was amazed. Several people had costumes on, not elaborate, but costumes for sure. Several were dressed in sheets with holes poked in for their eyes, looking like very sorry Casper the Ghosts. Others had wrapped strips of cloth around them to look like mummies.

"Don't you just love it?" Cassie said above the noise.

"How'd you do this?" Aspen looked at her, exasperated.

"I don't know. I invited a few people and told them to invite a few more. At last count we had more than one hundred here. If everyone comes, it'll be a lot more. Come on," Cassie said, pulling Leigh and Aspen toward the back of the hall. "We've got tons of food. Everybody brought something. I think people just were in the mood for a party and this happened to be the only one in town. I know you hate big parties," Cassie rushed on. "But, Aspen, you know everyone here. So it's not really like a big party. It's just some of our friends. Well actually, a lot of our friends." Cassie was beaming.

Leigh looked at all the people in the room. "You're amazing, Cassie Jenkins, truly amazing."

"Are Anne Jean and Skeet here?" Aspen asked, still anxious. *Take control*, she told herself. *Take control*.

"They are. Anne Jean dragged Skeet out tonight, although she said he groused that he wasn't going to have any fun. Look at him." Cassie nodded toward the corner of the room. Skeet was talking with the PR guy. They were laughing about something. Anne Jean was talking to some members of their group. She waved to Aspen.

"I don't believe it," Aspen said as she looked at Skeet and Tom.

"Believe it. They've been chatting it up big time," Cassie said. "And they're the two picking out the music. I think they've found they have something in common."

"Why did you invite him?" Leigh looked at Tom.

"I ran into him at the store and asked him what he was doing tonight. He seemed kinda lonely, so I invited him. I didn't expect he'd come, but he was one of the first to arrive. He even helped me finish with the decorating. I introduced him to Skeet, and the two haven't shut up." Cassie was pleased with herself. "Did you know he's divorced?"

"No, I didn't." Leigh had never socialized with Tom. "Will you excuse me?"

"God, she's so gorgeous," Cassie said as Leigh walked toward Skeet and Tom.

"She is and terrific also."

"I wish I could find someone like her . . . not as in a her, but as in a someone." Cassie waved her hand. "You know what I mean."

"Remarkably, I do."

Cassie slipped her arm through Aspen's. "I want you to meet some neat ladies from my dance group. You know most of them. Oh, by the way, I invited Linda and Melissa. They plan to be here. Linda said she's been out of town for the past two days, didn't say what. I figure a conference. Anyway, she said she'd be at the meeting Sunday. She is one strange city slicker, I'll tell ya." Aspen didn't feel she needed to comment. "Anyway, here's the group." Cassie introduced her and then went to greet some new arrivals.

"Hey, Aspen." It was Melissa. Linda was with her. "What a

great party. I've never been to one of Cassie's before," Melissa said, looking around. "She is phenomenal. Look at that, apple bobbing over there, and would you believe they're playing pin the tail on something over there?" Aspen looked to where Melissa was pointing. "I gotta go bob for apples. I haven't done that since grade school. We didn't do it in high school. It just wasn't cool." Melissa rushed off.

"I think I shocked you the other night," Linda said, standing way too close to her.

"You did. Is that what you intended to do?"

"No, I just thought—"

"You drop that on me, and what am I to think?"

"That maybe I was bragging a little to impress you."

"Were you bragging?" Aspen demanded.

"Sure," Linda said shamefacedly.

"Linda . . ." The music was even louder. "I don't know what to think." Aspen was angry.

"Look, we need to talk, but not here," Linda shouted into her ear. "Maybe Sunday, after the meeting." Aspen nodded.

"Can I have your attention please?" Cassie called over the din. "Can I have your attention?" The music and the conversation started to trail off. "First of all, I want to thank all of you for coming. This is a bigger turnout than I even expected. I know most of you know each other, but there are newcomers, so let's not be strangers. I want you all to go around the room right this minute and introduce yourself to someone you've not met before and spend a few minutes talking with them. Then move on to the next person." Cassie's face glowed. "And there's all kinds of food over there, so serve yourself, and as soon as Skeet and Tom quit reminiscing about Halloween music, we'll put on some dance music."

Tom and Skeet were beaming. They had switched to a song that talked about a ghost. Leigh was still helping them. She looked relaxed for the first time in weeks. Leigh glanced up and smiled.

"I see some students over there. I think I'll talk to them. Aspen, let's talk, after the meeting on Sunday, okay?"

Aspen scowled. "We need to."

"You're Aspen Brown," a woman she didn't know said. Linda, her back to Aspen, enthusiastically greeted the students. "I've been wanting to meet you and tell you how much I enjoy what you're doing to save the environment."

"Thank you, and you're?"

"Mary Springer, I just moved here . . ." Aspen listened to what Mary was saying.

"So what do you think?" Cassie said, by her side.

"I think you've outdone yourself." Aspen put her arm around her. "You are one special lady."

"I invited Brit and Harry, but they were on their way to Baltimore for some kind of astrology conference. She was disappointed she couldn't join us."

"Invite them next year."

"Next year, who knows?" Cassie said looking at the group. "If the spirit moves me, next year it may be a Columbus Day party. You know, Aspen," Cassie said raising her voice above the new song that was starting to play, "I think we should celebrate the holidays no one celebrates. It almost seems as though they're lost holidays."

"You're probably right. Next year I think you should plan the biggest Columbus Day party this town's ever seen."

"Really?"

"Absolutely."

"But you hate parties."

"I do, but being here tonight with Leigh felt right."

"You remember that next year when I ask you and you start to grouse at me about inviting the whole town."

Aspen looked at her quizzically. "I do grouse at you, don't I?"

"You do, but it's okay. I know you're trying to keep me from being disappointed or hurt. There's nothing wrong with that."

"There is something wrong with it." Aspen studied Cassie's face. "If I get in the way of your having fun."

"You don't really get in the way. Just sometimes I have to work extra hard to convince you that it's the right thing. I know I've had some pretty harebrained schemes over the years. You'll never forgive me for that tap dancing one. It was crummy that guy caught us, but more unfortunate that he had a big mouth. We should have sued the company. Isn't there some kind of law against invasion of privacy?"

Aspen laughed. "Not when the person is delivering something to your house. Anyway, I'm going to have to watch what I say. I don't have any right to make you feel less enthusiastic about life." Aspen reflected on that aspect of her personality.

"Forget it. I'm sorry I brought it up. Uh oh, there's your friend Linda." Linda was making her way toward them.

"Do me a favor, you go talk to her and I'll find someone else to talk to. Would you do that for me?"

"Sure, I can do that. I can keep her occupied the rest of the night if I have to."

"Just do to her what you do to me. Drag her off to meet a new group and then quietly fade into the background."

"Do I do that?" Cassie was surprised.

"You do that all the time," Aspen said as she waved to Anne Jean and started toward her.

Cassie intercepted Linda, and with just the gentlest of nudges, moved her toward a group of women about Melissa's age. Cassie was talking up a storm, and Linda was pretending to listen. When Cassie introduced Linda to the women, she talked some more and then, like a monk in monastery, quietly faded into the background. When Aspen looked back, the women were talking Linda's ear off.

Aspen rubbed the back of her neck.

"Tired?" Leigh was standing behind her.

"I am."

"I'm ready to go home if you are," Leigh said quietly.

"Fine with me." It was close to midnight, and a lot of the revelers had left. Skeet and Anne Jean had left an hour earlier. Linda and Melissa also had left. "Although I think we should stay and help Cassie clean up since I didn't get here in time to help her set up."

"Okay by me. Let's go see what she has to say."

Cassie was standing to the side of a group, not really listening to the conversation. "Hi guys," she said.

"We want to help you clean up," Aspen said.

"I don't have to clean the mess up tonight because no one's using the hall tomorrow. I figure if we all pitch in Sunday morning before the meeting, we can have it cleaned up lickety-split."

"I'm game," Aspen said.

"It was a great party." Leigh smiled. "One of the best."

"Agreed. You are special," Aspen said. Cassie was beaming.

"I really want you. I have all evening," Leigh said as soon as they entered the kitchen. Leigh was taciturn on the way home.

"Then what's stopping us?" Aspen asked quietly.

"Because I want to say something first." Aspen mentally squared her shoulders, uncertain what the question might be. "Aspen, I have been in love with women before, not a lot by today's young lesbian standards, but I've had my share. I've lived with a few." Leigh took her hands. "But never have I ever felt so linked with anyone like I feel with you, and it's not just the fantastic love making. I like being around you. I look forward to mornings and nights and just having you in the same room.

Maybe it's just me, but I get this inexplicable emotion when I look at you. Tonight watching you at the party—"

Aspen was surprised. "You were watching me?"

"I was." Leigh's eyes were kind. "I see the wonderful vibrancy you send out." Aspen looked down at her hands. "Don't be embarrassed." Leigh tipped her head back and looked in her eyes. "I know you hate big gatherings, but, Aspen, you radiate light and people are attracted to you. You're like that old stand of trees you love so much. You're the balm that soothes the people you're around, and I figured that out tonight and I'm very proud that I figured that out. You make me happy, for want of another word. I can have the worst day at the office and step into this kitchen, and it's not the welcome home kiss or the hug. It's you. You turn turmoil into tranquil just by who you are, and I cherish that. I love you."

"And I adore you," Aspen said caressing Leigh's cheek. "I wish I was as eloquent. I'm the one who teaches English, yet you're the one who adds color to sentences. I love you, Leigh, with a devotion and passion I've never felt before, but more importantly, I like each facet of you. I feel so safe with you."

"I love you so much," Leigh whispered against Aspen's lips, "and I—" It was the telephone. "Who the hell is that at this hour?"

"Your sister maybe?" Aspen said reaching for the telephone. "Hello. Yes, she's here. Who's calling?" Aspen put her hand over the mouthpiece. "The Maine State Police. They want to talk to you."

"Hello?" Leigh listened. "I can be there in about five minutes." Leigh's face was drained of color.

"What happened?"

"The woods behind the office are on fire."

"Oh! No!"

"It sounds bad, Aspen, really bad. I've got to call Jeff and Jay." Leigh dialed the telephone and then hung up. "I'll call them on my cell phone."

"Should I go with you?"

"I think it best you stay here." Leigh was distracted. "Where the hell did I put my jacket? Ah, the hell with it," she said as she closed the door behind her. Aspen heard Leigh's tires as they screeched out of the driveway.

"Come on, Miss Etta," she said putting on her jacket. "We're going to see what happened." Aspen grabbed the telephone on the first ring. "She's already on her way." It was Anne Jean. "Sorry, I thought it was the cops calling back. I'll wait right here," she said. "Come, Miss Etta," she said after she hung up. "Anne Jean and Skeet are coming to get us." Aspen looked out the window. There was a huge orange glow in the distance.

CHAPTER TWENTY-FIVE

Leigh stood next to the trooper. The rotating blue and red strobe lights from the town's lone fire truck and the fire trucks from neighboring communities made the night sky look like a dance hall. Firefighters in bunker gear were dragging hoses that looked like slow moving pythons toward the back of the office, the flames shooting high above the trees. The acrid smell of smoke filled her nostrils. The smoke and flames were blowing toward Anne Jean's house and the town. The area around the office had been cordoned off.

"How bad is it?"

"It seems to be concentrated in just that one section." The trooper nodded toward an area where only days earlier the protest rally had been held. "I think it was set to get us here and it got out of hand."

"Why would someone do that?"

"So we'd find this." He turned his flashlight on the front of the office. Leigh's eyes followed the light. Someone had spray painted in huge yellow letters *Go Home* all over the front of the building. But it was the deer that made her stomach pitch. They had left a disemboweled deer in front of the steps, its blood splattered across the porch. The blood looked shiny red in the light. "Looks like it didn't happen all that long ago, because the blood is still sticky," the trooper said.

"What's that?" Leigh said pointing at the door. The flashlight had skipped past it.

"The guts of a dead animal. I can't get close enough to see what kind of animal it might have been because I don't want to disturb any of the evidence, but I've called in the Maine Warden Service. I've also called for backup. It'll take about two hours for the detective to get here. He's in Bangor," the trooper said flashing the light on the door handle. "But right now, all I care about is that fire. We don't get that out, the evidence will be burned up." Firefighters ran past them. Two-way radios crackled as people were directed either to the right or the left of the fire. "Come on. Let's stay out of their way."

"We've got it surrounded and they're knocking it down now," the town's fire chief said as he walked toward them. Black soot covered his face. His bunker gear was wet and his fire helmet was sitting lopsided on his head. "We're lucky. Looks like whoever started it lit just one area. If there'd been a harder wind, we could have lost the town."

"How bad is it?" Leigh nodded toward the woods. She knew the fire chief from the diner.

"You got a mess back there, Leigh. Looks like you've lost maybe twenty acres." The chief's voice was grim. "We'll have spotters here all night. I want to make sure the fire hasn't gone underground. It gets in the roots and can burn for days and then start up again."

"Anything I can do, Chief, just let me know. Our company

president is on the way. I expect he'd like to speak with you at some point."

"I'll be around a long while."

"Is it safe for me to take her around back?" the trooper asked.

"Sure, go ahead." He looked straight at her.

"Did they try to break in?" Leigh asked as she followed the trooper.

"I didn't see any evidence of a break-in, but there's something around here I want you to see." He flashed the light under the windows. The same yellow spray paint had been used on the back, only this time it said, *Cunt, go home.* "I've read about what's going on with the development project. Have you been threatened by anyone?"

"No." Leigh was surprised. "I know that everyone's not happy with what the company plans to do, but, no, I've not been threatened."

"Well, I'd say that message was for you." Leigh stared at it. "I know you want to check inside, but until we process this, I can't let you." Another officer walked over and whispered something to him. "Jake here," the trooper said, nodding to the officer, "checked your house. They didn't do anything there, so if you want to go home, I'll let you know what we find when I'm done here."

"I'd rather stay. I've called my immediate supervisor and the president of the company. They're both on their way. My supervisor lives near Bangor. The president lives near our headquarters in Farmington, so it'll take a couple of hours for him to get here. I'd prefer to wait."

"Suit yourself," the trooper said, "but this is going to take hours."

The trooper swung his flashlight from the door to the doe. He motioned for one of the other officers to join him and then pointed at the doe and then at the door. Leigh looked at the deer, its red tongue hanging out the side of her mouth, one brown eye staring at her. She shivered. *Funny*, she thought, *I'm not cold.* The shiver came from disgust and anger. She'd seen vandalism before on job sites, a fired worker dumping sugar in the gas tank of a piece of wood-harvesting equipment, or kids spray painting equipment left behind, but never anything like this. She saw the large splashes of paint next to the messages.

"Officer?" she said to the trooper as he walked by. "How'd that happen?" She nodded toward the huge splashes.

He flashed his light on the ground. "They apparently filled glass jars with paint and threw them against the building. You can see glass here, there." His flashlight pointed at places on the ground. The trooper nodded toward some of the firefighters. "It looks like they're finishing up back there," the trooper said. "I just need to talk to them."

Some of the firefighters were rolling up their hoses. Leigh looked over to where a huge crowd of people had gathered and were being held back by police.

"You okay?" Leigh jumped at Aspen's voice.

"How'd you get here?"

"I hitched a ride with Anne Jean and Skeet. We came in the back woods road. I figured the cops would have the main driveway closed off. How bad is it?"

"Bad. Looks like they trashed the place and then set fire out back to get everyone's attention. We've lost twenty acres, maybe more. It could be worse."

"I saw the glow from the house. Skeet didn't want to drive in on the back road, but I insisted."

"You should have listened to Skeet. That fire could have turned and gone in any direction."

"We were fine."

"Where are they?"

"Over there." Leigh followed Aspen's nod toward some trees

to the side of the building. "They figured they'd stay out of sight."

"Miss, you can't be here," the young trooper said returning to Leigh's side.

"It's okay, officer. She's with me."

"Well, just stay back," the trooper said as he again went around to the back of the building.

"I will," Aspen said quietly. "Oh my God." Aspen gasped as her eyes settled on the doe.

"It's bad," Leigh said grimly.

"Who would do something like this?"

"Obviously people who don't like us." There was contempt in Leigh's voice.

"This is beyond dislike," Aspen said. "This isn't just vandalism, this is criminal." Aspen looked from the deer to the porch. "This is a really sick person."

"Maybe more than one person," Leigh said. "All four sides have been pelted with paint, and they had time to set the fire."

"You don't think—"

"I haven't thought." Leigh was angry again. She willed herself not to be angry at Aspen.

Aspen touched Leigh's arm and she jerked away. "Leigh, my group wouldn't do something like this."

"I know, but I'm just angry right now. Can we leave it at that?"

"Angry at me?"

"Just angry." Leigh took a deep breath. "Angry at the people who did this. I understand protest, but this is different. This isn't protest. This is a vile attack. Protest I respect. This I don't respect."

"Nor do I, Leigh."

"I'll tell you, this is more than I bargained for," Leigh said harshly.

"Could I ask the two of you to step back?" the young trooper said. "We need to take pictures, and I'm going to need a statement from you," he said to Leigh.

"A statement from me?" Leigh was surprised. "I know only what I see."

"No, about when you were last here, that kind of stuff," the trooper said pulling a notebook and pen from his pocket.

"I locked up around four o'clock on Friday. The only people here were my secretary, myself and our two foresters." She gave the trooper their names. She answered questions about who'd stopped by on Friday and if she'd noticed anyone hanging around. She also talked about the development project and the rally on Tuesday night.

"So was the rally contentious?" the trooper asked.

"Not at all," Leigh answered. "Actually, I thought it went rather well. My company offered some concessions that *some people* seemed to like."

"What kinds of concessions?"

"They plan to give a historic stand of trees that's next to the project to the town, along with fifty thousand dollars to maintain it."

"Not a bad offer," the trooper said.

"I guess it depends on which side you're on," Leigh said grimly. "Those who favor the project think it's a generous offer. Those who don't won't consider any offer short of our not doing the project."

"I heard about the layoff."

Leigh nodded.

"What happened to those folks?"

"Most were hired. A couple, as I understand it, are still looking for jobs."

"Do you have their names?" the trooper said, writing.

Leigh gave him their names. "I'm sure they didn't have anything to do with this," she added hastily.

"Maybe not, but I still need to talk to them. I also need to know where you went after you locked up."

"To a Halloween party here in town."

"The fire chief mentioned that. It was at the grange?"

"It was, and I'd say more than half the town was there. Which leads me to believe that this was done by someone out of town."

"Too early to tell." The trooper continued to write. "About what time did you leave?"

"Oh wow." Leigh inhaled. "I think around midnight. I'm not really sure."

"And where'd you go after that?"

"Am I a suspect here, officer?"

"Not at all, but we have to ask the question."

"Actually, I went to Ms. Brown's house," Leigh said, nodding at Aspen who had been listening. "We were talking when I received your telephone call. By the way, how'd you know to call me there?"

"When I got the report, I called your house first, and when I didn't get an answer, on a hunch I called Ms. Brown's house. I patrol this area, eat in the diner and hear stuff." The trooper looked away.

"Then you know that Ms. Brown and I live together," Leigh said evenly.

"I'd heard that. I didn't realize that you're Ms. Brown." His expression hardened.

"Then you know Ms. Brown organized the rally."

"I'd heard. I do have questions for you," the trooper said turning a page in his notebook.

Leigh listened as the officer asked Aspen many of the same questions, but listened more intently as she answered questions about her group and some of the people in it. "Anyone given to talking about doing more than just giving speeches?" he asked.

"Not at all, officer." *What about Linda?* Aspen thought. *It couldn't be. Linda had admitted she'd said those things to impress her.*

"Anyone new to your group?"

She began reluctantly. "A few people who've moved to town."

"Such as."

"Some from the college that've joined our group, some others. But mostly it's the same old protestors that've been around here for years. Me, Anne Jean Jones and her husband Skeet, Cassie Jenkins." Aspen also named off several more people in town, including two business owners.

"I'm surprised about those two business owners," Leigh said. The trooper was back looking at the front of the office.

"Why?"

"Because they'd make money off this development."

"That's something I've never understood. Men and women race to build fortunes, yet in the end, all anyone really needs is enough money to make them comfortable."

"I guess the rich have a different understanding of comfortable," Leigh said distractedly. "But then I'm not surprised you don't get it, Aspen." Leigh's tone was bitter.

"Leigh, I'm—"

"There's Tom." He was talking to two of the officers and pointing at her. "I guess I'd better tell them to let him in. He's going to have to try to put a positive spin on this."

"Leigh, we need to talk."

"Not now!" Leigh shook her head at how harshly the words had come out. "Look." She inhaled deeply. "I've got a lot to deal with right now. Why don't you wait over there with Skeet and Anne Jean?"

"Okay," Aspen said reluctantly.

"You can let him in." She turned her back on Aspen. "He's with the company." Tom ducked under the yellow tape.

"What the hell happened? I got a call from Jay. He's on his way."

"We've been vandalized and someone set fire out back where the rally was held."

"Do you think that environmental group did this?"

279

Aspen, who had walked away, turned and looked at Leigh. There was fear in her eyes.

"I . . ." Leigh took a deep breath and held it. She didn't know what she believed.

"How bad is it?" Tom wasn't interested in a response.

"Bad," Leigh said as they walked toward the front of the building. "I don't know what kind of positive spin you can put on this one," she said contemptuously. She breathed deeply. She was angry, and that anger was now running away with her emotions. She knew she had to let go of the anger, but each time she seemed to have it under control, she would look at the doe and the fury would come crashing down on her. Funny, she thought, holding onto rage made her feel better.

"Not positive, sympathetic," Tom answered without missing a beat. "Holy crap. Look at that." He surveyed the building. The cops had erected strobe lights, and the building looked like a scene out of a horror movie. "Was that alive?" He nodded toward the deer.

"At one time."

"What's that hanging from the front door?"

"Animal guts. The officers haven't identified it yet. They're waiting for someone from the Maine Warden Service to get here." Leigh looked behind Tom. "Looks like he's here and so is Jeff." Jeff was motioning to her. She waved for the officer to let him in.

"You okay?" Jeff asked.

"Yeah, I'm over the initial shock. Come on. I'll show you the mess."

"The cop said we've lost some acreage?" Jeff said following her.

"Out back. Twenty acres. Maybe more. It's where the rally was held. The fire chief said he's going to leave some men behind. Make sure it doesn't flare up."

"Good."

280

Jeff surveyed the building. "You said there's something out back?" Jeff asked.

"It's pretty bad." Leigh didn't know if she had the energy to walk back there again.

"Would you prefer we go back there alone?" Jeff asked.

"No, I'm fine." Leigh rubbed the back of her neck. "Come on."

CHAPTER TWENTY-SIX

The group was unusually quiet. Kathy from the art gallery and others were helping Cassie take down the decorations. Others were quietly talking. Linda was in the corner reading about the vandalism with Melissa hanging over her shoulder also reading. The newspaper had a spectacular picture of the fire on its front page.

Aspen stared at Linda. Linda did not look her way. *She said those things to impress you. She said those things to impress you,* Aspen repeated over and over until her head ached. Linda did not kill the deer. Linda did not set the fire. *You should have told the trooper,* another side of her conscience argued. *No, no, no. Linda loves the environment. She would never trash it to make a statement.* Aspen rubbed her eyes. She was tired. *She told you she was just kidding,* she repeated. She thought back to the night before. Linda couldn't have done it. She and Melissa had arrived at the party soon after she and Leigh and had remained there almost as long, she rationalized. *Linda is not the villain.* She's arrogant and portentous, but she's not a killer. They had to talk. Aspen sighed. She had to summon the energy to find out what Linda's truth was. But now, looking at her group, all she could summon was sadness. The numbness that had enveloped her the night before as she watched the fire burn her trees wouldn't go away. She had gone back to her house after Leigh had turned away from her, and she had wept for the dead deer and the blackened trees. She'd wept at the destruction and because Leigh had turned away from her. She wept because she was angry at Linda. She wept at Tom's question and Leigh's silent response. If Tom thought they had set the fire and killed the animals, then others in town did, too. Is that what Leigh believed?

The question hung out there like towels on a clothesline. *Stop it*, she screamed at her mind. *Stop it!* She wanted to go home, close her eyes and sleep. She looked at the group. Couldn't they see that sadness was all around her and if they didn't get away, it would swallow them, too?

"I think we need to get started," Cassie whispered to her. Her whisper echoed in her brain.

Dully, Aspen turned to the group. "We—"

"Did you catch what the governor said?" Linda asked no one in particular. She read out loud, "'The governor joined with environmental leaders from across the state in expressing his outrage at the vile act. He called for a return to civility.' Like he has a clue," Linda said sarcastically. "'He called them eco-terrorists and said his various department heads were organizing an emergency meeting to be held the first of the year.' How convenient. The election will be over. If it's so important, he'd hold it before the election," she scoffed. "I wonder if we'll be invited?"

"Well, the election is next week, so his staff needs time to plan something like that. Besides, the polls say he's going to win, so he probably figures what's the rush. I expect once it's planned, we'll be invited," Cassie said.

"I bet we will have to demand an invitation," Linda added. "He's a jerk and he should have his ass kicked out of office."

"At least he's not anti-abortion like that Republican guy," Cassie said. Linda gave her a dirty look. "Hey, I'm not happy with all his decisions, and I plan to hold my nose and vote for him, but there is no other choice."

"Whatever. I bet we still will have to beg to be invited, and I think—"

"If everyone's ready, why don't we gather around?" Aspen spoke over her. "We all know what happened last night," she began. Aspen then related what she had seen and about being questioned by the trooper. She also told them the police planned to question them.

"You're kidding," Paul Compton said.

"It's not unusual, Paul," Aspen said impassively.

"Why?"

"Because they think we did it." Linda was flippant. "As they say on television, we're the *prime suspects*. Other than the owners, we're the first people they're going to want to talk to."

"Well, we wouldn't do something like that," he insisted. "Man, I didn't expect this kind of stuff when I joined." He shifted uncomfortably in his chair.

"Hey, this is what it's about," Linda shot back.

"Not about destroying property," he responded.

"If it gets the point across, it's good." Linda glared at him.

"So you approve of something like this?" Anne Jean demanded.

"Why not?" Linda shrugged. "It's a tactic. Now the company is paying attention and so is the public."

"Would you do something like that?" Cassie was suspicious.

"I wouldn't!" Linda glanced at Aspen. "But I've known people who have," Linda said looking around the room. "Not here, but it happens."

"Like I said, I didn't bargain for something like this." Paul was scared.

"Look, Paul." Linda's voice was calm, but there was an underlying edge to her words. "If you want to drop out, do it. Better now than later when it could get even nastier."

"Nastier?" Cassie said.

"It could," Linda said.

"I agree with Paul. I didn't sign on for *nastier* either." Cassie's eyes were defiant.

"Hold on, folks. That's not what we're about." Aspen raised her hand to stop the onslaught of words. Her arm felt heavy. *Would Linda do this?* Her mind would not let go of the words. "I don't know who did this." She glanced cautiously at Linda. "And I have to believe no one in this group was involved." She faltered. "But the police have to ask. We've made it clear that we're opposed to this, and we have to make it clear we don't support this type of aggression. That fire could have destroyed more than trees."

"That's right," Cassie joined in. "I heard one of the firefighters say had it happened in August, Anne Jean would have lost her house. Hell, all of Codyville Plantation would have been destroyed. A few more acres and it would have engulfed the eagle's nest. It could have destroyed what we're trying to save. We can get our point across without destroying property." Cassie glared at Linda.

"It happens and I think we need to face it. I didn't do it," Linda said defensively. "But I don't condemn the people who did. Hey, this could have been a Halloween prank, or it could have been a message."

"It was a message," Aspen said quietly. The morning paper didn't say anything other than some messages had been spray painted on the building. "It was clearly directed at the company."

"You were there?" Linda said to Aspen.

"I was." Aspen was drained. She just wanted to go home and stop thinking.

"What did the message say?" Linda asked.

"The trooper asked me not to talk about anything I saw. Said it could compromise the investigation. I told him I wouldn't."

"I agree not talk about it with others, but you can tell us," Linda insisted.

"I can't."

"You won't." Linda stared at her.

"Choose whatever word you like, but I gave my word and that's it," Aspen said listlessly. There was no fight left in her. She turned away from Linda. Anne Jean was staring at her, concern in her eyes. "Look, I told Sandy I would give her our comments after today's meeting for the article she's writing, and I think we should focus less on cops coming to talk to us and more on what our position is with regard to what happened last night—"

"Ah, Aspen . . ." Paul cleared his throat. "If you don't mind, I'd prefer to let this all simmer down," he said putting on his jacket. "Maybe I could get involved later."

"It's okay. We're going to need lots of help later," Aspen added after a moment. The room was quiet as the convenience store owner left.

"Well, I think we need a show of hands as to who's in this for the long haul," Linda said standing next to Aspen. "No one said this was going to be a walk in the park, and I think we need to know who's with us and who's not. Now, not later. So I'd like to see a show of hands."

"Not so fast," Cassie said. "I want to talk first about what our position is with regard to last night and then if you need that *show of hands*," she mimicked, "you'll get it."

"Fine by me." Linda shrugged. "I think we want people to know that we didn't do it, but we don't condemn the people who did." Linda looked intently at the group. "There's all kinds of terrorism in the name of *good* causes, and some of it can get pretty ugly. I don't want people to think that last night wasn't important."

"Important how?" Anne Jean asked.

"It made a statement. People here realize we're serious and we don't want development. Look, folks, in one night those vandals or preservationists, whatever you want to call them, got more media attention than we'll get no matter how many rallies we hold, and speaking of rallies, I'm still miffed the company was able to put it over us."

"They won round one. So what?" Cassie said.

"They made public relations points. Look, folks, that's what this is about."

"I thought it was about right and wrong and preserving land," Kathy interjected.

"It is, but it's more than that. It's about winning."

Linda's words punctured Aspen's inner voice. Hadn't she also said that? But at what price was Linda willing to win? *Stop thinking about that*, she ordered her brain. At what price was Aspen willing to win?

"So what do you think?" Cassie asked.

Cassie had directed her question to Aspen. "Sorry." Aspen felt like her brain was in a fog bank. "I think this is about winning, but not like that. I think Linda's right. The vandals got media attention, but how does that play with people here? I don't think they're interested in winning by destroying property. I really don't."

"So who did this?" Jeremy asked.

"I don't know. I told the police last night it wasn't anyone in our group." Aspen couldn't look at Linda.

"Did they believe you?" Anne Jean asked.

"I don't know." Aspen thought back to the night before and the trooper whose face remained impassive as he questioned her about the group. "Anyway." She exhaled heavily. "Getting back to the issue at hand, I think we need to put together a statement outlining our position and condemning this senseless act." She wanted to go home. She wanted to sleep. "We've got to give a statement to the press."

"I agree we need a statement," Linda said, hands on hips. "And I think we talk about our position, but I don't think we condemn anyone. We should say something like this was unfortunate, but suggest there are people who believe in winning at any cost."

"We're not into vandalism," Cassie said. "That's not what we're about."

"Someone did us a favor last night," Linda said. "They got the media to sit up and take notice, and now they want to talk to us. They want to print what *we* think. We went from virtual obscurity, to public celebrity in one night. I got a call this morning from a friend of mine in Portland. She said it was all over the TV and radio stations there. That's coverage we couldn't have paid for. Last night was our ticket to the state. People know we have a major issue here."

"I agree with my aunt. I think we write out our position, hand out a press release condemning the vandalism and fire, but not the people who did it and move forward with what we said we were going to do," Melissa said. Aspen stared at her. Was this the same woman who had stumbled over her name just months before? Linda was beaming at her niece.

"Sorry, Melissa, I don't buy it," Anne Jean said. "I think we condemn the vandals. Otherwise, I don't think you're going to get a consensus from this group." The group murmured in agreement.

"My niece is right. I think we need to listen to our young people." Linda's voice was ice crystals. "Maybe, just maybe, this is the spark we need to make this company pack up their bags and go home. Our passive protest hasn't worked."

"We've just started," Cassie objected.

"And what did it get us?" Linda shot back. "The company

danced on our heads at the rally. Made us look like fools."

"Hang on, folks. There's no sense us going at each other," Aspen said trying to hold on to the meeting.

"There is if it means we finally take a stand." Linda persisted.

"I think we have visitors." Cassie nodded at the door.

The trooper Aspen had given a statement to the night before was there with two other officers. "Ms. Brown, I'm Trooper Smith. We met last night, or rather early this morning."

"I remember." Aspen did not smile.

"We thought since we're still in town, this would be a good time to take some statements. We heard about your meeting at the diner." Aspen wondered how long they'd been listening. She nodded in agreement. She wasn't surprised people had told police where they were meeting. She wondered what else they'd told them.

"Do we have a choice?" Linda asked.

"You do. You can consult your attorney, have one with you if you like." The trooper stared at Linda.

"It's fine."

"Do you need to talk to me again?" Aspen asked.

"No, not at all."

"We've been trying to put together a statement. We've yet to succeed." Aspen was tired of the arguing. Funny, she thought, she was actually relieved the police had arrived. The group was in disarray and she wanted to go home. Linda's words still burned in her brain.

"Aspen's right," Linda added brusquely. "Our *need* right now is to come up with a statement to give to the press. Can't this wait?"

"Are you with the college?" the trooper asked.

"I am. How'd you know?"

"Just heard things around town. Anyway, right now I have some questions for you, so you'd better figure out some other way to get your statement to the press." The trooper stared at her.

"Fine." Linda shrugged.

"Look, I'll call Sandy and say we condemn the act." Aspen glanced at Linda. "Tell her we'll have more to say later." Aspen heard the mumble of assent. "Is that all right with you, officer?"

"That's fine," the officer said. "We'd like to speak with the rest of you individually. I want to apologize ahead of time because it's going to take some time, but we'll finish as quickly as we can." Linda was clearly furious.

CHAPTER TWENTY-SEVEN

"You okay?" Anne Jean asked.

"I am," Aspen said, seated in Anne Jean's kitchen. After she'd left the group she'd gone home, called Sandy and given her a brief statement. Leigh was not there when she'd returned, and there were no messages. She was exhausted, yet restless. Aspen kept telling herself that it was her mind that was creating the walls that seemed to be closing in around her, but the panic of being closed in and buried was real. All day she'd felt scared and agitated and afraid to be alone, and the conflict at the meeting had only added to her sadness. So she'd gathered up Miss Etta and driven to Leigh's house, but she wasn't there. She'd driven to her office. Leigh's truck was there along with others. There were large white vans, and people were busy scrubbing away the memories of the night before. She wanted to go in but stopped. They'd all look at her and know her group was responsible for setting the fire. There would be accusations. She drove past the driveway. She had to flee. She was all alone, and for the first time in years, that prison of gloom she'd felt after her sister had died was again circling around her. She had to talk with someone. She drove to Anne Jean's.

"Aspen, that's not quite true, is it?"

She hesitated. "I had one of those gloomy attacks I'm okay now." Aspen could barely say the words.

"Are you really okay?" Anne Jean's eyes were on her. "The depression?"

"No, it was just a momentary thing. I'm fine. How'd things go with the cops?" She needed to focus on something else.

"Fine, I guess. Linda was downright contemptuous at first, but by the time the two cops got done questioning her, she was as docile as a lamb full up on mother's milk."

"Two cops?" *Should she tell Anne Jean about Linda?*

"After you left, the cops divided us into groups, kept her waiting until the end. Then two of them took her off to one corner and questioned her. I had to stick around because Cassie had to leave and I had to lock up. Anyway, when they were done, she'd lost a lot of her spunk. I can't figure out what's with her. I overheard her talking to the cops. They were clearly asking her if she was involved, wanted to know where she'd been before the fire. She denied she had anything to do with it, said she'd been at the party. Even got me to vouch for her." Anne Jean grumbled.

Aspen looked away. Anne Jean went on. "The way she was talking during the meeting worried me. It was so aggressive. I think she knows more than what she's letting on. At first I thought she was trying to impress us like she was this sophisticated protestor, but I've been thinking about it. I'm not saying she did anything, but I'm saying that her militancy may have influenced others. I'm really sorry she joined our group, and what's more, I find I really don't like her."

Aspen rubbed her hands together, back and forth, back and

forth. *She had to tell Anne Jean.*

"You know, Aspen," Anne Jean continued, "if it came out that she was involved or was stirring folks up, the proponents would paint us with that same brush like we're all ecoterrorists. I can tell you right now, we'd lose half our group. You saw the look on their faces when Paul walked out. I think a lot of them wanted to quit too, and if this happens again, we're going to lose them. Skeet and I talked about that stuff. Last night's done us in. We've lost a lot of our fight."

Oh, God, Aspen thought. She had to find Linda. They had to talk, and she had to find out the truth. Things *were* happening too fast. She was no longer in control. She was strangling on her fear.

"Are you all right? You look tired. Are things okay with you and Leigh?"

Aspen got up and restlessly walked around the kitchen. "She's right over there." Aspen pointed aimlessly toward the headquarter office. "They're meeting right now. I expect talking about us."

"I expect, but there's nothing we can do about it. Have you two talked?"

"I tried to talk to her at the fire. Tell her we weren't involved. She wouldn't even look me in the eyes. When she got home, she wouldn't talk to me. Last night our bed felt as big as a football field. This morning she got up and went to work. I don't know, Anne Jean, I have things to tell her, but I open my mouth and the words don't come out."

"She's struggling," Anne Jean said.

"Well, so am I." Aspen sat down.

"I know," Anne Jean said gently. "But Leigh has her own monsters right now, Aspen. Yes, she should talk to you, but maybe she's scared. If half the town believes we were the vandals, then what's Leigh to think? She loves you but doesn't really know what our group represents, how far we'd go to protect the environment. Deep down she knows you couldn't do something like this, but she hasn't got to that deep down part yet. Right now she's still dealing with the anger of the attack."

"Well, she should ask me!"

"Why so harsh?" Anne Jean was concerned. "I'm sure Leigh is confused right now. Since the announcement, she's been reeling between staying with the company and leaving. Between her love of what she does and her love of you. That attack last night was not just against the company. It was personal, and she's angry." Anne Jean shifted in her chair. "Aspen, you need to think about . . . ."

Aspen closed her eyes. An absolute sense of hopelessness had engulfed her. "What?"

"Compromise."

Aspen was annoyed. She couldn't look at her friend. "I knew you were going to say that."

"We have to compromise."

Was everyone turning against her? "God, not you too." Aspen rubbed her forehead.

"You can't accept the word compromise, can you?" Anne Jean stared at her.

"Why should I have to? It's just too final."

"I'm going to say something you're not going to like, but I need to say it. Aspen, for you compromise has always been like drinking poison."

"Ouch, that hurts." Anne Jean's words had cut deep. "I don't think that's true," Aspen feebly protested. "I've *grown* a whole lot in my life. That's how I see it. But Anne Jean, there's *growth* I've later regretted." She scratched at her legs with her nails. She was restless again. *Breathe deeply*, she told herself. Isn't that what her counselor told her to do? Breathe deeply. She stretched out her fingers and willed them to stop compulsively scratching at her pant legs.

"Aspen, although you may say the words—growth, compromise, whatever—when it comes to this issue, I don't think that compromise is an option, and that's deadly dangerous for you and Leigh. Aspen, I love you like a daughter, but when it comes to those trees, compromise is something you've always had difficulty accepting." When Aspen didn't respond, Anne Jean went on. "And I guess the question you have to answer is, what's more important? Saving a few trees, or Leigh?"

"I don't see that I have to choose."

"Ah, but you do, because last night someone made it clear that they're playing way more seriously than we are. What if that fire hadn't been stopped? Did you see the direction it was headed in?"

"Toward your house and the town." *Did Linda do this?* She repeated the mantra. She had to find Linda. Talk to her. If she did this, Aspen had to tell the police. *No, Linda didn't do this. She's an environmentalist. Environmentalists don't kill,* the other side of her brain repeated.

"Aspen, people could have been killed."

"But they weren't."

"What about next time?"

"Why does there have to be a next time?" Why was Anne Jean tormenting her?

"Aspen." Anne Jean touched Aspen's hands. "Skeet and I can't do this. We can't stand by and watch our house burn. We don't want to see anymore dead animals, dead trees. We have to compromise."

Aspen sat back. Even her friends were abandoning her. First Leigh and now Anne Jean and Skeet.

"Are you all right?"

"Yes." She couldn't tell Anne Jean about the tightness in her throat that refused to go away no matter how many times she swallowed. She had convinced herself it was from the tension of the night before, not the depression of the past. The old evil spirits that had gotten her in trouble before weren't back, because she was finally in control of her life. She inhaled deeply. Well, she didn't need them. "You have to compromise, not me." A steely calm had settled over her. "I've battled the mills, the state, everyone to make certain that what we have remains." She pulled her hand away from Anne Jean's soft grasp. She had to summon the energy to fight back. "I did that because I really believe trees deserve an advocate just like everyone else. We have advocates for the old, for babies, you name it, but few advocates for the environment. Look what we're doing to it right now. Look at all the compromises our federal government has made."

"It has and it's wrong, Aspen, but the fire last night made me realize that we might not win, because someone is playing for keeps. Aspen, we could lose more than just some trees. We could lose our integrity as a group. I expect the company's willing to give us concessions. They already did with the eagles' nest. Let's get together as a group, figure out what we want and put our demands on the table. Let's see what we get. Skeet and I aren't alone in this. I've had a few calls from some of the others, and they feel the same way."

"So I have to do it alone?" She stood up.

"No, Aspen. Hear me out. Skeet and I don't want to see another disemboweled deer or animal guts hanging from a door-knob."

Aspen rubbed the back of her neck. Her muscles were as taut as steel guide wires attached to a tower. *Why was Anne Jean making this so difficult?* She had to find Linda. Linda would tell her she had nothing to do with this and they'd talk to the group and then they'd all go on like before. Aspen rubbed her hand over her eyes.

Anne Jean went on. "I listened to Linda today and she scared me. Maybe Linda is just a lot of hot air, but maybe what she's been saying has encouraged other folks to act. I just don't know."

"I'll talk to Linda," Aspen said dully. "I can't believe she'd do something like that." She swallowed. Her emotions now were churning around inside her like an angry cyclone and Aspen feared they *now* were in charge.

"Oh, Aspen." There was sadness in Anne Jean's eyes. "You haven't heard me. You haven't heard a word I've said. This isn't about Linda. This is about a fight we are never going to win."

There was a buzz starting in her head again. It had been there the night before. She was agitated and restless. "I'm surprised at you," Aspen said looking at her friend critically. A headache was just at the edges, behind her eyes. It wasn't there a few minutes ago. Her throat felt tight. Her stomach was rocking back and forth. *Don't throw up*, she commanded her stomach. She knew these feelings. It was her emotional whirlpool. They had been there in the past and they were back and starting to suck her in alive. Once they almost did. She had to escape. She had to race away from those feelings. She'd had enough. Her friend didn't understand. She couldn't stay there any longer. "I thought you would understand." Sensing the tension, Miss Etta was standing looking from Anne Jean to Aspen. "I gotta go," she said getting up.

"Please don't," Anne Jean said reaching for Aspen's hand. "Let's talk this out."

She wrenched her hand away. "I can't, Anne Jean. I really can't. I feel like I need fresh air."

"Aspen, don't leave now. I've seen you like this before. Stay here." Anne Jean was alarmed. "Let's figure this out together. I didn't mean for this to upset you. I was only trying to—" There was worry in Anne Jean's eyes. Anne Jean reached for her again, but Aspen recoiled.

"I'm fine, really. This isn't like before," she lied. She had to lie because her whole body was shrieking for her to get out of there. "I'm feeling a little claustrophobic. I need fresh air. Look, I know you want to talk about this . . ." The words leaving her mouth were like the hiss of a tire. "But I need some space." Aspen pulled her jacket off the back of the chair. "We'll talk. I promise."

"Aspen—" She heard Anne Jean say as she closed the door behind her. Miss Etta was running to keep up. *Air*, she thought, *she needed air.*

Aspen pulled into her driveway. She didn't have the energy to get out of her car. She put her head against the seat and closed her eyes. The hum of the engine was comforting. Miss Etta cuddled closer.

She tried to focus on her day, but her thoughts were in disarray. She remembered leaving Anne Jean's house and driving to Linda's house, but her truck was gone. She searched for her around town, but couldn't find her. She'd driven past Leigh's office, but all the trucks and cars were still there. Disappointed, she drove home. She put her head down on the steering wheel and cried. The headache that had started at Anne Jean's was pounding inside her. She cried because she couldn't stop the pain in her head. Miss Etta, who had been licking her tears, barked. She had to get Miss Etta inside. She had to get back to the trees. She was tired. Utterly tired. She rubbed her hand across her eyes. She needed her trees. She needed to sit in her trees until her body was numbed by the cold and her memories deadened by the murkiness that she knew was starting to embrace her. *Her trees would comfort her.* She pushed open the car door. *Her trees would comfort her*, she repeated. She had to get to the trees.

CHAPTER TWENTY-EIGHT

"I've contacted a security company and they'll be here tomorrow." Jay looked at Leigh. They all looked a little raw around the edges. Leigh rested her head against her hand. The day before had been long and tiring. After the detective had finished, he had interviewed them about the layoff. Jay also told the detective about the former manager being fired.

After the police left, Leigh wanted to go home and sleep, but Jay insisted they check the logging sites to make sure that nothing else had been vandalized. By late afternoon Saturday, Jeff, Jay and Tom had gone back to their motel, but she'd felt wired. The tiredness she'd felt earlier was gone. Leigh didn't want to go home. She needed to walk. She'd thought about calling Aspen but Aspen was with her group. In the end, Leigh went alone. She'd walked to the river, but no matter how she tried to refocus her mind away from the destruction, Leigh couldn't recapture the solitude she usually felt listening to the river. Instead, the rushing water made her feel unsteady, as if her anger had connected with the rhythm of the river and was rushing through her. Soon she was angry at the river because the very thing that in the past had made her feel in harmony with life had failed her. When Leigh had gotten back to Aspen's house, she didn't want to talk, wasn't ready to talk. The disconnect she'd felt the night before standing in front of her office was real.

"I'm sorry we didn't install security cameras sooner." Jay's words startled her. "Are you okay?"

Jay had directed his question to her. "Yes, just tired."

"Well, this isn't going to be a long meeting. I have to get back to Farmington. Are you sure you're okay?"

"Just tired, really." Jeff and Tom looked equally exhausted.

"I've been thinking about a lot of things since yesterday," Jay started again. "Leigh, I'm moving you up to our Houlton office for the next three weeks. Bill's wife needs surgery, so instead of Jeff, I want you there. You've covered that office before."

"What?" She glanced at Jeff who looked down at the desk in front of him. Tom also wasn't looking at her. "I really don't want to leave. Bill said at the meeting he would be gone, but I thought Jeff would cover his office."

"He was going to, but I think this is a good move for you right now. It's just for a few weeks," Jay repeated.

"Jay, I think my leaving is a mistake. People will think I'm somehow at fault, or that you lack confidence in me."

"Jeff agrees with me."

She looked at Jeff. "Do you really?"

"Just for a while."

"Am I being transferred because this is my fault?"

"Absolutely not. First of all, it's not a transfer, it's a temporary assignment."

"I understand, Jay, but people here are going to think I'm being sent up there because I'm a woman or because I'm afraid of the guys who did this." Leigh rubbed her forehead. "People might think that maybe if a man had been the manager this wouldn't have happened. We all saw that message on the back door. I keep telling myself it wasn't personal, but it was directed at me."

"I talked with the detective this morning. He said the same thing. Said whoever did this has a gripe against you, against the company. So I just want to err on the side of caution. I want you in Houlton."

Leigh nodded, too angry to speak. *Tell him you're going to quit. Tell him to take his job in Houlton and stick it. But if you quit*, the other side of her brain argued, *the cowards who did this win.* The weight of the night was crashing down around her. All night she couldn't let go of the image that was etched on her memory board of the doe, her tongue hanging out, her eye begging for . . . for what? Leigh wondered. For life? Someone had maliciously killed that animal, dragged it to Leigh's office, its guts trailing behind it, and left it behind like a calling card. Whoever did this wanted her and the world to know that they were deadly serious about stopping the company, about stopping the project, about stopping her.

"You okay?" Jeff was staring at her.

"Yeah, like I said, just tired."

"Leigh, I'm really sorry." Jay was concerned. "I don't ever want any of my people to go through something like this again. Those messages—"

"I know." Leigh didn't want to talk about them again. When they'd arrived at the office that morning, it was clear that the trauma of the night hung over the building like morning fog clinging to branches. The outside walls looked like the psychedelic paintings of the Sixties, the yellow a burst of color in the gray morning, the front porch a carpet of dried blood. The cleaning people had not yet arrived, so they had to again go in the back door. The words written there seemed to anger Jay the most, and he tried to scrub them off with a brush he'd found in the bathroom, but all he did was smear the words, not the ugly message. Shortly after Jay's cleaning frenzy, the cleaning company arrived.

"I'm glad we're getting those security cameras installed," Tom said. "But I agree we err on the side of caution. I still think those environmentalists had something to do with this. I told the cops that."

After Aspen had left, the young cop had asked her the same question. She'd told him she didn't know who had done it, but she hadn't defended Aspen, hadn't defended her group.

"I think so too." Jay's words were clipped. "But like the cop said last night, it could be anyone." Jay stared at Leigh. "Anyway, you're going to Houlton today, right?"

"No, I'm not." Leigh summoned the energy to say it from deep within. She stared at Jay. *That felt good*, she reflected. For the first time in the last twenty-four hours, she'd finally done something—said something—that felt good.

"I don't understand."

Leigh swallowed. Here went her future, but there was no turning back. The hell with what people thought, she decided. The hell with the vandals. "Jay, I . . ." She looked at Jeff. "I'm not going to Houlton and I may not have a job after I say this, but I'm going to say it." She cleared her throat. "I thought if I stayed with the project, I might have been able to help influence the direction." She did not look at Jeff. She didn't need to tell Jay that Jeff felt the same way.

"I know," Jay said. "I know you're a team player."

"Team player, yes, just a different set of goals."

"I don't understand." Jay shifted uneasily.

"Whether last night happened because of pranksters, or kids, or environmentalists, the message was clear. Jay, people here are not going to accept the scope of the project we've dropped on them."

"They don't have a clue as to how large this is going to be. Unless . . . someone has said something." Jay was suspicious.

"No one's said anything. You, the company, have underestimated the folks here. They've figured it out. You could see the way those questions were that first night. Since then Tom, Jeff, me, we've gotten the same questions—how big is this going to get? We've stonewalled, but people know."

"So? The hell with people. We own the land. We have the governor's support. We can do what we want." Jay stared at her.

"I don't think so. Last night, the message was clear and I think we need to listen."

"I don't care if it was kids or environmentalist, whatever, the cops will catch the jerks. In the meantime, the project moves forward." Jay was livid.

"And there'll be more jerks after them." Leigh held her breath. "Jay, it's time to think about compromise."

"Compromise? I won't compromise with environmentalists, with the very people who probably did this. This is what they want. We can win this." He was resolute.

Leigh straightened her shoulders and stared back. "No, we can't. Last night broke new ground in protest here, and it's not going to go away. The cops may catch whoever did it, but there'll be others waiting to do more. Maybe even worse. Someone could get hurt next time. This project has angered a lot of folks, and those of us who live around here have seen and heard them. You're back in Farmington and you don't have a clue how angry people are. This project has split this town. We have people here who were best friends who are no longer talking to each other. Family members who are split over it. I think we're in for a rough ride ahead if we bull this project through."

"I see." Jay stared at her. "What about you, Jeff?"

"I think she's right." Jeff stared at Leigh. "In fact, I know she's right."

"Where do you stand on this, Tom?"

"I'm the hired gun. I can sell whatever you want me to. But you're asking, so I'll tell you. I can sell compromise. Make the company look really good."

"Well, I'm not ready for that right now." Jay was adamant.

"I'll have my resignation in in the morning," Leigh said quietly.

"I think that's appropriate." Jay looked fiercely at her. "You really are with her on this, Jeff?"

"I am. I think if we offer the town some concessions, we stand to win more. Not just in the PR stuff this guy does," he looked at Tom, "but in goodwill around the state. This is our first project. You said it yourself, you have plans for other places we own. We do it wrong now, we might not get to do those other projects. We show we can work with the community here. It can make a lot of points in the future."

Jay nodded. "I'll take two resignations."

Jeff sat perfectly still.

"What a jerk," Leigh said after Jay and Tom had left. She was angry that Jeff had been fired.

Jeff shook his head. "You're spinning faster than a windmill pointed at a storm. You're angry."

"I am, he didn't have to fire you."

"I've had worse things happen to me. Funny, all this tension's made me hungry. Let's go get something to eat, plus we need to talk about strategy."

"Strategy? What strategy? We've just been fired!"

"Hey, I need food, then I can tell you."

She wanted to find Aspen, tell her she had quit. "All right," she said reluctantly. Hadn't Jeff just put his job on the line for her?

"Trust me on this one," Jeff insisted. "I'll drive. That's if you feel okay driving with an old bugger like me."

"It's fine." Leigh picked up her jacket. She wanted to find Aspen.

Seated at the almost empty diner, Jeff folded his crippled hands together. "This feels rather good. I ain't ever been fired before. It was rather civilized, I might add, the way Jay handled it."

Leigh laughed. "I guess that's one way of looking at it. So what's this strategy thing you want to talk about?"

"I want to . . . how do you young folks say it? Push the limits."

"That's how we say it, but I don't understand." Leigh cocked her head and studied him.

"We aren't going to fax in our resignations. I want to hand deliver them tomorrow to Farmington, along with some suggestions."

"Suggestions?"

"Some areas where I think the company could compromise. We might never get another chance to get that information before Jay."

"Why would he listen to us now? We're sort of past employees."

"Like I said before, Jay's no dummy. He's gotten to where he is because he's a shrewd businessman. He's chewing on what just happened. He's upset about the vandalism, about the project, even about us. He left angry, but he's going to think all this through. Tomorrow, let's give him something to really chew on."

Leigh's chin came up. "I think we should fax him our letters of resignation along with a note that tells him to shove his job."

"Anger doesn't get it. Time to get over that. We still have a chance to make things right, say the right words. I need your help, though. We got to put down in writing some compromise ideas, that Jay could live with. Then we put them before the environmentalists. I suspect they're just as upset about all this as we are. I think we deal with them directly, instead of everyone running around trying to figure out what the other guy's thinking. I understand what that group's doing, and I agree we need to preserve and save as much as we can of the land. But I don't think you take every piece of land in this state and put it in a box and say nothing can ever happen to it. Land was put here to be used. Maine's been a good state. We put aside parks and refuges and places that will never be touched. But we can't do it with all the land. New people help pay the taxes. I think we can get the group to listen."

Would Aspen compromise? Or would her group consider this a win? She thought about Linda, and her jaw tightened. She couldn't stop thinking about Linda's militancy. "I don't know that they'd talk to us."

"We don't know if we don't try," Jeff said firmly. "You think she's responsible for this?"

He didn't have to say Aspen's name. "She says no."

"I didn't ask that. I asked you if *you* think she is."

"No, not her, but I don't know about people in her group." The words extracted from her throat with a knife. She thought about Linda again.

"You two talking?"

"Last night I turned away from her. I was angry, but I had to sort through what was going on in my head. I'm going to talk to her as soon as we finish."

"Let's order and let's write down some ideas, and then you go see that lady. You look as injured as a baby bird fallen out of a tree."

Leigh smiled tiredly. "All right, but I don't think Jay's going to like what we say."

"Does it matter? He's already fired us. But if what we say reaches him, then better said than left unsaid. Otherwise, we'll never know, and in the end, that's going to bug you more than being fired."

CHAPTER TWENTY-NINE

Irritated, Leigh tossed on the table copies of the concessions she and Jeff had come up with. After she and Jeff had left the restaurant they had gone back to her office and typed up their resignations and then labored over concessions they thought Jay could agree to. Jeff planned to hand deliver them in the morning. Would Jay approve them? Or would she be looking for a new job? Hell, she thought, he could approve them and she could still be looking for a job. She felt like she'd been set free. To hell with it if she didn't have a job, she'd decided. All she wanted was to make things right between her and Aspen. She had to apologize to Aspen for turning away from her the night of the fire.

Miss Etta was whimpering. "Come on, darling, I'm going to feed you. Looks like your mama hasn't gotten home yet." Leigh searched the kitchen and was disappointed that there was no note from Aspen. She'd checked the message machine. None from Aspen. There were two messages from Anne Jean asking Aspen to call her. The last one was urgent. Cassie also had called. Leigh fed Miss Etta and then went upstairs to their bedroom. Leigh sat down on the edge of their bed. She patted the white down comforter. How little comfort it offered now. She stared at her clothes hanging in Aspen's closet. Just hours before, she and Aspen had been in this same room dressing for the Halloween party and laughing about what it would be like. Now she wasn't laughing. She looked at her cell phone. Still no messages. She could call her, but what if she didn't answer? What if she was with . . . What if . . . Leigh shoved the phone in her pocket. Aspen was probably still meeting with her group, she decided. It was nine o'clock. She'd gotten home much later than that in past meetings.

All the way home she'd practiced what she would say to Aspen. She was going to tell Aspen about how angry she was at the vandalism. There would be no holding back. She would also tell her that she suspected that someone in her group may be involved. She wouldn't say Linda's name out loud. Then she would take Aspen in her arms and tell her that her anger was directed outward, at others, not at her, and that she was sorry she had pulled away, had turned her back on her in their bed. She would tell Aspen about the doe and how it kept staring at her every time she closed her eyes.

She stared out the window at the black night. She was disappointed. She had really wanted Aspen to be home, for them to be home together. Why hadn't Aspen called? Had someone in her group confessed they were behind the vandalism and now she was afraid to face her? What if Aspen and Linda were together right now and laughing about how this was really a win for their group? Stop it, she said to the jealous side of her brain. Leigh dialed Anne Jean. She had to find Aspen.

Miss Etta barked, and Leigh ran down the stairs. "Aspen . . ."

She opened the door. "Anne Jean?"

"Have you seen her?" Anne Jean's face was panicked.

"Aspen?" Alarmed, Leigh grabbed Anne Jean by the arm. "What's happened?"

"She left my house upset. I'm so angry at myself. I should have stopped her. I did nothing," Anne Jean cried. "I called here. No answer. I went looking for her. Skeet's out. Cassie's looking. It's been hours. I didn't realize, but she was falling into that depression again. I blame myself. I should have seen it coming."

Leigh looked at Miss Etta, and fear gripped her. "She must have dropped off Miss Etta. Wherever she was going, she didn't want to take her." Leigh grabbed her jacket. "I've got to find her."

"I'll go with you."

"You stay here and coordinate with Cassie and Skeet. I'll call you if I find her." Leigh squeezed Anne Jean's hand. "I'll find her."

Leigh drove past the grange. The parking lot was empty. She hesitated and then turned her truck toward Linda's house. Aspen had pointed out Linda's house one night when they were going to Cassie's. She drove slowly past Linda's house. There were several cars parked in her driveway, but Aspen's wasn't there. She was relieved. *Aspen, where are you?* She said silently to the night. She turned toward her office. Would she go to where she could watch the eagle's nest? The parking lot was empty. Leigh waited, a deadly dull pain inside. She tugged on her bottom lip. *Where are you, Aspen?* Leigh shook her head. Stop thinking in panic mode, she told herself. Think like Aspen, she said over and over. Think like Aspen. The trees. Aspen would go to the trees. But which trees?

She turned her truck toward the river. She would start where they had had their picnic. Maybe, just maybe, that's where Aspen went to find her peace. Leigh sighed. She remembered her own trip to the river just days before and how little comfort it had offered her. Don't think about that now, she willed her brain. Think about finding Aspen. Leigh turned into the trail parking lot. Aspen's vehicle sat there like a lone sentry in the night. She grabbed her flashlight. Leigh pulled the collar on her wool jacket up around her neck and her hat down on her head. It was the first day of November and it was damn cold. The wind had a bite. God, she hoped Aspen had worn her jacket. She hadn't thought to look before she'd left the house. Leigh shook her head. She had to find Aspen.

Leigh flashed her light on the trail and thought about the fun they had hiking across it the day of the picnic. Now the trail was black and full of leaves that pulled at her feet. She shined the light on the ground, her feet following the beam. The crunch under her feet was deafening in the silent night, and with each step, she hammered her brain demanding why she hadn't told Jeff she didn't have time to write up those concessions and gone home to Aspen sooner. A screech owl shrieked. Leigh jumped. She rounded the bend and flashed her light where they had sat talking, laughing and munching on tuna fish sandwiches on their picnic weeks before. Aspen wasn't there. She ignored the river. *Aspen would never* . . . There was one more spot she wanted to search, and if Aspen wasn't there, then she'd call Anne Jean. She would call for help to find Aspen. Leigh started toward the spot where they had made love.

Leigh saw the scarf first and shined her light in the tree. Aspen was crouched tight against the trunk, her eyes closed. "Aspen," Leigh whispered. When Aspen didn't move, Leigh tucked the flashlight under her chin and climbed. She reached for the limb Aspen was sitting on and pulled herself up. She touched Aspen's face gently with her fingers. "I love you, Aspen."

Aspen moaned. "Leigh, I feel so sad. There are things I have to tell you, but the words keep sticking inside me."

Leigh sat next to her. Aspen folded her body into Leigh's. "You're freezing. Come on, let's go home." Leigh held her close.

"I can't go home." Aspen cried.

Leigh didn't move.

"The night of the fire, when you turned away from me, I thought you hated me."

"Hated? Oh, Aspen, no. I never hated you." Leigh took Aspen's hand in hers. It was cold. She rubbed Aspen's hands. "After it happened . . ." Leigh contemplated each word. "I was angry. Angry at the world and at my company for the conflict it's brought to this town. I was angry at myself because I was a part of something I didn't believe in. I was angry at—"

"Me," Aspen said with finality.

"Never you."

"But that's what I thought. Afterward in bed, you turned away from me again, and I didn't know what to do with that."

"I was so wrong." Leigh looked intently at Aspen. "I don't do sharing my feelings well. I never have, and I feel so bad that I hurt you. Aspen, I'm so sorry." The words quivered in the air.

"No more than I," she said darkly.

"Come home."

"Leigh, I can't go back. I don't have the energy to carry on with the protest." Aspen wiped tears from her cheeks with the back of her sleeve. "I don't have the energy to save my trees." She cried uncontrollably.

Leigh pulled her tight against her and kissed the tears on her cheek. "You don't have to go it alone anymore, Aspen. I'll be there with you."

"How?" Aspen's voice was barely audible.

Leigh told Aspen about hers and Jeff's resignations and about the list of concessions they had written. She told her about Jeff's suggestion that the company and environmentalists sit down at the table and hash out their demands.

"You did that?"

"I did and now that I'm out of a job, that means we're in this together," Leigh said earnestly. "Aspen, let's go home. Let's fix this together."

"Leigh, the depression, it's back," she blurted. "I tried to make it go away, but it won't. It's just grabbed hold of my mind, and I feel like I'm trapped. I keep trying to push it away, but I don't have the energy. I thought I had control of it, but I was wrong. It's going to happen again. I know it. Leigh, my life's a wreck, and I can't deal with it anymore. You can't stay with me. You wouldn't want to stay with me."

"I do want to stay with you." Leigh felt good now that she had finally attached words to the emotional vortex spinning inside her. "Because I don't want to make the same mistake twice. Aspen, when my dad left home, I was elated. He took with him the fights, the drinking, the discord. Years later, I finally understood that he was dealing with depression, and he had dealt with it the only way he knew how. In a bottle. I've often wondered if we'd understood the disease, would my family life have been different? When my dad wasn't drinking, he was really a good man. When I couldn't find you, I was terrified that you, like my father, had gone away forever." Leigh looked at Aspen. Her face was masked by darkness. "When Jay told me he wanted my resignation, I felt liberated, not sad. When I thought I had lost you, I felt like a part of me had stopped breathing. I never want to feel that way again."

Aspen's voice was low. "All I could think about when I was sitting here was how I couldn't go back to that empty house, to your not being there. I couldn't think about anything else. I wanted you so much, needed you so much, that it hurt. Leigh, I've never felt that way before, and when I thought you no longer loved me, I couldn't deal with it. I came here, but the trees didn't take away my sadness. So I sat here, unable to move, unable to go home. I feel so safe with you." Aspen breathed from the depths of her soul. She had said it before.

"Come on. Let's go home. I have so much to tell you."

"And I have so much to tell you." Aspen touched Leigh's cheek. "Leigh, Linda—"

"We'll talk about Linda at home," Leigh said soothingly.

"No, I have to tell you now." Aspen wrapped her arms around the trunk. She stroked the bark with her fingers. "The night of the rally . . ." Aspen stared ahead. "Afterward, when I went with Linda, she told me about an incident back in Massachusetts. There was a fire at a company there. She made it sound like she was part of it."

"Did you tell anyone?"

"I was shocked. I've never had to deal with anything like that before. Later, at Cassie's party, she told me she was just kidding, said she was trying to impress me."

"A hell of a way to impress someone."

"I didn't know what to think. I really wanted to believe her. It made me feel better to believe her," Aspen hung her head. "Then after the fire, I felt so guilty. I felt like if I'd told someone, it wouldn't have happened. Leigh, it's all my fault . . . the fire, the animals, dead. It's all my fault."

"Aspen, no!"

"It is, Leigh," Aspen sobbed. "I never thought it would happen. I never wanted it to happen. You have to believe me."

"I do believe you, but, Aspen, you had nothing to do with this."

"I don't know." Aspen breathed out through tight lips.

"No!" Leigh said sharply. "It's not your fault. I probably wouldn't have believed Linda either." Leigh chewed on her bottom lip.

"You were suspicious of her from the beginning. You would have believed she helped set the fire and you would have told the cops."

"I don't know what I would have done," Leigh said honestly. "But know this." Leigh put her arm around Aspen again. "I love you and that's what we need to think about tonight. I don't know if Linda was involved with the fire or not. I am angry at her for making you a part of her secret. But right now, we need to go home. Fix this night. We will think about tomorrow, tomorrow."

Aspen put her finger against Leigh's lips. "Thank you for finding me. Thank you for loving me. Thank you. But the sadness is still there, and I'm so tired."

Leigh took Aspen's hand in hers and caressed it. "I know, but this time we fix it together. I owe you so much more, Aspen, more than I will ever be able to say in words."

CHAPTER THIRTY

Aspen sat down. She'd been cooking all day, and her legs ached from standing. Leigh was still at the office. It was two days before Thanksgiving and she was baking pies to take to Anne Jean's house.

Seated in her favorite chair, her eye caught sight of the red in the bowl. Aspen smiled as she pulled out the horsehair braid and thought about how much had happened since Cassie had put it in her hand. Miss Etta sniffed the braid and turned her nose away in disgust. "I don't blame you, little girl. Maybe we ought to dump this in the trash. Or better yet," she said smiling at the dog. "I think we're going to give this to Cassie. Maybe it'll bring her luck." Aspen put the braid back in the bowl and picked up the newspaper. She read the article about the fire investigation. The police were quoted as saying they had suspects, but nothing more. Leigh had insisted that Aspen tell the police what she knew about Linda, and reluctantly, she had. Aspen had rejoined the group, but was not as actively involved as before. Linda had quit the group in a huff after they had agreed to negotiate with the company after Jay called and said he was ready to sit down. Now weeks later, they had nailed down an agreement. The number of houses that the company had planned to build had been scaled back to half. The country club was to be reduced in size by several hundred square feet, and Cassie requested that three days each week the pool be open for municipal use. She wanted the kids in town to be able to swim, not just the kids whose parents could afford to join the country club. The group also demanded that the company put in place conservation easements on several thousand acres of land, guaranteeing public access for hunting, hiking, fishing and other traditional uses, and they'd asked for permanent restrictions on building within one thousand feet of the river. The last consideration was Aspen's. There was room for future development, and the group agreed it wouldn't resist it or the present plans. Jay had ordered Jeff and Leigh back to work. There was no mention of the resignations.

Miss Etta barked.

Good. Leigh was home. Aspen frowned when she saw Linda.

"We need to talk." Linda rushed in.

"About?" Aspen was taken aback by Linda's rage.

Linda's face was contorted. "You told the police about the fire in Massachusetts. Told them I was involved!"

"No, I didn't tell them you were involved. I told them what you told me. I also told them you said you were kidding." Linda paced around the kitchen.

"You sold me out." Linda ignored Aspen's denial. Her voice was shrill. "My life's been hell. I've taken a leave of absence from the college. They've already decided I'm guilty. You did this to me!"

"Linda, I haven't."

316

"I expected," Linda said as if she hadn't heard her, "that you of all people understood what I was about. I didn't think you'd rat me out to the police." Linda wouldn't let go of the words.

"I did not *rat you* out to the police."

"They've got nothing on me." Linda was arrogant. "So, little Miss Civic Mindedness, don't think I'm going to jail."

Aspen stared at Linda. She felt like someone had bopped her in the forehead with a mallet. She now understood why so many people didn't like Linda. She couldn't hide the contempt she felt for people who disagreed with her. "I don't—"

Linda ignored Aspen's words. "Then you turn around and sell out the land. What kind of environmentalist are you? You have no heart, Aspen. The going gets rough, and you get going."

Aspen's temper flared. "I admit that I hadn't considered compromise when we started. In fact, I was absolutely against it, but, Linda, the group's right, the cost of winning was too high."

"Protecting the environment shouldn't have a cap on it, and I thought that you of all people understood that. Compromise is losing, Aspen. Compromise is surrendering to the enemy. That's what you did. A little vandalism is nothing compared to what we are losing." Linda was furious, her fists clenched. She was leaning inches away from Aspen's face. Her eyes bled anger.

"We, Linda? This isn't your town."

"You're right about that. It isn't now. I had wanted it to be. I had hoped that—"

"Hoped what, Linda?" Miss Etta, who had been watching them, stepped closer to Aspen. She growled low in her throat. "It's all right, baby," Aspen said stroking her head. "I think you need to leave."

"Not before I have my say." Linda almost shouted the words.

"I think you've said enough," Leigh said. Her words startled them both. They had not heard Leigh's truck.

Linda spun around. "What are you, the big bad dyke, here to protect the little Mrs.?"

"No, I think the *little Mrs.* was doing just fine. I think you need to leave, Linda."

"It's a pleasure. Think about it, Aspen. You sold out those trees and me for what? A chainsaw-wheeling dyke? Think about what you lost, Aspen. Think about what this town lost."

"You all right?" Leigh said holding Aspen in her arms now that Linda had stormed out of the house.

"Just shaky." Aspen put her head against Leigh's shoulder. "She blames me for going to the cops, and she's mad because she feels like she's lost control of the group."

Leigh cuddled her close. "As to the first, you had no choice. She had no right dumping that secret on you, whether she was trying to impress you or not. As to the second, if you had any desire to save those trees, then compromise was the only solution. Aspen, Linda has a twisted understanding of give and take."

"I wonder if my depression hadn't come back where we'd be."

"We'll never know, but, Aspen, this wasn't your decision. It was the decision of a group of people who love this town. Are you going to tell them they sold out?"

"Never."

"Then why allow someone like Linda to make you doubt for even a moment that what you did was wrong? Linda doesn't like losing. Oh, she cares about the environment and is sincere about trying to protect it, but she cares more about winning and that can be very dangerous."

"Someone else said something like that to me not too long ago."

"Who?"

"Anne Jean." Aspen didn't want to think about Linda or the project. "You hungry?"

"I am. You okay?"

"Better than I was, but not perfect."

"Aspen, I couldn't live with perfect."

"I'm glad, because you'll never find it in this house. Even Miss Etta Betta, with her one eye, isn't perfect."

"Yeah, but Miss Etta sees more than most dogs. I love you, Aspen, I do."

CHAPTER THIRTY-ONE

"This is just so cool!" Brittany was bubbling with energy. "I've never attended a Thanksgiving dinner this big." There were twenty people seated around Anne Jean's dining room table. "It's like the stars are perfectly aligned and everything is just wonderful in the world." Brittany lifted her wineglass. "To family and friends. And to Aspen. We're so glad you're in our life."

"Hear, hear," Cassie said. She was dressed in an orange caftan with brown trim. Tom was seated next to her. Cassie was happy. They had been dating since the Halloween party. He was short like Cassie, and the second gnome on the lawn. Now that she'd gotten to know him on a more personal level, Leigh actually liked him.

"Well, I'm just glad—" Leigh frowned at the caller ID on her ringing cell phone, it was Jay.

"Don't answer it," Aspen said.

"I have to, it's Jay. Okay, if Jeff and I use your kitchen?" Leigh asked Anne Jean.

"I wonder what that's about?" Brittany nodded toward the kitchen.

"Don't know. I hope it's not a report of more vandalism. I've had enough excitement for one year." Anne Jean shuddered.

"I think we all have," Aspen said. "What was that about?" she asked Leigh, who was clipping her cell phone on her belt.

Leigh glanced at Jeff. "It appears they caught the guys who vandalized the office and set the fire." There was a surprised look on everyone's face. They all started to talk at once.

"You're kidding! Who?" Cassie said above the commotion.

"You tell them," Jeff said to Leigh.

Leigh glanced at Aspen. "They've arrested two students from the college." Aspen turned ashen. "They've also arrested Linda as an accessory. It appears she didn't start the fire, but they think she influenced the two young men. She's apparently been hold-ing meetings with some of the students from the campus. Her niece is being questioned by the police right now. They haven't charged Melissa. Anyway, the police have the three in custody. They called Jay a few minutes ago."

Aspen couldn't move, couldn't breath.

"I knew it," Cassie spit out. "I didn't like that woman from the beginning."

"Well, I certainly pegged it right. I said it was the environ-mentalists." Tom blushed. "I didn't mean like you guys . . . I just meant, like Linda . . . that kind of radical environmentalist . . . not that I think you guys . . ."

Cassie laughed. "Give it up, Tom. You're digging a deeper hole. I'm not mad, sugar, I knew who you meant." Tom was red-faced and embarrassed.

"Well I suspected her," Anne Jean said quietly. "After the fire, she was just too militant, too full of herself."

"You know what really burned my butt, pardon the burn pun?" Cassie was irritated. "That fire could have hurt Anne Jean and Skeet and destroyed the town."

"But it didn't," Skeet said. "And that's all that matters."

"You're not angry?" Cassie asked Skeet.

"No, just happy we're all together." Skeet put his arm around Anne Jean. He smiled at his children and grandchildren.

"And it's finally over." Anne Jean smiled at Skeet. "That's what we have to stay focused on."

"You okay?" Leigh touched Aspen's shoulder. She nodded. "If you guys'll excuse us, Aspen and I need to talk alone a minute."

They went in the kitchen. "You okay?" Leigh asked.

Aspen nodded, her back to Leigh. "I'm angry."

"You have every right to be."

"Leigh, my life almost slid backward. If it hadn't been for you, I'd have been right back in that hellhole of depression." Aspen's face crumpled. "But I'm so angry at Linda. She put everything I believe in on the line. People are only going to remember that an environmentalist burned the trees and killed those animals."

"People will forget," Leigh said softly.

Aspen bit her lip worriedly. "What they'll forget is that two college students and an instructor were involved. But what they'll be saying years from now is those damn environmentalists almost burned down the town. They won't differentiate between the Lindas of the world and the Aspens."

"I'm really sorry Linda was involved because I know the pain this has caused you. I'm angry at her because of that."

"Me, too," Aspen answered bitterly. "Strange woman, she boasted that she got off before, maybe she'll do the same this time."

"Maybe, but Linda's got bigger problems, because in this community, she already stands convicted."

Aspen put her arms around Leigh's waist and sighed. "I love you, Leigh. I really do, and I'm so glad you're in my life." Aspen laid her head again Leigh's chest. "Weeks ago Cassie gave me a piece of horsehair braid with red ribbons on it."

"Why?"

"Because she's Cassie. She'd read in some book that a horsehair tail brought you luck. So she went out and found a horse, cut off a swatch of his tail, put red ribbons around it and gave it to me. At first I thought it was just another one of Cassie's funny little ways. Now I'm not so sure. I came across it a few days ago and was going to throw it away. I think that tail brought me luck in the form of a woman named Leigh Wright."

Leigh took Aspen in her arms and kissed her. "Let's keep that horsehair tail," Leigh whispered against her lips. "For luck."

REALITY BYTES by Jane Frances. In this sequel to *Reunion*, follow the lives of four friends in a romantic tale that spans the globe and proves that you can cross the whole of cyberspace only to find love a few suburbs away . . .   978-1-59493-079-9 $13.95

MURDER CAME SECOND by Jessica Thomas. Broadway's bad-boy genius, Paul Carlucci, has chosen *Hamlet* for his latest production. To the delight of some and despair of others, he has selected Provincetown's amphitheatre for his opening gala. But suddenly Alex Peres realizes that the wrong people are falling down. And the moaning is all to realistic. Someone must not be shooting blanks . . . 978-1-59493-081-2 $13.95

SKIN DEEP by Kenna White. Jordan Griffin has been given a new assignment: Track down and interview one-time nationally renowned broadcast journalist Reece McAllister. Much to her surprise, Jordan comes away with far more than just a story . . .

978-1-59493-78-2 $13.95

FINDERS KEEPERS by Karin Kallmaker. *Finders Keepers*, the quest for the perfect mate in the 21st century, joins Karin Kallmaker's *Just Like That* and her other incomparable novels about lesbian love, lust and laughter.   1-59493-072-4 $13.95

OUT OF THE FIRE by Beth Moore. Author Ann Covington feels at the top of the world when told her book is being made into a movie. Then in walks Casey Duncan the actress who is playing the lead in her movie. Will Casey turn Ann's world upside down?

1-59493-088-0 $13.95

STAKE THROUGH THE HEART: NEW EXPLOITS OF TWILIGHT LES-BIANS by Karin Kallmaker, Julia Watts, Barbara Johnson and Therese Szymanski. The playful quartet that penned the acclaimed *Once Upon A Dyke* are dimming the lights for journeys into worlds of breathless seduction.   1-59493-071-6 $15.95

THE HOUSE ON SANDSTONE by KG MacGregor. Carly Griffin returns home to Leland and finds that her old high school friend Justine is awakening more than just old memories.   1-59493-076-7 $13.95

WILD NIGHTS: MOSTLY TRUE STORIES OF WOMEN LOVING WOMEN edited by Therese Szymanski. 264 pp. 23 new stories from today's hottest erotic writers are sure to give you your wildest night ever!   1-59493-069-4 $15.95

COYOTE SKY by Gerri Hill. 248 pp. Sheriff Lee Foxx is trying to cope with the realization that she has fallen in love for the first time. And fallen for author Kate Winters, who is technically unavailable. Will Lee fight to keep Kate in Coyote?
1-59493-065-1 $13.95

VOICES OF THE HEART by Frankie J. Jones. 264 pp. A series of events force Erin to swear off love as she tries to break away from the woman of her dreams. Will Erin ever find the key to her future happiness?   1-59493-068-6 $13.95

SHELTER FROM THE STORM by Peggy J. Herring. 296 pp. A story about family and getting reacquainted with one's past that shows that sometimes you don't appreciate what you have until you almost lose it.   1-59493-064-3 $13.95

WRITING MY LOVE by Claire McNab. 192 pp. Romance writer Vonny Smith believes she will be able to woo her editor Diana through her writing.   1-59493-063-5 $13.95

PAID IN FULL by Ann Roberts. 200 pp. Ari Adams will need to choose between the debts of the past and the promise of a happy future.   1-59493-059-7 $13.95

ROMANCING THE ZONE by Kenna White. 272 pp. Liz's world begins to crumble when a secret from her past returns to Ashton.   1-59493-060-0 $13.95

SIGN ON THE LINE by Jaime Clevenger. 204 pp. Alexis Getty, a flirtatious delivery driver is committed to finding the rightful owner of a mysterious package.
1-59493-052-X $13.95

END OF WATCH by Clare Baxter. 256 pp. LAPD Lieutenant L.A. Franco Frank follows the lone clue down the unlit steps of memory to a final, unthinkable resolution.
1-59493-064-4 $13.95

BEHIND THE PINE CURTAIN by Gerri Hill. 280 pp. Jacqueline returns home after her father's death and comes face-to-face with her first crush.
1-59493-057-0 $13.95

18TH & CASTRO by Karin Kallmaker. 200 pp. First-time couplings and couples who know how to mix lust and love make 18th & Castro the hottest address in the city by the bay.   1-59493-066-X $13.95

JUST THIS ONCE by KG MacGregor. 200 pp. Mindful of the obligations back home that she must honor, Wynne Connelly struggles to resist the fascination and allure that a particular woman she meets on her business trip represents.
1-59493-087-2 $13.95

ANTICIPATION by Terri Breneman. 240 pp. Two women struggle to remain professional as they work together to find a serial killer.   1-59493-055-4 $13.95

OBSESSION by Jackie Calhoun. 240 pp. Lindsey's life is turned upside down when Sarah comes into the family nursery in search of perennials.   1-59493-058-9 $13.95

BENEATH THE WILLOW by Kenna White. 240 pp. A torch that still burns brightly even after twenty-five years threatens to consume two childhood friends.
1-59493-053-8 $13.95

SISTER LOST, SISTER FOUND by Jeanne G'fellers. 224 pp. The highly anticipated sequel to No Sister of Mine.   1-59493-056-2 $13.95

THE WEEKEND VISITOR by Jessica Thomas. 240 pp. In this latest Alex Peres mystery, Alex is asked to investigate an assault on a local woman but finds that her client may have more secrets than she lets on. 1-59493-054-6 $13.95

THE KILLING ROOM by Gerri Hill. 392 pp. How can two women forget and go their separate ways? 1-59493-050-3 $12.95

PASSIONATE KISSES by Megan Carter. 240 pp. Will two old friends run from love? 1-59493-051-1 $12.95

ALWAYS AND FOREVER by Lyn Denison. 224 pp. The girl next door turns Shannon's world upside down. 1-59493-049-X $12.95

BACK TALK by Saxon Bennett. 200 pp. Can a talk show host find love after heartbreak? 1-59493-028-7 $12.95

THE PERFECT VALENTINE: EROTIC LESBIAN VALENTINE STORIES edited by Barbara Johnson and Therese Szymanski—from Bella After Dark. 328 pp. Stories from the hottest writers around. 1-59493-061-9 $14.95

MURDER AT RANDOM by Claire McNab. 200 pp. The Sixth Denise Cleever Thriller. Denise realizes the fate of thousands is in her hands. 1-59493-047-3 $12.95

THE TIDES OF PASSION by Diana Tremain Braund. 240 pp. Will Susan be able to hold it all together and find the one woman who touches her soul? 1-59493-048-1 $12.95

JUST LIKE THAT by Karin Kallmaker. 240 pp. Disliking each other—and everything they stand for—even before they meet, Toni and Syrah find feelings can change, just like that. 1-59493-025-2 $12.95

WHEN FIRST WE PRACTICE by Therese Szymanski. 200 pp. Brett and Allie are once again caught in the middle of murder and intrigue. 1-59493-045-7 $12.95

REUNION by Jane Frances. 240 pp. Cathy Braithwaite seems to have it all: good looks, money and a thriving accounting practice . . . 1-59493-046-5 $12.95

BELL, BOOK & DYKE: NEW EXPLOITS OF MAGICAL LESBIANS by Kallmaker, Watts, Johnson and Szymanski. 360 pp. Reluctant witches, tempting spells and skyclad beauties—delve into the mysteries of love, lust and power in this quartet of novellas. 1-59493-023-6 $14.95

ARTIST'S DREAM by Gerri Hill. 320 pp. When Cassie meets Luke Winston, she can no longer deny her attraction to women . . . 1-59493-042-2 $12.95

NO EVIDENCE by Nancy Sanra. 240 pp. Private investigator Tally McGinnis once again returns to the horror-filled world of a serial killer. 1-59493-043-04 $12.95

WHEN LOVE FINDS A HOME by Megan Carter. 280 pp. What will it take for Anna and Rona to find their way back to each other again? 1-59493-041-4 $12.95

MEMORIES TO DIE FOR by Adrian Gold. 240 pp. Rachel attempts to avoid her attraction to the charms of Anna Sigurdson . . . 1-59493-038-4 $12.95

SILENT HEART by Claire McNab. 280 pp. Exotic lesbian romance. 1-59493-044-9 $12.95

MIDNIGHT RAIN by Peggy J. Herring. 240 pp. Bridget McBee is determined to find the woman who saved her life. 1-59493-021-X $12.95

THE MISSING PAGE A Brenda Strange Mystery by Patty G. Henderson. 240 pp. Brenda investigates her client's murder . . .   1-59493-004-X $12.95

WHISPERS ON THE WIND by Frankie J. Jones. 240 pp. Dixon thinks she and her best friend, Elizabeth Colter, would make the perfect couple . . .   1-59493-037-6 $12.95

CALL OF THE DARK: EROTIC LESBIAN TALES OF THE SUPERNATURAL edited by Therese Szymanski—from Bella After Dark. 320 pp.
    1-59493-040-6 $14.95

A TIME TO CAST AWAY A Helen Black Mystery by Pat Welch. 240 pp. Helen stops by Alice's apartment—only to find the woman dead . . .   1-59493-036-8 $12.95

DESERT OF THE HEART by Jane Rule. 224 pp. The book that launched the most popular lesbian movie of all time is back.   1-1-59493-035-X $12.95

THE NEXT WORLD by Ursula Steck. 240 pp. Anna's friend Mido is threatened and eventually disappears . . .   1-59493-024-4 $12.95

CALL SHOTGUN by Jaime Clevenger. 240 pp. Kelly gets pulled back into the world of private investigation . . .   1-59493-016-3 $12.95

52 PICKUP by Bonnie J. Morris and E.B. Casey. 240 pp. 52 hot, romantic tales—one for every Saturday night of the year.   1-59493-026-0 $12.95

GOLD FEVER by Lyn Denison. 240 pp. Kate's first love, Ashley, returns to their home town, where Kate now lives . . .   1-1-59493-039-2 $12.95

RISKY INVESTMENT by Beth Moore. 240 pp. Lynn's best friend and roommate needs her to pretend Chris is his fiancé. But nothing is ever easy.   1-59493-019-8 $12.95

HUNTER'S WAY by Gerri Hill. 240 pp. Homicide detective Tori Hunter is forced to team up with the hot-tempered Samantha Kennedy.   1-59493-018-X $12.95

CAR POOL by Karin Kallmaker. 240 pp. Soft shoulders, merging traffic and slippery when wet . . . Anthea and Shay find love in the car pool.   1-59493-013-9 $12.95

NO SISTER OF MINE by Jeanne G'Fellers. 240 pp. Telepathic women fight to coexist with a patriarchal society that wishes their eradication.   1-59493-017-1 $12.95

ON THE WINGS OF LOVE by Megan Carter. 240 pp. Stacie's reporting career is on the rocks. She has to interview bestselling author Cheryl, or else!
    1-59493-027-9 $12.95

WICKED GOOD TIME by Diana Tremain Braund. 224 pp. Does Christina need Miki as a protector . . . or want her as a lover?   1-59493-031-7 $12.95

THOSE WHO WAIT by Peggy J. Herring. 240 pp. Two brilliant sisters—in love with the same woman!   1-59493-032-5 $12.95

ABBY'S PASSION by Jackie Calhoun. 240 pp. Abby's bipolar sister helps turn her world upside down, so she must decide what's most important.   1-59493-014-7 $12.95

PICTURE PERFECT by Jane Vollbrecht. 240 pp. Kate is reintroduced to Casey, the daughter of an old friend. Can they withstand Kate's career?   1-59493-015-5 $12.95

PAPERBACK ROMANCE by Karin Kallmaker. 240 pp. Carolyn falls for tall, dark and . . . female . . . in this classic lesbian romance.   1-59493-033-3 $12.95

DAWN OF CHANGE by Gerri Hill. 240 pp. Susan ran away to find peace in remote Kings Canyon—then she met Shawn . . . 1-59493-011-2 $12.95

DOWN THE RABBIT HOLE by Lynne Jamneck. 240 pp. Is a killer holding a grudge against FBI Agent Samantha Skellar? 1-59493-012-0 $12.95

SEASONS OF THE HEART by Jackie Calhoun. 240 pp. Overwhelmed, Sara saw only one way out—leaving . . . 1-59493-030-9 $12.95

TURNING THE TABLES by Jessica Thomas. 240 pp. The 2nd Alex Peres Mystery. *From ghosties and ghoulies and long leggity beasties* . . . 1-59493-009-0 $12.95

FOR EVERY SEASON by Frankie Jones. 240 pp. Andi, who is investigating a 65-year-old murder, meets Janice, a charming district attorney . . . 1-59493-010-4 $12.95

LOVE ON THE LINE by Laura DeHart Young. 240 pp. Kay leaves a younger woman behind to go on a mission to Alaska . . . will she regret it? 1-59493-008-2 $12.95

WHEN THE CORPSE LIES A Motor City Thriller by Therese Szymanski. 328 pp. Butch bad-girl Brett Higgins is used to waking up next to beautiful women she hardly knows. Problem is, this one's dead. 1-931513-74-0 $12.95

UNDER THE SOUTHERN CROSS by Claire McNab. 200 pp. Lee, an American travel agent, goes down under and meets Australian Alex, and the sparks fly under the Southern Cross. 1-59493-029-5 $12.95

SUGAR by Karin Kallmaker. 240 pp. Three women want sugar from Sugar, who can't make up her mind. 1-59493-001-5 $12.95

FALL GUY by Claire McNab. 200 pp. 16th Detective Inspector Carol Ashton Mystery. 1-59493-000-7 $12.95

ONE SUMMER NIGHT by Gerri Hill. 232 pp. Johanna swore to never fall in love again—but then she met the charming Kelly . . . 1-59493-007-4 $12.95

TALK OF THE TOWN TOO by Saxon Bennett. 181 pp. Second in the series about wild and fun loving friends. 1-931513-77-5 $12.95

LOVE SPEAKS HER NAME by Laura DeHart Young. 170 pp. Love and friendship, desire and intrigue, spark this exciting sequel to *Forever and the Night*. 1-59493-002-3 $12.95

TO HAVE AND TO HOLD by Peggy J. Herring. 184 pp. By finally letting down her defenses, will Dorian be opening herself to a devastating betrayal? 1-59493-005-8 $12.95

WILD THINGS by Karin Kallmaker. 228 pp. Dutiful daughter Faith has met the perfect man. There's just one problem: she's in love with his sister. 1-931513-64-3 $12.95

SHARED WINDS by Kenna White. 216 pp. Can Emma rebuild more than just Lanny's marina? 1-59493-006-6 $12.95

THE UNKNOWN MILE by Jaime Clevenger. 253 pp. Kelly's world is getting more and more complicated every moment. 1-931513-57-0 $12.95

TREASURED PAST by Linda Hill. 189 pp. A shared passion for antiques leads to love. 1-59493-003-1 $12.95

SIERRA CITY by Gerri Hill. 284 pp. Chris and Jesse cannot deny their growing attraction . . . 1-931513-98-8 $12.95

ALL THE WRONG PLACES by Karin Kallmaker. 174 pp. Sex and the single girl— Brandy is looking for love and usually she finds it. Karin Kallmaker's first *After Dark* erotic novel. 1-931513-76-7 $12.95

GUARDED HEARTS by Hannah Rickard. 240 pp. Someone's reminding Alyssa about her secret past, and then she becomes the suspect in a series of burglaries.
1-931513-99-6 $12.95

ONCE MORE WITH FEELING by Peggy J. Herring. 184 pp. A lighthearted, loving, romantic adventure. 1-931513-60-0 $12.95

TANGLED AND DARK A Brenda Strange Mystery by Patty G. Henderson. 240 pp. When investigating a local death, Brenda finds two possible killers—one diagnosed with multiple personality disorder. 1-931513-75-9 $12.95

BACK TO BASICS: A BUTCH/FEMME ANTHOLOGY edited by Therese Szymanski—from Bella After Dark. 324 pp. 1-931513-35-X $14.95

WHITE LACE AND PROMISES by Peggy J. Herring. 240 pp. Maxine and Betina realize sex may not be the most important thing in their lives. 1-931513-73-2 $12.95

UNFORGETTABLE by Karin Kallmaker. 288 pp. Can Rett find love with the cheer-leader who broke her heart so many years ago? 1-931513-63-5 $12.95

HIGHER GROUND by Saxon Bennett. 280 pp. A delightfully complex reflection of the successful, high society lives of a small group of women. 1-931513-69-4 $12.95

LAST CALL A Detective Franco Mystery by Baxter Clare. 240 pp. Frank overlooks all else to try to solve a cold case of two murdered children . . . 1-931513-70-8 $12.95

ONCE UPON A DYKE: NEW EXPLOITS OF FAIRY-TALE LESBIANS by Karin Kallmaker, Julia Watts, Barbara Johnson & Therese Szymanski. 320 pp. You've never read fairy tales like these before! From Bella After Dark. 1-931513-71-6 $14.95

FINEST KIND OF LOVE by Diana Tremain Braund. 224 pp. Can Molly and Carolyn stop clashing long enough to see beyond their differences? 1-931513-68-6 $12.95

DREAM LOVER by Lyn Denison. 188 pp. A soft, sensuous, romantic fantasy.
1-931513-96-1 $12.95

NEVER SAY NEVER by Linda Hill. 224 pp. A classic love story . . . where rules aren't the only things broken. 1-931513-67-8 $12.95

PAINTED MOON by Karin Kallmaker. 214 pp. Stranded together in a snowbound cabin, Jackie and Leah's lives will never be the same. 1-931513-53-8 $12.95

WIZARD OF ISIS by Jean Stewart. 240 pp. Fifth in the exciting Isis series.
1-931513-71-4 $12.95

WOMAN IN THE MIRROR by Jackie Calhoun. 216 pp. Josey learns to love again, while her niece is learning to love women for the first time. 1-931513-78-3 $12.95

SUBSTITUTE FOR LOVE by Karin Kallmaker. 200 pp. When Holly and Reyna meet the combination adds up to pure passion. But what about tomorrow?
1-931513-62-7 $12.95

GULF BREEZE by Gerri Hill. 288 pp. Could Carly really be the woman Pat has always been searching for? 1-931513-97-X $12.95

THE TOMSTOWN INCIDENT by Penny Hayes. 184 pp. Caught between two worlds, Eloise must make a decision that will change her life forever.
1-931513-56-2 $12.95

WHEN GOOD GIRLS GO BAD: A Motor City Thriller by Therese Szymanski. 230 pp. Brett, Randi and Allie join forces to stop a serial killer. 1-931513-11-2 $12.95

MAKING UP FOR LOST TIME by Karin Kallmaker. 240 pp. Discover delicious recipes for romance by the undisputed mistress. 1-931513-61-9 $12.95

THE WAY LIFE SHOULD BE by Diana Tremain Braund. 173 pp. With which woman will Jennifer find the true meaning of love? 1-931513-66-X $12.95

SURVIVAL OF LOVE by Frankie J. Jones. 236 pp. What will Jody do when she falls in love with her best friend's daughter? 1-931513-55-4 $12.95

LESSONS IN MURDER by Claire McNab. 184 pp. 1st Detective Inspector Carol Ashton Mystery. 1-931513-65-1 $12.95

DEATH BY DEATH by Claire McNab. 167 pp. 5th Denise Cleever Thriller.
1-931513-34-1 $12.95

CAUGHT IN THE NET by Jessica Thomas. 188 pp. A wickedly observant story of mystery, danger, and love in Provincetown. 1-931513-54-6 $12.95

DREAMS FOUND by Lyn Denison. Australian Riley embarks on a journey to meet her birth mother . . . and gains not just a family, but the love of her life.
1-931513-58-9 $12.95

A MOMENT'S INDISCRETION by Peggy J. Herring. 154 pp. Jackie is torn between her better judgment and the overwhelming attraction she feels for Valerie.
1-931513-59-7 $12.95

IN EVERY PORT by Karin Kallmaker. 224 pp. Jessica has a woman in every port. Will meeting Cat change all that? 1-931513-36-8 $12.95

TOUCHWOOD by Karin Kallmaker. 240 pp. Rayann loves Louisa. Louisa loves Rayann. Can the decades between their ages keep them apart? 1-931513-37-6 $12.95

WATERMARK by Karin Kallmaker. 248 pp. Teresa wants a future with a woman whose heart has been frozen by loss. Sequel to *Touchwood*. 1-931513-38-4 $12.95

EMBRACE IN MOTION by Karin Kallmaker. 240 pp. Has Sarah found lust or love?
1-931513-39-2 $12.95

ONE DEGREE OF SEPARATION by Karin Kallmaker. 232 pp. Sizzling small town romance between Marian, the town librarian, and the new girl from the big city.
1-931513-30-9 $12.95

CRY HAVOC A Detective Franco Mystery by Baxter Clare. 240 pp. A dead hustler with a headless rooster in his lap sends Lt. L.A. Franco headfirst against Mother Love.
1-931513931-7 $12.95

DISTANT THUNDER by Peggy J. Herring. 294 pp. Bankrobbing drifter Cordy awakens strange new feelings in Leo in this romantic tale set in the Old West.
1-931513-28-7 $12.95